A Deceitful Bait

Mercer Addison

Windtree Press
4660 Northeast Belknap Ct
Hillsboro, Oregon 97124
http://windtreepress.com
www.merceraddison.com

Publisher's Note: This is a work of fiction. Names, characters, places, and incidents are a product of the author's imagination. Locales and public names are sometimes used for atmospheric purposes. Any resemblance to actual people, living or dead, or to businesses, companies, events, institutions, or locales is completely coincidental.

Book Layout ©2013 BookDesignTemplates.com
Cover design by Gilded Heart Designs at http://gildedheartdesign.com
Ordering Information:
Quantity sales. Special discounts are available on quantity purchases by corporations, associations, and others. For details, contact the "Special Sales Department" at the address above.
A Deceitful Bait/Mercer Addison. -- 1st ed.
ISBN 978-0-9891947-4-7 ebook
ISBN 978-0-9891947-5-4 print book
ISBN-10:0989194752

Dedication
This is for my daughter Whitney, aka Whitney Bug.
This for my son Michael, aka Toadie.
Hey, kids, who knew?

We all live in suspense, from day to day, from hour to hour; in other words we are the hero of our own story.

—Mary McCarthy (1912-1989)—
American Writer

Chapter One

Manhattan
September, 1918

"Miss DeLane—you're needed on stage!"
Shouted words and loud knocks shredded the fog that was Jonathan Drake's brain. His eyelids fluttered open. He stared into the glazed, emerald-depths of Zelda DeLane's eyes, his lover. He lifted his head to see he was prostrate on top of her body, poised like a puppet with cut strings.

Her mouth gaped open.

Red gore from her sliced throat matted her blonde hair, it coated both their nude bodies and pooled on the uneven floorboards. The coppery smell of Zelda's life hung like a curtain, invading his nostrils.

His insides clenched.

"Miss DeLane what's wrong in there?" Mick the stage manager pounded on the locked dressing room door.

"Zelda—no—no—no," Jonathan sobbed, knowing she was

beyond help. Struggling to his knees, he discovered a knife clenched in his right fist. The knife wasn't his. He recoiled at the devastation, and gaining purchase on the blood-slicked floor, pushed to his feet where he glanced around searching for his clothes. The expensive tuxedo he'd worn was nowhere in sight. Also gone were his shoes, socks and hat.

Still fuzzy, he felt the back of his head, his hand now sticky with blood. His or Zelda's? Fright from the unknown goose-fleshed his skin.

Mick's deep voice bellowed through the wood as he rattled the doorknob. "Miss DeLane—open this door or I'll knock it down."

Fear crept up Jonathan's spine.

Christ.

Nothing made sense. It was like an elaborate play was being put on and he the unwilling star. The stage was Zelda's dressing room that held an ornate privacy screen, a brocaded love seat, her dressing table and chair. In short, there was no place to hide, no window to escape out of, and no curtain being lowered to signal the end of the first act.

Another slam against the door splintered it open. Mick tumbled inside the room, landing hard on his hands and knees. Spotting Zelda's dead body, stunned surprise creased his craggy features. He glared at Jonathan and bellowed, "Damn you, Drake—ya killed Zelda. I'm gonna snap ya in two." He scrambled to his feet to become a looming no-neck enforcer.

"Mick, I didn't do this—I love her, for God's sake." Panicked, Jonathan yelled back and started for the doorway.

Follies dancers craned their necks through the gaping hole. They screamed.

"You're not goin' anywhere." Mick, with murder in his eyes, came on fast. "Somebody call the police—now." He reached for

Jonathan.

Seeing his escape route cut off, Jonathan switched the knife from his right hand to his left and swiped at Mick.

Mick lunged. He grabbed Jonathan's wrist and bent it backwards. Paralyzing pain shot through Jonathan's arm as Mick pried the knife from his hand. The deadly blade clattered to the floor where their churning feet kicked it under the love seat.

Jonathan grunted, he scratched Mick's arm and gouged at his eyes.

Mick seized Jonathan by the hair, yanked him forward, and put him in a headlock. His arm tightened like steel around Jonathan's neck, squeezing, cutting off his air.

Choking, his head ready to burst, Jonathan crashed against the dressing table. He snatched a round box of powder from the table top and ground it into Mick's face. The white snowy substance covered the man's head and shoulders, creating a lilac vapor trail. Blinded, Mick staggered backwards sending cosmetics and perfume bottles crashing onto the floor.

In a haze, coughing, trying to breathe, Jonathan grabbed Zelda's long sequined cape from the love seat and wrapped it around his body.

Again Mick charged. Jonathan ducked, leaving Mick with a handful of turquoise and black fluffy feathers. Bolting from the dressing room, Jonathan plowed through a group of sequined women. He batted at the tall purple and pink feathery headdresses attacking his face. They grabbed at him, trying to disrobe him, stop him. Their nails raked his skin—he swatted their hands away.

Another stage worker appeared out of nowhere. Unlike Mick, this guy was slight of build. Jonathan slammed his fist into the man's face knocking him to the floor. Pain radiated from Jonathan's split knuckles to his shoulder.

He darted out the back exit and into a dark alley lit only by a single lamp over the door. A stray cat jumped off a wooden box and hissed at him, its eyes glowing in the dim light. Behind Jonathan, the metal door slammed open and a quick glance over his shoulder showed the men piling out after him.

His bare feet slapped against wet cobblestones, the grit sharp like needles, hurting. Cold air whipped against his skin puckering it, the flimsy cape provided him with no protection. Not knowing what to do, Jonathan sprinted down the sidewalk next to Broadway, into the dazzling glittering lights of theater marquees.

People stared, women screamed, and men tried to shield the women's eyes from the strange sight of a naked man draped in sequins racing down the street. Cars honked, carriages pulled up short, and he continued to run.

Behind him voices rang out. "Stop that man—he's killed Zelda DeLane. Stop him!"

People were slow to react, allowing him time to veer off into an alley, dodging smelly trash, moving fast, away from the bright lights, away from what money could buy in entertainment, away from the familiar and into the unfamiliar. After being on the move for what felt like hours, he dared to stop and catch his breath against the side of a brick building. The back of his scalp throbbed from being clobbered. Perspiration covered him causing the cape's sheer material to cling like a second skin. A quick glance showed he was on Eleventh Avenue, in an unfavorable part of the City, heading toward crowded tenements. The air smelled of rotting garbage and of the nearby Hudson River.

Miserable from the chilly air, it helped him to think, and to chase away his confusion. His last clear thought was being in Zelda's private dressing room where they had time between acts to make love. Their foreplay was always fun, fast, and sometimes rough. Zelda, his blonde beauty, liked being spanked, pinched, and rough sex, but tonight he didn't get that far. Having watched her striptease for him, she'd stood in front of him wearing only a white satin dressing gown that was parted to reveal all her pleasures. She put one foot on the chair between his thighs and made sure to press her toes tight against his crotch. Getting hard, his erection strained against his trousers. He ran his hand up her well-shaped leg. Her smooth skin was titillating, but not as titillating as the golden tuft of curls between her legs. His breathing became ragged.

"What does my star desire tonight? I'll do anything, anything you want," he whispered.

"I want your cock inside me," she said and ran her tongue around her lips indicating exactly where she wanted him.

He slid his fingers between her hot folds, claiming, pinching, exciting her, making her moan with deep-throated pleasure.

Zelda's moans stopped, her head snapped upright, fixed on something behind him, her eyes widened. "Jonathan— someone's—"

The blow was sickening, the pain sharp against the back of his head...

...A man and woman staggered by. Holding each other up, they paused to stare at him. The woman giggled and pointed, begging the man with her to say she wasn't seeing things, that indeed a man wearing a glittering sheer cape with peacock feathers wasn't cowering against the building.

Jonathan pushed off the brick wall. Leaving their laughter behind, he headed west, deeper into territory he'd never dared enter before.

Chapter Two

Liberty Fitzgerald gripped her black medical bag and stood on the rooftop staring out at a city enshrouded in a gray morning mist that the sun failed to penetrate. The early hour found Liberty getting ready to call on her first patient of the day.

Working for Lillian Wald's public nursing service, Liberty's job was to bring health care to the poor. Show them proper preventative care, how to keep their homes and persons clean, and ward off diseases. Most of her patients lived in reeking two-room apartments stuffed with people living in squalor, and some or all of them sick. Her assigned territory was Midtown West and also the tenement area known as the notorious Hell's Kitchen where thousands of people were getting ready to survive another dismal day.

Yawning, Liberty walked toward the roof of the neighboring tenant building. She liked to travel this way, going from rooftop to rooftop. Depending on what floor her patients lived on, it was easier on her twenty-eight-year-old body to go down the stairs inside the buildings than to trudge up the winding staircases all day long.

Nattily dressed in her starched uniform consisting of a white blouse, long gray skirt, and a gray woolen cape that came to her hips, she'd be filthy and vomit crusted by day's end. Sometimes she wondered why she bothered to start out so clean, but knew the answer, it made her feel good, professional. But what didn't make her feel good was the constant danger she was in, the threats by irate husbands who forbade her to ever step foot inside their homes again. She'd been given black eyes, bruises, and a cracked molar, all of which made her question if the job was worth the anguish, especially for the small amount of pay she received. However, the physical abuse she endured didn't even come close to the deadly diseases she was constantly exposed to. The Spanish Influenza being one of the nastiest that made its presence known last spring. Liberty became violently ill with the flu in April, but fought like a demon to get well.

Gathering the hem of her straight skirt, she pulled it up and tucked it inside her waistband, revealing bloomers, white hose and scuffed white high-top shoes. She climbed the short ladder then dropped down onto the attached rooftop of the next building. After releasing her skirt to swoosh back into place, she bent to brush away a smudge on it, and straighten her cape.

A few hairpins jostled loose releasing strands of hair to tickle across her face and nose. Cursing under her breath for having inherited curly, wayward hair the color of a ripe pumpkin, she removed her brimmed straw hat and tidied the mess.

Foraging in her medical bag, she found her identity card and tucked it into the front crown of her hat between the ribbon and brim. A time saving step that kept her hands free and allowed her to enter a tenant's home before the door was slammed in her face. Some liked seeing her arrival, while others shied away with distrust. The distrustful, new and still smelling of the land from where they immigrated were so ingrained with old customs that no amount of threats could make them change their ways. Others were so poor they couldn't afford a bar of soap. The destitute always scrambled Liberty's heart, leaving her determined to help them, despite themselves.

Her long legs propelled her to the door on the roof that would lead inside the building and to her next patients, the O'Grady's, a family of six, with an argumentative father who knew all, yet knew nothing about cleanliness and keeping illnesses away.

She reached for the doorknob when a sound stopped her. The soft moan came from the backside of the enclosure surrounding the door opening. Curious, she eased over to peer around the side.

Her hand flew to her mouth.

A naked man, well as naked as one could be with a shimmering cape wrapped around him, sat on the floor of the roof, his back against the wall, shivering. His head tilted forward, his black hair covering his forehead.

He didn't see her.

Liberty's muscles tightened, and with self-preservation taking over, she dashed back to the outer door, threw it open, and hurried inside. The door slammed loud behind her.

"Who's there?" The stranger's deep voice muffled through the door. "Help me…"

Liberty hesitated. She started to turn back and see if the man was ill. No doubt in his head. Why else would he be dressed as such and on a rooftop? Had he escaped from the insane asylum? If so, he might be dangerous. Presented with something out of her nursing routine, she wasn't sure what to do.

'Mind your own business,' she scolded.

As if it were glowing hot, she snatched her hand away from the doorknob and started down the dimly lit inner stairway, pausing when she heard him call out again. She teeter-tottered. Help him. Don't help him. The reason she was here won out. *People in need are waiting for you. See to your patients.* This time she entered the top floor. Strewn with trash, broken toys, the odor of cooking food flooded the hallway. Still thinking about the man on the roof, Liberty paused before the O'Grady's apartment.

She knocked and after announcing who she was, it wasn't long before the door was opened a few inches to allow the owner to peer out.

"'Tis good to see ya, Miss Liberty." Mrs. O'Grady, thin and worn looking with hair escaping her bun, asked her in.

All the tenement apartments looked alike. Small, crowded, a living room, kitchenette, a bedroom, and the only bathroom outside and in the outer hallway to be shared by all tenants. The O'Grady's abode was no different. Cots for sleeping leaned against the corner while a broken-down sofa was pushed against another wall. A quick glance around ensured Liberty the cluttered apartment was at least clean. Only the smell of breakfast lingered, fried bacon.

"Is Mr. O'Grady here? Or one of your sons?" Liberty thought to enlist their help in dealing with the man on the roof.

Mrs. O'Grady shook her head. "He's gone off to work. Found a job cuttin' patterns in a factory. My lads were up and out before the sun. But, Nellie's here. I'm afraid she's not feelin' well." She frowned, forcing wrinkles into deep grooves.

Relieved she wouldn't have to deal with the stranger just yet, Liberty asked, "Where is Nellie?"

"As soon as my mister left, I put her in our bed." She motioned for Liberty to follow.

They walked through the small kitchenette into the lone bedroom on the other side. The room held a bed, a dresser, and nothing more. Liberty went to the young girl who lay beneath a drab patchwork quilt pulled up to her neck. Nellie's brown hair was darkened with perspiration and pulled away from her face. Her blue eyes glazed with fever stared back.

Liberty smiled at her patient and leaned over the girl to feel her forehead. Sweaty heat filled the back of Liberty's fingers.

"How long have you been ill?"

Mrs. O'Grady answered for her. "Around four days or so."

"Do you hurt anywhere, your stomach?" Placing her bag on the floor, Liberty reached inside it to take out a thermometer.

"I hurt all over...feel terrible...so sick," Nellie whispered.

"I need to take your temperature, please open your mouth, Nellie," Liberty said and tried to be gentle.

Nellie obeyed and clamped her lips shut over the long glass rod.

While timing the thermometer with her watch pendant that hung from her neck, Liberty tried to concentrate on Nellie, but the man on the roof and his call for help worried her just as much. What if he had the flu or typhoid, certainly either contagion would make one lose their mind.

Removing the thermometer that read close to one-hundred-four degrees, Liberty took Mrs. O'Grady aside and put her arm around the frail woman.

"Mrs. O'Grady, Nellie's extremely ill. I'm going to call the health department. Typhoid Fever and the Spanish Influenza are very much alike when they first appear. No matter what, both contagions are serious and we need to know what your daughter has."

"Mother, Mary and Joseph," she muttered and crossed herself. "Are ye sayin' my wee Nellie may die?"

"Either illness can infect your whole family. I'll need a doctor's confirmation."

"Nay, ye will not!" The voice belonging to Mr. O'Grady rang out as he stood swaying in the doorway. Unkempt in a wrinkled brown suit and looking like he hadn't slept in weeks he held a small silver flask in his hand. "I'll not have the feckin' health department doctors...snoopin' in me home. You're bad enough...

nurse…hic…bad enough." Tipping his head back, he gulped the drink, allowing the booze to trickle down his chin.

Mrs. O'Grady gasped and wrung her hands on her dingy apron. "Husband, what are ye doing home? I thought ye had a job to go to." Her eyes held defeat. One more thing to try and overcome, a drunken husband, a sick child, and both were deadly.

"I did have…hic…job, was fired." He pointed a finger at his wife. "Why is Nellie…sic…in our bed? Move her…hic…want to lie down." Holding tight to the doorjamb with one hand, he postured, and pointed his whiskey flask at Liberty.

Liberty stood to face Mr. O'Grady whose breath was heavy with whiskey. "Your daughter's very sick and she can't be moved from this bed. Whether you like it or not, I must call the health department and get a doctor in here." She turned her attention to Mrs. O'Grady. "Please cool her off by putting a wet washcloth on her forehead. I'll go make that phone call."

Liberty closed her bag and started to leave when Mr. O'Grady's meaty fist exploded against her jaw whipping her head backwards. Pain rattled her ears as she slumped to the floor…

…"Nurse—Nurse Fitzgerald, please wake up!"

Something slapped against the back of Liberty's hand, forcing her to fight against the painful haze developing her.

"Please wake up!" Again the rapid tap—tap—tap.

Groggy, Liberty opened her eyes to see a worried Mrs. O'Grady kneeling on the floor next to her, patting Liberty's hand, trying to bring her back to the world of the living.

Liberty gingerly felt the right side of her jaw and the lump now forming. The metallic taste of blood coated her tongue. She removed a freshly starched handkerchief from the cuff of her blouse and spit bright blood into it. She tongued the cut on the inside of her cheek, made by the lower back tooth that Mr. O'Grady came close to knocking out. Tears of pain started, and she allowed Mrs. O'Grady to help her to her feet.

"I'm so sorry. Are ye sure you're all right?" The woman asked and bent to pick up Liberty's hat and put it back on her head.

Mr. O'Grady was passed out across the bed, open-mouthed, snoring, and Nellie was nowhere in sight.

"Where's Nellie?" Liberty tried to compose herself, which wasn't easy when she wanted to beat the meanness out of Mr. O'Grady of whom she didn't give a rat's turd about. He was fortunate she'd taken an oath to *do no harm*, or she would gladly flay him with a broom or whatever weapon was available.

"She's back on the cot in the living room. Ya need to leave now, before my mister wakes up."

"How long was I out?"

"A couple of minutes, maybe less. I'm not sure. Please just go."

Ignoring the woman, Liberty went into the living room where Nellie, in a sweating stupor, lay on the cot with a meager blanket covering her. "I'm going to make that call now. Please put another blanket on her."

Mrs. O'Grady twisted the material of her apron into a tight ball. "If ye think your jaw hurts, that's nothin' to what he'll do to me when he finds a doctor and the health department here."

There wasn't much Liberty could do about a drunken wife-beater. The situation ran rampant in the tenements. She also felt little sympathy for Mrs. O'Grady at the moment.

"And that, Mrs. O'Grady will be mild compared to what the influenza or typhoid fever will do to you and the rest of your family if this illness isn't identified. Let me do my job." Pulling on her cape and grabbing her doctor's bag, she left the girl in her mother's care.

Liberty trudged down eight flights of dark and gloomy stairs to the entrance hall and where the telephone hung on the wall outside the manager's door. She gave the needed information to her clinic and requested a doctor. After replacing the receiver she decided to do her civic duty and go check on the stranger. Civic duty, ha, she almost choked on the thought. The nutcase on the roof might do worse to her than Mr. O'Grady did. Once again she spat into her handkerchief to see that her mouth had stopped bleeding.

She let out a deep sigh and started back up to the top to find out if he was still there or not. Reaching the rooftop door, she opened it and peered out. Seeing and hearing nothing at first, she eased around the wall that enclosed the stairwell hoping to find him gone. He wasn't. He was in the same place and position as earlier.

Misery seemed to cloak him better than the flimsy cape.

His head came up at her approach, his eyes wary, yet hopeful. "I need help," he said in a raspy voice. Using the wall to steady himself, he got to his feet.

The vision before her wasn't right. Liberty told herself to turn and go the other way. Instead, she followed her basic instincts and approached. Her eyes swept over the disheveled dark-haired man with bare skin showing through the shimmering cape of sequins and peacock feathers. Upon closer observation underneath the sheer blue material she spotted what appeared to be dried blood on his neck, hands, and abdomen. She gulped saliva and clutched her bag against her bosom using it as a shield.

Clearing her throat, she managed to say, "I'm a nurse. How can I help you?"

He stared at her as if trying to absorb her words. "You're a nurse?"

"Yes." She pointed to her identification on her hat band. "I'm a qualified degree-carrying nurse. I see you're hurt, bleeding."

"Well, so are you." He had the nerve to point out the obvious.

"Don't worry about me." She tongued the inside of her

mouth, the cut.

He held his hands out, turning them over, staring at them as if they weren't his own. "I can explain some of my predicament, but not all."

"Where are you wounded?"

He lowered his head and pointed to the back of it. "Here. My feet are cut from running barefoot, but I don't think you can help that."

"Let me warn you, I'm armed. I've been hit today by a drunk and I don't plan on letting it happen again."

"How are you armed?" he asked, staring at her with curious blue eyes.

"Just never you mind. Don't tempt me, that's all I'm saying. I'm short on tolerance right now." Mustering courage, she closed up the gap between them. "Please turn around so I can see your scalp."

While doing as told, he wobbled. His arm shot around her waist like a vice.

She gasped. For someone hurt, this man was strong, too strong.

"I'm sorry," he said. "Please trust me. I'd never hurt you." He released her as fast as he'd grabbed her.

Wanting to believe him, Liberty steadied her knees, her nerves. She parted his dark hair where it was matted with con-gealed blood and could see a gash several inches long. His scalp was swollen and bruised.

"This cut needs stitches. I'm afraid I'll have to do it here. Let me help you to sit." She took his offered left arm.

Using his free hand he fought to keep the cape modestly wrapped around his hips. Her eyebrows rose, that sheer thing didn't allow one iota of privacy, but he needn't worry, she'd seen many a man's genitals in her line of work. She helped him sit on the gritty surface of the rooftop.

Liberty opened her bag and took out a roll of gauze bandages, a long needled syringe, and a bottle of iodine. While filling the hypodermic needle with Novocain she saw him flinch and tried putting him at ease.

"Do you mind allowing a nurse to doctor you?"

"I don't have much choice, do I?" His voice suited him, deep and distinctive.

"Please listen, this shot in your scalp is going to hurt, so I suggest you refrain from yelling out and attracting attention." Without further ado, she pushed the needle through his skin shooting the anesthetic inside the cut.

"God—almighty!" He sucked in air and whistled through his teeth in short spurts. Grabbing onto the material of her skirt, he balled it between his fists and held on as if she was a life raft and he was drowning. She'd seen it so many times, a grown man turning into a whimpering child when it came to needles or pain.

After clipping his hair as close as she could get it to the cut, she threaded her needle and started closing the wound. "Not much longer," she soothed while stitching away. "Just a couple more. Whatever you were hit with was deadly. You're lucky you're not in a coma."

"Maybe less pain if I was."

Her lips quivered at his feeble joke, and it hurt her mouth to even do that. She took her scissors and snipped the catgut close to his scalp. Checking her work, she was quite satisfied, next came a generous dab of Iodine. Good thing he was still numb and couldn't feel the sting. She finished her doctoring by wrapping gauze around his head making him look like a wounded soldier.

"Let me look at your feet."

"They're all right."

"I said—let me see your feet." She knelt in front of him and lifting his long leg, settled his foot in her lap. Seeing cuts and bruises, she took her tweezers from her bag and began digging grit out of the cuts.

His toe's curled at her administrations. "I hate having the bottoms of my feet touched," he said between clenched teeth.

"I'm sorry, but if I don't get the dirt out, they'll become infected. The streets are filthy with garbage, urine, spit, and other unmentionables." Her eyes met his and she raised her brow at him.

When she was certain she'd removed all the debris from both his feet, she took her bottle of Iodine and used the glass wand from inside it to dab the antiseptic on his cuts. He yelped and kicked the bottle across the roof where it landed, shattering the glass container.

"Damn," he cursed. "You could tell a person you're going to put that stinging fire water on them." He pulled his left foot up past his right knee and blew on his sole.

Glaring, she got to her feet. "Really? Well you could warn a person you're going to kick their medicine all to heck and ruin it. That was my last bottle."

"Maybe I did the next patient a favor." He continued blowing at his foot.

When she started putting her supplies away, and without him even uttering a thank you, or, I'm sorry I broke your antiseptic bottle, he had the gall to ask.

"Would you mind helping me out?"

"I thought I just did, and with no thanks from you," she said getting perturbed. "Is there someone I can call for you, family—"

"No!" his words exploded.

Taken aback by his venomous outburst she hesitated before saying. "Then I don't know how I can help you any further. I've offered to contact your family but you don't want me to. I have patients to attend to. I must go. So if you need further assistance you better tell me before I leave."

His newly found strength collapsed and he sagged against the wall. "I can't explain right now, but I can't involve anyone in this mess I'm in. Since I don't understand what's happened to me, I can't expect anyone else too."

Give her a sick or wounded person and she could be of great assistance. But this strange predicament was something she'd never encountered before and she wasn't sure if she wanted further involvement. She closed the leather strap on her bag.

"So, you want me to just accept finding a naked man on a rooftop? Sew your head up and go on about my day? You're right, I don't understand. You need to explain more."

"I'll tell you everything once I'm off this roof." His blue eyes, a startling contrast to his black hair, held her, pleading. "I need clothes."

For the life of her, Liberty didn't know what further compelled her to want to aid this man, but putting him in the category of a sick and helpless animal helped somewhat. That comparison made up her mind.

"You'll have to remain here until dark. I'll come back with something to fit you."

"I can't stay here that long, it's too blasted cold." He fisted the useless material tighter, pulling it taunt against his body, to no avail.

Liberty removed her cape and put it around his shoulders trying to cover the flowing gossamer fabric. "It isn't much, but my cape is wool and will be of some warmth until I can come back." She wanted to laugh at the funny sight he made, wearing her cloak that came to his waist, hairy legs protruding below gossamer fabric, instead, the cold air nipped at her, and she almost took it back.

He pulled the garment close. "Ah…miss, I've changed my mind. Would you please make a telephone call to my father, tell him where I'm at?"

Hearing a please in his request, she agreed. "I can do that. There's a telephone inside on the main floor. Who do I call?" She narrowed a look at him, gauging, always processing her thoughts. Was she in danger? She couldn't be sure. Yet if she was, he would have moved against her by now, wouldn't he?

"Do you have a pencil—paper?" he asked.

"Yes, use the back of this." Liberty opened her bag and taking out her list of patients for the day, she turned the paper over and handed him the pencil. She looked at her pendant watch that showed she was already late for the next patient, a tenement across the way, easy access from joined rooftop to rooftop.

He began scratching on the paper. "Contact my father, Lincoln Drake at this telephone number. I'm his son, Jonathan. Talk to him directly and no one else. If he's not there, try this other number. If you can't reach him personally do not leave a message." Returning her paper and pencil, he slumped against the stairwell enclosure, resting his head against the boards. "Jesus." He fingered the gauze going across his forehead and glanced at her. "One other thing. Please tell my father I'm innocent."

Innocent? One strong word with a ton of meanings, and one that conjured up all sorts of nasty thoughts. Liberty's eyes narrowed at him. "I don't know what that means. It frightens me. You might not like what I'm going to say, but I'm saying it anyway. I have a patient to call on in the next tenement. I'll see them and then I'll make the telephone call to your father. I'll try to buy you something to wear. After that I want no further involvement with you."

Pushing away from the wall, his eyes tipped downward to meet hers. He clutched her woolen cape tight against his body in a white knuckled grip. "I'll not harm you in any way. I promise. The word of a Drake carries a lot of weight in this city."

Well, the name meant little or nothing to her right now. She nodded and started to walk off when his voice floated after her.

"Does Nurse Nightingale have a name?"

She stopped to stare at him. This time his attempt at making a joke didn't amuse her in the slightest.

"I'm Liberty—Liberty Fitzgerald. Miss Fitzgerald to you."

Chapter Three

Detective Frank Jones stood next to detective Ernesto Scala. Miss DeLane's body had recently been removed by the medical examiner and taken to the morgue. The only thing left of the Follies star was the pool of congealed blood.

Jones and his partner were here since being called onto the scene late last evening. Tired, Jones yawned and pulled out his pocket watch. Seven a.m. He figured they had another hour of work here before leaving.

At fifty-two Jones was considered an old man. More than one of his superiors hinted that he might do well behind a desk, or step aside. Part of Manhattan's police department for thirty some years he'd been given the nickname of *Sherlock* for always solving his case. Even with his reputation of being dogmatic and thorough, there were plenty of young policemen who wanted his job. In order to keep his job, he needed to prove himself, and in order to prove himself, he must find and bring the killer, Jonathan Drake, to justice. This was the kind of case any and all detectives dreamed of, practically having the killer dumped on their doorstep. If anyone was guilty, it was Mr. Drake. Yet, cases that appeared open and shut were not always so open and shut. And Jones knew it better than anyone.

Jones glanced at Scala, his partner of ten years. Scala, born in America to Italian immigrants from the old country, used to take pride in his appearance. But in recent years, he'd let himself go by becoming pudgy and showing up for work in wrinkled suits. Years ago, he'd been slim with curly black hair and sharply dressed. Now at the age of forty-five, Scala's tragic past and this job itself aged him. He usually smelled of Jack Daniels and carried a flask, something Jones typically overlooked. Despite his partners many foibles, the one thing Jones knew for certain was that Scala was the only cop he wanted beside him.

Right now, Jones's keen eye took in the room, satisfied that they hadn't missed a thing. Numerous footprints scattered throughout the powder on the floor gave off a cloying smell of lilacs. Scala's black pants legs were dusted with the stuff from where he'd earlier flattened his body against the floor and peered under the fancy brocaded love seat to find what they sought. A bloody knife.

Scala took out a handkerchief from his suit pocket and wiped perspiration from his face. "I think we're done here."

"Bag up those clothes." Jones ordered a uniformed policeman standing close by and pointed toward the male evening attire they'd found neatly folded behind the star's dressing screen. "Shoes too."

"Don't forget the knife." Scala flicked his head toward the deadly blade on the dressing table. "Time to interview the remaining dancers and crew." He removed the diminutive flask from his suit coat pocket and took a sip.

"Breakfast?" Jones said with some sarcasm. More than anything he wanted to help his friend, but that door closed a long time ago and no one, not even a mother's dying plea could sway Scala. "Put it away," he mouthed at Scala, and indicated with a nod toward the blue-coated policeman who was glancing their way as he picked up the bagged evidence.

Scala saluted Jones with the silver flask, and belligerently took another sip. He capped the flask before hiding it inside his pocket.

They went out into the area backstage where the detained dancers had wilted onto the floor. Some were propped against the wall while others lay haphazardly against the other. Feathery headdresses and high-heeled shoes were in a pile next to them. The male dancers and the lone singer that were on stage during the time of the murder had been interrogated earlier and sent home. Two women with measuring tapes around their necks, and their wrists adorned with pincushions stood chatting in French to each other. Next to them was the rigging crew.

Jones perused his lists of names and signaled to a big gruff looking man.

"Ah…Mick Brown?" Jones said. "Stage manager?"

The man got to his feet and approached. "Yeah, that's me."

"You're the one who broke down the door to get inside and fought with Drake?" Jones said, and patting the breast pocket on his suit, took out a cigarette case and clicked it open to reveal a dozen purchased cigarettes all in a neat row. He claimed one and striking a match against the sole of his shoe, lit up, the gray smoke spiraled upward into the rigging. "Tell us what happened."

"I already told ya," he said with a scowl.

Jones flared. "Look, smartass, if I tell you to tell your story a hundred times, you will. Understand?" Moving close to the big man, he blew smoke into the stagehand's face.

"Aw right, aw right. Yeah, I caught Jonathan Drake with the knife in his hand—still dripping blood. We fought. I would have kicked his ass if he hadn't thrown that damn powder in my face. Blinded me."

"Which hand was he holding the knife in?"

The stagehand's dark brows lowered over his eyes. "His right. I've already answered that."

Seeing their prime witness was getting angry and tired, and weren't they all, Jones pointed at the showgirls who had peeked into the dressing room to see Jonathan Drake standing there with the knife in his hand. One of the gals dabbed at her tears, while another appeared bored, and yawned. Knowing how keen competition was between the performers, he wondered if the tears were being faked. For sure most of the dancer's right here would be begging to take Miss DeLane's place. Yet, their testimony was crucial to the investigation.

"I need to talk with each of you again," Jones said.

Before Jones could start his interrogation, a short, compact man in a gray suit came up to him puffing on a cigar.

The man held out his hand. "I'm Sidney Brawley, the theater manager. Terrible thing, terrible loss—terrible loss. How can I be of help?"

"Well, first things first. We want the theater closed until our investigation's complete."

Sidney Brawley paled and sputtered. "Shit—how long will that take?"

"Just a few days. Relax. We don't want this to go on any longer than you do." Jones stroked at his gray mustache.

"Do you know how much money we will lose in two days? That is if I can believe you will be done in two days." Sidney puffed his cigar, clouding the air with its stringent odor.

"That should give you time to replace your star, right?" Scala said. "You need to leave and let us do our job so we can be done and outta here." Dismissing the manager who could only stand there staring, Scala turned his attention back to the dancers.

They left the theater a little after eight. Jones knew his wife, Clara, no longer went through the motions of being a dutiful wife waiting by the home fires to prepare a meal for her chronically late husband. Their two sons were out on their own. Frederick the eldest at twenty-eight was married, lived upstate New York, and had his own law firm. Garth, three years younger, joined the police department and was a cop in another precinct.

"Want to go eat breakfast instead of drinking it?" Jones asked Scala.

"Sure, I could use something solid instead of liquid."

They entered the café, open twenty-four hours, and one that catered to the theater employees and actors. The room was crowded, noisy and the talk bantered around was of Zelda DeLane's death.

Jones spotted a booth just emptying by four people and instantly claimed it. The male waiter with a long grubby apron tied around his waist hurried over to clear the table. As he rattled plates and cups into a pile onto a tray, he took their order of eggs, bacon, sausage, and strong coffee, no cream, no sugar, just black.

When the food and coffee was delivered, Scala added drops of whisky into his steaming cup. He shook the flask next to his ear.

"Aw, just enough for another cup."

Jones stared at his partner's flaccid face, the dark eyes now trained on him and knew he should back off, but he couldn't. "Don't refill that damn flask. Give it up."

"Shut up. No lectures, don't need 'em." He forked his eggs, spilling the yolk to run into the toast.

"Maybe you do. Thought it might be getting easier on you by now." Jones buttered his toast and spread blackberry jam on it. He took a bite, and then another, devouring the slice, and then picked up his fork and started on his eggs.

Scala simply stared at him. "Must have something to do with identifying my dead wife's body. Seven months pregnant with our first child. Stacked like cordwood alongside hundreds of other bodies." He shuddered.

"Scala," Jones said, now sorry to have brought up the past that was always in the present, looming. "I know—I know, but fourteen years is time enough to mourn. You need another woman in your life, someone who can take your mind off the tragedy, off that damn General Slocum disaster."

"You mean someone who can try to stop me from drinking." Scala pushed his half eaten meal aside and drained his spiked coffee. "None of your business is it."

"Only when you drink on the job, which nowadays is always."

"Do I make mistakes?"

"No, Ernesto, you don't. It's just..." Let it go, he told himself, let it go.

Chapter Four

With her jaw a constant ache, Liberty found it hard to keep her mind on her work, but somehow she got through her next visit and trudged down ten flights to the main floor. She entered the foyer in search of the wall phone, but when she got there a man was using it, so she waited at a polite distance until he finished.

While leaving, he smiled and tipped his hat at her.

She lifted the black earpiece off the cradle and, putting it to her ear, clicked the cradle up and down several times.

"Number please," said the switchboard operator.

Liberty read the first number on the paper for the operator and waited.

"Drake's residence," answered a female.

Liberty wasn't expecting this. She stuttered, "May...er...may I speak with a...er Mr. Lincoln Drake?" She picked at the flowers on the faded wallpaper.

This time the woman sounded cautious. "He isn't here. May I ask who is calling, please?"

A young boy in knee pants ran by bouncing a red ball. The noise echoed loud in the confined hallway.

"I'm sorry, I didn't hear you. Would you mind saying it again?" Liberty asked.

"I said Mister Drake isn't here. Who are you?"

Disappointed, Liberty said, "Mr. Drake doesn't know me. Please, I need to know where he can be reached, it's important."

"One moment, please."

Minutes ticked by before a man's deep voice came on the phone. "I'm Lincoln Drake, are you a reporter?"

Reporter? From what? A newspaper? Baffled, Liberty's words tumbled out. "No, I'm not a reporter. I'm calling on behalf of your son, Jonathan Drake."

When Mr. Drake didn't say anything for several seconds, the pause set Liberty's pulse on a rapid course.

At last he spoke. His voice steady yet forced. "I thought you said you weren't a reporter."

Liberty wanted to slam the earpiece back in its cradle. What was going on? "I'm not a reporter. I'm just someone who happened upon your son."

"I can't tell you anymore than I can the detectives standing here next to me. So, I suggest you take your slimy newspaper and do you know what with it."

Why was Mr. Drake insisting she was a reporter and mentioning the detectives? Not being totally dumb in the ways of secrecy, she was fast to figure out he didn't want the police to know that she knew Jonathan Drake's whereabouts. She told him about finding Jonathan on a rooftop, and that he needed help.

"I don't know my son's whereabouts and if I did I wouldn't tell a reporter. Once again take your filthy newspaper and—"

Liberty's words rushed out, "He said to tell you he's innocent." She heard Lincoln Drake expel a loud breath. She rattled out questions. "Mister Drake, I don't know what he's done. Am I in danger?" It was Liberty's turn to let out a shaky breath.

"No damn you—you're not! And don't call here again."

Perplexed, she asked, "Do you want me to call you again—tomorrow?"

"Yes. You heard me right."

The line went dead and she hung up before the operator could come back on. The kid with the ball returned and she waited until he pushed open the front door and ran outside.

She in turn placed a phone call to Emma Taylor, her boss at the Henry Street organization. Liberty told Mrs. Taylor about Mr. O'Grady punching her, that her jaw was swollen, she had a bad headache, and asked if her friend Helen Cartwright could take her patients for the rest of the day? Emma, in a concerned voice, asked if Liberty was going to be all right, did she need to see a doctor.

"No," replied Liberty. "If I do I'll let you know."

"I'll send Miss Cartwright to call on your remaining patients. Please take care of yourself and I'll see you tomorrow."

Liberty took a trolley to the shopping district that teemed with people, food carts, honking automobiles, and clopping horses. Sidestepping a pile of steaming manure on the street, she hurried across.

In case of an emergency she carried a small amount of money in her doctor's bag. Ducking into a clothing store that smelled of new fabric, she nodded at the female store clerk who approached.

"May I be of assistance?" The matronly woman was all business with her hair piled high, a pencil over one ear, and an apron covering her blue dress.

"Yes, I need ready-made clothing for a man, thank you." Liberty followed the clerk down the aisle toward the clothes.

"Here's what we have." The clerk paused in front of a shelf with stacked goods. "I'm afraid the war in Europe limits us, but with our own factories sewing more of what we need, our shelves aren't so bare now." She smiled at Liberty. "What size do you require?"

Liberty had to guess. She stretched her arm up to match his height. "He's tall, around six-feet, long legged, slim at the waist...er...well..." She made her arms into a circle that would reach around his waist. "This is about right."

The clerk clucked her tongue and shook her head. She grabbed a measuring tape from her pocket and measured inside Liberty's arms. "Most unorthodox, I must say."

"He's a distant uncle that's come to visit and I want to surprise him with new clothes. I'll take the black pants, and a white shirt."

"What's his shirt collar size?"

"What?" This was all becoming too much for Liberty. Visualizing her hands around Jonathan Drake's throat, she formed another circle. "Measure this," she said, and would really like to be squeezing his neck about now.

Liberty paid for the pants, a shirt, and a pair of black socks, which was all she could afford. When she came back outside, a boy selling papers stood on the corner holding a newspaper aloft, calling out the news.

"Follies star brutally murdered. Read all about it."

She quickly put a nickel in his grubby hand and took the offered paper. A sea of people rushed by, some knocked into her, some went around. Food cart vendors yelled for customers to stop by. The thick aroma of cooking onions and sausage coming from the carts beckoned, but she tried to ignore the mouthwatering smells and instead stopped to lean against a store front. She put her package and her medical bag at her feet and allowed the paper to unfold, revealing the bold headline.

Zelda DeLane, darling of Foyle's Follies murdered.

A grainy picture of the star on her back and in the throes of death glared out from the page. *Jonathan Drake, son of the hotel magnate Lincoln Drake, found on top of the lovely Zelda...*

Murder.

Jonathan Drake.

"Tell my father I'm innocent."

Innocent.

The words bounced around in Liberty's mind like the ball being kicked by the youngster. She folded the paper and shoved it underneath her armpit. Grabbing her bag and package, she walked with determination. My God, the man was the son of the owner of *The Drake.* Mr. Lincoln Drake who she'd just had a phone conversation with. She'd seen the hotel from a distance. Smart, fancy, and definitely for the rich, the very rich.

Murdering someone was a whole lot different than being out of your mind. She thought Jonathan was a nutcase, perhaps escaped from the mental institution. Well, maybe he was a nutcase and a murderer rolled into one. How was she supposed to handle that? Not handle it at all. What if she didn't go back? What if she just ignored that she'd ever found him?

Innocent.

She resented finding him in the first place. More than upset with herself for even going back to see if she could be of service. Certainly, angry for buying clothing for him. Would it make her an accomplice? She wanted her uneventful and scheduled life back. Cure the sick, improve the poor.

Down the street was the local police precinct, where two blue uniformed policemen came out and strolled in her direction. She hesitated but a moment before she hurried toward the station and the two officers. When she was directly in front of them, they touched the brim of their hats and started to go by.

"Excuse me," she said, and met two pair of eyes staring at her in question.

The tall one's sharp gaze took in her face, the bruised jaw and said, "If you want to put in a complaint about the man who hit you, an irate husband I assume, you can go to the precinct and do so. We don't take complaints here on the street."

"No, that's not it. This is," she said and pointed at her news-paper. "The news—the Follies star—do they know for sure this Jonathan Drake murdered her?"

The heavier of the two chuckled and rested his hand on his baton. "Nothing's for sure in life. But, they have a good case against the man accused."

The other one with sharp features stared at her in thought and stroked his graying goatee. "Why the interest in a murder or mur-derer you obviously know nothing about?"

She frowned and said, "I'm just curious. So…if a person…er, this Jonathan Drake, is found guilty of murder will he go to pris-on?"

Again the sharp-featured policeman answered. "No, if he says he's innocent, there will be a trial. If he's guilty, he'll go to Sing Sing where he'll roast in the chair." He looked her over. "I'm afraid someone of yer place in society wouldn't know anything about rich Jonathan Drake, now would ya?"

Belittled by his snide remark, her jaw tightened and she slipped into her father's Irish dialect. "Sure'n yer right. I know nothin' about the Drake's, what with me being the daughter of a poor Irish immigrant and all." Even if her life depended on it now she wouldn't tell them anything. Maybe it did. But with them both standing there looking down their noses at her, she would be damned if she'd say another word. They were mere policemen, while she, a trained nurse was better educated than the both of them put together. If anyone should be putting on airs here, it was her.

"Thank you for your time," she said.

Again, good manners made them tip the brims of their hats at her as they walked on.

Clutching her packages a little tighter, Liberty continued back toward the tenement and the man waiting there, innocent or not.

Chapter Five

Alice Montgomery leaned against the fluffy pillows supporting her back. Her honey-blonde hair was pulled up into a mass of curls on top of her head. Wearing a rose-colored negligee, she was all lace and silk.

At the sound of a loud knock on her bedroom door she watched as the door swung open and her husband, Talon, entered. Tall, distinguished, and razor sharp as his name suggests. His midnight black hair, straight and graying at the temples was pomaded into place against his scalp. As always, he was impeccably dressed in a black suit that showed off his wide shoulders and disguised his forty years of age. Alice, ten years younger than her husband, felt that she looked older especially after a restless night. She was tired.

Stopping next to her bed, he pulled up a chair where he flipped the New York Times open. His eyes, the color of a cold gray sky, locked onto hers.

"You will never believe what is in the paper," he said and waved the front page at her, his thin mouth set in a cynical twist.

"No, and I guess I won't if you don't stop waving it around

like a flag of surrender, and give it to me. You might calm yourself, while you're at it." She brushed a tickling strand of hair from her cheek and looked at the paper Talon held up so she could read.

The words, so fatal in telling, shouted in bold headlines that Zelda DeLane, the darling star of Foyle's Follies had been murdered by one Jonathan Drake.

"Hmmm," she said. "This Zelda DeLane's murder means more to you than it does to me. I'm trying to remember if I went to one of her performances. If I did, it was no doubt so uneventful that I can't bring it to mind."

"I'm surprised you don't say something about Jonathan Drake. I always figured he'd end up in a pickle someday. Although, I can't say I thought him capable of murder." He handed her the paper so she could see the gruesome pictures of the lovely Zelda.

She stared at the newspaper, studying it for the longest of time, how horrible to see such an intimate display on the front page. She'd never seen a dead person before, and was more than thankful the grainy black and white picture toned the puddle of blood down some. An insert of Jonathan's face was in the corner of the death scene. She handed the paper back, where Talon placed it on his lap, the rest of the news forgotten.

She leaned back against the pillows as pain seized her in its familiar grip and squeezed, radiating from her lower back to crawl up her spine making her want to scream. Instead, she said in a calm voice. "I cannot believe Jonathan Drake's capable of murder either."

Talon nodded. "If I remember correctly he was courting you before we married. True?"

Alice balled the sheet into her hands. Yes, how true. The past seven years she'd been married to Talon made the years before that seem a lifetime ago. "Yes, dear, it's true. Isn't it also true you've had more than one peccadillo with dancers from all the theaters? Miss DeLane included?" She dared him to try and wiggle out of that one. He didn't. Only sat there and smiled at some re-membered vision of the Follies star, locking Alice out of his thoughts, making her temper flare. But a flaring temper took too much strength, something she didn't have to flitter away, so she didn't take the bait.

Across the room in a fancy tall gilded cage were two love birds. Alice's pets. And the only love going on in this room, and right now they preened, chirped and groomed the other's feathers.

"Be sure and have Miss Bishop take you outside for some fresh air. It will do you good."

She glanced out her bedroom window. At the gloomy sky filled with clouds threatening rain. "I'm thinking I might catch my death out there. I wonder why you would suggest such a thing."

But he only smirked and shrugged.

"I'm assuming you're going to the store soon?" she said, again gritting her teeth with pain.

"Of course, why wouldn't I?"

"No reason. When you see Daddy downstairs would you give him my love?" she asked, her way of letting Talon know she was through conversing with him. "Oh, and please summon Miss Bishop for me." All she had to do was use the bell cord herself to let her maid know she desired breakfast, but giving Talon orders made her feel better.

Talon leaned forward, and she was quick to offer him her cheek to kiss. His lips barely brushed her flesh before he straight-ened. He reached over her head and pulled the long brocaded bell ringer. "Now, Miss Bishop is sent for. Anything else?"

When she shook her head no, he started to leave but paused by the bird cage and put his finger in the cage, beckoning, but the birds only fluttered around. "You might have the bird shit cleaned out of the cage, it reeks." He glowered her way and then left, his tailored suit coat brushed against his hips with each step.

"Make sure Miss Bishop heard the bell," she called after him.

She took a deep breath and stared at her elegant surroundings. Lavender brocaded chairs, a love seat to match, mahogany pillared headboard and footboard polished to perfection, a mirrored dressing table with perfumes from Paris and horsehair brushes with silver handles. Wallpaper with colorful birds graced the walls. Across the room was an armoire bursting with clothing.

Her wheelchair, that she despised, was nearby.

She'd been told many a time by her father to thank her lucky stars for being born wealthy and how she owed her good fortune to her great-great-grandfather who had migrated from France and started *Grand's* department store. Small and unassuming at first, her father, Charles Grand, boosted how over the years he'd turned the store into a growing enterprise, one that rivaled Macy's.

Alice lacked for nothing. But even more so, she should be thankful her father's money bought her a husband, and that her father set Talon up in *Grand's*. Talon surprised everyone with his keen business acumen and made a success of the department he was in charge of. Talon imported trinkets and knickknacks from all over the world, he filled *Grand's* with what Alice called junk. But people loved to collect junk, and to her delight, put more money in the bank for her to spend.

Her mother, Yvette, from France, was in her hub of high society, her forte, yet Alice knew she despaired of never having a grandchild to spoil. A grandchild, who if born would be close to three-years-old by now. Although she tried, Alice would never forget the details or the man's face when he stepped out from the bushes in Central Park, startling her horse, causing it to rear up, and bouncing her on her behind. Four month's pregnant she'd miscarried, and was left partially paralyzed. The doctors told her the miscarriage was just as well since her being so damaged might hinder the child's development. And now pain instead of a husband was her constant companion.

When first married to Talon, Alice's parents insisted on the newlyweds living with them. The Grand's mansion was huge and Alice and her husband had an entire floor all to themselves. After Alice's accident a special elevator was installed to ferry Alice and her wheelchair between floors.

The door opened and Jenny Bishop breezed in holding a heavy tray laden with a silver coffee pot and covered dishes. Miss Bishop at forty-three was a tall, big-boned woman with large brown eyes and chestnut colored hair tucked into a neat bun.

"Good morning, dear Alice, good morning." Her comely face lit up with a wide grin.

"Is it? Just one minute with Talon sours the whole day for me. He wants the birdcage cleaned. You can use today's paper to line the bottom of it."

Miss Bishop nodded. "The one with the news about the murder? Miss DeLane?" Her smile was most secretive.

"Exactly."

Miss Bishop put the tray on the nightstand and poured coffee from the silver pot into a dainty cup decorated with roses. She added three sugar cubes and cream, and after stirring it well, she put it on the tray and then placed it across Alice's lap.

Alice accepted the cup and saucer, and sipped slowly, allowing the hot liquid to warm her insides. She nibbled on the toast, the poached egg, but ignored the bacon.

"Is he gone?" she asked, and dabbed the corners of her mouth with a rose-colored napkin.

"Yes, he is. Both he and your father left a short time ago. Your mother is off to have breakfast with some senator's wife. Would you like your opium now or after I exercise your legs?"

"Now. I'm in too much pain to allow you to even touch my

legs. Please, the opium."

"Tsk, tsk, my dear, Alice. You always say that, but I'm to follow doctor's orders, and that is to work your legs, make them stronger."

"It's been over three years since my accident, and I think if my legs were going to get stronger they would have by now."

"Your nurses before me were lazy, that's all."

Yes, indeed, those in Alice's employment before Jenny were lazy. My word, Alice thought, had two years already passed since Jenny came into her life, and all it took was an ad for a nurse companion. One who could lift an invalid, get her meals and take care of her. Alice held court and interviewed Jenny who appeared friendly enough, wise in the ways of nursing and answered every question asked. Jenny proved to be invaluable. But it was the other things Jenny could do above and beyond the call of taking care of Alice that set her heart to pounding, and her waking up each morning with a greedy anticipation.

Alice pouted and watched as Jenny pulled the bed covers away to bare her legs, which had gone from shapely to thin with little use. No wonder Talon turns away, she thought, I certainly would.

The oil Jenny put on her legs smelled rather nice, and she endured as Jenny massaged and lifted each leg, peddling it as if Alice was riding a bicycle. Alice could feel something in her legs, a nerve tingling, felt Jenny squeezing her muscles hard. Yet, whenever she tried to stand, her legs felt liquefied, and refused to hold her. The doctors cautioned her that this feeling was caused by her damaged spine, and despite her being able to feel pain in her lower extremities, she would never walk again.

Jenny went to the large armoire and after several minutes returned with an opium pipe delicately carved from ivory. She lit the long slender pipe and handed it to Alice who eagerly accepted it.

Alice lay there inhaling the pungent, mind-altering smoke that crawled into her lungs, wondering how she ever made it through a day without opium. It made life bearable. Her Jenny made it even more so. She relaxed, the pain dulled as she melted into the soft mattress.

"You're my savior, Jenny…my savior."

The tug on the ribbons of her negligee bodice foretold they were being untied. Parted, the cool air hit her bosom making her skin pucker. And then the feel of moist spit as Jenny's tongue lapped Alice's breasts, her nipples, kissing, sucking, taking the sting away of a husband who didn't love her, wanted nothing from her or her body. She and Talon's love making had been wonderful, full of excitement, experimenting, and ended with Alice expecting a child. A child she desperately wanted, a child to pamper, to treat like a doll, something she and Talon created. Certainly he would love the child as much as she would. Alice opened her eyes, her pretense that Talon was kissing her, gone, instead it was Jenny. Jenny, who had removed her own clothes, and Jenny whose large firm breast Alice now suckled like a baby.

"Suck harder, Alice. Hurt me, bruise me," Jenny ordered.

Alice languished in the throes of heat that only Jenny could bring to her. She moaned, allowing Jenny to do what she wanted. Her body felt liquid, her surroundings blurred. Alice offered the pipe to Jenny and held it while she drew the opium deep into her lungs. Putting her mouth over Alice's, she shared the smoke, all the while her fingers caressed Alice's folds, stroking, playing the man. Jenny's hand took on a frenzied rhythm, causing Alice to climax, the jolt so wantonly delightful she didn't want it to end. She clasped Jenny's hand tight against her, pressing it into her cleft. That she still had some feeling below her waist made Alice thankful, but she was even more thankful for Jenny.

"Do it again, please…" Alice begged.

"You're greedy, my Alice. Not right now, in a minute." She bent to kiss Alice on the mouth, her tongue seeking the sweet tastes. Jenny finally withdrew from her side and removed the pipe from Alice's grasp.

Pulling on a fancy silk robe, Jenny left the room to fill the claw-footed tub. Alice lay there listening to the water splashing. Bubbles, lots of bubbles, would make her feel better. Even the floral bouquet that wafted from the bath soothed.

Jenny returned. "Let me help you into the tub. It's hot, filled with jasmine bubble bath." She slipped the negligee off of Alice. Despite the fire in the fireplace, the chilled air peaked Alice's nipples. Naked, she allowed Jenny to lift her from the bed and put her into her wheelchair.

Still groggy from the drug, she was wheeled into the large bathroom, where being strong as any man, Jenny placed Alice in the bath, and slipped a neck pillow behind her head. The water was hot, almost too hot for Alice's tender skin, but she allowed it, thinking the hot water would help her muscles. Steam rose and water did a slow drip from the faucet.

Jenny lathered the sponge with jasmine scented soap and ran it over Alice's body, washing one toe at a time. Alice smiled at her nurse and Jenny returned the smile, her brown eyes alight as she continued to wash between Alice's legs.

"Join me," Alice urged.

"Not today. Tonight, I will come back to your bed."

"I don't know how I ever got along without you. I'm so thankful you're here, for me, for me alone, never to share…never to…"

Alice's head tipped downward toward the water, and Jenny was quick to tilt her chin upwards out of harm's way.

Jenny kept an eye on Alice, making sure she didn't slip underneath the water again. Dropping the sponge in the water, she sat in the chair, relaxed, and let the opium take over. Opening her robe, she caressed herself, skimming her fingers over her breasts, her abdomen, to her bush exploring, just like Miss Reed taught her to do. Ah…Miss Reed, beautiful Miss Reed with the blonde hair so like Alice's. Oh…yes, Jenny and Alice had much in common. Both were an only child. Both had ambitious parents, only Jenny's didn't rise to such glorious heights as the Grand's…

…Born in a small town in Connecticut, Jenny turned out tall for her age with glossy chestnut-colored hair and large doe eyes. Highly intelligent, but with strict parents, she had a sheltered up-bringing. That is until she was sent to an all girl's school where she lost her virginity to a female mathematics teacher. In the tenth grade, she excelled at math and was awarded a ribbon for her high grades in all her courses, but the blue ribbon for math made her the proudest.

Her math teacher, Miss Reed, asked Jenny to come to dinner at her home to further celebrate. Miss Reed, young and unmarried, and who always walked around the classroom tapping a wooden ruler against her palm, was a different woman this night. To six-teen-year-old Jenny's surprise, Miss Reed opened her door wearing her golden-blonde hair billowing around her shoulders. Jenny fol-lowed Miss Reed's hourglass figure adorned in a low cut, pink dress amassed with ruffles and lace, into her home. A warm and inviting home filled with a woman's preference of flowery décor.

During dinner, Jenny couldn't help but notice Miss Reed's silken skin, her long elegant neck, and the way she was constantly putting her hand over Jenny's. After dinner when Miss Reed sug-gested they have a glass of sherry, Jenny nodded.

They drank far too much of the amber liquid, and when Miss Reed asked for permission to kiss Jenny, she let her. Miss Reed's moist tongue slipped inside Jenny's mouth, and that act alone brought intense feelings between Jenny's legs. When she asked

Jenny if she was a virgin, again Jenny nodded. When Miss Reed asked if Jenny minded if she took off Jenny's clothes, Jenny agreed. When Miss Reed led Jenny upstairs to her bedroom and proceeded to strip her, Jenny allowed her to touch her breasts, she allowed her to touch her all over. She climbed into the bed and that feeling between her legs intensified even more, especially when Miss Reed took Jenny's hand and mapped her body with it by putting Jenny's hand into the most delicious spot of all, Miss Reed's cleft. She taught Jenny that one-plus-one equaled more than two, it equaled all sorts of decadent delights. This was the start of many dinners between the two. Jenny graduated from school with the highest marks ever for a woman in math.

Jenny left Miss Reed and the school behind to work for her father in his pharmacy. But mixing medicine in a drug store started to pale and Jenny wanted adventure, so she left home. She falsified nursing credentials and work references. She moved to Philadelphia where she started working as a nurse companion for rich and spoilt women who thought they were sick but really weren't. Jenny became adept at mixing remedies that helped her employers enjoy life. When they started craving too much or became addicted she simply packed up and moved on.

Her parent's died and she inherited the pharmacy. Not wanting to live in Connecticut, she sold the store to simply pay off her father's debts, leaving her with nothing. She moved to New York City and answered an ad for a nurse companion and that woman turned out to be Alice Montgomery. Jenny watched and listened and realized how lonely and starved for affection Alice was. Jenny, wormed her way into Alice's good graces, flattered her, told her how beautiful she was and how anyone, man or woman would be lucky to have her. Not knowing if Alice would be offended and fire her, Jenny took the risk, she made the first sexual advance towards Alice. All it took was Jenny undressing Alice for a bath, a quick kiss on the lips followed by kissing her breasts, and asking if Alice missed being made love to, and would she allow Jenny to show her how? She convinced Alice their love making wasn't wrong. They'd fallen into a sexual relationship, which both were sure to keep from Alice's husband and parents...

...Noticing Alice's mouth had slipped under the water; Jenny hurried to pull her upright, splashing water on the floor.

"Alice—Alice, wake up. It's time to get you out."

Next time she would have to use less opium and think less about Miss Reed, and past sexual romps.

Talon sat at his desk mulling over the news in the paper. A soft knock on his office door made him glance up to see Mrs. Beamer the secretary opening the door and announcing visitors. Two men he didn't know approached. After flashing their badges at him, they took off their hats.

Across the hall his father-in-law sat in his office watching them like a hawk. Talon suggested they close the door behind them.

The older and taller of the two spoke. "I'm detective Jones and this is detective Scala. We'd like to ask you a few questions concerning your relationship with Zelda DeLane."

Taken aback, Talon could only stammer and said the first thing that came to mind. It was the wrong thing to say. "I...I...have no relationship with Miss DeLane."

"That's not what we've been told," Detective Jones said. "Folks working at the theater said you are...were...one of Miss DeLane's lovers and you made weekly visits backstage to her dressing room."

Talon took a pencil from his desk and rolled it between his hands. "Yes. We were friends. On occasion I'd take her out to eat after her performance."

"On occasion, not regularly?" The taller of the two spoke.

"That's what I said."

The short heavy-set cop offered an opinion. "We hear that over the years you make it a habit...of...taking out theater stars."

Talon dropped the pencil and stood. "Your name is...Scala, right? Well, tell me, has a law been passed against fucking any woman I choose?"

Scala answered with authority. "No. Most married men do just that. Play around, dip their cocks in as many pussies as they can. That's not why we're here. We want to know about you and Miss DeLane."

Talon shrugged and smirked. "There's nothing to tell. She had a hot cooch and I have a hot sausage in my pants. We clicked. We fucked. Book's closed."

Jones stood toe-to toe with Talon. "Don't get smart with us. Do you know a Jonathan Drake?"

Talon backed up putting space between him and the cop. "Now you're asking questions I can answer. The Drake's are old friends of my wife's family. I only know of Jonathan Drake through them. Apparently, Jonathan was an old flame of my wife's, years ago, when she was young and starting her search for a husband. Lucky for me, they didn't mesh."

Jones narrowed his eyes as if thinking. "Do you have any idea where Drake might be hiding?"

"No, not at all. Like I said, I didn't have much to do with the Drake's, or with your murderer. I hope you find the bastard and fry him. He took a lovely woman away from the world."

Jones and Scala put their hats back on.

"If you think of anything else other than him being an old beau of your wife's, let us know." Jones adjusted his fedora.

Talon opened his office door for them. "How about I treat

you both to a new suit? New shoes maybe?" He flicked his fingers across Jones's suit lapel.

Jones brushed Talon's hand away. "Not necessary, we don't take bribes."

"Not a bribe. Just being friendly." Talon ushered them out of his office.

From across the hall, he caught Charles Grand's caustic stare. One that he'd put up with ever since he'd married Alice and been ensconced in the office across from his father-in-law. The feeling of dislike was mutual. Talon nodded before closing the door and returning to his desk.

Talon, more than anyone, knew he was an enigma, a chameleon, who left his old life behind in San Francisco for a new life started here in Manhattan. Upon his unheralded arrival in that new life, he went to work for Dillard's department store as a sales clerk. From there he worked his way up to a buyer. He lived modestly, purchasing ready-made clothes, keeping his shoes shined, his hat dusted. His frivolous spending was on a weekly whore. Then eight years ago, he happened to be in Central Park, sitting on a bench when a beautiful woman appeared on her horse. The sun haloed her blonde hair, her cheeks were rosy, her ass on the saddle small and rose neatly with the gentle gait of the horse.

"Who is that lovely woman?" He'd asked the man beside him.

The man's bald head swiveled to where he was now looking at the back of the vision of loveliness as she rode on. "Her? Oh…that's Alice Grand. You know…of the Grand's department store fame. Got yer eye on that now do ya? Well, if ya don't have money, like several million or so, don't bother to introduce yourself." He threw his last peanut to a chattering squirrel and left.

Talon sat there, determined to have Alice Grand and all that came with her. He formulated a plan, one that he hoped would work. He found out Alice's riding schedule. He found out everything he could about her family, their business dealings.

He put himself at the park on the day that Alice rode by. He was quick to spook her horse, and even quicker to stop it from throwing her. She came off the horse and into his arms. Devilish handsome, he knew he'd caught her attention. And he did. She couldn't take her eyes from him, and insisted on introducing him to her parents and made sure they knew he'd saved her from getting hurt. After introductions were made, her father showed him his gratitude by giving him a job at Grand's.

He introduced Alice to his apartment and his bed where he educated her on how to lose her virginity in the best of ways. While she bounced up and down on his cock, he told her he wanted to marry her, but alas how could he when he didn't have much money? But, what Alice wanted, she got. And just getting over a broken heart courtesy of Jonathan Drake, she wanted Talon.

Their wedding was on a grand scale. Her side of the church was filled to the brim. His two pews reserved for family remained empty. She didn't care, but her father did. He had Talon investigated; discovering he hailed from San Francisco where his mother died during the earthquake. That Talon was a man of no means, but of determination to become someone who was. Charles Grand forewarned Talon that if he hurt Alice in any way, he would be out on his ear without so much of a blanket to cover his ass.

Talon, desperate to get on Charles's good side, suggested that Charles branch out and build stores in Chicago and San Francisco. Following his advice, Charles built a store in Chicago and it was prospering, doing as well as his store in Manhattan. This smart suggestion had elevated Talon's status in Charles' eyes and made him aware of Talon's business acumen.

During his marriage, Talon watched with great disappointment as Alice miscarried two babies. He became saddled with a wife who couldn't walk. Her brilliant blond hair dulled to him, her skin became waxen, and his desire for her faded. And now his very future in the Grand family was tarnishing more each day.

The door to Talon's office opened and Charles walked in. "Would you mind telling me what the detectives wanted with you?" His eyes were sharp, almost daring Talon to lie.

"They wanted to know my involvement with Zelda DeLane, the murdered actress at the Joyeux Theater."

"And?"

"I had little to tell. Just because a man attends the performances often isn't a reason to suspect him of anything."

"Are you a suspect?" Charles frowned.

"No, I am not. I wasn't even there that night. I believe I worked late at the store."

Charles opened the door to leave, but paused, his hand on the doorknob. "Both you and I know that you don't attend the theater to merely watch the shows. I warn you, Talon, don't bring shame upon my family and house." He closed the door behind him.

Talon shrugged and smiled.

Chapter Six

Jonathan waited for the tall redhead to return, wondering if she'd bring the police. He knew if the tables were turned, he'd bring the authorities with him, point a lofty finger at the fugitive, give a statement and be done with the person. He'd go on his lavish way and think nothing more about it, only what he read in the papers, if that.

Last night he'd scrambled up a fire escape and vaulted himself onto this rooftop somewhere in what is called the Hell's Kitchen area. Not a safe place to be, but for right now he was hidden from prying eyes and grasping hands trying to tear him apart.

He stood and moved his legs around trying to get the circulation going. Just to put weight on the soles of his feet felt like shards of glass piercing his skin, but he needed to get warm. He went to stand next to the tall ledge where he reached inside the capes he wore and peed against the brick and mortar of the building.

Moving away from the puddle of urine and strong smell, he peered over the high ledge to see rattling automobiles below. The streets teemed with people; everyone was in motion going about their business. Across the street in another building and alleyway, a woman leaned out of her window and pulled a clothesline toward her. She started hanging long johns, pants, shirts and other articles of clothing to flap in the brisk breeze. He shivered. Even with the wool cloak the nurse gave him, the early morning cold was going through him like a blast from the north.

The back of his head throbbed, and gingerly putting his fingers against the gauze dressing, he felt a lump the size of a goose egg. The nurse did a good job and in truth he wanted to wail like a baby when she shoved that damn needle in his scalp.

He took Zelda's long cape and drew the shimmering blue material across his hand, fingering the delicate peacock feathers around the hem, seeing for the first time how intricate they were, the vibrant and bold turquoise and blue colors. My God, Zelda had looked enchanting on stage as she pranced around wearing a four-foot-high headdress made entirely of peacock feathers. Her cape, that when she raised her arms out created magic, her body lithe, and with little else on made the audience gasp and clap with pleasure. He'd clapped loudest of all.

He brought the indigo material to his face smelling Zelda's perfume. Lilacs.

Zelda.

Zany, zestful, Zelda. The golden girl of the Follies. His girl, no make her his lover who he'd dated over the past year. At first, she'd made it clear to him that he wasn't the only man in her life and he had to share. And in the beginning of their relationship, her rules were fine with him as long as when he and Zelda were together she acted like he was the only man in the world, time wise and sex wise. But being no stage-door-Johnnie, his hours with her became valuable and he insisted on having her to himself.

They'd met at a party for a new Follies production. Since the theater owner was courting investors, Jonathan, along with his thick wallet, was invited. The party was on the rooftop of the Joyeux Theater where a new production had just taken place and where lights were strung giving off a festive atmosphere. The night was filled with warm breezes and the strong perfume from the female performers. Zelda wasn't Jonathan's first trysts with a star. He liked women, high society daughters, performers, it didn't matter much, they were all the same to him. Back home he kept a drawer full of baubles, expensive bracelets, necklaces, French perfume, anything to give to his latest conquest.

How well he remembered the exact moment his life changed, when he lost his vision of who he was while watching Mr. Foyle approaching with his latest star, Zelda DeLane, draped over his arm. The blonde beauty glowed, her smile dazzled, her nipples pointed through the soft fabric of her dress. She held out her gloved hand to slip into Jonathan's, embroiling him, snaring him like a rabbit. He felt his life as he knew it leave him and travel into Zelda.

After introductions, Foyle disappeared, leaving Miss DeLane with Jonathan. He handed her his cocktail and watched her ruby-red lips sip the pink liquid, her eyes, pea green, stared up at him, and then raked over his body in calculating measurements. Almost a bet, a dare, and the flick of her penciled eyebrow was a promise of more to come. And it had, in waves like a roaring ocean, in rippling tides of sex, parties, and card games of strip poker with just the two of them.

He gave her diamond bracelets wrapped around his penis, easy for her to find, simply nibble her way down his shaft and claim her prize.

They knew him by name backstage. Saturday nights became his night with Zelda. While he wanted to monopolize all her time, she made it clear to him that she had her life to live. Rehearsals, new songs to learn, new dances to perform, new costumes to be fitted for, all took up her time.

Backstage, most of the showgirls preened over him like he was the only man in the world. But they couldn't turn him away from Zelda. He'd arrive at the theater, go to his usual box in the balcony, watch Zelda enthrall the audience and then meet her in her dressing room. They thought nothing of a quick tryst between shows. When her door was locked everyone knew not to bother them. If she was done for the night he waited for her to change, and from there they would go to a nightclub, dance, and be amongst the last to leave.

He'd classify himself as a lover that he knew everything about sex but in truth knew little. Zelda introduced him to sex in a way he didn't know existed. Bondage, hurtful, kinky. She promised to be faithful, certainly what they had together, sex and otherwise was enough for her. Wasn't it for him, she would tease.

But as backstage gossip had a way of slithering around, insinuating she was sharing her treats, he got wind of the rumor. He cautioned her never to make light of him, that she would regret it if she did. And yet, as persistent stories were whispered from showgirls red lips into his ear, he was becoming what he dreaded ever to become, the butt end of the joke.

Was it less than a week ago they were together at her apartment, sipping martinis, eyeballing each other over the rim? When he asked her about the gossip, she pouted acting hurt he'd even listened to such nonsense. When her eyes glistened with tears and she threatened to call it a night, he took her glass and put it on the table. Tilting her chin up, he leaned down to cover her mouth with his. Light nibbles at first, and then they were tearing each other's clothes off, running toward the bedroom where she was quick to fall on her satin-covered bed and him doing a nosedive to land on top of her. Laughing, he pulled her legs apart and nestled into her golden curls. He tongued her clit, making her squeal and beg for more, always more. When he finally took his engorged cock and shoved it into her jewel box, she matched him thrust for thrust. Later, satisfied and smelling of sex, they lit cigarettes, and she made him promise to never again distrust her...

...Right now, he leaned his arm on the cold stone of the building's ledge, trying to recall, wishing he still had the note from Zelda asking him to attend her Friday night performance instead of Saturday night. She wrote that her mother was sick and wanted her to come home to Chicago. How much truth was in her story, he didn't know and didn't want to know. She did have a mother living in Chicago and said she would be gone but a week.

Tired and with his wounds aching, Jonathan returned back to the enclosure around the stairwell where he sat down. He wondered if the nurse, Miss Fitzgerald was able to contact his father. Certainly, his parents would never doubt him. Well, maybe the old Jonathan they'd form a solid stance behind, but this new person he'd become, he wasn't so sure what they'd do or think.

He'd been cautioned by his father to stop his carousing at the theater. That he was making a name for himself and it wasn't in building skyscrapers.

"Jonathan, you're provoking society and it isn't good for your business. You know how proud of you your mother and I are, but you're starting to tarnish our good name and yours. Use the degree in business and architecture you have and make something of yourself. Boost yourself up in your mother's and my eyes. Boost yourself up in society's eyes. Stop with this playboy role you're doing and build something constructive."

He knew that his father wanted him to design new hotels for him. That he hinted of opening a chain on the west coast from Seattle to Los Angeles. He wanted Jonathan in charge of building them, to oversee all aspects. And Jonathan agreed. But as much as he loved drafting and creating, he also found Zelda's greedy smile and sexual appetite an even bigger lure.

He wasn't always this way. After graduating with two degrees, and with his father's help, he'd opened his own architect firm. Jonathan admired the men who designed the Brooklyn Bridge, and those who designed and built Union Station, drilling through dense soil and rock to create the subway. Yet, he doubted very much he'd ever leave his stamp on anything substantial, not the way he was going.

His father's hotel, *The Drake*, was starting to look dated and worn. It was time for it to outshine the eleven-story Waldorf, and certainly to go higher than the sixteen-story Astor. Promises Jonathan made to his father to do so. He loved his father and thought highly of him and knew he'd become a big disappointment to him.

He wondered about his mother, how she was taking this latest escapade. *Escapade?* Hell it was more than an escapade. His mother, a British aristocrat and after living in the states so long had softened in her lofty views somewhat. But still she lived within high society's code of ethics. Jonathan figured his predicament had her prostrate in bed, unable to hold her head up.

The same could be said of his sister, Lona, only she was a fence sitter. She could fall one way and land on the side of the rich, fall the opposite and she could land on the side of the women's movement and fight for the right to vote. Maybe her love for him would come through and she would side with her big brother.

Sitting here right now freezing his ass off, accused of murdering the woman he loved, he wondered how he was going to find out who killed Zelda. Who in the hell would want to frame him and why? With his lackadaisical lifestyle, there wasn't a thing to set him up for. No money exchanged here. While he was unconscious the murderer could have slit his throat with ease. Was he the intended target, if not to die, then to frame? Why? Certainly the knife in his right hand when he's left-handed was a plant.

His only hope was Miss Fitzgerald. Several pigeons landed close by. They cooed, strutted and pecked at debris. Jonathan flapped his hand and shooed them away.

The sun was disappearing behind the tall buildings when Liberty trudged up the eight flights of stairs and came out onto the roof. She found Mr. Drake leaning against the wall sound asleep. Careful not to disturb him, she put the package next to his lap and placed two silver dollars on top of the brown wrapper. She headed back the way she came, thinking she could wash her hands of him at last.

She got as far as the stairwell when the money clanked together and Mr. Drake spoke.

"Don't tell me you're leaving me, Miss Fitzgerald. Not after going to so much trouble to bring me clothes and money."

Stopped in her tracks, she turned with a start, and watched as he got to his feet.

"Before I left here, Mr. Drake, I thought you were mentally disturbed. Now I know differently. You're a wanted man, and I assume the cape you're wearing belongs to the woman you're accused of murdering. How do I know you won't slit my throat the second I turn my back?" She rolled up the newspaper and tossed it at him.

He caught the paper, and unrolling it, started to read. Liberty watched his jaw flex and his eyes squint in disbelief. Finished, he tapped the paper with his knuckles.

"I didn't do this, I didn't kill her."

"How can you say you didn't do it if you can't remember anything?"

"Because I loved Zelda. I'm not a man of violence. I like to think I'm more of a…ah…well…a lover." He shrugged, and picking the package up, tore the paper wrapping off which fluttered away to land against the wall of the roof. "Miss Fitzgerald, if I wanted to harm you I had plenty of opportunity to do so earlier. And, if I'm such a devious murderer, I could have gone inside this building and killed anyone who got in my way. Stole clothes— money and scrammed."

He dropped both capes he wore to the floor and kept facing her as he pulled on the pants, situated his privates, and buttoned the fly. The pants were too short, but he only smirked and told her that her measurements were off. He pulled the shirt on and buttoned it up, the neck fit just right.

"I'm not going to ask how you got the size of the shirt collar right, I'm certain I already know." He grinned while tucking in his shirttail.

Watching him pull on the socks, Liberty had admit the old adage; *the clothes make the man*, or something like that held credence, because with just a shirt and pants on, Mr. Drake was transformed. His stance became erect, he was now too handsome for her tastes, his hair too dark, his eyes too bold, and yet...

Picking up her cloak, he approached and draped it over her shoulders. He closed the top button with dexterity, his large hands lingering, making her heart lurch with his closeness.

He tilted her chin up to stare at her face. "You and I look like we've gone several rounds with each other."

She flicked her head away from his grip. "Yes, I'm sure we do."

"Don't worry," he said, his warm breath tickling her ear. "I'm not going to harm you." He took Zelda's cape and proceeded to fold it. "Would you mind putting this in your medical bag?"

"No, I can't. What if I'm caught with it?" My word, what more did the man want of her?

He darted an unfriendly glare her way as he unbuttoned his

shirt and tucked the shimmering material inside, instantly turning his flat abdomen into a pot belly. "Did you speak to my father?"

"Yes, I did. Also two policemen."

"What do you mean policemen? Did you turn me in?" He glanced passed her, trying to see if anyone followed.

"If I'd brought the police, or told them about you, you'd already be in handcuffs." She watched him relax.

"What did my father have to say?"

"Not much about you at all. He basically played a game with me on the phone. He kept insisting I was a newspaper reporter and told me the detectives standing next to him were looking for you. If I got his underlying message right, he wants me to telephone him again tomorrow. But, you can make that call yourself. Can't you, Mr. Drake?"

"How can I when it's not wise to show my face?"

Becoming indignant, she tapped her foot. "You have made me lie for you. Certainly those policemen indicated that an accomplice is just as guilty as the person committing the crime. What's next, Mr. Drake—what's next?"

"I suspect getting me off this roof and into someplace safe where I can prove my innocence. Do you live close by?"

"What?" she said, never thinking for a second he would want to come home with her. "Oh...no—no—no—no! I'm not taking you to my apartment."

"Why not? I can't stay here."

Liberty thought of the consequences if she helped him any further. Not good, not good at all. She'd done enough for him. "You can stay here. I'll call your father back and tell him where to find you. Another night here will not kill you, I'm sure." She started backing away toward the stairwell, but one look at his face, his eyes pleading with her, had her stopping. And then there was Lincoln Drake's explosive words that his son wasn't dangerous came back to her. She was tired, her jaw throbbed, and all she wanted right now was to be home and take care of her aching mouth. Instead of leaving him here to fend for himself, compassion trumped fear, and she found herself offering to help him even further.

She approached him and beckoned. "You'll have to lean on me, like you're hurt, and I'll help you get away from here."

"The way I feel, that will not be hard to do," he said, trying to joke, but failed.

With Jonathan leaning against her they made a pitiful pair of nurse and patient. She managed to steer him through the hordes of people returning home from work and had no trouble doing so. Vendors were shuttering their food carts reminding her that this out-of-sorts day she'd not eaten since breakfast. With no time to dwell on hunger, she helped him onto the trolley where several men gave up their seats for the wounded man. She plastered on a sweet smile when their eyes fell upon his shoeless feet and then looked at her. No questions were asked, and no suspicions aroused, at least she hoped not. When the swaying trolley had him nodding off, and his head lulling against her shoulder, she elbowed him back into an upright position.

The closer they got to her home the cleaner the streets and sidewalks became. They finally reached her apartment building in the Chelsea district located between West Eighteenth Street and Eighth Avenue. Identical narrow, red brick buildings were dissected with small alleys.

"This is where you live?"

"Yes." She pointed at the structure on a corner lot where tall windows facing front were shielded by white lacy curtains. Around the side was another window framed by a metal fire escape that zigzagged from the top of the building to almost street level. "I'm on the third floor. In my building there are only two apartments per floor which is a luxury."

People passed them until one man stopped to ask if she needed help with the injured man. She thanked him and said she could manage. And she did just that, she wrapped his arm around her neck, and putting her arm around his waist they made it inside.

Climbing three flights of stairs had him moaning and saying ouch with every step they took. She took joy in his every groan.

Chapter Seven

With their arms still intertwined, Liberty guided Jonathan down the long hall to her apartment. Unlocking the door, she pushed it open to allow him in first.

Glad to be home, safe and sound, she switched on the overhead light fixture and glanced around her tidy place. Her living room consisted of several sturdy pieces of furniture, a velvet camel-backed sofa, blue in color, and a chair with a crochet doily on the back. Cornered between the sofa and chair was a round table, its top polished to a sheen. On top of the table was an hour-glass shaped electric lamp with rose pink floral globes. Over a dozen porcelain knickknacks of human figures, animals, and birds also covered the table top. Her one concession to penny-pinching was to buy a pretty for herself every so often. An oval-shaped rug covered the wood floor making it appear cozy. The dining room located off the living room and under an arched entry held a table and four chairs. Next to the arched entry was a long cheval mirror.

While Jonathan stood in the middle of the room looking around, she removed her cape and hat and hung them on the coat stand. Her doctor's bag she placed on the floor next to the sofa.

"My kitchen is on through the dining room. And that's my bedroom." She pointed at a closed door a few feet away and located on the same wall as the entry to the dining room. "I don't have a bathroom in here. If you need to use it, there's one back outside and down the hallway. We passed it coming in. It's shared on this floor. The other apartment has a family of three, so it's fairly quiet here."

Moving with caution on aching feet, Jonathan approached the tall window in the living room and parted the lace curtains to peer out. Night was coming on and streetlights were being lit. He allowed the curtain to fall back into place. Unbuttoning his shirt, he removed the cape and folded it.

"Put it on the table there." She indicated the round table in the corner. She then led him through the dining room and into the kitchen where there was a cook stove, a sink with running tap water, cabinets, and a counter top to prepare meals on. A window was on one wall, and once again, he parted the floral curtains that concealed the fire escape.

"Not much of a view is it?" he said.

"No it isn't. But if there's a fire and I need to get out fast, I'll not care about a view."

He limped back into the living room where he appeared undecided about what to do next. Finally, he spoke. "The bathroom's back out in the hallway, you say?"

Liberty frowned; he could at least comment how clean and nice her home was. But then why should he, this wasn't something he was used too. Instead of lecturing him, she said, "Let me get you a bar of soap so you can clean up."

Going into her bedroom, she opened the dresser drawer and took out a clean towel and washcloth. She paused before the mirror over her dresser and tilted her head to stare at her jaw, which was swollen and taking on a purple color. Leaning forward she put her finger inside her mouth and checked the cut on the inside of her cheek. Darn that drunken Mr. O'Grady, she scowled. Jonathan Drake was right; she did look like she'd been in a boxing ring. Her red hair as usual escaped its bun and curly tendrils stuck out about her head in a fiery halo. Freckles dotted her face and ruddy cheeks. She tucked her hair back into place, somewhat. Why should she care what she looked like, there was no impressing this man who had blood on his hands.

Going through the dining room and back into the kitchen, she grabbed the bar of Palmolive soap from the sink and the bathroom key from the hook where it hung. She took it all back into the living room and approached Mr. Drake who was sitting on the sofa, waiting. He sprung to his feet.

She handed him the skeleton key for the bathroom. "Please don't let anyone see you. Oh…don't forget to clean the room after you're done."

"I'll be careful." He accepted the towel and soap. "Scrub the tub out when I'm finished." Turning his back on her, he limped out of the door.

While he was gone, Liberty filled the tea kettle with water and put it on the stove. Waiting for it to heat, she sat at her dining room table and thought over the events of the day. Jonathan Drake didn't appear to be dangerous, not according to his father anyway. She had to rely on those words. Hers was a structured world and she didn't like threads of it snapping. She compared it to the cat-gut she used to stitch wounds, so incredibly strong that one needed scissors to cut it. Jonathan Drake's appearance in her life broke that thread with little or no effort. Making her realize just how vulnerable she was after all.

Tomorrow she had to return to work. She also planned on calling Mr. Lincoln Drake again to tell him to come get his son.

She didn't care how he did it, only that he did. If her father or brother knew she harbored an accused killer in her home they'd storm in and break him apart.

She'd always thought of herself as being as tough as her father and two brothers. Nothing fazed her father who had bundled his family up and brought them from Ireland. Everyone else in the family but Liberty was born in the old country. She was still in her mam's belly when the ship they were on sailed by the Statue of Liberty. Mam declared then and there if she had a girl she would name her Liberty, and she did. Liberty was an impressionable fifteen when the typhoid fever took her mam's life more than thirteen years ago. While wiping the sweat from her mam's brow, seeing her sink into a morass of fever and delusion's, Liberty decided to become a nurse, to help fight the contagion's flowing through the tenements like water in the surrounding rivers. However, days like today and coming home all bruised and battered made her wonder why she kept on with it. A job as a store clerk was looking better all the time. If Nellie O'Grady had typhoid, it would mean isolation for Liberty for a couple of weeks. Life as a nurse compared with being a soldier in the trenches, dodging shooting bullets of diseases.

Her father, Keegan, worked in a furniture factory where he carved wood into beautiful furniture. He had promised his dying wife to keep their small family together, and he'd done so. Knowing the great love her dad carried for Mam, it's a wonder his life didn't stop when she died. But he struggled on, raised them and worked long and hard hours to save for Liberty's nursing education. Liberty believed she'd inherited his strength, and certainly her mam's contemplative attitude.

Liberty's favorite brother Teague was older than her by eight years. He had a shock of red hair and teasing eyes. He'd also enlisted in the army, and now fought overseas in the war. She'd begged him not to enlist, worried he could be killed or maimed, but her wants concerning his life held little. Bursting with pride in his solder's uniform, he would tease her, tell her she acted like their mam, and to quit worrying about things she couldn't control. How could she not worry about where he was and what he was doing? Stories of mustard gas used by the German's to blind soldiers, and of machine guns mowing them down in trenches were reported in the papers daily. Just before Teague left for Paris, he'd moved their dad into his flat. Her dad would drop by often to visit and bring Liberty the occasional letter from Teague meant for the whole family.

Blaine, her thirty-three-year-old brother, had bitterness coming out his pores. He hated his station in life, hated being poor, hated the rich, and in short didn't have much thought about Liberty's profession as a nurse. He'd told her more than once she was wasting her time trying to teach people hygiene when all they had to do is walk out their doors and sink up to their arses in squalor. She often wished Blaine had inherited their mam's soft approach on life, found the good in everything instead of finding the bad in the smallest detail. Blaine and his wife Marybeth had two boys, ten and eight, and Liberty could already see distrust starting in their wee eyes. Despite the mixed emotions and feelings her family had about life, she loved them all dearly.

The tea kettle's piercing shrill startled her from her musings and forced her to go snatch it off the burner. Pulling the stubborn top drawer open that often stuck, she pushed cooking utensils out of her way and freed the metal tea strainer, which she stuffed with tea leaves. After filling the teapot with scalding water she covered it with a tea cozy and placed it on the table. Next came two cups from the cabinet that she placed next to the small dish of sugar cubes on the dining room table. Spotting a few bread crumbs on her lace tablecloth, she swiped them into her hand and disposed of them in the garbage pail underneath the sink.

Jonathan rose out of the claw-footed bathtub filled with scalding water. He'd scrubbed himself so hard he'd turned beet red. He pulled the plug in the tub and watched the pink tinted water form a miniature whirlpool as it drained. Instead of getting out, he got on his knees and turning the faucets, he sloshed fresh water over his body. When at last he felt clean, he stepped from the tub onto the black and white tiled floor and dried off.

He didn't expect much but the simplicity of the room was still a shock. Small and chilly there was a pedestal sink, the bathtub, and a toilet with the water tank mounted high on the wall.

Using the towel, he wiped the foggy haze from the mirror. The mirror was cracked in one corner. The gauze bandage wrapped around his head came off in the tub and he'd thrown it on the floor, a constant reminder of the grisly murder and him getting hit.

My God, was it only yesterday at this time he was home in his parent's mansion, soaking in a tub of hot water with gilded fixtures, enjoying all the luxury money could buy? And wasn't it this time yesterday he'd donned his dress clothes, tied his white bow tie against his white shirt? And wasn't it this time yesterday that he put a wad of bills in his money clip, left his fancy bedroom, and got into his dad's chauffeured automobile?

He ran his hand over his dark stubble, thinking about his expensive razor and nice smelling shaving soap. Again he felt the rasp of his whiskers. He needed a shave but what he needed even more was a beard, a disguise of some kind. The last person he wanted to be right now was Jonathan Drake.

From where she sat on the sofa, Liberty watched her front door creak open and Jonathan Drake enter. Never had someone looked so out of place in her home as he did. Even in ill-fitting pants, shirt, socks and no shoes, he looked like money, walked like money, and talked like money. When he glanced around, out of habit, she stood and motioned him to join her. Rather awkwardly, he handed her the towel and soap. He smelled clean, of Palmolive soap. Water dripped from a curl of jet-black hair hanging over his forehead. Without thought, she took the towel and dabbed at his hair, hoping to dry it and stop it from dripping on her clean floor. She also glanced at the stitches on the back of his head, happy to see the wound had stopped bleeding. Chastising herself for being such a mothering type, she walked with grace back into her kitchen where she put the towel and washcloth in the sink for now.

When she returned, he was still standing in the living room and she suggested they go into the dining room and have tea. While he slipped into the chair across from her, she poured him a cup of the brewed beverage with its strong piquant odor.

Getting comfy, Liberty dropped three sugar cubes in her tea, Jonathan didn't bother. He emptied his in one long swig while she blew on hers trying to cool it off. When she took the first sip, the hot liquid nipped at the cut making it sting. Grabbing her napkin, she instantly spit her tea out to splatter onto the white fabric.

"Ouch!" she exclaimed, and took short spurts of air. "Ouch— ouch! Darn that hurts!"

Jonathan stared at her as if she lost her marbles. "It appears you put up with a lot from your patients."

"Yes, and now I can add not being able to drink tea or eat because of it. I'd forgotten about the cut inside my mouth."

"You're not going into work tomorrow looking like that?" he asked.

"I could have a broken leg and still have to work." She

laughed at the surprised look on his face. "No to the broken leg and yes I will have to work but first I have to go to the health department office."

"But you will telephone my father again tomorrow?" He fingered his cup and saucer.

Still unable to enjoy a sip of tea, she refilled his cup. "Yes. Between my patients, I'll call. He made it obvious to me that policemen were with him. He was trying to convince them you were not there."

His brows knit together and he blew out a breath lifting his dark hair off his forehead. "You gave him my message? That I'm innocent, right?"

"Yes, I did."

"Did he say anything after that?"

"Not much, it was pretty obvious he couldn't talk. Are you hungry?"

When he nodded, she stood and went into the kitchen to heat the stew she'd made the night before. Her mother's recipe, good old Irish stew, thick with sausage and potatoes. While ladling the stew from the pan on the two-burner stove, she chastised herself for being foolish enough to bring him here. Anxious, she peered around the doorjamb, but he was busy playing with the spoon, practically flipping it in the air, his thoughts elsewhere for sure.

She took the tray and put two bowls of soup, bread and butter on it, and carried her burden into the dining room where she placed a hot bowl in front of him. The other she put where she would be sitting, and then took her place at the table.

"Would you like to say grace?" she asked.

"I'll leave that up to you but only if you make it short, I'm starving." He had the nerve to say.

At least he waited for her to finish the prayer and for her to start eating before he did. Manners, she scoffed to herself, how noble of him to remember them.

She gingerly took a small bite, trying to keep it away from the right side of her mouth, which was impossible to do. So she gave up and watched Jonathan spoon the food in his mouth like he hadn't eaten in weeks. When his bowl was almost empty he slowed down and bit into the buttered bread.

"I need money. Ask Dad to get some to you. I don't care how you do it, just do it."

Liberty studied him for a moment. Now that she had him safely tucked away here, she thought he was an insolent, bossy ass.

"For someone who is an accused murderer you're asking a lot. Why should I help you beyond today—tomorrow after I make contact with your father? Maybe you should turn yourself in and get your innocent-self cleared of any wrong doing?"

"Murder is a whole lot more than wrong doing, Miss Fitzgerald. I'm innocent and I don't plan on simmering in the electric chair at Sing-Sing." He finished the stew then nudged his bowl aside, and politely burped into his napkin.

"Tell me what happened."

"Like I said before, I don't know. One second I was kissing Zelda's leg...we were about to have...er...make love. The next thing I remember is waking up with her underneath me, dead."

Liberty ran her finger over her lips and glanced over at him. "Did you already have your clothes off?"

"No. I was fully dressed, shoes included. Hadn't gotten that far," he said and cleared this throat. "Foreplay...ah...you know."

"No," she quipped and felt her skin go hot. "I don't."

A loud knock sounded against her door. "Liberty? Are ye home, lass?"

"Quick—my dad's here. Hide in the bedroom, under the bed." Again, she wondered why she was helping him. Here was the perfect chance to get rid of Mr. Drake. Her father would rather see him jailed than her helping him.

Once again, she acquiesced.

As Jonathan streaked for the bed, she followed and made sure to shut the door securely behind him. She then hurried to let her father in. He stood there, wrinkled, back slightly bent, wild red hair escaping from under his worn cap, and always, just for her, a twinkle in his gray eyes. In his gnarled and big-boned hands was a wall shelf.

"Dad, I forgot you were coming by, or did you not tell me?" She stepped back to allow him to enter.

"Thought I'd surprise me daughter by droppin' by. Made ye another shelf with left over wood. Thrown on the trash heap it was." He paused and squinted at her face. "What happened to me lass? Did someone attack ye? Are ye hurt otherwise?"

"No, Dad. A drunken father of a patient of mine didn't want me calling the health department. I'm fine, just a little bruise, that's all." Smiling, Liberty kissed her father's cheek. His Irish lilt was as strong and endearing as ever, even after living here for twenty-nine years. She'd grown up listening to it, loved his lyrical voice, which rang of the old country. He smelled of wood shavings, wood stain, turpentine, and had a few specs of sawdust on his shoulders and cap. "Thanks, Dad. As you can see, I have plenty of knickknacks to go on it." She pointed to the table with its menagerie.

"Women," he scoffed. "Must be a female thing to keep buyin' such when ye have run out of room for 'em." He carried the three-layered shelf, stained dark walnut, with curlicues on each end, and held it up against the wall between the dining room entryway and the bedroom door.

"How 'bout here?" He turned to look at her.

She nodded. "Yes, right there will be fine." She watched as he took his hammer and nails from his work apron and with a few loud strokes of his hammer, mounted the shelf. When he finished, she collected her treasures, and arranged them on the shelves one by one. She still had room to buy even more.

"Have you eaten your supper yet?" she asked.

He removed his cap releasing a shock of reddish gray hair. "Nay, thought I'd be able to eat with me daughter."

Before she could stop him, he headed into the dining room and drew up short at the dishes on the table. "Appears ye've already had yer supper, aye?"

"Yes, my friend Helen Cartwright stopped by. You remember her? She works with me at the Wald foundation. But there's plenty for you." Thankful she and Jonathan hadn't finished off the stew, she cleared the table before putting a bowl down for her father. She refilled the kettle and put it on to heat.

"Have you heard from Teague?" she asked.

He buttered a piece of bread and shook his head. "Nay, not lately. Yer brother's a constant worry for me. I read daily about the hardships of the war over there. Teague was brash to join up."

"At least Blaine's safe from being drafted."

"Aye, I'm mighty thankful the army's not taking men with families. Not yet, anyway."

"I'm hearing the war will be over with soon. Now that we've entered it and are helping out, it sounds as if the tide has turned. Let's pray so."

"Can't be soon enough for me." He spooned a piece of sausage floating in the broth, put it into his mouth and chewed thoughtfully. "Yer mam's recipe, aye?"

"Of course, none other. Do you miss her still?" She blew on her tea letting it cool.

His brow furrowed into deeper lines. "Aye, I miss her something fierce. Thirteen years isn't that long ago. It seems like only yesterday she was taken from us. And with ye, my girl, lookin' just like her, you're a reminder." He reached over and patted Liberty's hand. "She'd be just as proud of you as I am, being a nurse and all. And, yer brothers, can't short them for a second. Blaine's family, Teague's being in the army. Me offspring are a button-buster of pride for sure." He grinned. "Aye, she'd be most proud."

A slight noise coming from the bedroom had Keegan turning his head. "What was that?"

"Nothing…" Before she could stop him he was already on his feet and charging across the living room where he threw open the door to her bedroom.

They both peered around the tidy room and at the bed with the wooden head and footboard, made by Keegan. The dressing table with the round mirror was about the only thing he hadn't made. Here too, several wall shelves were loaded with figurines.

Opening her wardrobe door, Liberty let out the breath she'd been holding. "Oh…Dad, it's nothing. A blanket fell from the top shelf in here." She picked up the bulky quilt, and was startled to see Jonathan's tall body, crouched over trying to hide behind her clothes. She quickly shut the door and put the quilt on her bed. Could the man never listen to anything he was told? Hide under the bed? She guessed not.

Her father's eyes swept the room one last time before leaving. "Want to make me another cup of cha?" he asked.

"Sure thing, Dad." She quickly obliged, suggesting they have their drinks in the living room. "I want to admire my shelf again."

He grinned and shoving his hands in his pants pockets went to wait for her in the living room where he stood before the shelf, admiring his own handy work.

Jonathan felt like a pretzel amongst the few clothes hanging there, and could kick himself for not sliding underneath the bed. He'd had a close call thanks to his disobedience.

He needed to get money from his dad and find a new hiding place. Then what? How was he going to convince anyone of his innocence when he couldn't convince himself?

The wardrobe door opened and a highly agitated Miss Liberty Fitzgerald stood there, tapping her toe against the floor, her red hair a swirling mess around her head.

God, he disliked redheads, freckles, and tempers. Give him a sleek blonde with alabaster flawless skin. He stepped out of the closet dragging with him a few dresses that slid off their hangers and wrapped around his wide shoulders.

She rescued her clothes and letting out a deep sigh of agitation put them back on the hangers. "It would be much easier on the both of us if you'd follow instructions."

"At least you didn't tell your father about me."

"The thought crossed my mind several times. But like I said, once I get money from your father, you can disappear."

His brow flicked upward, his grin bland. "That's something I've been thinking about. But, I wouldn't get far with my face on every newspaper in the City. I can't get caught before I prove my innocence. And another thing, I sure as hell didn't bang my head to give myself this injury. No, someone else did it and that someone killed Zelda."

Like the clouds parting to let sunshine spill out, and for the first time since finding him, all of it made sense to her. His deep cut. She finally believed he was innocent.

Liberty grabbed the quilt and the spare pillow from her bed and placed them on the sofa where Jonathan sat drumming his fingers against the sofa's arm.

"You know, I could fit my whole bedroom and then some inside your entire apartment."

"I'm just sure you could. But, your big fancy bedroom's a long way away and out of reach right now—isn't it?"

Her barb shut him up. Picking up her doctor's bag, she turned on the lamp and went to sit in the chair. She took out her list of patients she would be calling on the next day. There weren't as many as today and some were repeats. She found it hard to get people to change their habits, and those were the repeats on her list, the ones who after losing members of their families called begging for her help. The oldest, from the old country were the hardcore unwilling to learn or be changed. Some she converted, some she didn't.

She watched Jonathan stand and go to the wall shelf. He stood there with his arms crossed studying the knick-knacks.

"This is the shelf your father just put up?"

"Yes, it is."

He reached over and picked up a figurine, the one with a French couple sitting on a fence kissing. After looking it over, he put it back.

"Please be careful," she said, eyeballing him.

He took down each one, studied it, and then put it back, until finally he bobbled one and caught it a mere inches before it hit the floor. Red faced, he turned to see if she was watching.

She was. She jumped to her feet, sending her papers to scatter onto the rug, and hurried to his side. "These are irreplaceable, and I assure you each one has a special meaning."

"Really? Did you buy this in France?" He pointed to the one on the top shelf, a man dressed in eighteenth century clothing, with a maid looking like Marie Antoinette beside him.

"No, I've never been out of the country. If I was to go some-where, it'd be Ireland where I could meet some of my cousins."

"I thought most of Ireland has immigrated here to America and Manhattan." He smirked.

She couldn't help but stare at his blue eyes rimmed with jet black lashes. "You really are a snob, aren't you?"

He shrugged his shoulders. "I guess so. Never gave being a snob much thought."

"Sure you have."

"Have what?"

"Thought about being a snob. Actually, I believe you work hard at being one." She huffed back to her chair and after gathering her work assignments, sat down none to gracefully.

He sauntered back to sit in the exact same spot he'd vacated. Again, drumming his fingers, until he finally leaned forward to stare intently at her. "Miss Fitzgerald, I don't like being here anymore than you like having to put up with me. But, I do know one thing, if I'm going to leave, I've got to have a disguise and that's where my father's money will come in…with your help of course."

"What kind of disguise? And where do I buy such a thing?"

Jonathan started talking, telling her all she needed to do.

Chapter Eight

Liberty stood next to her boss Emma Taylor's desk in the Wald Foundation office. Mrs. Taylor, one very strait-laced, gray-haired woman, stared at Liberty's battered face with a good deal of concern.

"Miss Fitzgerald, the reports back, and Nellie O'Grady has typhoid. Her whole building has been quarantined. Which means you will need to curtail your activities—"

"But, I can't do that," Liberty interrupted.

Mrs. Taylor held up her hand to silence Liberty. "It's just as a precaution. You have never had typhoid—"

"My mother died from the fever, if I was to get it, you'd think I'd come down with it before now. Mrs. Taylor, I have to work."

Emma Taylor took out the company's checkbook and filled out a check. She handed it to Liberty. "I'm giving you your paycheck today, early by one week. I value your work, Miss Fitzgerald and want to see you back here."

There was a soft knock on the office door and Helen Cartwright, Liberty's fellow nurse at the foundation, poked her head in.

Helen, barely five-two, blonde headed, and with a buck-toothed grin, entered. "You sent for me, Mrs. Taylor? Liberty, hello," she said and clasped her hands in front of her.

"Miss Cartwright, I want you to take over Miss Fitzgerald's patients for the next couple of weeks."

Helen's eyes widened as she leaned forward to stare at Liberty's jaw. "Are you all right? Did a patient hit you?"

Liberty tried to smile, but it hurt the inside of her mouth to do so. "Yes to both your questions. I'd appreciate it very much if you could help me out for a while."

Helen rapidly nodded, again showing her buck-toothed grin. "I've had both the flu and typhoid fever, so I should be fine out in the field." Her brown eyes danced with what she must see as an adventure.

"But, you are not armed against an aggressive husband or father who doesn't want you there. Just be careful, Helen," Liberty said with a warning. She tucked her check into her medical bag, and saying her goodbyes, left.

Liberty rode the subway to the other side of the City and to the upper class area where *The Drake* hotel stood in all its glory. She approached the concierge's desk inside the well-designed Drake hotel and waited for the tall slender man sitting behind the desk to focus his attention on her. Dressed in her nurse's uniform, clutching her doctor's black bag, she never felt or looked more out of place. *The Drake's* lobby had fancy upholstered chairs and sofas in rich supple leathers, cigarette stands, and tall potted ferns swaying gracefully. Women with plumed hats and men in smart pin-striped suits hurried to and fro, all with purpose. Well, Liberty's purpose wasn't so grand, and she wanted to get it done and over with. In short, she'd spent last evening with a conceited Jonathan

Drake, wanted him gone, and that was her reason for being here.

"I'm Mr. Edgar Hill, concierge for The Drake. How can I be of assistance?" Mr. Hill peered at her through his wire-rimmed glasses. Immaculately dressed in a black suit with a white starched shirt and black bow tie, a white handkerchief poked from his breast pocket.

Liberty opened her doctor's bag and removed the note she'd written her instructions on. "I'm to meet a Mister Lincoln Drake. Please tell him that Miss Fitzgerald is here."

"One moment," he said and picked up the telephone. "Mr. Drake. There is a Miss Fitzgerald to see you." His sandy colored brows arched upwards as he hung up the phone. "I'm to escort you to Mr. Drake's office." He indicated for Liberty to follow.

The door closed behind Liberty and she approached the large walnut stained desk. Lincoln Drake, Jonathan's father stood and walked around to meet her. Wearing a dark brown business suit, he was shorter than his son by several inches, his hair was more gray than black. His mustache and beard were neatly clipped and held interesting patterns of dark and light hair. Liberty noticed his eyes were the same brilliant blue as Jonathan's.

He accepted her hand within his and squeezed it followed by a pat. "I'm Lincoln Drake, as you know by now."

"And, I'm Liberty Fitzgerald."

"Liberty. Interesting name. Were you followed?" He indicated for her to take the nearby chair.

"How would I know? This isn't something I do daily, Mr. Drake." She sat on the leather tufted chair, careful to adjust her skirt around her legs.

"Of course—of course it isn't." His gaze slide over her. "You're a health nurse with the Wald Foundation? I've heard of the good work your association does."

"Yes, and it's been an interesting day for me. I'm surprised you know of our existence."

"You'd be further surprised to know I give to your employer Lillian Wald's charities, the house on Henry Street. I'm not an ogre who stomps on those who you perceive are beneath me. But enough said, how's Jonathan holding up?"

His admission of giving money to Lillian Wald's charity astounded her. What astounded Liberty even more was his perception of what she thought of him, classifying him as a rich snob. He was different than his son, which to her was a good thing.

"Since Jonathan Drake is a stranger to me, I'm not sure how to answer. I stitched the cut on the back of his head, which he claims he got at the Joyeux Theater, backstage, during his…well…his being with Miss DeLane."

"A cut on the back of the head? Well that must account for something, doesn't it? He would never hurt himself on purpose."

"I'm sure you read in the papers he was wearing Miss DeLane's cape when he fled and nothing else."

Mr. Drake nodded. "Odd, don't you think? Did he tell you he was fully dressed when he was at the theater?"

"Yes, he did. He said he woke up on top of Miss DeLane's dead body, both of them covered in blood and him with a knife in his right hand. He says it was planted there by the killer. He said to tell you he is so sorry for putting you and his mother through this. But to believe him when he says he is innocent."

Lincoln sat back in his chair, his brow wrinkled in thought.

Liberty rattled on. "He's at my place, wearing ill-fitting clothes, no shoes, but other than that I guess he's holding up." She rested her bag on her lap and stared at Mr. Drake, resisting the urge to tell him that his son was a spoiled elitist.

"By the way, Jonathan wears a size eleven shoe." He opened his desk drawer and pulled out a wad of bills. "Here's six-hundred. Tell Jonathan to use it wisely. The police are following me, they are watching my home, the hotel here. From the way you're dressed, I hope you haven't drawn attention to me...er...us." He knuckled his beard.

Liberty sat there, staring at the stack of bills that would take her years to make. Just when she'd thought she'd misjudged the man he insults her. Her first inclination was to refuse his money and throw Jonathan Drake out the second she got home.

"Mr. Drake, I've just been put on leave from my job. I've got a bruised face from an irate drunken man who didn't want a doctor to see to his sick daughter. I've made many calls on people who you would normally not even talk to, or cross the street to avoid, so don't speak against my way of dressing again. I wear my nurse's uniform in pride. I'm also putting my own life in jeopardy by helping your son. Did you know I could be jailed as an accomplice?"

Chastised, he smiled at her. "I'm sorry. I see how you've misconstrued my comment. I only meant that it is most uncommon for a health nurse to call upon my hotel. A doctor, yes, but never a health nurse. Please take no offense, as none was intended. My wife, our family...er...all of us are thrown into chaos concerning Jonathan." He took out a cigar and clipped the end off. He lit it and stared at her through gray coils of smoke. "What can I do to help both you and Jonathan?"

"Is there somewhere you can hide him? A room here?"

"This is and was one of the first places the police searched. Put my guests out when that happened. Like I said, they are watching this place closely. I haven't even mentioned you to my wife, my daughter. Some secrets are best never voiced." He took another puff, sending smoke roiling.

She waved the smoke from her face. "I expect once I give this money to Jonathan, he will leave my home and go somewhere else to hide."

Alarm creased his features, Mr. Drake stood and dabbing out his cigar, came around his desk. "Where can he go? He'll be arrested. There is nothing he can do behind bars to prove his innocence. I beg you, do not turn him out. You'll be as good as putting him in Sing Sing if you do."

"Mr. Drake, I can't keep—"

"For a short time only. I know my son. Jonathan will be able to prove he didn't do this." He took the money from his desk and handed it to her.

Feeling totally defeated, she put the money in her bag. "Size eleven?"

"Yes. Most of Jonathan's clothes are tailor made so I can only guess at the size he wears." He took out his pen and started writing. When finished he handed her the fancy stationary. "I'm here always. Call me and we'll make arrangements for you to meet me again. Just be careful when you do come. Tell Jonathan I need to know how to help him."

"I'll be sure and give him your message."

"I'd escort you to the front door, but with the police out there, I can't." He took her hand and affectionately patted it. "I can't thank you enough, Liberty Fitzgerald. But someday, I expect I will. By the way, did Jonathan tell you he's left handed?"

"Yes, he did." Liberty gathered her bag, and after saying goodbye, she left the fancy hotel and fifth avenue behind.

She strolled down Broadway taking in sights she never bothered with before. The street was noisy and packed with horse drawn carriages, and black automobiles driven by uniformed chauffeurs. People clustered everywhere. She found herself on 42nd street staring at the Joyeux Theater where Foyle's Follies were held. Black bunting surrounded the entry doors. An easel, holding a giant, black-draped photograph of Zelda DeLane, was positioned right next to the box-office. Next to Zelda's picture was a large sign announcing: *The Show Must Go On. Theater opens tomorrow night with a new star.*

So much for mourning, Liberty scowled at the thought.

Liberty studied the smiling seductive blonde with the perfect features. In full costume, Zelda was wearing a tall peacock head-dress. She held her arms straight out beside her sultry body, allowing the cape to cascade from her slender arms, showing off the beautiful material. The cape was the one she'd found Jonathan wearing. No wonder everyone thought he was guilty. Why would anyone want to snuff such a vivacious life? Why would Jonathan Drake cut her throat and not make a clean getaway? And without clothes? None of it made sense.

"Hey, Miss, did ya know the star?" A shaggy blonde-haired youngster stood next to her. Dressed in knee pants and a soiled white shirt, he didn't appear to belong here anymore than Liberty did.

"No, I didn't know Miss DeLane. I had business nearby and just stopped to look."

"Curious, then." The kid scuffed his shoe sole against the sidewalk. "I'm Fitch. I run errands for the theater manager."

"Then you must know...er...have known Miss DeLane? Mr. Drake?"

Fitch scratched his armpit while shaking his head. "Nope, didn't know him well. But I did deliver messages from Miss DeLane to Mr. Drake. He'd give me good tips. Don't know why she didn't use the telephone." He turned to stare at the picture of Zelda DeLane. "Sure was pretty. She gave me candy."

The kid started to trace the star's face with his finger just as the door swung open and a gruff looking man stepped out. He used his foot to push the doorstop into place anchoring the heavy door wide open. Two men exited the theater. The shorter of the two put his fedora on, while the other already had his hat on. They paused next to the man.

"We'll be in touch. Keep Miss DeLane's dressing room locked tight until we say otherwise."

"Yes sir, Detectives," said the big burly man putting his hands in his pockets. Spotting the lad standing next to Liberty, he signaled. "Fitch, you're needed inside."

Upon seeing Liberty, both the detectives tipped the bill of their hats and hurried off.

Fitch turned toward Liberty. "Gotta go. Nice talkin' to ya."

People were starting to queue up to buy tickets. Liberty walked south and crossed over to Sixth Avenue and Twenty-Third Street where she paused in front of the large department store, *Grand's*. A step below *Macy's* in elegance, but a working man's type of store with cheaper prices. It had everything in it she would want or need for the man back in her apartment.

After seeing Zelda DeLane's picture, talking some with the messenger boy, she was beginning to have second thoughts about her further involvement. And of course, Mr. Lincoln Drake's urging her not to put his son out of her apartment was another big factor. And there was the big if. *If* Jonathan Drake were innocent, she'd never forgive herself for not helping him.

Red brick surrounded the large glass window displays while the entrance to *Grand's* had tall white columns that spoke of stylishness inside. Liberty joined the throngs of shoppers entering, while others came out chatting and laughing from the exit door. The store was a hubbub of shoppers, mostly women, some pushing baby prams while others had a maid tagging along behind them.

Grand's was overwhelmingly huge. Several levels high, the bottom floor contained household goods and children's clothes. Men's and women's clothing was on the second floor. Avoiding the elevator, she walked up the wide staircase where she came out onto the floor sectioned off by numerous racks of women's wear. Beyond the women's was the men's section.

A neat looking female clerk approached with a wide smile and offered to be of help. Liberty accepted. Remembering the sizes Mr. Drake had wrote, she strolled through the store with the sales-clerk following her. Liberty, pretending she was shopping for her husband, picked out a pair of brown shoes, tie, shirt, socks, long underwear, and a ready-made black suit coat with matching pants, and handed them to the clerk to ring up.

Liberty would have to go to a drug store and buy shaving stuff and hair oil. She hoped the store wouldn't be closed before she got there. With her purchases stuffed inside a shopping bag, she took the elevator to the first floor, and started to leave when a knickknack display caught her eye.

Like a child picking out her favorite candy, Liberty walked down the aisles looking at the shelves loaded with porcelain figurines of all types. She picked up a delicate ballerina. She didn't have a dancer and it would look good in her collection.

"May I help you?" a deep voice floated behind her.

Startled, she fumbled the delicate dancer. Before it could hit the floor a hand shot out catching the figurine.

Straightening up from the catch, a tall, dark-haired man, laughed, crinkling the skin next to his gray eyes. "It would have been a shame to break such a pretty thing." He was dressed in more expensive clothing than most salesmen, and certainly his suit alone cost more than all the clothing she'd just bought. The man was quite attractive.

"Oh, thank you so much for saving it. I...er...I was just admiring this. I collect figurines."

"Did you want to purchase this?" he asked, his large hand dwarfing the delicate dancer.

"Yes, yes, I do."

He indicated for her to follow him to the counter. He took Liberty to the front of the line where she listened to the other customers standing there grumbling about pushy people and line crashers.

While adding up Liberty's purchase, a female clerk smiled at the man beside her. "Are you helping us out today, Mr. Montgomery?"

"Be nice to the customer, isn't that our motto?" He grinned showing white teeth, one overlapping the other slightly. He even wrapped the delicate figurine in butcher paper and handed it to Liberty.

The clerk seeing Liberty's puzzled look, leaned close to say. "This is Mr. Montgomery, the store's general manager. Mr. Grand, his father-in-law owns this store."

Being told information she really didn't need to know, Liberty put her prized purchase in the shopping bag and started to leave. Mr. Montgomery hurried to her side and insisted on carrying her shopping bag for her

"I take it you're a health care nurse," he said indicating her uniform and doctor's bag.

"Yes, I am."

"I see. Well here we are." He opened the front door and stepped aside for her to exit. When she held out her hand for her shopping bag, he glanced inside it. "Purchases for your husband I see. He's a lucky man. I only hope he wasn't the one who bruised your face." He handed her the bag and returned back inside.

Liberty made it to the drug store in time to buy the necessities Jonathan would need. She stopped by a haberdashery shop and bought a hat using Mr. Drake's size written on her paper. On her way home she passed a shop filled with costumes and decided to go in. The owner, small and wiry came forward with a bored look on his face.

"May I help you?" he asked.

"I hope so." She grinned. "I'm going to a costume party and want to go as a man." She described what she was looking for.

"Follow me." He pointed toward the back of the shop. He took her to where a row of manikin's heads was adorned with all colors of wigs, beards and mustaches. She fingered them. The hair tickled her fingers, making her grin. She held a reddish brown mustache up to her face and laughed at the results. "I'll go with the blonde wig, beard and mustache. Oh, and glasses, I need glasses. I can't wait to trick everyone at the party."

The salesman showed her how to use spirit gum to apply the mustache, and remover to take it off. He also suggested blond eyebrows, something she would never have thought of. She grinned and spent more of Lincoln Drake's money.

The City was starting to darken, and she hurried toward the trolley line when she passed a millenary shop with its window filled with displays of wide brimmed hats and colorful scarves. Seeing it was almost closing time, she hurried inside the shop filled with feathers, ribbons, and chatting women trying on hats. Not one for frills and lace and all the stuff that made a female feminine, Liberty was drawn to a ready-made black straw hat. It had a wide brim and a crown trimmed with a black and white striped ribbon that ended in a wide bow going vertical on the left side. Liberty cocked the hat at a jaunty angle and looked in the mirror. It was a great hat, nothing like she'd ever worn or owned before. The hat instantly transformed her from a nurse to a tall elegant woman.

"That one looks like it was made for you." The rosy cheeked milliner wearing an apron with a measuring tape around her neck approached. "I actually made the hat for someone else, but if you'd like to purchase it now, you can take it with you."

"What about the customer it's for? Won't she be disappointed when she comes to buy it and it's not here?"

The milliner laughed and shook her head. "Not really. I can make another in no time. Her order will be here when she arrives."

"I'll take it." She spent more of Lincoln Drake's money and this time on herself. After all, she should get compensated for her troubles. And Jonathan Drake was a whole lot of trouble.

The sun was starting to set when she arrived back at her apartment. Loaded with purchases, her doctor's bag, and the glorious hat on her head, she put the key in the lock and entered her home.

Jonathan jumped up from the sofa and approached. He took the shopping bags and her doctor's case from her and put them on the sofa. His gaze took in her hat. "Father must have given you money?"

"Yes, he did. And I was frugal with two exceptions. One, you've already spotted on my head, the other...well...let's just say I added to my porcelain collection." She opened her bag and handed him the wad of money from his father. "I've been put on a two week leave from work. One of my patients was diagnosed with typhoid fever. It's a precautionary measure, just to make sure I'm not infected. Have you had the fever?"

"I'm not sure. I remember some kind of illness going through my whole family when I was in my teens. We all recovered." He fanned the money and counted the bills, before putting them on the corner table. "This makes me wonder what happened to my wallet. My money clip. I had both when I went into Zelda's dressing room."

"They must be with your clothes wherever those are."

When he started to dump the bags contents on the sofa, she practically shouted, "Please be careful—I have a breakable in there." She hurried next to him and snatching up the wrapped figurine, she put it out of harm's way on the table.

Standing in front of the cheval mirror that stood in the corner of the living room, he held the suit coat against his body. "By the way, that hat looks good on you. Makes a different person...er...well, other than that ghastly nurse's hat you wear, this one is splendid...er...hell...I should shut up." He tried on the suit coat and put on the fedora. His mouth curved up in a practiced sneer. "It'll do."

He gave the other items of clothing a brief glance. Then his gaze fell on the wig, beard and mustache. He took the blonde wig and put it on, again he approached the mirror. It was a drastic transformation. He put on the wire-rimmed glasses and held the beard and mustache against his face.

Liberty stood next to him, her mouth parted in awe.

He grinned at the stranger staring back, a bookish looking man, a teacher perhaps, certainly not the womanizing rich playboy he was known for.

"My word," she said. "You look nothing like yourself—nothing at all. With that disguise, you can leave here and not be caught. Don't you agree?"

Jonathan didn't say anything, not even a pun or retort was directed her way. Instead, he took off the wig, the facial hair, and put them on the sofa. Turning toward Liberty he studied her with such deep intensity it not only puzzled her but also frightened her. When he began to unbutton her white blouse, surprised by his actions, she slapped at his hands.

"Stop it! What do you think you're doing?"

He tipped her chin up to meet his eyes. "I know what I'm doing. Don't be frightened, I'm not going to rape or harm you. I want to see something. It's the hat. It transforms you into a worldly looking woman. Would you strip down to your corset and underwear?"

"Mister Drake, I don't know what you have in mind, but I'm not sure I like it." She stepped away from him as if that small amount of space could help her.

He placed his hand over his heart and pledged. "I promise that I have only honorable thoughts when it comes to you, Miss Fitzgerald." His handsome face was contrite, a little boy pleading for something he shouldn't have.

"All right, but only if you stay across the room from me."

She was relieved to see him back up to be stopped by the wall. Liberty unbuttoned her blouse and put it over the back of the chair. Next came her gray tight skirt, also to join the blouse. She stood in her white, thin-strapped corset cover. Beneath it was her corset and white lacy drawers. When she pulled a long hatpin from the hat, and started to take the hat off, he held up his hand and asked her not to.

She obliged, but when he took a step toward her, she hurried behind the chair using it as a shield, and the hatpin as a weapon.

"Miss Fitzgerald," he said, "I've seen many a woman without her clothes on. For sure, much less than what you're wearing. Don't be shy, I'm only going into your bedroom and get the cape."

"You mean the cape Miss DeLane wore in the revue?"

"Yes." He glanced at her before continuing into her room.

Jonathan returned shortly with the glimmering cloak across his arm. He paused next to Liberty and her freckled covered skin. Arranging the cape around her shoulders, he guided her toward the mirror where he stood next to her. His hand stroked his chin, all the while thinking she would make a great dancer, tall, with long legs, and a winsome body. He removed her hat and pulled the pins from her hair and watched as it cascaded in a fury of fiery curls and waves to the center of her back. With dexterity and practice, he reached under the fabric and slipped the corset cover straps off her shoulders sending the lacy undergarment to puddle on the floor. Next, he unlaced her corset and allowed it to join the others.

She stood bare breasted covered only by the sheer turquoise material. When her gaze met his in the mirror, she crossed her arms to cover herself. He took her wrists and lowered her arms.

"Don't be uncomfortable. You're truly beautiful, you're like a fire radiating a glow all around," his voice was low with desire, and he told himself it was because she was a female standing before him with wonderful looking breasts. That was the reason he was vibrating with want, or was it need?

He turned her toward the mirror and pulled her body against his. When he kissed the soft skin at the nape of her neck she stopped him by removing his hands.

"Please don't," she said. Grabbing up her clothes she hurried inside her bedroom leaving him standing there.

As they sat eating their evening meal, stew again, Liberty cleared her throat. "I was at the Joyeux Theater today."

His brow furrowed, questioning. "Really? You could have told me sooner."

"We were busy with other things." Her cheeks started to burn.

"Did you see anyone of interest?"

She took a deep breath. "A young boy named Fitch introduced himself to me. Two detectives came out of the theater. They told the man at the door to keep Zelda DeLane's dressing room locked."

Jonathan kept hitting his spoon against his empty bowl. His mind appeared to be a thousand miles away.

She reached over to stop him. "Why did you want me to put on the cape? Didn't it bring back unwanted memories of Zelda DeLane?"

Jonathan wiped his mouth with the napkin and tossed it on the table. "Yes it did. Believe me or not, but it hurt like hell. It hurts every time I think of her. Zelda was…well…she was a complex woman. At times she used people, well men actually. She used us to get what she wanted, which included sleeping with owners of the theaters so she could achieve her status as a star performer. Zelda was also witty, fun to be with, extremely sexual, and I loved being around her.

"However, if I was to show up without an expensive gift for her, that would be the end of me. Zelda was also a taker. My love for her wasn't the love and marriage type of love, it was a convenient love. That's why it's so important for me to find out who killed her. I want revenge. I want the person responsible to fry in Sing Sing. And that's the reason I wanted you to wear Zelda's cape. So I could see how much of a star you look like."

She put down her spoon. What Jonathan just shared made her realize he wasn't going to die from a broken heart concerning Zelda. That Liberty's caring about him wasn't going to infringe on any sort of grief he might be suffering, if any. She thought about the cape and being bare breasted. Today's happening with Jonathan aroused sexual desires in her that she'd long suppressed. She'd never had a true boyfriend, just crushes on fellow college students, and a few dates. While studying for her degree in nursing, she didn't have the time to bother with anything bordering on love, sex, or high jinx as she called it. She'd been kissed many a time, but never with passion. No, there was much more in the way Jonathan kissed the back of her neck, the heat from his lips, his hands, delicious, and the stirring between her legs incredible. She warned herself, the man could make moldy bread tastes fresh. He knew his way around a woman's body like his own.

"Why is it important if I look like a Follies star or not?"

"Because, I want to know everything that goes on backstage

at the theater. If I'm going to prove my innocence, I have to start where the murder happened. I can change my appearance but not my voice. This is where you can help me. Especially with you being off work for a while. Be my eyes and ears where I cannot."

"I can do no such thing!" Her words rushed out. "There's no way I can go to the theater and snoop for you."

"Ah...but you can. I bet you can even dance if you wanted. You could try out to be a dancer."

She sucked in a deep breath, and squared her shoulders. "What are you suggesting?"

"That you audition for the revue. You're taller than most women, hell, truth be told, you looked imposing just standing there wearing the cape. Imagine what you'd look like with the whole costume on. Regal."

"No—no—no!" She pushed away from the table and hurried back into the living room where she paused like a statue, and mutinied against his very suggestion.

He followed her.

"Mr. Drake, you have your disguise, clothes, money. Anything else you need you can get from your father. Please, just go."

His hands clasped her shoulders and she found herself being turned to face him. *Don't let him get the upper hand, she thought.* She swallowed and met his gaze and his mouth when he dipped his head. His lips worked against hers, his strong arms encapsulated her until there was no air between them. She was drowning in his heat. He'd managed to work his way into her life and body. His fingers stroked the back of her neck, until finally she broke the kiss.

He kept his hold on her. "With you next to me, we can find the killer. Without you, I can't."

She didn't know what to say. Part of her wanted to help him, feel the excitement of a lifestyle she'd never known or even wanted too, until now. He was opening a door that once she stepped through; she might never be able to come back. Trying to clear her mind that he so enveloped, she went to stand next to the shelf and took down the ballerina figurine, the one Mr. Montgomery saved.

"What about my job? I have to return in two weeks," she asked, running her finger over the dancer's porcelains leg.

"You'll have a new one which pays you more in one week than what you now make in a year or more."

That news alone was staggering to her. Making that kind of money she could donate some to the Henry Street settlement. She could help out her family. But realization came crashing in.

"Just one problem, a big problem, I can't dance or sang." She replaced the dancer on the shelf and went to plop, very unladylike, on the sofa.

He joined her. "You'll have to prove to me that you can't do either one of those things."

"How?"

"Right here and now. Dance for me. Sing."

Her cheeks flared red. "I need music, something to accompany me."

"I'll order a gramophone, some records."

"No."

"Yes. Tomorrow, it'll be done." He laughed and instantly sobering, he took her hand within his. "Liberty Fitzgerald, I'll repay you someday for what you've done." He brought her hand to his cheek and then turned his face to capture her hand with his lips.

The Drake's mansion was located on Fifth Avenue alongside the Astor's and others whose rich status showed in the wealth of their homes. The mansion, a tall brick affair, towered three stories high, and had a black wrought iron fence acting as a border between it and the sidewalk.

Lincoln Drake, along with his wife Earlene and daughter Lona sat around the table unable to enjoy dinner. The mood brought to mind the painting of *The Last Supper,* only no betrayal here, more like being rounded up for the firing squad.

Their untouched food jelled on their plates. Only the wine glasses saw interest and were refilled more than once. With Jonathan's empty chair a constant reminder as to why he wasn't here, nothing could change the fact they were worried sick.

The fancy electric lamps cast the normally bright room into a morass of gloom. Mrs. Osborne, the head housekeeper, who along with the maid Gladys Finlay, stood peeking around the doorjamb, a concerned look on both of their faces.

Mrs. Osborne, appearing to gather her courage, approached the three, and folded her hands in front of her apron. "Do you want something else to eat? Would you like cook to fix something special?"

Lincoln, who usually left such matters to Earlene, now spoke. "We've lost our appetites, Mrs. Osborne. Thank you anyway. Why don't you come back later to clear the dishes?"

The housekeeper started to leave but paused. "Mr. and Mrs. Drake, I'm speaking for the staff when I say we don't believe Jonathan is guilty. We...er...well, we just don't."

Gladys came forward to bob her head in agreement.

"We thank you for your support. Tell the others won't you?" Earlene said.

Both women left, talking amongst themselves as they did so.

Lincoln's gaze alighted on his wife of thirty-four years. Once beautiful, and now at the age of fifty-five, her face had settled into an attractive grace. She occasionally lamented how she disliked the gray now threading through her chestnut colored hair. She voiced her dislike concerning the lines that formed next to her mouth and brown eyes. But to him, and he told her many times, she was as beautiful as the day they met during a hunting trip to Scotland. The rich American, the rich English beauty, he promptly forgot about shooting grouse and pheasants. He was always quick to remind her how she'd bagged his heart that day, and still did.

Earlene put her hand over his, her touch light and warm. "Lincoln dear, have you heard from Jonathan? You would tell me if you did?" Her voice, soft with its British accent was filled with questions, yet her face was pinched with worry.

Lincoln tried to smooth the lines, gentle her fears, but knew nothing he said would help. "No, I haven't. You'll be the first to know when I do." And he hadn't, not in the flesh or on the phone, only through Miss Fitzgerald's messages. He hated lying, but lying was the only way he could safeguard his son. To him, what he just said was a half-truth. He could tell just how hard Earlene ached for their son. She was like a mother lioness with her cubs, always trying to protect them. Yet, the spoiling of her two children had perhaps been the making of Jonathan's Achilles heel.

Lona, who'd kept quiet until now, spoke. "Daddy, do you think he killed the Follies star?"

"No!" Both Lincoln and Earlene spoke at the same time.

Lincoln, disgusted, stared at his daughter. With her black hair and dark brown eyes, she was as pretty as any actress, but right now he wanted to send her to her room. He spoke in anger. "I'm surprised as hell that you'd even entertain such a thought. Dangerous, Lona, very dangerous. Jonathan is innocent. Your brother isn't capable of such a dastardly act. I must help him get to the bottom of this, anyway I can, and anyhow I can." He pointed a finger at his wife and daughter. "If Jonathan tries to contact either one of you, you must tell me immediately."

Earlene smoothed the sleeve of her blue dress. "Lona, do you truly feel your brother is capable of killing someone?"

Lona put her cloth napkin on the table. "Not really. The Jonathan I know wouldn't hurt a fly. It's just that all the newspapers imply he's guilty, especially with how they found him."

"It sounds like you believe what the papers say. Have you read all of them?" Lincoln was curious.

"No, not all, but they all say the same thing. That Jonathan was…er…ah…naked and on top of Zelda DeLane, the star, and she was nude…well…and Jonathan had a bloody knife in his hand." Her face turned a deep scarlet. "It doesn't look so good for Jonathan, does it?"

Earlene narrowed her eyes at Lincoln and postured, her long neck rigid, her mouth set in a deep gash. She finally spoke. "But…where is Jonathan? Don't tell me he's running around Manhattan naked as the day he was born. Are you sure you haven't heard from him? Stashed him at the hotel somewhere?"

Lona tapped her mouth with her finger, unconsciously or consciously, staring at him. Lincoln knew he was transparent to both Lona and Jonathan, and had been for years. His firm gaze met hers as she searched for lies. Lona, who was good at ferreting out indecisions within others couldn't ferret out her own indecisions. She failed to dedicate herself to any cause, and was inclined to take her mother's side on the issue of high-society.

"Have you heard from Mr. Townsend lately?" Lincoln tried to change the subject but wasn't sure it was the best way to go, not with Lona's fiancé fighting in France for his homeland, Britain. And from the sad look on his daughter's face, he knew he'd made a bad blunder.

"No, Daddy. I'm so worried about him. I know Britain's in the thick of the fighting over there. And Darrell being an officer leads his men into battle. His last letter said how lucky he was to be in France for so long and not be wounded or worse. I remember when the war started and Britain thought it would last just several months. How silly they all were."

"Yes, I have to agree," Earlene said, and took a sip of red wine. Darrell's parents, the Townsend's were old friends of hers. Earlene kept in touch with her British acquaintances, and before the war started, returned to England often, always taking Lona with her. It was during one of those visits Lona and Darrell fell in love and became engaged.

Lincoln stared at his daughter. She'd matured into a lovely young woman and he'd missed it. He'd never asked Lona how she felt about marrying Darrell, leaving that part of his daughter's life in his wife's capable hands. Maybe he should ask. Certainly if he'd been more involved with Jonathan's life, had stood firm about his career and not playing so hard, Jonathan wouldn't be on the run for murder.

Earlene interrupted his musings. "Today, I received a cancellation from my *Ladies Society Club*. At their discretion, they said, until this horrendous mess with my son is cleared up. That's two memberships canceled within as many days."

"Well, it appears the women at your clubs are narrow-minded to believe the worst. You're better off without them." He pushed his chair back and stood. "Think I'll have a cigar in my den." Nodding at both Earlene and Lona, he started to leave when Mrs. Osborne came into the room.

"This telegram just arrived for Miss Lona."

They all stared at the small piece of paper as if it carried a disease and couldn't be touched.

Lincoln stepped forward and accepted the message. "Thank you, Mrs. Osborne."

Lona's face blanched. "Please read it for me, Dad." She gripped the arms of her chair.

Lincoln opened the sealed envelope. "It's from Mr. and Mrs. Townsend." He took a deep breath and began. *"Dear Miss Drake.*

We've been informed our darling son, Darrell was killed in action. Will send more information as we receive it. Regards, The Townsends."

Lona remained as still as a statue. Finally she was able to move. Her delicate hand shook as she reached for the telegram and read it for herself. "Mother, it's as if I'm reading about a stranger. Perhaps they are mistaken. Maybe Darrell's just been wounded, taken prisoner, anything but dead." Her eyes glistened with tears as she slowly got to her feet. She took one step before she started to faint.

Lincoln caught Lona as she slumped toward the floor. He scooped her up into his arms and with Earlene at his side he hurried into the sitting room where he laid his wilted daughter on the sofa.

"Lona—Lona!" Earlene patted her daughter's hand. "My God, Lincoln, what horrible thing is next for our family?"

Chapter Nine

Returning from buying a few groceries, never more than she could carry comfortably in her shopping bag, Liberty entered her apartment. Met by silence instead of a brooding Jonathan, she put her purchases on the kitchen counter. She opened the cupboard and put the few cans away. The potatoes and turnips she placed on the counter intending to make a stew.

Searching for Jonathan, she checked her bedroom. Empty. Wondering where he was, hoping he hadn't been arrested, she hurried out the door toward the bathroom.

No Jonathan.

He'd left without saying goodbye.

Puzzled, she went back into her apartment and sat on her sofa. The quiet was too quiet, she missed his laughing eyes, his devilish attitude, his smile, heck, she even missed his annoying presence. How could that be? How had she allowed herself to be taken in by him? She could ask herself these questions until the sun failed to shine and she'd never know the answers.

Dejected, she decided that tea was the answer for now, and

put the kettle on. The kettle's shrill whistle cut the silence, a reminder that the man she was trying to help had abandoned her. The kettle's whistle also masked other sounds, so when large hands came around her waist in a hug, frightened, she yelped and dropped her cup, shattering it against the floor.

"Sorry about that. I'll buy you another. Shut your eyes," he said, and putting his hands on her shoulders, turned her around. "You can open your eyes now."

She opened her eyes to stare into the face of a strange man. Surprised, her hand covered her mouth, suppressing laughter.

A blonde-haired Jonathan returned her stare, his grin now surrounded by a blonde mustache and beard, even his eyebrows were blonde. "I'm sorry to have frightened you. How do you like my disguise?"

Amazed, Liberty touched his cheeks, his beard. The glasses made him bookish looking, his short, blonde wig parted on the left, further enhanced the façade. Dressed in his ready-made suit, he'd become a simple man, a man who eased through life in the shadows of others.

"Yes, it'll work. Had I passed you on the street, I wouldn't have recognized you."

"Good, because we are going to try it out tonight."

"Walk the streets?" She made him a cup of tea and handed it to him. "I hope the steam from the tea won't loosen your mustache."

Ignoring her joke, he said, "Miss Fitzgerald, I'm taking you to the theater tonight, the Joyeux to be exact." He grinned, again the transformation fascinating.

"I'm not one to go out with strangers," she quipped and laughed.

Delighted, he grabbed her hand. "Close your eyes again, Miss Fitzgerald, I have a surprise for you."

He led her into the living room where he'd dumped some packages on the sofa and a Victrola player now sat on the top of her side table.

"Now you can open your eyes," he urged.

"Oh…my…word. Jonathan." Thinking it was like Christmas in September, Liberty's gaze took in a new Victrola with its large trumpet speaker setting on her corner table, and where wrapped purchases, along with a hat box cluttered her sofa.

He handed her one of the wrapped gifts. "This is for you. Open it."

With care, she removed the plain brown wrapping paper and unfolded a pretty dress, cerulean blue in color, and held it against her body for inspection. The stylish dress with its slim skirt hit just above her ankles. It had a black slash tie, long sleeves and scooped neck, both trimmed with wide pleats.

"You can wear it for either day or evening, preferably evenings," he said, and grinned. "And, I got you these." He stood back while she opened the rest of her gifts.

Next was a warm coat, tan in color, with double breasted buttons. After draping the coat over the back of the sofa, she opened the hat box and removed the hat. It was a dark navy blue and brimless. She stood in front of the cheval mirror and tried it on. The hat, so different from what she was used to, snugged against her head with a toile veil ending below her nose. Her bruise now a faded yellow was starting to disappear.

Peering at him through the veil, she wrinkled her nose. "This veil tickles. I've never owned a hat with one on it. I'm not sure if I like it. Certainly, it'll take some getting use to."

"Well, then, it's time you had one. It makes you look sophisticated." He took her by the hands and guided her back to the sofa where he insisted she sit down for the next surprise. Going to his knees, he took her one foot in his hands and darting a devilish glance her way, he proceeded to remove her shoe.

"What are you doing?" she asked, a look of curiosity covered her face through the veil.

"Be patient," he said and after popping the lid off the shoe box he removed a pair of black dressier heels.

"Here my lady," he teased while taking her right foot and working the shoe on, he then did the same with the left. "What we have here is a high heel shoe that comes with three detachable buckle sets, a rhinestone one, a set of dressy black leather bows, and just plain pewter buckles for day wear. I suggest you wear the rhinestones when I take you out on the town."

It sounded as if he meant to stay for a while. She was sure that with his disguise he'd want to leave here—her. He got to his feet and helped her to stand. She preened at the shoes while turning her ankles this way and that.

"Jonathan? Why do this? You need your money to last."

He ignored her questions. "Not too bad for off-the-rack at Macy's. And, my pretty girl, shall we try out those new shoes and see how well you dance in them?"

She sat amongst the finery and removed the hat which she held in her lap and played with the veil. "Are you sure you want to go to the Joyeux? I mean back to the place where you're known?"

"I can sit here and wait to be caught, or I can try out this masquerade and see where it gets me. The thought of Sing Sing prison scares me to death. But being unable to see my family, those I love most, frightens me even more. There's an old saying, *you don't know what you've got until you lose it*. Well truer words have never been spoken. I might be a lazy, good-for-nothing-son, but I'm willing to change all of that just to have my arms around my mother and sister. My dad goes without saying. Understand?"

She had nothing to contribute, he'd said it all. This was certainly a different side of Jonathan, and she'd feel the same way if she was kept from seeing her family. His poetic words deepened her commitment to help him anyway she could. Her resolve deepened even more when he tilted her chin and brushed his lips against hers.

How, in such a short time, did she allow her feelings for a man to overtake her life, and those feelings to become something akin to love? Like the statue she was named for, she always thought of herself as strong and steadfast. Where did that woman go, she wondered?

"How about that dance?" He put on the large black disk, and wound the Victrola up using its crank on the side. He lowered the arm with its needle onto the disk and the tinny sounds of a man singing, *For Me and My Gal,* flowed from the bulbous trumpet.

Jonathan bowed before Liberty.

"Ah…miss…may I have this dance?"

Liberty couldn't help but grin and curtsy back. "Yes sir, you may." She held out her arms and he slid his hand around to the small of her back. He took her hand within his and they danced.

Jonathan was all grace. Liberty wasn't. Her new shoes were stiff, she felt silly, clumsy, and thought Jonathan must be comparing her to the graceful women of his past. If nothing else, his nearness came into sharp focus and she couldn't help but smell his fragrant shaving soap.

He dipped her, making her laugh and hold on tight to his strong shoulders. His eyes twinkled as he looked into hers. "I'm going to make a dancer out of you, or die trying."

"Don't say that."

He twirled her around and around. She became dizzy. Again he dipped her close to the floor.

"Stop it," she squealed, "You'll drop me."

"Never." Still leaning over her, he slowly brought her to safety against his chest and straightened up, his hands caressing in the way only Jonathan had of doing.

She bit her lower lip while staring at him, his eyes.

He broke the spell, and moved with grace to put on another record. A slow waltz by a female singer. Again, he took her in his arms and danced moving his body against hers.

"Jonathan, this kind of dancing is nothing like the tap dancing they do on stage."

"Mmmm, you're right, it's not. Are you complaining?"

"No."

Inside the Joyeux Theater, and with Liberty's arm tucked within his, Jonathan followed the page who escorted them to their seats. Helping Liberty sit in the maroon-velvet seat, he couldn't help but be proud of the way she handled herself, with self-assurance, style, and grace and felt she would fit in here with no problems. After placing her purse on her lap and with her eyes shining with excitement, she warmed him with a wide smile. Pan-cake makeup covered her fading bruise, and the cut inside her mouth now healed. The dress he'd bought her was a perfect fit, it showed off her tall figure, had just the right aura of evening attire, not too fancy, but just right. She'd swept her hair up, fitting the hat over the elaborate do. The webbed veil came just below her nose, and he noticed she rolled it up so she could see without interference. He settled into his seat on her right.

Liberty opened her program and leaned close to him. "They have a tribute to Zelda DeLane in here."

"I'm surprised. I noticed the one out front but it was too hard to see with all the people milling around it."

The opulent theater he knew so well seated several thousand. The closed curtain across the stage was also a deep velvet maroon in color. Gold filigree swirls framed the balconies and cloaked the lighting sconces on the walls casting large diamond shapes all over creating light and dark shadows. The orchestra in the pit directly before the stage was warming up. Violinists plucked at their strings; the reed and brass sections practiced scales and mingled with the many voices throughout the Joyeux to form a chattering musical choir.

He glanced around, his gaze going to his family's box seats in the balcony on the right. Empty. As the theater filled, body heat forced the women to use their programs to fan themselves with.

"My word, I can't help but feel like a goldfish in a bowl," Liberty said while pointing a gloved finger at the box seats on the left where dozens of faces hid behind opera glasses scanning the crowds below them.

For a moment, Jonathan looked to where she pointed. He knew right away who was behind the small binoculars directed at him and Liberty.

Alice Montgomery.

Using his program as a shield, he coughed, and pressed his body against the seat, hiding his face from prying eyes. "That's what happens when you sit here on the main floor. My family's box is up to the right. Don't look, you might draw attention to us."

He was relieved when the lights dimmed and the curtain opened. Hopefully the start of the show distracted others as well.

He watched Liberty's mouth slightly part in awe when the showgirls gracefully flowed onto the stage, filling it with long limbs, sky-high headdresses with plumes of feathers. Glitz and glitter dazzled the audience. She laughed at the comedian, and sighed as the new star, Capucine, came out on stage to sing a trilling love song. Thundering applause accompanied the large maroon and gold curtains as they swished closed for intermission.

As the house lights came on to help patrons down the aisles, Jonathan glanced toward his box seats. A chill ran through his body. He was more than surprised to see his father and his sister Lona, sitting there. Secretly, he'd wished his father would appear, but not his sister. He wondered if his father attended the revue with the hopes of seeing him. No, how could he? Besides, how would his father know what he would look like?

As Jonathan stared upward, his father put opera glasses to his eyes and Jonathan could swear his father nodded at him. Knowing his father would recognize Liberty in an instant and realize that he was behind the blonde masquerade made him do a slow nod back. The show soured for Jonathan, and wanting to avoid any kind of innocent meeting with his family, he decided to leave.

"Seen enough?" Jonathan turned to Liberty and forced a grinned.

Reluctance fleeted across her face. "No, I could stay here forever. It's all so wonderful. But, I guess we shouldn't over extend our luck."

He leaned close and wrapped her shawl around her shoulders. "My father's here."

"Oh…my…where?"

"In my family's balcony seats. Don't look. He knows you. And now he must realize it's me in this getup."

A brief glance upwards confirmed his suspicions, as his father was no longer there.

They joined the wave of people in the aisles taking advantage of the intermission. Jonathan walked directly behind Liberty, his hand against the small of her back. His mere touch felt exciting to her. When they reached the crowded lobby filled with chatting people, cigar, pipe, and cigarette smoke, she started pushing toward the exit.

A lone voice spoke. "Don't tell me a lovely woman like you is alone tonight?" Right beside her was the man from Grand's department store, the one who rang up her figurine. Dressed in a black evening suit, every shellacked hair in place, and if possible he was even more handsome tonight than at the store.

"Oh...I remember you from Grand's. You were most helpful. Ah...Mr. Montgomery isn't it?"

Apparently pleased she remembered his name, he grinned. "Yes, that's right."

She used her rolled program to lightly tap his forearm. "And, I'll have you know, I'm not alone, my escort is right here." When she turned to introduce Jonathan, she realized in horror they hadn't made up another name for him. But he'd pulled a Houdini act and disappeared. Relieved, she said, "I guess he's gone to refresh himself."

"Are you enjoying the revue?" he asked.

She smiled and said, "Yes, it's breathtaking."

"I don't think I've seen you here before." His gray eyes took in her apparel.

"No, you haven't. Oh...one time about five years ago, I went to the Schubert and watched Caesar and Cleopatra, but that was nothing like here. It's quite glamorous isn't it?"

He stared beyond her, searching, and said, "Are you sure you're here with someone? I don't see anyone claiming you. You're much too lovely to leave standing here alone." His finger traced up her arm in a slow sensuous path.

"Truly, I'm here with my male friend. He left to go...to...well...over there." She removed his hand and pointed to the alcove where the men's room disappeared behind blue velvet curtains. "It was nice seeing you again, but you'll have to excuse me, I don't want to miss any of the show."

She moved away from him and headed toward the other side of the lobby and the restroom for ladies. Searching for Jonathan and not seeing him, she turned to leave when she bumped into Lincoln Drake's chest. Startled, she dropped her program.

"I beg your pardon," he said and bent to retrieve it.

She watched as he switched her program with his. Straightening, he tucked the rolled paper inside her hand. Nodding and saying he was sorry, he turned away, and melted into the crowds making their way back inside the theater doors.

Liberty ducked outside and gulping in fresh air looked around. Still not spotting Jonathan, she pulled her shawl tight and started walking down Broadway. Cars rattled by, and horse drawn carriages clopped along carrying laughing people. To her, the evening was magical and she wouldn't allow anything to take away the feeling she'd felt while watching the performances.

A few blocks away Jonathan, silent as a cat, fell in step with her giving her a start.

Liberty put her hand on her heart as if to stop its rapid pounding. "Don't do that," she said, her gaze going over a blonde Jonathan. "And try not to disappear again. I didn't know what was happening. One thing I did figure out though is we must invent a name and occupation for you."

"I beg your forgiveness, I consider myself lashed and whipped into shape and will never let it happen again. However, what happened back in the lobby was too close." His eyes twinkled and whistling between his teeth, he entwined his arm within hers. She gladly accepted it, needing the strong comforting feel of him.

"Yes, indeed. I didn't think I was going to get rid of Mr. Montgomery. I take it you know him and that's why you left?"

"I didn't want to take the chance of Talon Montgomery recognizing me. How is it that you're acquainted with him?"

Liberty stopped walking and paused in front of a window display filled with women's hats of all shapes, some wide brimmed, some not. "I don't know him, not really. He waited on me one time at Grand's when I was buying clothing for you."

"Latched onto you is more like it. I bet he slithered close to you and whispered in your ear how beautiful you are, and he'd like to help you with your purchases, and then he took you to the counter and got the clerk to ring you up."

Liberty looked at his reflection next to hers, a blonde, moody, bookish and somewhat jealous man stared back.

"The answers yes, to all those things. Who is he? Is he a close friend of yours?" She turned to look him in the eye.

"I'd never classify Talon Montgomery as a friend of mine. Acquaintance at the occasional card table perhaps. He's married to Alice Grand whose father owns Grand's department stores. It's just that their store, Grand's isn't far from my father's hotel. So being in the business, everyone knows everyone. Talon's a woman-izer and seeks out single attractive women. I noticed he was look-ing at us through binoculars from his booth. You must have made quite the impression for him to come trawling as we left."

"I certainly gave the man no encouragement. Truly, I hadn't thought about him since we talked at the store. I'll say one thing though; at least he didn't recognize you." She smiled. "Your own mother wouldn't recognize you. Well your father did and that was because he knows me. By the way, your father bumped into me and switched our programs. He didn't say anything other than to excuse himself." She handed him the brochure with the colorful painting of the revue star, Capucine, on the cover.

A smile formed around his mouth as he unrolled the program. "Dad's written in here. He wants to meet with you and asked that you call sometime this coming week. He warns to be careful, he's still being watched. Two detectives, named Scala and Jones, were at the theater tonight and were sitting not far from you and I. Damn they remind me of a sticky spider's web." He paused and brought the brochure closer to his eyes. Disbelief covered his face.

"Oh my—God," he blurted.

"What is it?" She leaned close.

"Dad writes that my sister's fiancé was killed in France."

"Oh…my, I'm so sorry to hear that. Did you know him well?" she said.

"Yes…yes, I did. Darrell was a fine man who loved my sister very much. They planned on getting married when the war ended. I hate this war. It's taken so many lives."

Liberty squeezed his arm. "I do hope my brother Teague remains safe."

"I'm sure he is. Don't let this news make you sad or worry about your brother. Enjoy the evening as intended."

They strolled on, arm-in-arm, past row houses where muted conversations could be heard from within. A few men sat on their stoops smoking and visiting with neighbors. Cooking smells of late dinners lingered to mingle with the night air that turned crisp and in the grasp of fall.

Finally reaching her apartment they allowed another couple living in the building to go ahead of them. All of their footsteps rang out on the stairs. Tonight Liberty minded the long trek, she was tired and wanted to get her new shoes off to ease the blisters on both heels. She'd have to bandage them. Jonathan's grip on her arm became firm and it wasn't long before they were in front of her door where he took her key and opened the lock, pushing the door open for her to enter. He removed her shawl and hung it on the hat rack, his suit coat and hat followed.

Liberty slipped off her shoes and crossed her arms, rubbing them as if she was cold. Cold was the furthest sensation from her mind, she'd felt Jonathan's body close to hers all evening. When his arm would accidentally brush against hers, it felt good. Anymore, the only heated body she was used to touching was a fevered brow. Not even realizing it, she'd missed out on so much.

The cheval mirror reflected them as Jonathan filled up the space behind her and began kissing the back of her neck. His lips were white hot, as caressing as a breeze as they trailed down her neck and onto her shoulder. She closed her eyes and let the moment flow over her.

"Tell me to stop and I will," he said, and turning her to face him, he rolled up the veil on her hat. He lifted her chin with his finger and bent to kiss her cheek, her chin, and gently press his lips against the faded bruise on her jaw.

"Please, stop. You muddle my mind when you do that. I lose my will." She moved away from him, knowing if she remained within his embrace she couldn't stop him. Trying to command her body back from wicked desires she removed her hat and gloves and placed them on the table. "Would you like something to drink?"

"Yes, a brandy. Liberty, I'd never force you to do anything you don't want to."

"I know. If I didn't trust or believe in you, I wouldn't allow you here." She went into the kitchen, and after pouring them both a finger of the strong spirits, returned with the amber colored drinks.

They clicked glasses. She sipped. He emptied his in one gulp.

Liberty sat on the sofa, took a deep breath, and another sip. The brandy burned all the way down. She liked the feel.

Jonathan returned after refilling his glass, this time more generous than Liberty was. He sat beside her, allowing his arm to brush against hers.

"You look extraordinary tonight. A lot of men noticed you."

She smiled at him, liking how he looked in a white shirt and dark brown vest. "You sound jealous."

"I am."

"Don't be. Our first step is to get you free of this mess. Then you go back to your life and I can get back to mine. And, by the way, don't think for an instant that I can sing and dance like those women on stage tonight, because I can't."

"Yes, you can."

"No, Jonathan, I can't. I'm not talented. I'm clumsy. Besides, there might not be an opening for me to try and get. We'll just have to make other plans."

"The plan is to get you behind the scenes as a dancer. That might lure the killer out. Please, I know of no other way to do this."

He took her hand and brought it to his lips. He chuckled, and loudly kissed up her arm to her neck where he stopped to nibble.

"Do I have to sleep on the cot tonight?" His face was hopeful.

"Yes, Mr. Drake, you do. Just pull it out and make your bed." Again, she slipped out of his enticing embrace.

Across town in the Drake's mansion, Lincoln Drake holding a decanter of brandy and two glasses, slipped into his wife's sitting room off her bedroom. Earlene, gorgeous in a rose-colored dressing gown, was sitting on a brocaded stool brushing her long hair. When she started to stand, he told her to remain there, and he placed the glasses and decanter on her dressing table. Taking the brush from his wife's slender hand, he began brushing her hair. Her hair, long, brown and laced with gray, crackled with each stroke of the hairbrush. He pulled it away from her swanlike neck and couldn't resist leaning down and kissing her alabaster skin. After so many years of marriage, she could still make his heart flip, as it was doing right now. Her eyes, brown and gentle, were the thing he loved best about her. Especially now, in the mirror, her smile reached her eyes and were filled with love for him.

"Lincoln, dear, do you remember when you gave me this comb and brush set for my birthday? It's so lovely. I think of you every time I brush my hair. I suspect that's what you thought would happen when you bought it for me."

He chuckled. "You know me too well. Is there no secret I can keep from you?"

"Yes, there are secrets you might try to keep from me." She turned and took the brush from him. "I'd like that drink you walked in with. How about you, thirsty?"

He helped her to her feet and filled each glass a neat two fingers high. Earlene accepted the liquor from him and gave a toast to their son being cleared of any wrong doing. They clicked their glasses together.

"Yes, here's to bringing our son back home." He longed to tell her about seeing Jonathan at the theater tonight, but couldn't. The less Earlene knew the better for her. To know that Jonathan had Miss Fitzgerald on his side was a blessing. And what a clever disguise Jonathan wore. If he didn't have Miss Fitzgerald with him, Lincoln would have walked right by his own son and not known him. He thought Jonathan had brass balls for daring to go back to the murder scene and be amongst those that thought him guilty. He was proud of his son's moxie.

Earlene took a seat in one of her floral brocaded chairs next to the fireplace that a small flamed crackled in. He claimed the one next to hers.

"How was the revue?" she asked. "I hope it took Lona's mind off her grief. I'm glad you insisted on taking her."

He reached over and patted her bejeweled hand, hoping to smooth away the furrows that formed on her brow. "I'd say it went well. Despite her grief, Lona appeared to enjoy herself. They have a new singer called Capucine. She's French, and I could hardly tell what she was saying when she sang. Also, no one asked me about Jonathan which was a great relief to me." He hesitated and then blurted, "Earlene, I think our son is all right."

She tilted her head at his comment, and leaned forward. "Do you know something about Jonathan that you aren't telling me?"

"No. But if he needed help, somehow he would have gotten word to me. I can only say that not hearing from him is good news for us." He said things he shouldn't and could kick himself for the hope he'd put in Earlene's eyes.

"Oh." She looked crestfallen. "If you say so. But you must admit, we—I've spoiled our son. Now I regret having done so." She sipped the brandy, her pretty face in thought.

"Dear, why don't you take Lona, and go upstate to our summer home for a few months. Leastways, until I can get a handle on what's happening with Jonathan?"

Again, that troubled stare as she worried her bottom lip. "If I didn't know any better, I'd say you're trying to get rid of me—your family. To what means?"

"I'm thinking of you, the stress of the scandal and all. This is going to get ugly, very ugly. Right now guests are coming in droves to the Hotel because of its association with Jonathan. Later, if he's caught, patrons will give The Drake a wide berth."

"You mean we may go bankrupt?" She sat her unfinished drink on the table.

"I don't think it'll get that bad." He stood and removed his suit coat, bowtie, and starched collar. Earlene, getting the signal, came to him and helped him out of the rest of his clothes. One thing in Earlene's favor is that she never barred her door to Lincoln, and he never took a mistress. Didn't see the need. Never wanted too. His wife and family meant the world to him. He loved her too much to ever want to take another woman to bed.

They joined each other in Earlene's big four-poster bed with all the feminine fluff imaginable. He slipped his arm behind her head and pulled her close, waiting. She snuggled even closer, kissing his cheek.

At last she said, "I'm not going to our summer home and leave you alone. Nor do I want to be gone, especially if Jonathan needs me. Also, my love," she turned to him and rubbed her finger across his mouth. "I believe you're lying. And if you're lying, you are trying to keep news from me. And if you're trying to keep news from me, you have heard from Jonathan. And if you've heard from Jonathan then you are trying to keep him safe by not telling me. And now my sweet, husband, two kisses on the lips means you have heard from our son and he's safe. A chaste kiss on my cheek means otherwise, that you positively know nothing concerning Jonathan's whereabouts."

Lincoln couldn't help but shrug. He gave her two kisses in rapid succession on the mouth.

Puzzled, she pulled back to stare at his face. "That was two kisses, was it not?"

"Yes," he said, "Definitely two."

Chapter Ten

The next morning after attending the theater, Alice was up early. She'd taken care to dress in a long-sleeved white blouse with a wide collar and lacy cuffs, and a skirt of brown. Her hair was done up in a French twist and her makeup just right.

She insisted that her companion Jenny Bishop take her downstairs to have breakfast. Since Alice practically stopped eating any meal with Talon or her parents this was a rare occasion indeed.

As Jenny pushed her, Alice rested both hands on the arm rests and listened to the bulky wheelchair's squeaky wheels announcing her entrance into the lavishly decorated dining room.

Talon was all by himself at the long mahogany table, eating his breakfast with only his newspaper to keep him company. Alice watched in glee as her startled husband came alive and immediately stood to acknowledge her.

"Alice! This is a pleasant surprise," he said. Immaculate in a brown suit and dark brown vest, he moved the chair next to him out of the way allowing room for her wheelchair. He helped Miss Bishop situate Alice's chair close to the table.

She snapped her white monogrammed napkin open from its crisp fold and placed it on her lap. "Please don't be so shocked to see me, darling. It's not good for one's heart." Alice's smile for Talon was so sugar-coated it would satisfy any sweet tooth.

"I'd say I'm more pleased than shocked. You have to admit it's a rare day you leave your room to eat, let alone join me for breakfast."

"Yes, I thought it's about time I left my ivory tower and be social. I must have missed Mother and Father?"

He shook his head, "No, they haven't been down yet, but since this is Sunday they usually go to church, and then come back for brunch."

Feeling like an outsider who had to be told by her husband about her parent's plans, Alice felt a stab of jealousy. "Jenny would you please get me some eggs, bacon and toast. Oh, and coffee, please bring me a cup of hot coffee with plenty of cream in it. And, would you open the curtains? I swear it looks like a morgue in here, all dark and sinister. Don't you agree, Talon, doesn't it look sinister in here, especially with all this furniture left over from the Victorian age. That's what I'll talk to mother about, getting a new table and chairs. Light and airy, get out of the dark ages I say."

Jenny flung open the dark purple-velvet curtains allowing the morning sun to filter in and fall upon the table where Alice sat. She then took a plate and filled it with Alice's request.

"Jenny, would you be a dear and go see if cook has made scones?"

Talon shattered the shell on his poached egg then spooned the dripping contents into his mouth. Glancing over at the window he shrugged and commented. "The curtains being opened does make it more pleasant in here. To be truthful, I'm always in such a hurry when I eat breakfast that I've failed to notice the furniture I'm sitting on."

Alice sipped coffee from a porcelain cup with pink roses and a gold rim. The cup with its matching saucer was from a large set of china. Her mother's dishes of course. Alice didn't have anything to call her own in this house. Well, maybe her clothes. She couldn't even call Talon hers. "I see…well I hope to change all that. It's time I started joining you for meals, even going about the City more. I do love getting out and going to the theater, and I do thank you for taking me. It's just…I so…well I've come to hate how people stare at me in this chair. I got an eye full of it last night at the theater."

But then, even she had to admit to spending most of the evening peering through her opera glasses at the masses and taking in the latest fashions, the glittery feathery hats, gowns, and people in general. She perused for the longest time a certain couple, a striking redheaded woman and a blond nondescript man who reminded her of someone. Who? Protected as he was beside the woman, she was afforded mere glimpses of the man. Yet, while sitting in her wheelchair during intermission in the grand lobby, Alice noticed this same woman was stopped by Talon and he'd had a conversation with her. The woman's mystery escort had disappeared. Perhaps they weren't a couple after all.

"Who was that woman you talked to at the revue last night?" she asked and dabbed her mouth with her napkin.

His brow crinkled in a frown as he held his coffee cup. "Which woman? I believe I talked to more than one woman last night. Your friends, our acquaintances in surrounding boxes, who are you referring to, my dear?" His cup clanked against the saucer.

"The tall redhead in the lobby. She's someone you'd never forget, quite imposing I may add, quite imposing indeed." She buttered her toast and spread marmalade across its hot surface.

"Ah…yes, the redhead. I hardly know her. She was a customer in Grand's a few days ago. I waited on her. She was buying clothes for her husband." His smile was almost feral. "Does that make you feel better that she's married?"

"I've never known you to let a little thing like marriage stop you before." Her words were direct, sharp, and she wanted them to sink into Talon's brain. She was making him aware that she always knew when he was getting ready to have an affair, having an affair, or ending an affair. She might be wheelchair bound, but nothing got by her, and if she had to admit, her skills at sleuthing had enhanced gloriously.

"Ah...so this is the reason for your early appearance. So you can question me about last night. And here I thought it was my charming company you sought." When she started to protest, he held up a hand to silence her. "My dear wife, you know when I have a little peccadillo I don't waste my time on women without money. Isn't that a requirement of yours? They must be rich, so when I dip into their...ah...caves of modesty my penis will not be tainted by poverty, disease, and most of all I'll not be blackmailed by some destitute dredge seeking a better life?"

Alice's mouth fell open at his directness. Tit-for-tat. And he played the game much better than she. When did he start hating her so much that he didn't care what he said? His gaze, gray, cold and directed at her certainly made it clear.

"Perhaps I made a mistake joining you for breakfast," she said in a flat voice.

"Perhaps you have." He reached over and taking her hand within his, kissed her palm. "But, listen to me, sweet wife. What is between your legs still functions quite well. It isn't paralyzed." He dropped her hand and went to his knees next to her. His hand snaked under her skirt, stopping at the juncture of her legs. His fingers began questing, moving through her bloomers, reaching bare skin, poking inside her cleft, pinching her clitoris between his fingers.

"Do you feel that?" he asked and pinched harder.

Her lips parted and not from shock. Waves of pleasure started within and threatened to burst out of her skin.

He abruptly stopped, stunning her. He stood and wiping his hands on his napkin, tossed it on his plate. "I'm going to the store for a while."

"It's Sunday, the store is closed."

"We'll be taking inventory soon. I need to get ready for it without interruptions. I hope your day is planned with all sorts of fun things for you to do." This time he leaned down and kissed her on the mouth, his tongue searching inside hers. Finally, he broke the kiss and whispered, "Don't worry, darling. My tongue hasn't been inside any tainted pussy's here lately." He laughed and pushed his fingers inside her mouth. "But my hand just was."

When her teeth grazed the skin of his fingers, he cautioned, "Tsk...tsk...don't you know good girls don't bite." He jerked his hand back and stared at her for a moment before turning on his heels and walking out.

Alice wasn't aware when Jenny came back into the room. Talon just now showed her more sexual attention than he had in several years. Thinking of Talon's smart-alecky words about her privates not being paralyzed made her smile. She then tipped her head back and laughed out loud.

"What's so funny?" Jenny asked.

"Nothing, just something Talon said to me. My coffee's cold. I'd like a fresh cup. Did you find those scones I asked for? I am extremely hungry all of a sudden." She watched as her mother and father entered the room. They were getting old. Their hair had gone completely gray; her father's face florid with loose jowls, and her mother's mouth was pursed with winkles.

Her mother might be showing her age, yet she was still a vision of loveliness. Dressed for church and the cool fall weather, she was wearing a brown coat along with a black hat with the wide brim turned up. The hat, free of adornments had only a veil affixed over her face.

Wearing his Sunday best and anxious to leave, Alice's father pulled his watch from where it nested inside his watch pocket and looked at the time. "Sorry we can't join you for breakfast, but we're off to church," he said while replacing his watch. "Why don't you join us? A little bit of preaching will do you good."

"No thank you. I'm tired and am going back upstairs."

Yvette clutched her purse against her bosom. "Alice, mon chéri, it's so good to see you in such good spirits. When we return from church perhaps our little family can have brunch together, oui?" She looked so hopeful that Alice grinned and nodded at her.

"I'd like that very much, Mother. Maybe we could go shopping together this week?"

"Oui, we can do that. Would you have Jenny close the curtains in here when you're through? I don't want the furniture to fade." Pointing to where the sun rays skittered across the dark mahogany table, she leaned down to give Alice a kiss on the cheek.

Alice watched her parents leave, their voices echoing behind them.

Silence coated the room like a thick fog.

Jenny came up behind her and Alice felt familiar hands cupping her breasts sending spikes of desire raging through her, more so than Talon ever could. Leaning over, she kissed Alice's neck.

"I heard. Close the curtains." Jenny did her bidding, and pulled them shut putting Alice back in a gloomy room.

Jenny turned and with a bright smile, asked, "Would you like to go to your room and have your opium pipe? Me?"

"Yes, Jenny, I'd like to have both."

Talon stood at the end of the bed looking at Josette Jackson. Lying nude with her legs spread wide enticing him to join her. Josette, a dancer in the Joyeux Follies, was a delightful fuck that he'd been seeing for several months. He'd also been juggling his time between her and Zelda. Not one to keep only one woman dangling, Talon chose to keep many, and now with Zelda dead, he would be on the lookout for another conquest. Liberty Fitzgerald was on his mind to fill the gap left by Zelda's demise.

When he first started seeing Josette, the vibrant dancer intrigued him, but he hated coming here to her small flat that wasn't the cleanest. He insisted on clean sheets and ordered the place picked up before he arrived every Sunday afternoon. Josette complained about washing the sheets, that she didn't have time, so he paid for a woman to wash the sheets and keep the place clean and tidy. Just for him, he cautioned her, he wasn't about to share his clean nature with any other man she might be seeing.

Right now, he watched Josette trace her finger around her breasts, down her abdomen to disappear inside her brown bush, and pout her cherry-red lips at him. Her bleached blonde hair had a dark grow out, giving her a frowzy appearance. Despite that, her blue eyes and flawless skin beckoned for his touch.

His grin stretched across his face as he untied his shoes and removed his socks. Next off were his suit coat, then his trousers, then his shirt and under garments, all neatly arranged on the wooden valet he kept here.

"Get between the sheets," he ordered, and she complied. Lifting the top sheet he inspected it to make sure it was clean and crisp. She knew to put his sheets on when he was there and to take them off after he left. They smelled fresh, and satisfied with them, Talon lowered himself next to Josette's scrubbed body.

"What do you have for me today?" she asked.

"In place of what? My cock satisfying you?" He took her hand

and put it on his erection.

Knowing what he liked, she continued her administrations trying to please him. When he started breathing faster and lifted his hips off the bed and groaned, she suddenly stopped. "No, I mean what present did you bring me?"

Unable to believe that she dared stop what she was doing, he suppressed his anger. He turned onto his stomach and crawled on top of her. "Naughty, Josette," he said and laughed. "Like always, I have a present for you, but you have to earn it first." He kissed her neck to her bosom and moved to capture a nipple in his mouth. He bit down, causing her to gasp and tears to come to her eyes.

"Ouch, stop it!" she cried out and tried to push him off of her. He captured her wrists within his large hands. He grinned and changing breasts, he bit the other one and proceeded to suck and tongue her until her cries turned to pleasure.

Having enough of foreplay, he grabbed his engorged cock and entered her. He was large, and didn't care if he pleased her, only himself, as his hips set up a rhythm, making the bedsprings groan. He grabbed her by the shoulders and riding her like a horse quickly came inside her.

She laid there, tears still in her eyes, until finally she turned to him. "Do you care for me at all?" she asked, with heartbreak in her every word.

He took a cigarette off of the night stand and lit it. Lying next to her again, he pulled the smoke into his lungs and blew it out in a gray cloud. "To answer your question, of course I care for you."

"Would you leave your wife for me?" she asked and fidgeted with the bed sheet, daring to glance his way.

He took another drag and blew smoke rings before he started laughing, a belly laugh that made the bed jiggle. "Not on your life. You're a second-rate dancer with little income and who has nothing to offer me."

Her smooth brow pulled into a frown and she put her arm across his chest and played with his chest hair. "What if I did have something to give you that your wife couldn't? Would you leave her then?"

Wondering just where she was going with this, he sat up and dabbed the cigarette out in the ashtray. "I can't imagine what you could give me that she can't." He stared at her smeared lipstick, at her mussed hair, and found that everything about her disgusted him.

She swallowed and blew out a breath. "A child, I could give you a baby."

He drew in a sharp breath and somehow knew that was what she was going to say. "Are you pregnant?"

Josette did a meek nod and bite her lower lip.

"How do I know it is mine?" he asked, remaining cool and detached.

She pulled the sheet around her bosom and looked like she'd been slapped. "There has been no one else but you. I want to know if you are going to stand by me, help me with this child."

Ah...yes...another child to be brought into the world only to be abandoned by its father. Talon never knew his father, or what happened to him. The story told by his mother is that his father worked on the railroad. One day he took a train out of town and never returned. This was not in the cards for Talon.

Talon was livid that Josette allowed herself to get caught. And with her being caught, she was trying to snare him. Better women than Josette Jackson tried and failed. His mind was awhirl with the awful news. He wondered what she had in mind. If Alice ever found out about this baby, it would be disastrous and kill his marriage. Not that he was in the grips of a wonderful marriage, his stank. But it was his marriage to get out of in his own way.

He slipped from the bed, and going to his suit coat, removed a small package. "Here is your present. Certainly it can't compare to your surprise for me. Don't worry, my dear, I'm going to take care of you." And how he was going to achieve that started to form, little-by-little, piece-by-piece until his plan fell into place.

Josette moved over to the side of the bed and dangling her legs over the edge, she accepted the present from him. Removing the ribbon and opening the black velvet box, she smiled at him and removed a gold locket with a heart pendant. "Oh…it's beautiful. Please put it on me." She lifted her long hair off of her neck and turned her head so he could shut the clasp.

He affixed it and ran his hands around her neck admiring the pretty bauble. He tilted her face upwards and bent to kiss her.

"It looks nice on you."

"Thank you, Talon. Thank you so much." She beamed at him.

"That's no way to thank me." He took her by the back of the neck and forced her to take his aroused penis inside her mouth. He shut his eyes and pressed his body against her face, waiting for his reward. "Be a good girl and show me just how much you give thanks."

Sunday afternoon Liberty left Jonathan alone and went to have dinner with her brother Blaine and his family. A regular event, and if she didn't show up they would all be pounding on her door wanting to know why. Blaine lived in an apartment about a mile north of where she lived, in a nice neighborhood, certainly a huge step away from the squalor and tenements that the City was tearing down and rebuilding.

Liberty wore last year's best dress, a one-piece draped shift with an inset belt and a fancy collar and sleeves. The hem came to her ankles showing off her new shoes, bandaged heels and all. She carried a tote bag loaded with groceries.

Marybeth Fitzgerald answered the door on the third knock. Standing beside her were Shawn and Kenny, her two little boys. Both boys were anxious to rush Liberty, but were held in check by their mother. Well rounded with another pregnancy and about six months gone, Liberty's sister-in-law looked tired. Strands of blonde hair escaped her bun, and her dimpled cheeks were rosy from what Liberty suspected was heat from the oven. She wiped her hands on the white apron stretched over her maternity top. Her brown eyes held warmth as she welcomed Liberty with a big hug.

"Liberty," she said, and gave Liberty's back several loving pats. "It's so good to see you. Please come in. Your dad's already here arguing with Blaine."

Liberty no sooner stepped inside when both boys hugged her around the hips, impending further progress. They smelled of Palmolive soap and were dressed identically in white shirts and brown knee pants. The scuffs on their shoes were polished over with brown polish. Kenny, the youngest at eight, was endearing with blonde curly hair and blue eyes that now stared up at her. She ruffled his curls making him giggle. Sandy-haired Shawn, named after some relative back in the old country, was two years older than Kenny and several inches taller.

Liberty bent to extract herself from their grip and to give each of them a smooch on the cheek, which they loved getting but acted like they didn't. They both made fake motions like they were wiping off her kisses.

"Would you boys please take this to the kitchen for me?" Liberty handed them the heavy tote, and acting important, they headed for the kitchen.

Marybeth watched them go and took Liberty by the arm. "Liberty, dear, the boys do love you so. They have talked of nothing but you coming here today." She tried to push a straggly hair back into place. "You'll have to excuse the mess, but I have orders due out this coming week."

The mess, Marybeth spoke of, was sewing cluttered in a corner of the living room next to her Singer sewing machine. Colorful fabrics had been made into little dresses, shirts and blouses for children, and stacked high. Liberty knew her sister-in-law's sewing helped to supplement their income.

Otherwise, their home was tidy, with tan colored walls, a picture of Jesus Christ being crucified hung on one wall while a cheap landscape painting hung above the sofa. All the furniture, tables, chairs and sofa were rejects from the furniture factory that both Keegan and Blaine worked at. Keegan had re-upholstered them in a color popular at the time, blue velvet. Marybeth's knitting basket sat beside the rocking chair and was filled with pink yarn. Pink for the girl she wanted to have.

Keegan and Blaine came in from the kitchen area holding cups of hot tea. They were wearing their Sunday best, plain black suits with vest over white shirts. Both of their faces sported bushy mustaches.

"Liberty, glad ya made it." Blaine welcomed her with words. Tall and skinny, he remained where he was.

Her father, who made up for her brother's lack of social graces, kissed her cheek. "Here's me sweet lass. Glad to see yer jaw is better." Smelling of wood chips and shaving soap, his face lit by just looking at her.

Keegan took the rocking chair while Blaine sat in a stiff backed chair, leaving Liberty the sofa.

"What happened to your jaw?" Blaine asked. His gray eyes were curious. He might have their dad's big nose, and eye coloring, but not Dad's easy going manner. Blaine's usual bitter attitude made Liberty think that he was found beneath a tree.

"I was hit by an irate man who didn't want me to bring a

health department doctor to his place."

Blaine shrugged. "I would have done the same. Nosey doctors aren't allowed in my house."

"You would have hit me to keep them out?" Liberty didn't believe a word Blaine said.

"Lass, are ya still workin' then?" Keegan asked.

"Actually, I'm on a two week leave because I was exposed to the Typhoid fever. Exposed by the daughter of the man who hit me."

Keegan scoffed. "Ye would have the fever long before now. Yer mam died with it."

Liberty looked fondly at her dad. "I know and that's what I told my boss. But she wants me to remain home to make sure I'm all right."

"Other than you gettin' hit, how is your work?" Blain asked.

"I've been busy. I swear people like being filthy and live like pigs. It's so hard to get them to even use a bar of soap. They act like they are going to melt if they let water get close to their skin."

Blaine allowed a smile to cut his stern mouth. "Can't blame them now can ya. It's not much of a life poor people live."

Liberty wanted to punch her brother. "It's not much of a life to die in the throes of some horrible disease and pass it along to other's while you're doing the dying. Just once I'd like to see you believe that the work I do is helping others, that we're making progress. It's the filth that folks live in that brings on the diseases. Living cleaner would help tremendously."

Blaine cocked his head and shrugged, giving Liberty this round.

Liberty smiled as her two nephews came over to her. Kenny held a carved wooden car with spinning wheels. Liberty knew who made the car, her father.

Shawn leaned against her knees and held a shiny tin bank with a monkey poised to play a drum. "Auntie Liberty, do ya have a penny? I want ya to see what the monkey does."

"I've already put enough pennies in your bank to pay for ten banks." She grinned and leaned over to retrieve her purse off the floor. She took out a penny and put it into the bank's opening for the coin. The monkey made jerky motions as his arms went up and down beating on the drum. They laughed at his antics and Liberty put another penny in.

"I have something else for you, a surprise," she said and delighted in watching their faces as she pulled from her purse sticks of hard stripped candy that were quickly snatched by short stubby fingers. "You can have this after you eat your dinner, not before."

"Gee, thanks, Auntie Lib," Shawn said.

"Thanks, Auntie Lib," Kenny echoed his brother.

"Are you learning a lot in school?" Liberty asked.

Both heads bobbed at the same time.

Marybeth appeared in the doorway to the kitchen, "Boys, leave your aunt alone and go play until dinner." She signaled Liberty to join her. "Would you mind mashing the potatoes? It's hard for me to do with this girth."

"You're not having twins are you?" Liberty studied her sister-in-law. At six-months along, she was much larger than when she carried either one of the boys.

"God forbid, don't say that. I don't know what I'm having. I feel like a cow." She lifted her skirt to show how swollen her ankles were.

Liberty took her sister-in-law by the shoulders. "Sit, that's an order. I can get this dinner on the table without you." Putting on an apron, she went to the stove where she removed the pan of boiling potatoes, drained the water off and putting in butter and seasonings, proceeded to mash them. She removed the roast from the oven and used the drippings to make gravy. With ease she pulled the dinner together and put the food on the table.

They gathered around the table and joined hands while her father in his heavy Irish accent gave thanks. Blaine dished food for his sons before filling his own plate. She knew how hard it was for her brother to make ends meet. Blaine was a foreman at the factory, and confided to Liberty how tough it was at times to tell his father what to do, especially with dad so set in his ways.

Blaine surprised everyone when he said, "I'd like to move across country, to California maybe. I'm fed up with everything here. You can't walk down a sidewalk without tripping over people. I'd like my boys to have a better life."

Keegan scoffed and pointed his fork at his son. "I'll tell ye about a better life. Ye wouldn't last a minute in the old country, not iffen ye think this is a livin' hell. That was hell. No jobs. The men were a bunch of drunken slobs, the whole lot of them. Livin' in Ireland was like livin' in the gutter. Oh…iffen ye had money, ya lived well. Ye can thank the good Lord I had enough sense to bring ye to this country."

"Amen to that," Blaine mocked and carried it even further by making the sign of the cross and pressing his hands together as if praying. "Dad, I was too young to remember much of the old country, but I could kiss your feet for bringing us here." He forked a piece of meat on his plate and sopped it in the gravy.

Liberty listened to the lively exchange between her brother and father. Always the same words, always the same telling their father how grateful they were to be here in this country. But the bright façade was long gone. She couldn't blame her brother for wanting out. She'd gotten a good dose of society's cut and dried partitioning of the rich and poor. If her father had any idea of the company she was keeping, Jonathan's secret, he'd take a strap to her and beat her. He was a loving father, yet stern when it came to his offspring. He found it hard to give up old customs, yet had cast off the silly or bad ones, and embraced his new country, even when he first landed on American soil and was packed into a tenement so tight he couldn't breathe. Liberty knew they owed a lot to their father, working hard, moving them out of the lower East Side to a better place across the City, skirting Hell's Kitchen and the Irish that congregated there. He never thought he was better than anyone else, but he certainly knew he didn't bring his wife and two sons from Ireland to exchange one rat hole for another. He worked hard and so did his wife to get them away from the crowded tenements. They'd done it. And he had a right to be proud of his accomplishments.

Keegan glanced over at Liberty. "Did you read in the papers about that murder at that theater?"

Liberty choked and spewed water into her cloth napkin. Turning red, she coughed and finally composed herself. "Yes, I did."

"Hope they find the man and do it soon. Put him away in Sing Sing for the rest of his life. I understand they fry murderers in the electric chair in that prison," Blaine said and belched behind his fisted hand.

Her father pointed his fork at her. "You need to be careful. No tellin' where this man is."

"Dad, I'm safe. The man has money, and as Blaine puts it, would never stoop to be amongst the poor. He is probably long out of this country. Wouldn't you be?"

Her father directed his gaze at her. "I'd never murder anyone, so can't rightly say. It takes a cold-blooded person to kill another. Especially a defenseless young lass. Did ya see her picture? Right pretty, aye. She could have been an Irish colleen, fer sure."

"Who got killed," Shawn asked, looking at his dad.

"No one you know." Blaine rolled his eyes at Liberty. "Do we have a dessert, Marybeth? Thought I smelled apple pie baking."

"Yes, we do. I'll let Liberty serve it when everyone is ready.

That murder does give me the chills. Please do as your father says and be careful, dear sister-in-law." Marybeth wrapped her hands around Liberty's. "Do you have someone special in your life, a man perhaps?"

Liberty tried to stop the flush from spreading on her cheeks but couldn't. A dead giveaway. "Really, no one to speak of. I'm much too busy with my work."

Her father's eyes narrowed. "I'd say my girl isn't tellin' the truth."

"Well, I say I am. Besides, if I was seeing someone, I'd bring him around to meet you." She put her napkin on the table and got to her feet. "Anyone want a piece of that pie Marybeth made?" At everyone's brisk nods, she excused herself and went into the kitchen that still smelled of roasting meat, potatoes and a touch of cinnamon. How could she possibly explain Jonathan to them? Just this morning she'd removed the stitches from his scalp. Would she bring the blonde Jonathan or the dark-haired gorgeous stranger who would certainly set any woman's heart tripping. No, it was best to say nothing at all. Not until his name was cleared. And then she was certain that would be the last she'd see of Jonathan Drake.

While Liberty ate dinner with her family, Jonathan had gone out. In disguise, it was easy to blend in with the crowds. Like a magnet to metal, he was pulled to Broadway where he stopped in front of the Joyeux Theater. In between the matinee and the evening performance the marquee's glittering lights were off making everything look drab and somewhat dirty with trash blowing around.

A barrel filled with torn posters and pictures was on the sidewalk not too far from the doors of the theater. He wanted to see Zelda's poster again but it was gone, and now he saw why. Zelda's picture and the tribute to her had been thrown into the rubbish. Not even left up a week after her death showed Foyle's callousness toward a star that had made thousands for his company. Like all things in death, Zelda would eventually slip into the ages like a faded star, her name archived in the annuals of the theater, her talent and wonderful voice forgotten. Well, he would never forget the melody of her voice, her laugh. Yes, he would always remember. And, if he couldn't solve her murder, his name would be right there beside hers, forever labeled a murderer.

Even news about Zelda was starting to dim in the newspapers. No longer front page worthy, yesterday he'd read a snippet in the New York Times that Zelda's body was being sent by train to Chicago for burial. He should be thankful for the reprieve.

A large poster of Capucine, the French singer he'd watched with Liberty, was plastered all over the place. CAPUCINE. A one-name and hopeful legend.

Come see Capucine, an import from France. She'll beguile you, her voice will dazzle you.

He'd got a good dose of her beguiling charisma last night. Her hair was dark and from what he could tell so were her eyes. She was all that a man desired, sultry and slim, with a come-hither stare. The Egyptian costume she wore barely covered her charms. She piqued his interest but that was all. Where before he would see to it that he met the alluring Capucine and brush up on his French, Liberty now consumed his thoughts and her lovely face now wavered in front of him.

Death wasn't new to the theaters. Throughout the years, they'd found more than one entertainer having killed themselves in some gruesome way. Stars, or would be stars, were a fickle lot, and wore their egos on their sleeves. Jonathan thought one had to be a little off their nut to want to perform. Certainly, those that lacked talent refused to believe they had none, and he'd seen plenty who couldn't dance their way across the stage. And now he planned on putting Liberty into this mad culture. There was something about Liberty, strong and selfless, and he figured if she couldn't do this no one could. Who was he kidding, there was no one else. He put his hands in his pockets and jiggled some change. Thinking to see if there was something to salvage of Zelda's poster, hopefully her face, he started toward the garbage barrel when the theater door flew open.

Mick Brown, the stagehand, along with Fitch came out carrying rolled up posters. Jonathan's heart lurched and for a moment he thought to get the hell out of there. But, it's now or never where his disguise was concerned. He forced himself to stand his ground, see how things go.

Go?

Damn it, Jonathan, he cussed, *you are walking on eggs here.*

Be careful.

Trying to stop his knees from shaking, he watched Fitch put a bucket of glue and brush down on the sidewalk. Jonathan sucked in his breath and waited to be noticed or ignored.

Mick tipped the bill of his cap, and said, "Need ya to move. Time to change the attractions posters."

Fitch whistled a tune and ignored Jonathan who stepped back and watched. If these two didn't recognize someone in disguise when they worked around actors made up all day, then he'd done a damn good job of it. He folded his arms and tapped his one finger against his lips, watching.

Mick tore off the poster of the showgirls putting on the skit that had played last night. Fitch replaced it with one of them forming a chorus-line and kicking high. Capucine was out front wearing little in the way of a costume, a high majorette's hat, her bare hips showing clear up to her waist. The advertising was of a new show.

The show would have been Zelda's. Jonathan remembered

her being fitted for the daring costume. He'd grumbled about her showing so much skin, but she'd only laughed.

Mick, ignoring Jonathan, climbed the ladder to replace burnt out lights. He unscrewed them and tossed the lights down to Fitch who caught them and chucked them in the garbage.

"You come to the theater often, mister?" Fitch picked up pieces of poster paper and stuffed them in the garbage.

Jonathan shook his head and put a cigarette in his mouth. No good in talking to a kid who he'd sent on numerous errands and tipped generously, and who would recognize his voice in an instant. Not wanting to push his luck any further, he took a long drag from his cigarette and left. He walked on, stopping to gaze at window displays, looking as if he had all the time in the world. He couldn't help but pause before another theater and glance back. Fitch stood watching him.

Chapter Eleven

The following Monday evening, Jonathan, with his hands jammed in his pants pockets, rattled change, unmindful of the clatter he made, simply waiting for the woman he'd grown quite fond of to return from shopping. He went to the window to peer out, hoping to see her coming down the sidewalk. He parted the curtains and watched two men, one who he recognized from a family portrait as Liberty's father, wrestling what appeared to be a drop-leaf secretary up the apartment's front stoop.

"Damn!" Jonathan hurried into the bedroom where his clothes hung in the wardrobe. In one giant swoop, he gathered his garments into his arms and shoved them under the bed. Satisfied that no loose sleeves poked out, he became a flurry of activity grabbing his shaving supplies, his disguise, and pushed them under the bed to join the rest of his stuff.

On his way out, he took the bathroom key, his wallet, and left. Outside the door he could hear the two men huffing and cursing and the loud banging of furniture echoing up the stairwell. He headed for the bathroom.

"Dammit, Dad, could you have made this any heavier?" Blaine said.

"Mind yer cussin', lad. I'm all about surprisin' yer sister with this. Took me months to make and it's a thing of beauty, aye?"

"Didn't say it wasn't nice, just sayin' the feckin' thing's heavy as all get out. Where do you plan on puttin' this in Liberty's small livin' room?"

"I have a perfect spot in mind."

"Does she know yer plannin' on doin' this?"

"Nah. Stop here on the landin' a few minutes. Got to catch me breath."

They put the tall secretary down and Keegan leaned against the wall taking deep breaths, sounding like the bellows at a blacksmith shop. He pulled his handkerchief from his back pocket and wiped his face.

Blaine grinned at him. "Well, now, ol' man. Maybe this wasn't such a good idea after all."

Not one who liked being called old, Keegan straightened and motioned for Blaine to lift his end of the cabinet.

Blaine shook his head and suggested. "Dad, let's take the top half off, leave it here and come back for it after we get the bottom half inside Liberty's apartment."

Keegan wasn't accepting the suggestion, nothing easy for him. "We're almost there. Might as well get it over with."

Between them they managed to reach Liberty's front door. Keegan took a spare key from his pocket and opened the door.

They hefted the secretary into the living room. Exhausted, they both collapsed on the sofa.

Again wiping the sweat from his face and neck, Keegan's gaze fell on the Victrola resting on top of the table next to the sofa.

Getting to his feet he went to look at the record player with the large trumpet shaped megaphone. Removing his hat, he started to hang it on the rack alongside a man's black suit coat hanging there.

"What the hell?" he bellowed. No daughter of his was going to live in sin. What in heaven's name was Liberty up to?

"Well...well...would ya look at that Victrola. Looks like Miss Hoity Toity is comin' up in the world. Won't be long before she'll be too good for the likes of us. Wonder when she planned on telling us about it." Blaine started for the player.

Keegan pointed at the coat rack. "That's what caught me eye, not the damn noise maker." Again that protective instinct a father felt for his children clamped around his heart. Not his Liberty who was so damn responsible she could have written a book about responsibility. Not his daughter.

"I'll be damn. Appears my little sis is human after all. " Blaine took the coat off the rack. A big coat for a tall man. "This could fit me." He felt inside the pockets and took out a couple of ticket stubs for Foyle's Follies. He cut his eyes over at his father.

"What the hell?" Keegan blurted.

"Ya already said that." Blaine reminded. "I'd say Liberty's company must have forgotten his coat."

"Would ye forget such?" Keegan hurried into his daughter's bedroom and jerked open the wardrobe. Nothing there but her clothes. He fingered a pretty evening gown that he'd never seen her wear. Didn't know she owned such a thing. He picked up a hat box and opened it to find a big frilly hat in it. Never saw Liberty wearing such as that either.

Blaine leaned against the doorjamb staring. "Find anything of interest?"

"Nah, just some pretty frocks I've never seen her in." He held the evening dress out for his son to see.

Blaine let out a soft whistle. "Well, now, that's pretty. Not something we normally see her wearin'. Secret life, secret sister."

"Maybe," huffed Keegan, still rattled at what he'd found here. He resisted the urge to open the drawers on her vanity dresser; it wasn't nice to go through a woman's under things. But on top of the dresser was a Joyeux Theater Program, blue in color, with a colorful picture of an actress called Capucine. A hussy in Keegan's mind. He took the program and after rolling it up, stashed it in his back pocket.

Blaine, already heading back into the living room, tossed over his shoulder. "Let's ready the desk. It's getting late. I don't want to be late for dinner. Marybeth gets cranky."

Putting the tall walnut-stained secretary in its place, they began cleaning it. Keegan tried to concentrate on what he was doing but his discoveries in Liberty's home made it hard to do. Blaine used his neckerchief to dust off the curlicue top, sides, and claw feet. Keegan cleaned the ornate glass that was embedded on the two door openings. Leaving them open, he wiped off the three shelves inside. Next he lowered the desk's writing top and swiped at the dust inside the cubby holes. Leaving the writing top down, he placed Liberty's fountain pen, ink bottle, and stationery on it. He stood back to eye his handiwork.

"Looks like it's always been here," Blaine said, and smiled spreading his red brush of a mustache. "Good work, Dad."

Keegan scratched his head, and putting his hat back on, took one last admiring look at his handiwork and had to admit, he'd done a darn good job. He removed the program from his pants pocket and placed it on top of the desk, anchoring it with an ink bottle.

They left, both thinking about the mystery that was now Liberty, and got into the truck borrowed from the company they worked for, and drove off.

Liberty, carrying a shopping bag and close to home, stopped a block away and watched her dad and brother get into the truck. Her first inclination was to run over them and give her father a hug, invite them in for tea and gobble up precious moments with them. But, not knowing why they were here, she held back. What about Jonathan? Had they surprised him? Thought she was a kept woman? Needing to know what happened, she watched the truck rattle down the street and turn the corner, and then she couldn't get home fast enough. She pounded up the stairs and practically flew inside. Holding onto the doorknob to keep from falling on her face, she stared at Jonathan lazing on the sofa, reading the paper, acting as if nothing happened.

"Don't tell me you stayed here and met my father and brother?" She put her hat on the rack and her shopping bag on the floor. The tall secretary-desk across the room caught her eye. "Oh…my, they brought this in, didn't they?"

Jonathan folded the paper and stood to greet her. "I spotted them out on the sidewalk, so I stashed my stuff under the bed. I hid in the bathroom. Nowadays, I'm always hiding from something or someone it seems." He sounded bitter.

She removed her coat and put it over the back of the chair. "Are you positive you got everything of yours out of sight?" She prayed to herself that he had. She would wilt and cave in under a cross examination from her father and brother.

"Yes, I'm positive, quit worrying."

She approached the tall beautifully made desk, silently thanking her father who spent a lot of time on it. On top of the writing space was the program from the theater and with Mr. Drake's message inside. "Did you put this program here?"

Looking puzzled, Jonathan shook his head.

"Then either my dad or Blaine did. Your dad's message to you is inside it. We can only pray they didn't read it." Any enjoyment of the desk was quelled at the thoughts her dad and brother were letting her know that they had found the brochure. She also won-dered what they thought of the Victrola.

"I called my boss, Mrs. Taylor just to check in. She said there is a lot of sickness going around. They are hoping it's not that deadly flu from last spring, but they believe it is." Liberty sat on the sofa wondering about the implications of that and voiced her opinion. "If so, I feel extremely guilty about the time I'm away from work."

"Did you tell your boss you might need more time off?"

"Yes. I asked for another two weeks. Mrs. Taylor agreed, but I have to be back after that. I really wanted to wait and see if I'm hired at the theater before I even asked for the additional time. And, I must say, Mr. Drake, I doubt very much that the theater will hire me. Maybe to be a ticket taker," she said and scoffed.

Jonathan cranked the Victrola and put on a record titled *The One I love*. He took her hand and propelled her back to the sofa. He sat next to Liberty and shifting her around on the sofa, put her feet on his lap and removed her shoes. He then started to massage her insoles, her feet, her calves, making her relax. His hands were mag-ical, working away sore muscles.

"That feels so good. I shouldn't allow you to do this, but don't stop." She sighed and turned her eyes to Jonathan who was in profile, concentrating on her toes. He was a beautiful male and she wanted him for herself. But that could never be. She was poor. He was rich. Once his name was cleared, he would move on and forget all about her. If only she could shelter him forever, hide him away, like a fairy tale story. Hers to cherish and keep.

He turned a sly grin on her. "The hose you're wearing is get-ting in the way of my massaging your feet properly. You should take them off."

When he hit a sensitive spot on the bottom of her foot, she yelped, squished her toes tight and tried to bolt but he held fast.

"Ticklish?" Laughing, his hold on her foot tightened even more as he traced feather light swirls on her soles.

She squealed and fought. He released her foot and dived onto her, pinning her against the sofa cushions and him. She stopped fighting and lay still. When his eyes darkened with passion and his mouth slowly descended on hers, she met him with equal fervor. Her hands threaded through his thick hair to the back of his head, cupping his scalp, relishing in the feel of him. She forced her tongue against his, seeking, sucking. When he started to unbutton her blouse, she let him. He pushed her corset cover up allowing her breasts to pop free, and allowing him to claim them both. His eyes became appreciative as he kneaded her breasts gently and ran his thumb over both nipples making them hardened.

She unbuttoned his shirt and he helped pull it off where it joined her blouse on the floor.

"Let's get off this sofa," he suggested.

She nodded and stood. The cheval mirror showed them standing there, disheveled lovers.

He unbuttoned her skirt, allowing her to step out of it. Next off were her undergarments, her corset, drawers, and hose. He was deft at his job. She didn't care, her body quaked and quivered.

"Your body is like an alabaster carving," he said and continued, "Only you're more beautiful. With your red hair and bush, you look on fire. Your freckles make your skin warm, colorful." He ran his tongue across her shoulder. "Silk, you feel like silk."

Her hands were quick to remove the rest of his clothing. They both stood in front of the mirror and she watched as his member rose, stiffened. He pressed his hard body against the back of hers, his heat became her heat. He brought his hands around to cup her breasts, pinching the nipples. Still cupping her one breast, she watched his other hand slid down her torso to end at the juncture of her legs. His fingers slid inside her. Her legs went weak with sensations she never felt before. His hand began to move fast, rubbing, a frenzied caress. Her skin flushed, she spread her legs wider. She clasped her hands around his neck, holding tight, as he turned her body into sheer ecstasy.

He groaned and spun her in his arms. His kiss was heady, his tongue searched her mouth.

"You like watching us?" he said.

She nodded, somehow liking being a voyeur, as if she was watching two strangers through a window making love. She couldn't explain why, only that she did.

"Liberty, I want more, much more than you can give me standing here," he moaned and sank to the oval rug, taking her with him. "Now it's your turn to please me."

Her hand went to his sacs, touching the delicate velvet feel of them. She ran a lone finger up the side of his penis, feeling its strength in rigid veins and muscle. Taking his length within her hands, she found a rhythm, kissing his lips, her tongue delved while she worked magic.

"Oh...God," he said in a tormented groan, his hips starting to move. He grabbed her hand, stopping her. "Let me fuck you."

His callous words threw cold water on her. When he started to roll on top of her, she pushed against his chest, barring him.

"No, we can't." She lay beside him, her passion smashed.

"What's wrong? I thought you wanted me." His erection withered.

"I should thank you for bringing me to my senses, stopping us," she answered, not meaning her words at all.

"I'm not sure how I did that," he said, and getting to his feet, helped her to hers. He took her by the chin, forcing her to look at him. "Please, I don't want you to think any of this has cheapened you in my eyes or othewise. It hasn't. We're two adults who have needs. You're wonderful."

She dipped her head in agreement, but not really. It would have been so much better if he'd said he was in love with her and wanted to make love to her. But he didn't. He wanted to fuck her. Fuck, a filthy word for sex, not romance. Fuck her like he did all his theater conquests. She accepted her clothes that he handed to her and started dressing.

He picked up his pants and pulled them on, followed by his shirt. As he concentrated on buttoning it, he talked. "Liberty, you need to be forewarned that the performers at the theater can be a crude bunch. Or rather I should say they are artistic thinkers, who enjoy sex with whomever they want and as often as they want. They are free spirited. I don't know what I did right now to change your mind about us having sex. Just know that I find you desirable and still want you." He tucked his shirt inside his pants.

She buttoned her blouse and shrugged. "As a nurse, I've seen it all and touched it all. I can handle over-sexed people. It was just the moment, Jonathan. Nothing more."

"I guess we should eat and then start your dancing lessons, huh?" His grin was half-hearted, his face covered with puzzlement.

"I suppose," she agreed.

This wasn't the path Liberty envisioned her life taking. She didn't know the first thing about working as a dancer, a singer. But in order to find out who killed Zelda, she was going to have to get in the trenches.

Chapter Twelve

Liberty clutched Jonathan's arm as they waited for the Joyeux Theater's personnel manager to meet with them. Her legs felt liquid and she couldn't stop fidgeting. Why had she allowed Jonathan to talk her into this mess? And mess it was. She couldn't dance, and lord knows she'd tried, poor Jonathan with the patience of a saint, shook his head in dismay at her feeble attempts. Her size eight shoes kept stepping on his toes. Nor could she sew, well not much, give her catgut and skin and she could make the best stitches ever, but give her thread and fabric it was a different story. Certainly not enough to try and pass her off as a seamstress and sew the elaborate costumes. What she did have going for her was her height and long limbs, but she didn't think that would be enough to get her hired.

The door to the office flew open and a short overweight man rushed in smelling of hair oil and whiskey. With the flair of someone who always gets his way, he paused to light a cigar and blow gray smoke toward the ceiling. Only then did he bother to take a breath and acknowledge Liberty and Jonathan.

MERCER ADDISON

"I'm Sidney Brawley, manager. Most people call me Sid. I hire, I fire."

Jonathan took the offered hand. "Emery Edison here, agent to the lovely, talented, Miss Liberty Fitzgerald," he said, "I also hire and fire." He winked while looking at the shorter man.

Liberty held out her gloved hand. "Nice to meet you, Mister Brawley." Her knees trembled along with her hands.

"No need to be nervous. I don't make it a habit of eating dancers for lunch." He clasped her hand in a tight grip, trying to calm her nerves. "Like I said, call me Sidney or Sid."

"Mister Sidney," she said and wanted to kick herself for sounding so stupid.

Sidney puffed his cigar and circled Liberty like he was stalking game. His eyes, sharp and brown, went over her from head to toe. He grabbed a large headdress from the chair next to his desk. "Take yer hat and dress off," he ordered.

Liberty complied and pulling the hat pins out of her wide-brimmed hat, handed the large chapeau to Jonathan. Her mutinous glare at him warned him to say something and do so now.

"It's not necessary for Miss Fitzgerald to remove her clothes. I can personally guarantee that her body is beautiful."

But Sidney wasn't having any of it. He pointed his cigar at her. "This ain't a place for modesty. Off with it all. I want to see your legs, breasts. Lady, I see tits and tails every day, so don't act shy."

When it looked like they might be thrown out on their ears and without a chance for Liberty to do some sleuthing backstage, Jonathan took her aside. "Remember I warned you this would happen. Act like you're in an anatomy class, nurse. Close your mind, anything to get the job."

"You're going to pay for this, Mr. Emory Edison," she whispered.

"That's my girl," he said and crossed his arms.

Seething inside, Liberty removed her new blue dress and stopped when she stood in her one piece corset cover and drawers. The top with delicate embroidered roses, had tiny straps going over her shoulders, and her drawers came to just above her knees.

Feeling she was showing plenty, she said, "This is as far as I go, Mr. Brawley, I'll not parade around here like a prized cow at an auction. My tits as you so crudely put it, are great, just ask my agent." She glared at Jonathan who coughed and cleared his throat. "And, my legs are fine. If you need to see for yourself, come here." Gesturing at the manager to come closer, she pushed her straps off her shoulders, and lowered her corset cover just enough to show her nicely shaped shoulders and cleavage. She then pulled her drawers up revealing her legs through white hose. And with that done, she situated her undergarments back in place.

"Freckles, you have freckles." After putting the tall headdress on Liberty's head, Sidney twirled his finger in the air indicating where and what he wanted her to do. "Don't have anyone yer height. Let's see ya walk, Miss Modesty."

Liberty prayed, *let this work, let me do well for Jonathan's sake.* With the heavy headdress flaring out about her head like the tail on a peacock, she mimicked what she'd seen the dancers and singers do the other night at the theater. Without holding onto the monolith resting on top of her head, she put her left hand on her hip and sashayed with the grace of an actress who'd been on the stage for years. Laughing, she spun around, smiled and dipped into a deep curtsy, just like Jonathan taught her to do. The extravagant headpiece remained in place.

Sidney's mouth stretched into a grin of approval and he clapped. "Good—good. Now, let's see if you can sing. Get dressed and follow me." He snatched the headdress from her head, and put it on the chair.

With Jonathan's help, she put her dress and hat back on. Sidney then opened the office door and led them down the hallway and into the rehearsal hall where he stopped next to the piano and the man playing it.

"Meet George Gershwin our rehearsal pianist. George, this is Liberty Fitzgerald and her agent, Emery Edison. She wants to join the revue. Thought if she can sing we will start her off as a background singer and dancer. With those gams of hers, she could be in our *Legs Galore* revue."

The long-faced pianist gave her the once over. He paused long enough to take the cigarette out of his mouth and give them both a quick nod.

Well, this is where the rubber tire goes flat. Liberty trying to remain calm shot Jonathan a look of *help me out of this mess right now.*

Jonathan cleared his throat and stepped forward. "Mind you, my little song bird here has a slight cough, but I'm sure you'll be able to hear how well she sings." He clasped both her shoulders and squeezed as he whispered, his mustache tickling her ear. "You can do this just like we practiced."

She whispered back, "I'm not so sure." And tried to swallow, but couldn't.

"What songs do you know?" Gershwin asked her.

"Ah…" she lost her voice and mind at the same time.

Jonathan stepped in. "How about, 'Oh Johnny, Oh Johnny, Oh!' "

Gershwin tickled the ivory keys, his fingers flying over them, the song a snappy tune that most people knew. He started singing, "Oh Johnny," and indicated for her join in.

She did, and to her relief, she didn't sound half bad. Found she had a rather fondness for singing, and that Mr. Gershwin made it easy with his willingness to sing along with her, even with a cigarette dangling from his mouth and ashes tumbling down the front of his white shirt. She tapped her toes. Sidney Brawley joined in and so did Jonathan. A most catchy tune for sure and she wanted to kiss Jonathan for suggesting it.

A large man hurried into the rehearsal hall and paused next to Sidney. Catching his breath, the man barely gave Liberty and Jonathan a second glance. Gershwin stopped playing and stood. The man leaned close to Sidney's ear and spoke. He used his hand to shield his words from the others.

"Christ!" Sidney emitted a low growl. "Can things get any worse?" He started off and then checked himself. "Listen," he pointed at Jonathan. "Looks like I have a opening. I'll sign yer girl to a month-long contract. See how she works out. But I gotta tell ya, I hope she can dance better than she can sing. Ya start out at sixty dollars a week. What's yer stage name, honey?"

At the drop of a hat, Liberty said the first thing that came to mind. "Liberty la Roux. The red head, that's me." She watched Jonathan let out his breath, but his eyes were on the large man who returned his stare.

"Nice—nice, it's catchy, I like it. You start tomorrow, be here at nine sharp for rehearsals. I'll have your contract ready then." He signaled to the man next to him. "Mick, c'mon. Take me to where Josette Jackson is. Christ," he continued to mutter.

A bunch of showgirls walked in chattering. The name of Josette cropped up repeatedly. They got in a long line and as George pounded the keys, they began to dance, high kicking in unison.

Now forgotten, Jonathan led Liberty out of the rehearsal hall. The sidewalks were plush with people buying tickets, sightseers gawking and snapping pictures with their Kodak cameras. Busy, the streets were clogged with vehicles on the move.

Jostled by people in a hurry, Jonathan tilted his head and said, "Would you like an early lunch, a soda?"

"Yes, to both," she answered, and then beamed a grin at him.

He took her arm and wrapped it within his. "I can't believe

you pulled that off. Things got a little dicey when Mick came in."

"Who is Mick?"

"Mick Brown. He's the stage manager who found me with Zelda dead...well, you know."

"Do you think he recognized you? I thought he was looking at you rather curious."

"Me too. But my disguise must have worked or he would have grabbed me. Wonder what he wanted and what was so urgent that Sidney Brawley stopped our interview?"

"I was wondering the same thing. His face actually paled when that Mick person spoke to him."

"I'm curious, that's for sure. Maybe you'll find out tomorrow." He patted her arm that was woven within his. "You know I can't go with you to rehearsals. Don't want to press what little luck I have. You'll need tap dance shoes and a rehearsal outfit. I know of a place off of Broadway that caters to the theater dancers. We'll go after lunch and purchase some things for you."

She looked at him, meeting his blue eyes. "You need to be careful with your father's money. It has to last. At least until I get paid at the theater. Imagine, me, performing at the Follies." She allowed just a little bit of pride in.

He opened the door to the Bistro Café and held it for her to enter. Wonderful smells of cooking food, meat and exotic dishes, wafted about. The café was busy with chattering men and women. A friendly male waiter wearing a white starched apron seated them at a booth against the wall.

Jonathan put his hat on the rack next to their booth and patted his hair down, making sure his wig stayed in place.

Liberty removed her gloves, but left her hat on. "I know Mr. Brawley wants me to sign a contract for a month. It's a good thing I asked for an extra two weeks off from my nursing job, but that's all I'm willing to give. If I can't find out any information during that time, it's not there to find, and I guess it's back to nursing for me."

Jonathan leaned back against the booth and fit his fingers together. "Even with you making more money as a background dancer than you do as a nurse?"

She felt he was attacking her lifestyle, her career. "Yes, even so. I know I've been disenchanted with my profession here lately. But overall I still feel a certain gratification at being a nurse. Let me just say that I wasn't fond of Mr. Brawley's attitude that women are put there for him to ogle. He reminded me of a man who has sexual inadequacies so severe that all he can do is look, touch, and slobber over. You told me the theater people were crude and highly sexual. But you failed to warn me about Mr. Brawley."

"I didn't know that would happen, honest. I've never been to an audition before." He started to read the menu.

"That's right," she said and smiled sweetly. "All your women friends at the theater were already hired and bedded?"

He glanced across the table at her. "I'm sorry, Miss Fitzgerald. But you did handle the situation quite well."

She picked up the menu. "You better hope so."

Jonathan grinned at her and changed the subject. "What tickles your fancy?" He wanted a nice juicy steak. He'd been living on soup, stews, and hash, and right now he craved something different.

When she looked undecided, he tried putting her at ease. "Order a steak. The meat will put a glow in your cheeks."

"I'm not used to spending much on food. Oh...look, they have ice cream sodas here...oh."

"Then you shall have one for dessert. Why don't you let me order for us?"

When she acquiesced, he did indeed order. Steak, potatoes, gravy, peas, and a chocolate soda for dessert. He also requested red wine and two glasses.

Picking this restaurant was a test for Jonathan. It was where he'd dined with Zelda after a performance. They would close the place down as words tumbled between them. With heads together they shared kisses and he'd tell her how wonderful she was. She craved adoration and couldn't get enough. Jonathan shook his head trying to dispel Zelda from his mind. He wanted to concentrate on the pretty woman across from him. Vibrant Liberty la Roux, fire and warmth. Liberty's green eyes were full of smiles for him as she spooned her ice-cream soda. He hadn't paid much attention before, but Liberty's face had great bone structure. Today at the theater, her movements were graceful and coordinated. Of course he knew what delicious curves were underneath her clothes, but it was as if he was seeing her for the first time.

Detectives Scala and Jones were in one of the upper reserved box seats at the Joyeux. Called in to investigate another death, a young dancer named Josette Jackson was found hanging from a balcony. The box with its gilded front was located second from right to the stage. Another box was beside it and closer to the stage. Only the rich could afford this type of seating, and Scala knew he never would. But since the death of his wife, he wasn't much for revues, plays and such.

Two deaths in less than three weeks were more than any theater needed or detectives wanted for that matter. Scala and his partner weren't even close to solving the first one yet. Jones was pointing out camera shots to the photographer, making sure he was getting the perfect picture for later use. Flashbulbs gave off a magnesium smell as the cameraman followed orders. Below, on the main floor, another camera's flash lit up the area taking pictures from that angle. Finally finished with his work, he moved his tripod to allow room for the detectives.

Scala stared over the ledge at the dancer's naked body suspended high above the seats below. She reminded him of a broken bird, unable to fly, her arms dangled at her sides. He ordered the two policemen waiting by the entrance to come in and pull her body into the balcony's box. Her clothes, he took notice of, were neatly folded on one of the velvet chairs.

Loud voices caught his attention, and he turned to look at the two men barred from the area by the same policemen. He recognized one of them he'd interviewed during Zelda's DeLane's murder.

"Hey, let me in there. I'm the stage manager." The large man tried to push pass the burly policemen to no avail.

Jones stepped out and confronted the theater personnel. "Ya have to remain here. Let us get her body down first. She isn't so pretty to look at anymore. Where's the kid that found her?"

"That would be Fitch. He's waiting below, in a seat." The stage manager offered.

"Make sure he stays put."

Scala was careful not to trip over the taunt rope that was tied to a column beside the balcony's entrance. The police were slowly pulling the other end that held Josette. With a lot of grunting and cursing, the two men managed to get the slim dancer to the floor of the balcony. Her face was swollen purple, her eyes bulged red with broken veins, her tongue filled her mouth and protruded.

Jones lifted one of her hands where the fingernails were broken off to the quick. "Don't look to me like this was a suicide. I'd say she fought like hell."

Scala inspected her hands, the fingers long and slender. "Yeah, but she could also have changed her mind about killing herself and fought the noose around her neck. It could go both ways. Yet I'd say whichever way, this dame fought, and she fought hard. Naked, same as the other star. But I can't see Jonathan Drake coming back here and doing another one." He noticed her pubic bush was dark brown, and the hair on her head bleached blonde with dark roots. He could never understand why men in the theater thought a blonde was more beguiling.

"Maybe, maybe not. Who would have thought he'd off a Follies star, or anyone for that matter. Looks to me like he's gone off his nut. Maybe he plans on doin' away with the whole troupe."

"We'll have our answer when we find Drake and he's covered with claw marks from this little lady's fight." Scala shook his head, thinking he'd never get used to seeing death. He called over his shoulder at the stage manager. "I want to know whose private box seats these belong to."

"I can tell ya that right now," the voice boomed. "It belongs to the Drake family. You know, Lincoln Drake, Jonathan Drake's father."

Scala and Jones stared at each other.

"Give me her dress," Jones ordered the cop standing by and taking it from the offered hand, he took the floral material and with reverence settled it over the dancer's lithe body. "All right, let the two guys in," he said and watched as they hurried over.

Mick Brown knelt and lifted the dress to reveal Josette's face. The other man, rotund, with lips curving around a cigar stuck in his mouth, nodded over Mick's shoulder. Visibly shaken, they met Scala's and Jones's hard stare.

"That's Josette Jackson for sure," Mick said.

"Jesus," said the other, "I don't understand what's happening here." He puffed on his cigar and offered his hand to Scala and Jones. "I'm Sidney Brawley, in charge of all personnel. I hire and fire."

"Did you fire Miss Jackson?" asked Jones.

Sidney held his cigar between thick fingers. "No, but I threatened. Her performance wasn't up to snuff here lately."

Scala wrote on his notepad. "What do you mean, not up to snuff?"

"She'd been sick most days. Isn't that right, Mick?" He elbowed the man beside him.

Mick nodded his shaggy head. "Yeah, sick. And she was moody, crying. Like I told ya when Miss DeLane was killed, I'm the stage manager, so I'm around the gals a lot. I make sure they are on stage on time. I take care of them off stage. I'm friends with all the dancers and stars."

"In other words you do their bidding," Scala said.

Mick met Scala's keen stare. "I try. Performers are a queer bunch. Temperamental as all get out. But, they like me."

"Did this Josette like you enough to confide in you what was bothering her?" Scala poised his pencil over his notebook.

Mick glanced at Sidney Brawley. "No, she didn't. Guess she couldn't."

Commotion outside in the hallway forced the policeman to stick his head inside. "Sir, the men from the morgue are here."

Jones nodded. "All right. We need to clear out."

Scala said, "Let's go and talk to other dancers. I want to see her dressing table. Might find a suicide note."

Jones scoffed. "You don't believe that any more than I do." He pointed at Mick. "Go bring the kid. What's his name?"

"Fitch." Mick left.

This time Jones wrote the kid's name in his notebook.

The detectives paused next to the long table surrounded by mirrors with encircled light bulbs giving off a bright glow. Powder puffs and makeup cluttered the length of the table top.

Mick having returned with Fitch stood in the doorway with him. The dancers were brought over from the rehearsal hall.

Scala approached. He blew his nose on a white handkerchief and shoved it back inside his suit pocket. The powders and perfumes were getting to him. Either that or being a man without a wife for so long left him not used to smelling these frilly feminine things. And this was an abundance of odors, all mingling into one giant sneeze. And he did just that. Out came the hanky again and he blew hard.

"Hey, kid, Fitch is it?" Scala asked.

Fitch squirmed until Mick told him to be still. "Tell the cops what ya saw," Mick ordered.

"I was goin' through the seats, looking for change that falls out of pockets. I get to keep what I find. I found a necklace in the aisle...well...the locket...a heart. That's when I saw her danglin' like a bird." Tears came to the kid's eyes. "I liked Josette, she was nice to me." He removed his hand from his pocket and handed over the gold heart-shaped locket to Scala.

Scala glanced at it. The chain was missing from the necklace, leaving only the gold heart. This gift was from someone with money. He closed his fists over it and stuck it in his pocket. He'd turn it in to evidence later.

"Which dressing area belongs to Miss Jackson?" Jones asked Mick.

He pointed to the end dressing table. "That's Josette's."

Jones leaned forward to look at a picture stuck in the frame of the mirror, one of Josette with some of her fellow dancers. She was pretty, petite and looked full of life. He opened the drawer and rifling through it shoved aside makeup brushes, powder puffs, ribbons, lipsticks, and garter snaps. He picked up another picture, this one of Josette dancing and being held by a man with his back to the camera. A random snapshot taken while out on the town. Finally, pulling the drawer completely out, he bent over to stare inside the cavity and spotted a folded-up piece of paper stuck inside the wooden slide. He retrieved the paper, and unfolding it read the two sentences written in bold masculine strokes.

"Josette, I'm done with you. Why don't you try and blame someone else for the baby? It's not mine." Not a suicide note, but certainly a reason to commit the deed.

"Let's talk with the dancers, anyone close to Miss Jackson," Jones said and handed the note to Scala. Jones barked out an order to Mick. "I want every dancer—every person working at the theater—brought in here so we can question them." He ordered the policeman standing next to the door. "Give every damn person here paper and pen and make them write this note word for word." He studied the picture of Josette and the man entwined in an embrace, dancing.

They ordered the men to get into one line, and despite a lot of grumbling they did make headway. Royce Valentino, an upcoming singer from England came forward to say that he'd been dating Josette.

"I'm saying that I dated Josette until about three months ago. She told me she'd met someone else and for me to get lost." Royce ran his hands through his dark wavy hair, his eyes darting from one detective to the other.

Scala met the singer's gaze. "Do you know if she had relatives here in the City? Where she lived?"

"She never mentioned any family. And, yes I can give you her address."

Royce accepted the offered notebook and wrote in Miss Jackson's address. While he was at it, Scala made him write the words on the note. His spidery scrawl didn't match.

"Do you know who this man is or where the photograph was

taken?" Jones showed him the picture of Josette dancing with a man.

"No to both questions."

None of the men's handwriting in the theater matched the note. Nor did any of them look like the man in the picture, but one man recognized the inside of the ballroom where it was taken. He said it was the Silver Club over in Harlem.

Josette's landlady, Mrs. Chester, an older woman with a big bosom pushed open the door to Miss Jackson's flat allowing the detectives inside.

"Do you want me to remain here?" she asked.

Jones nodded. "Yes. We have questions for you. Is that your apartment across the way?"

"Yes, I live right over there. That way I can see who is coming and going in the building."

Jones smiled half-heartedly. "Do you have a family's address or someone we can notify about the young lady's death?"

Mrs. Chester thought for a moment. "I have a name written down, someone upstate in Buffalo. I will say one thing though and that is after Miss Jackson started seeing this latest boyfriend, her place became neat as a pin."

"Are you saying she was not so clean before she met this guy?" Scala asked.

"That is correct," she answered and put her hand in her apron pocket. "The girl was a regular slob, couldn't hardly wade through her place."

Scala poised pencil over paper. "Can you describe her boy-friend to us?"

Mrs. Chester stuck her bottom lip out. "Yes, I can. He always came on a Sunday afternoon. The man was well dressed in a tailored two piece suit."

Jones, getting excited, said, "What did he look like?"

"Now mind you, I can't see too well. Need glasses, I think. He wore a hat, pulled low. But whenever he took it off, his hair was dark...black like."

Jones showed her the picture of Josette and a man dancing. "Is this the man?"

She took the picture from Jones and squinted at it. "It's hard to say, it could be him, but I'd never swear to it on a bible."

"Anything else we need to know?" Scala asked.

Mrs. Chester smiled and said, "Miss Jackson had her laundry done weekly. Sheets and all."

Scala's pencil scratched over the paper. "Do you know which laundry?"

When she nodded, and gave the name, Scala fired off another question. "How did this man arrive here? Did he drive himself? By taxi? Walk?"

"Sometimes he would walk. Other times he arrived by taxi."

"Same or different taxi?"

"I'm not sure. I don't always stay by my window. Whenever Miss Jackson was working she asked me to take the laundry delivery in so she'd have it. Said something about the man she was seeing insisted on clean sheets. He was a neat person, that's what she said."

Jones walked inside and looked around. Everything was so clean a person could eat off the floor. He opened bureau drawers and shifted frilly undergarments around. He spotted a Joyeux Theater brochure and opened it to see Miss Jackson amongst the dancers. Opening another drawer, he pulled out a scrapbook and sat in the chair to look it over. The scrapbook was filled with photographs of Josette and friends at nightclubs. Colorful theater brochures with her in the chorus line were numerous.

Scala leaned over Jones's shoulder to stare at the pages. "Bring that back to the station."

They found little else, no laundry tickets, nothing. It didn't appear that the young lady wore jewelry as there was none to be found. Her hairbrush was free of hair. Her clothes, what few she owned, hung neat in the closet. Her tap shoes and regular shoes lined up like perfect soldiers at drill.

They left with their clues that to the detectives were not very revealing.

Lincoln Drake, inside his den and with a drink in hand, paced in front of the large fireplace. For what seemed to be a thousand times since he'd weakened and indicated that he knew something about their son's whereabouts, Earlene became relentless trying to pry the information out of him. Again and again, he told her that the less she knew the better off she'd be.

"Earlene, I'd like you to go to our summer house upstate. Stay out of this. Not only for our son, but for Lona, subtle rumors are swirling around the City that the flu has returned."

Earlene fingered the red ribbon tied at her white blouse's neck. "The flu? I haven't heard. But then, I don't get out much since my social friends and my charity leaders have turned away from me. Can you at least tell me if Jonathan's all right?"

"No, I can't. Earlene, I don't want you to become involved with this. I know how hard all of this has become," he said.

"Well, I'm thinking of Jonathan and how hard this must be for him. What if he needs me and I'm off upstate? This certainly sounds like abandonment to me. No, darling, I'll not be going. I'll weather this storm with you, by your side."

Lincoln finished off his brandy and set the glass down. He turned to take in his wife standing there. Worry creased new lines and love for their son showed in each wrinkle. "Well my dear that is your choice. But I'm wondering if we should send Lona to stay with my sister in Massachusetts. This is no easier on Lona than it is for you. She has lost so much here lately. Perhaps a change of scenery will do her good. Take her mind off of Darrell to say the least."

"Again, I must say no. I want her close. Lona's a comfort to me, and I believe I'm of a comfort to her concerning Darrell's death."

"Earlene, have you noticed that policemen still guard our home and hotel like we're the criminals?"

"Yes. Lincoln, I know perfectly well what's going on around me. Why can't you confide in me? Is it because you think I can't keep such news to myself? Well, I can guarantee when it comes to our children I can seal my lips quite tight." She pointed at him. "And, did you ever think I might have something of value to add—information to give Jonathan that might help him?" She flounced onto the closest chair and glared at him.

If Lincoln wanted to tell her anything and it was on his tongue to do so, he swallowed his words. He'd already done enough harm. The less anyone knew about Jonathan and Liberty Fitzgerald, the better for all concerned. After the short note to Miss Fitzgerald the night of the Follies, he wasn't able to contact her again.

Chapter Thirteen

Despite her inhibitions, Liberty joined the ranks of over-worked, jealousy-ridden dancers who saw her as a threat. They didn't make any bones about her being new, and at first refused to befriend her. Only one became friendly with Liberty, twenty-year-old Magnolia Moore, an auburn-haired beauty with flashing brown eyes. Magnolia, one of those rare females who didn't have a mean bone in her body, realized Liberty didn't know how to tap. She took Liberty aside and taught her the basics, *heel toe—heel toe—slide—slide—slide* and the novice *shuffle off to buffalo*. Just enough to make her look good.

They ate lunch together, shared their backgrounds, well Magnolia shared hers, Liberty made up some of hers, leaving out her college education and being a health nurse. Her parents indeed came from Ireland, she was named after the Statue of Liberty, her mother was dead, her father and brothers were still alive. Her one brother fought in France. She did say in a warm sincere voice that she was in love with her manager, Emery.

Magnolia, a chatterbox, told about being born and raised in Illinois. That she left home at the age of fifteen. Or rather, she ran away from home. She escaped domineering parents with a vaudeville troupe touring the state, and joined an act featuring a family of six singers and dancers. She stayed with them until she turned eighteen. When the act played the Orpheum in New York City, she claimed the theaters and the lights on Broadway reeled her in. Magnolia also found love at the Joyeux. She loved Leon, the older of two tap-dancing brothers, and he returned her love with a shiny engagement ring. Both brothers accepted Liberty and would sometimes join them for lunch, usually sitting on a prop backstage or in the rehearsal room. Liberty could well see why Magnolia fell for Leon. With his thick brown hair and dark expressive eyes that shone with love whenever Magnolia was around, it was obvious this was no passing flirtation. Leon, at twenty-seven was older than his blond-headed brother Leroy by two years. Both guys could tap so fast their feet became a blur. When they tried to out tap each other, their shenanigans would draw a crowd, stop rehearsals, and bring thundering applause from the troupe crowding around them.

Leroy flirted with Liberty but she squashed that infatuation in a hurry by telling him about Emery.

Fitch, the boy messenger Liberty had talked to that day in front of the Follies, would bring them sandwiches from a nearby delicatessen when they ordered them. He also exchanged chatter with the small group. Liberty discovered that Fitch was an orphan who lived backstage. He slept wherever he found a place to bunker down in the theater. Fitch's darting gaze and ability to fade into the background made Liberty think he might know more than he ever let on. She needed to get him alone, pull out information she was sure he possessed. But, the theater people were a close knit bunch and most of them eyed her with suspicion. She was afraid that she would run out of time before she could help Jonathan.

Liberty found Magnolia's easy smile a welcome relief from the hateful stares she garnered from Capucine, star of the *Leg's Galore* revue both she and Liberty were in. After a week on the job, she couldn't figure out what she did to the star to alienate her. Stage performers were not an easy crowd to be with, Liberty found trying to wade through a ton of conceited personalities was like climbing up the stairs of a fire escape, tricky, dangerous, but could be accomplished if one took their time. She already missed her nursing job with a passion and couldn't wait to go back. And with her extended time off she had less than three weeks to find out all she could.

Liberty's tap shoes clicked against the floor as she headed toward the sewing department located in a building behind the theater. Wearing her rehearsal clothes of black tights, a short skirt that came to her knees, and a dark blouse, she hurried along. Sent to be fitted for her first costume, she entered a large room where half a dozen women sat at clacking sewing machines, pumping foot pedals and feeding delicate material through the needles. Bolts of fabric were stacked everywhere, adjustable sewing mannequins wore fabric, headdresses hung on the walls, and more racks than she could count were filled with colorful costumes. She noticed quite a few dancers from various shows were trying on costumes.

She paused next to a sewer who was pushing colorful fabric underneath the needle, her foot rapidly worked the wrought iron pedal beneath the machine. The woman stopped to remove the fabric and clip the thread. Finally, she gave Liberty her attention and asked what she wanted.

"I'm to see Josephine Hébert," Liberty said.

"Back there," the sewer indicated at the door in the back.

Liberty went to where she was directed and knocked. A lone seamstress greeted her. The woman, of medium height with an ample bosom, had a pinch of gray in her black hair that was carelessly twirled into a French knot at the back. "Hallo, I'm Josephine

Hébert, but you may call me Fifi. And you are…Liberty La Roux, oui?" she said, her voice lyrical with a French accent.

"Yes." Liberty held out a hand that was ignored.

"You look more Irish than French, but then La Roux means red-hair." She shrugged. "I don't like your hair color. You should bleach it. Do you have freckles all over?"

Surprised at the question Liberty didn't have time to answer before she was handed a colorful robe to put on and ordered to strip nude. Going behind the dressing screen, Liberty did as told. She came out from behind the screen clasping the robe tight.

"Hurry—come here," Fifi said and removed Liberty's hands from the robe. "No need to be so modest, oui."

Liberty stood with her head high, her arms at her side, and watched as Fifi pulled her robe open and stood appraising her body. Her eyes locked onto Liberty's breasts as if they were ripe peaches and she wanted to bite into one.

"Your breasts are nice and firm, but you do have those damn freckles all over. However, they do not distract, they add something…er…I cannot say what." She shrugged.

Liberty steeled herself for what Magnolia told her would come next. *"Just give into it," Magnolia had said. "She can have you fired immediately if you don't play along. The woman's a joke amongst us dancers. We call her 'Fifi the Feeler.' It's how she gets her kicks. If you can't handle her frisky fingers you're in the wrong business."*

Pushing a dress form veiled in purple glittering material next to Liberty and with a wide smile on her red lips, Fifi put her measuring tape around Liberty's chest and measured. She then took pins from the pin cushion on her wrist and pinned the purple material to the dummy. She started cutting, the scissors snipping fast. Again, her attention was back on Liberty who she looked in the eye while cupping both breasts, feeling, running her hands over Liberty's skin in a most intimate way.

"*Non*, these freckles do not distract at all."

She stopped her groping long enough to transfer the measurements to the dummy. Going to her knees she ran her tape from ankle to crotch, her knuckles skimming Liberty's pubic area. Affronted, Liberty drew in a deep breath which was misconstrued as passion.

Fifi stood and ordered, "Spread your legs."

Liberty bit her lip and fisted her hands. "I don't understand, didn't you get my inseam measurements the first time?"

"Oui, I did," Fifi's eyes narrowed. "But I want to make sure I have them right. You don't want to be tripping on your gown's length, now do you?"

Allowing the seamstress to stretch the measuring tape again, Liberty shut her eyes and pictured Jonathan touching her, that it was Jonathan who was being so intimate with her. When Fifi stood with a satisfactory smile on her face, she spoke. "You weel do just fine, *chère*. I expect to have many fittings with you, *oui*?"

"Yes." Liberty smiled back when in reality she wanted to slap the woman's face. "I expect so. Were you seamstress to Zelda DeLane? Poor lady, how sad."

Fifi's face clouded. The seamstress appeared to be thinking about something, and said, "Oui, I was th…." She shook her head and continued, "I mean to say, I agree, so sad. She will be missed, but you ma chère, your body is better, perfectly proportioned. And you're so tall. You weel be made a star in no time."

"Did Miss DeLane let you touch her like this?"

"Oui, and more. We indulged each other. I did this to her."

Fifi kissed Liberty who shut her eyes against the woman's tight lipped invasion. Liberty acted like she was a nurse with a patient which was the only way she could touch the seamstress's burgeoning breasts. But when Fifi indicated she wanted more by starting to unbutton her blouse, Liberty gently pulled away.

"You were here at the Follies when she was murdered?"

"Oui, I was here that night, actually in…weel, I was helping with costume exchanges. There is always a seam that rips, something that needs last minute adjustments."

"Did you see anything out of sorts, someone that shouldn't be here?"

Fifi's eyes were sharp and assessing. "Why are you asking such questions? It is none of your concern, oui." She studied Liberty. "Do you have a steady beau?"

Liberty made her face go sultry like and ran her tongue around her lips. "No, I don't. The only man in my life is my agent. And he's so…so…somber and not much fun. You, I like." She winked at Fifi.

A soft knock on the door reminded Fifi another girl was ready for a fitting. Liberty practically dove behind the screen and let out a deep breath. While she dressed, she heard Fifi talking to the next performer. Liberty stepped aside for the young dancer to slide behind the screen.

On her way out, Fifi gave Liberty a time to come back the next day for her first fitting.

Welcome to the sordid backstage world of the theater Liberty told herself.

When she told Jonathan about the seamstress, his face darkened. He said he didn't like what she'd been put through, but accepted it for what it could get them. He'd gone backstage enough to know what went on, and Zelda had told him about various seamstress's, how they loved to feel the women's bodies, how most of them disliked men and demanded the right to touch and have sex with the young girls. If they didn't cooperate they could be fired. Zelda claimed to enjoy the fondling, the orgasms they brought on. She often told him that a woman was as good in bed as a man. But when he asked how a cold dildo felt compared to his hot shaft-of-delight, she would laugh and say there was no comparison, Jonathan won hands down and fingers up.

Liberty mentioned to Jonathan that other than Fifi's roaming hands and withheld information, she wasn't able to ask too many questions about Zelda's murder. But, she felt that Fifi knew something that she was keeping quiet about.

With the death of Josette, a pall fell over the troupe. Magnolia told her all about the hanging, the day Liberty had come to apply for a job. How coincidental is that?

Just this day, the detectives returned to the theater. They talked to Liberty asking her if she knew anything about the hanging. How could she when that was the first time she'd walked into the theater to apply for a job there?

Where was her agent they asked?

Out looking for more clients, she said.

Where was his office, they asked?

He lives with me, she answered, and watched the interesting looks that passed between them. They wanted to talk with everyone in the theater that day, would she make sure her agent, this Emery Edison, came to their precinct? Yes, oh yes, she smiled, he would come by real soon. She'd gone home in a frightened dither. She hadn't missed the intense stares of both detectives. Those two would dig and dig until they found Emery Edison didn't exist beyond the past month. Surely, a keen-eyed detective could see through the fake hair Jonathan wore in public. Liberty panicked, telling Jonathan he must leave, it wasn't safe for him to be there. And weren't they foolish thinking by putting Liberty in the lion's mouth, they could sleuth their way to finding the killer. Well, it was backfiring like a tin-lizzie starting up.

"Jonathan, let me go to your father, see if he can hide you

somewhere. Get you out of the country on a ship to Canada, anywhere to keep you safe." Liberty paced her small living room. "Maybe you can enlist in the army under an assumed name?"

Setting his drink on the side table, he took her by the arms and stopped her. "I'm not going into the army. Nor can I leave the country. If I do, it'll make me appear guilty. I want you to go to Dad, get more money. If he can find a better place for me to hide, then so be it." His eyes stared into hers, and she melted against him. Her face turned into his palm that now caressed the side of her cheek, pushing back her wild hair. "I hate the thoughts of being away from you, not knowing what is going on. When I leave here that is exactly what will happen. My God, I've come to rely on you so much. Tell me how I'm supposed to live without this?" His hands covered the sides of her head tilting her face to meet his gaze.

His warm lips pressed against her forehead, then traveled over each eyelid, her nose, finally parting to cover her mouth. Jonathan cloaked her body, her being, and she opened her lips accepting him. While bestowing hot kisses on her neck, he unbuttoned her white blouse and parted it. His hand rubbed the delicate fabric of her corset cover.

"And this?" He kept up his teasing, his fingers did a slow swirl over and around her breasts, softly caressing, chuckling when her nipples hardened.

"And this?"

Her blouse hit the floor, her corset cover straps were forced off her shoulders, and he continued his seduction with moist kisses. He put her hand over his groin, his hard penis. "And this," he whispered, "Do you want me in you?"

Losing her voice, she could only nod, and when he started to lift her, a knock sounded on the door.

"Oh…hell," he muttered and grabbing Liberty's blouse tossed

it to her. He snatched up his coat and hat, and looked around the room for anything of his left lying about. He headed into the bedroom where he shimmied beneath the bed.

"Who is there?" Liberty called out while buttoning her blouse and tucking it back into her waistband.

"Detectives Scala and Jones."

Liberty recognized Scala's voice. She opened the door and met the detectives with a wide yawn that she covered with her hand. "Hello. I'm afraid you woke me from a nap." She patted her hair that Jonathan had so effectively mussed. "I'm surprised to see you here." Like a sentinel she stood within the open door.

"Mind if we come in?" Jones asked, his gaze already going beyond her.

"I can't refuse you, now can I?" She stepped back, allowing them entrance into her world.

Not bothering to remove their hats, both men entered, their broad shoulders shrinking her living room, their heads turning, taking in everything they could about her home.

Clasping his hands behind his back, Scala went to peer at her shelf with the knickknacks on it. He picked up her latest acquisition, the one she'd purchased at Grand's. The delicate ballerina shrunk in his meaty fists. Liberty was concerned he might shatter it, but he simply turned it over to look at the bottom before replacing it back on the shelf.

"Do you collect figurines, Detective Scala?" she asked, praying they couldn't hear her heart thumping.

He grinned at her. "No, but my late wife collected this kind of stuff."

"I see," she said. "I'm sorry to hear that your wife has passed away. My father made the shelf for me." Why did she say that? She didn't need to bring her family into anything.

"Your father?" Jones pulled out his notebook and pencil.

"Yes. I don't care to talk about him, he's dead," she said in a shaky voice that threatened tears.

Scala shrugged at his partner and shook his head slightly. "We're here to talk with your agent...ah...Mr. Edison."

Liberty sighed and furrowed her brow. "I'm sorry, but he's not here."

It was Jones' turn to furrow his brow. "Not here, as in he'll be home soon, or not here as in he'll be gone for a while?"

Liberty almost jumped at the detective's suggestion, but her mind said watch out, don't take his bait. "I don't know. He wasn't here when I got home. And not knowing where he's off to, I can't give you a time when he's expected. You're welcome to wait for him if you'd like. Would you care for a cup of tea, coffee, or a brandy?" She folded her hands, darted a genuine smile at them, and waited patiently for their answer.

"No thanks. Does he have an office here in Manhattan?" Scala asked.

Liberty shook her head, careful not to make a mistake, she answered, "No. I'm his first client. It takes money, and with me just starting out, and...well...he lives here with me. Recently we haven't been getting along so well." She leaned forward to make sure they were included in her gossip. "Personally, between you and me he's not such a good agent. He should have gotten me more money, but my interview was interrupted by that shocking happening, you...know it's why you're here...Josette's hanging. Terrible, thing just terrible, that poor girl."

"I take it Emery Edison's your lover?" Jones asked.

"Yes," she didn't hesitate and smiled, "But I'm afraid he's not very good at that either." She guffawed and broke into a hardy laugh.

The tenants upstairs made thumping noises and children's voices could be heard. Next came a male voice shouting at the kids to shut up. Liberty looked at her ceiling and rolled her eyes.

"That must be hard to live with," Scala said. "Oh, one more thing. Where did you work before Foyle's?"

"Here and there. I'm a registered health nurse, but found I wanted to do something different. I was tired of going into tenements with sick people, putting myself at risk. Besides, the pay was bad and I want—no, I need to make more money. It's not against the law to change jobs or a profession is it?"

Ignoring her question, Scala's pencil was busy scribbling across his notepad. "Who did you work for as a nurse?"

Liberty felt she was being boxed in and they did it with such ease. "I worked for Lillian Wald's health care organization. You must be familiar with her organization?"

Ignoring her question, they took their notes, and asked more of their own. How long did she work there? They wanted to know more about her family. Did she have siblings? She answered each question as truthfully as she could, yet felt the noose tightening around her neck for helping Jonathan. She fully expected them to check the rest of her apartment, pull Jonathan out from under the bed. Instead they closed their notebooks and put their pencils in their breast pockets.

Jones locked eyes with Liberty. "We'll take our leave now. Tell Mr. Edison to come down to our precinct first thing tomorrow. We'll be expecting him," he said with a good deal of authority.

They doffed their hats at Liberty and left.

When Jonathan shimmied out from under the bed and came into the living room, Liberty was peering out the window. She pointed at her front door, put her finger across her mouth and shook her head at him to be quiet.

She took a towel, a washcloth and soap, and taking her key, she motioned for Jonathan to go back inside the bedroom. With her arms full, she opened her door and smacked right into Scala's chest. The confrontation made her drop her supplies.

"Oh…I didn't expect you to still be here. I thought you'd left," she said and watched as the older detective retrieved her towel and soap. "I was on my way to the bathroom." She pointed down the hallway. "Did you need something else?"

"No, we were discussing some issues," Scala said. "C'mon, let's go." He nudged his partner and they started to leave.

Liberty locked her apartment door then headed toward the bathroom. Her heart was knocking so hard she thought they could hear it as they went down the stairwell. Reaching the bathroom, she turned the occupied sign outward and was never so glad to step foot inside her destination. How fearful Jonathan must be and like her, felt the law was closing in on them.

She ran water in the bathtub, and taking off her clothes, she dipped her poor blistered feet in the hot water. As the water stung her heels, she sank into its warming depth, knees up, and lowered her body under the water. Sitting up, she used the French lilac-scented soap that Jonathan bought for her. First she washed her hair and then her body. She ran the sponge between her legs liking the feel of wantonness it gave her. She pretended it was Jonathan who held the sponge, who plied her with pleasure.

Jonathan nudged the lace curtain aside, just enough so he could see the street and the two detectives still standing in front of the stoop. Talking to each other, they both glanced back at the building and Liberty's window. Jonathan moved back. He and Liberty had a close call. And now, he had to go to the police department tomorrow. Disguise or no disguise, they would see through it immediately. They were trained to notice such things, a small amount of spirit gum showing on his cheek, his mustache that might become askew or loose. No, there was no way he could show his face at the precinct. Like a sealed bank vault, everything was closing in on him. He needed more time, but didn't think he was going to get it. When the detectives figured out Emery Edison didn't exist, they would come after him.

His one fear was Liberty being hurt, possibly jailed for harboring a fugitive. She was the number one person in his life right now and he wanted to protect her. Maybe she was right, maybe he should hide out at The Drake. He would miss not having Liberty to cuddle up with, miss her grin, her giggle, her strength, her guidance; in short he would miss everything about her.

The door opened and Liberty came in, the scent of Lilac's filled the room. Her wet hair fell to her waist but was already starting to form curls. She put her bath supplies on the floor and came over to him.

"What are we going to do?" she asked.

"You're not going to do anything. I am. I'm leaving here. If you don't know where I'm at, then you will not be able to tell the police anything."

She sat beside him and grasped his hand within hers. "No. You must be there for my first performance. I agree, the time has come for you to leave here, but I selfishly want you there in the audience."

"I guess if I was absent for your grand entrance it might appear odd. All right, I'll stay until your big debut. But then I must leave." He stood and went to put on a record, 'The One I Love.'

Chapter Fourteen

Inside her father's department store, Grand's, Alice was being pushed in her wheelchair by Jenny. Alice, wearing last year's tan coat with its ermine collar and cuffs, and her red hat with the broad crown and black bow looked like the latest fashion. Even though women were being urged to wear out their clothes instead of buying new, it was hard for women to quit shopping and ignore new fads, especially Alice.

Her father, most astute in business, turned to buying ready-made clothing from local factories. Merchandisers had stepped up when the Paris fashion houses shut down because of the war. And now, young and upcoming designers from the States were becoming known. Charles Grand labeled them the latest fashions from New York that were equal to Paris in quality. Buying off the rack was starting to catch on, even with the rich.

Alice was meeting Talon and her parents for lunch, but first she wanted to shop, to buy new undergarments, things that felt good against a woman's skin. One could only recycle and wear corset covers and drawers so long before they became shabby, and

Alice abhorred shabby.

Jenny maneuvered Alice's chair to the lift and where a smiling, chatty elevator operator took them to the second floor. The operator opened the door to a flurry of customers, mostly women. Grand's had advertised heavily in the papers about their summer sale and the new winter clothing line they were introducing.

At Talon's suggestion her father also installed a restaurant on the third floor. It was a big hit amongst female shoppers, a chance to rest, eat, and shop some more. What a novelty, one could practically live in the store. Not to mention the delicious odor of cooking onions and meat permeated the store like a giant beckoning hand.

Women who recognized Alice as the daughter of the store's owner stopped to fawn over her. Like a queen on her throne, Alice preened and glorified in their compliments.

"My, dear, please tell your father what an amazing job he has done with the store. The lure to the café is positively mouth-watering."

"My sentiments exactly," said another stranger.

Even if their comments were meant for her father, Alice smiled back at every grinning face.

"Thank you. I'll tell my father what you've said, he'll love hearing it."

Jenny continued pushing Alice towards women's wear.

"Alice," her father's voice wafted behind her wheelchair. "How perfectly wonderful to see you, dear girl. You're looking healthy, don't you agree, Miss Bishop? Doesn't she have a rosy bloom on her cheeks?"

Jenny nodded at Charles Grand. "I agree with you, sir. Must be the excitement of buying something new."

Alice glanced at her father's gray hair, his drooping walrus-shaped mustache, and met his soft brown eyes. "You can stop talking about me as if I'm not here," she scolded and pushed out her bottom lip. "Daddy, some of your customers just said wonderful things about the store."

"That's most heartening to hear. One always worries if they are doing the right thing, meeting customer's demands."

"It would appear that you are. Where's Talon? He's supposed to meet me here and help me shop."

Charles smiled at Alice. "I'm sure he's around here somewhere. Probably busy with customers. Let me take you to the women's better clothing section, more expensive, and you can pick the store clean if you so desire." He leaned down to kiss her forehead.

"Where's mother?" Alice patted her father's cheek, resisting the urge to pull his thick droopy mustache like she'd done when she was a little girl.

"She's meeting us in the restaurant. Ah…here's my son-in-law as we speak."

Talon came up behind Alice and bending over her shoulder, uttered something for her ears alone. She smiled and stared at him. Her smile faded when she noticed that he had a nasty looking scratch on his cheek. "Darling, what happened to your—"

"Mr. Grand," Talon interrupted her and grinned at his father-in-law. "Why don't I wheel Alice about? I never get to spend much time with her. We'll meet you for lunch."

Charles Grand pulled out his gold pocket watch and clicked it open. "All right. I'll see you later. I'm going upstairs to my office. Ah…Talon, don't forget to fill out an accident report. Also have all the shelving bays checked to make sure they're secure. Don't want a customer getting hurt." He replaced his time piece and again kissed Alice's cheek. "If I run into your mother before lunch I'll tell her you're here." He left, stopping to glance here and there at the counter displays, and to talk to a department employee.

Talon slowly pushed Alice's wheelchair toward the women's section. "I'll be glad when the war is over and Paris and every country involved can get back to normal. I have missed having Paris fashions in our store," he said.

Alice nodded and reached out to feel the sleeves on a blouse as she rolled by. "Yes, even traveling by ship was halted years ago…well…after that ship was torpedoed with so many people onboard. What was it called?"

"The Lusitania," he answered.

"Yes, yes that's right. Mother's worried about her relatives in France. And now this flu has her frightened even more. So," she said with a sigh, "It seems there are a great many things in this world to be scared of."

Talon leaned over and said, "I understand. The epidemic is getting worse. But try and put all of that from your pretty head and take in all the wonderful things in the store. What are you looking to buy?"

"Undergarments, dresses, maybe a warm coat." She plucked at her ermine cuff. "This is last years and I'm tired of it."

He wheeled her around and stood aside while she fingered the material of dresses and other garments. Her nurse, Jenny, along with a salesclerk, became loaded down with all sorts of clothing.

"Jenny, please remain here while they ring up my purchases. And make sure they deliver them today. Don't forget to join us for lunch at the appointed time," Alice said, and smiled.

She waited until Jenny left before confronting him. "Darling, did you really get that scratch on your face by a shelf falling on you? It looks as if a fingernail made the mark."

His eyes were icy as they met hers. "I can't help what it looks like. If I say a display shelf fell over on me, then it did. Almost killed me." He fingered the cut and when he did so, long red gouges on the back of his hands were revealed.

Alice didn't ask about them, she didn't want to be lied to and assumed his latest mistress was the one who did the clawing and not a display shelf. Instead, she asked Talon to take her to meet everyone at the restaurant.

He did just that, and headed for the elevator to take them to the third floor. While being pushed close to the stairs Alice spotted a tall red-headed woman coming toward them up the stairs. Alice recognized her at once. She was the same woman Talon was talking to at the Joyeux Theater awhile back.

All of a sudden Alice's chair tilted sideways, almost pitching her out onto the stairs.

She screamed.

"Help!" Talon yelled.

Alice grasped the wooden arm rest and held on for dear life. Her purse tumbled onto the stairs, and her heart followed.

Pandemonium broke out as several customers along with the red-headed woman grabbed the chair and helped to right it. With Talon pulling the chair from the other side, they maneuvered the bulky apparatus back on the floor and away from danger.

"Oh—my—word! Thank you so much," Alice said, her voice still shaking. And only when she paused to take a breath, did Talon speak.

"Alice—Alice, I'm so sorry. I didn't realize the wheel was so close to the stairs." He dropped to one knee, and taking Alice's hand, he rambled on about how sorry he was, begging her forgiveness, and how glad he was that she wasn't hurt.

Getting to his feet he took in the customers standing there and reassured them that Alice was all right. "Thank you so much for helping to save my wife. I don't know what else to say. You have averted a horrible tragedy here today." He shuddered and reached into his pocket. "In appreciation for your valor, here's a coupon for a free lunch." He passed them out to the two women and lone man standing there.

The tall red-head handed Alice her purse. "You dropped this. Are you sure you're not hurt? You were jostled quite violently. Maybe you should see a doctor?"

Alice took the woman's hand and squeezed. "I'm all right. Really, just frightened out of my skin." Tears came to her eyes and she took a hanky from her purse and dabbed at them. "My heart's calmed down too. I think it'll stay put." She gave out a meek little laugh and still shaken turned to look at her husband. "Talon, please invite my savior here to dine with us.

"Yes, since you were the one who helped save Alice the most, you must have lunch with us. That's where we were headed before this terrible accident."

"Almost accident," Alice said, "But we can thank your fast actions, Miss...er...Misses?"

"I'm Liberty Fitzgerald...Miss Fitzgerald. And there's no need to buy me lunch."

"Yes, yes there is," Alice was quick to answer. "You'll be able to meet my parents, too."

They were in the lift when Alice spoke. "Talon, what happened back there? Why did you push me so close to the stairs?"

Talon Montgomery shot their guest, Miss Fitzgerald, a questioningly glance before addressing his wife. "I didn't mean too. My God, I feel awful, Alice. I was distracted and simply pushed you too close." He took her hand and kissed it. "Forgive me? I'd rather cut off my arm than ever cause you harm."

Who was he trying to convince? Her or Miss Fitzgerald whom Alice knew Talon was somehow acquainted with. There probably wasn't a woman in the state he wasn't familiar with. And, cut off his arm? What was that play acting all about?

The operator announced their floor and he pushed her toward the restaurant.

"Alice...ma chère." Her mother called out.

Alice watched her petite mother hurrying up to her. "Mama," she said and held out her arms as tears wet her cheeks.

"Ma chère, you're white as a ghost, what has happened?" Her face, matronly, yet still pretty, looked frightened.

Talon quickly said, "We had a near mishap. Nothing to worry yourself about."

Her mother's cheeks paled under her rouge. "What kind of mishap? Let me be the judge of...er...if it was an accident or not," she searched for the right words, her accent, if hard to understand, was delightful.

"My wheelchair started falling down the second floor stairs. But I was saved by a group of customers, and this lady right here." She groped for Liberty's hand and pulled her forward. "Mama, this is Miss Liberty Fitzgerald who saved me."

It was her mother's turn to grab Liberty's hand and pull her into a tight embrace and then release her. "Bonjour, Miss Fitzgerald. I'm Yvette Grand. God knows I cannot thank you enough." She kept patting her own bosom as if to mimic her heart pounding. "You will have to tell me all about it during lunch. I'm assuming you are joining us, oui?" Before an answer was given, she acknowledged Talon with a nod of her head. "Were you pushing my daughter?"

"Yes, I was."

After being seated at the round table, Yvette Therriault Grand took her daughter's hand and stared at her anxious face. Yvette also took in her son-in-law's composed features and wondered about the near mishap on the stairs. She wasn't particularly fond of Talon Montgomery, and after having personal conversations with Alice, decided that after seven years of marriage there was little love shared between her daughter and Talon.

Another thing in Alice's life that Yvette compared to her own was how Yvette met and married Charles Grand who was in Paris scouting out high fashion clothing for his store. A successful department store handed down through several generations of Grand's and now placed firmly in Charles' capable hands. Yvette Therriault's family owned high-couture fashion houses. Charles' reputation was impeccable and he was rich. Talon Montgomery had no reputation when he met Alice. Practically penniless, he lived paycheck to paycheck.

And Talon's lack of money was a constant bother to Yvette, for she knew that being penniless could cause a person to do things they normally would never do.

When Alice was born, Yvette couldn't have been happier with her healthy child who ran in the park and was both her and Charles' to spoil. Yvette was amazed at how Alice had grown into a beautiful woman who'd mesmerized many a beau at dances. Yvette had hoped that Jonathan Drake would fall in love with Alice, but it was not to be. Instead, Talon was the chosen.

Looking at Alice now in her wheelchair, Yvette couldn't help but think back at how devastated they all were when Alice fell from her horse. Yvette brought in doctors from all over the world and all of them told her that Alice's paralysis might cure itself in time but that was rather doubtful. There would be no grandchildren to spoil.

Still holding Alice's hand, Yvette couldn't help but notice her son-in-law kept staring at Miss Fitzgerald. A very pretty Miss Fitzgerald, who was wearing a fashionable dress, and whose bright hair was knotted in a French coil, and half hidden beneath a wide-brimmed hat. This Miss Fitzgerald helped to save her precious Alice's life, and Yvette wanted to learn more about her.

"Miss Fitzgerald, do you have family fighting in the war?"

Miss Fitzgerald seated across from her nodded. "Yes, yes I do. My brother Teague is in the army and fighting in France. You're French, Mrs. Grand, so you must have relatives still there?"

A slow sad smile creased Yvette's mouth. "Oui. My brothers, all in their seventies, are too old to fight and have shuttered their fashion houses in Paris. They have moved to Switzerland. My great nephews have joined the cause and now fight for our country. I fret for them all and wonder what will be left of my beloved family and France."

Two empty chairs, one on each side of Liberty, remained and with place settings on the table, Liberty knew others would be joining them. And they did in the way of an older man who came up first and put his hands on Mrs. Grand's shoulders and bent close to buss her cheek. From the looks exchanged between the two, Liberty knew they were still very much in love.

"Charles, ma chère, how good of you to join us, we've been waiting," Mrs. Grand said and smiled adoringly at her husband. "Darling, we have a guest. Miss Liberty Fitzgerald, this is my husband, Charles Grand. He owns this fabulous store." She chuckled at the obvious.

Liberty, like any lady would, remained seated and acknowledged the store owner by saying, "I'm pleased to make your acquaintance."

"Likewise, I'm sure." Charles kissed Liberty's hand before he took the empty seat between his wife and Liberty. With his old-fashioned mutton-chop sideburns he reminded her of a man who was mired in the past.

Alice filled her father in on her narrow escape and how Miss Fitzgerald helped to save her from a terrible fall down the stairs.

A minute later, a tall, robust woman approached and stood

behind the empty chair on Liberty's left. The woman was comely with a square chin and wide mouth. Her brown hair was pulled up and disappeared into a short brimmed hat.

Alice hurriedly exclaimed, "Oh…good…Miss Bishop at last. Now we can eat…I'm starving." But in good manners, Alice found the time to introduce her companion and nurse to Liberty.

When a waiter arrived to take their orders, Mrs. Grand insisted Liberty order the most expensive meal on the menu, Liberty did as told. Why not, she thought, she didn't want to join them, but now that she was, she was going to take advantage of it.

Mr. Grand sipped his coffee and placed his cup in the saucer. "Tell me, Miss Fitzgerald, what is it you do besides saving people…especially my daughter?" He directed a friendly smile her way.

"I'm a certified and registered health care nurse. I did work for the Lillian Wald foundation and the state of New York." She picked up her fancy teacup and taking a drink, decided it needed more sugar and dropped in another cube.

Alice, from her wheelchair appeared to perk up at the mention of a nurse. "You said you did work for the Wald foundation, where do you work now?"

Seeing no reason to lie to these people, Liberty acknowledged Alice and answered her question. "Right now, I'm a dancer in Foyle's Follies."

All eyes were on her. She effectively stopped them from taking another drink or eating another bite.

Mrs. Grand's mouth parted and she said, "You have a college degree in nursing, oui? Then you will have to explain why you are now a dancer in the theater. It makes no sense to me." Her brown eyes were full of questions.

"Yes," said Alice, "I'm equally curious."

Only the men remained silent, yet both stared at her in admiration as if to imagine her on the stage and dressed in very little.

Liberty cleared her throat, replaced her cup in its saucer, and spoke. "It has everything to do with money. I make more money being a dancer than I did being a nurse. Plus, the risks I took going into people's homes. Some were very sick, and some of the men were downright abusive to me. If I have my choice of getting the Spanish flu or getting blisters on my feet—blisters win hands down. Just because I'm a nurse doesn't make me Florence Nightingale, or Lillian Wald for that matter. I'm not like either woman, nor will I ever be."

Alice joined in and revealed to all. "My Talon here goes to the theater as often as he can. Did you know that star that got murdered—ah...Zelda DeLane?"

Liberty smiled at delicate Alice. "No, she was murdered before I was hired on. Mr. Montgomery, since you go often, were you there the night Miss DeLane was killed"

Talon's dark eyes flashed over his napkin as he wiped his mouth. "As a matter of fact I was there that night. Horrible— horrible thing to happen to someone with such talent and beauty."

Alice smiled and said, "And my Talon knows talented beauties, don't you dear?"

Charles Grand glared at his daughter, cleared his throat and signaled for the waiter to bring them dessert and more coffee. "I'm not a big patron of the theater, but find if someone wants or needs to work there, then all the better for them. We have to have our entertainment and someone has to do the job."

"Sort of like being a mortician, a horrible job in anyone's mind, but someone has to do it and aren't we all glad someone does," Liberty said, and stared at Mr. Grand who threw back his head and roared with laughter.

Talon choked on his coffee.

Alice laughed.

Mrs. Grand spurted in her cup.

Jenny Bishop took a bite of cake. "Ohhh," she said, "This chocolate cake is delicious. Mrs. Montgomery try yours, it might put some meat on your bones."

Liberty, rather enjoying the ability to shock, bit into her cake. "It is delicious."

"I agree," boasted Mr. Grand.

Mrs. Grand tried the dessert and finding it to her liking turned to her husband. "I believe the cooks you have hired will do just fine. I'm sure this restaurant will become quite popular and the main meeting place for people to gather here at Grand's." She smiled at Liberty. "What do you think, Miss Fitzgerald, of our restaurant and of our store?"

"I don't eat out a lot, but I do like to shop here. I must agree however, the food is wonderful. But since I don't have a lot of money to spend here, I'm sure my opinion doesn't matter much."

"No, Miss Fitzgerald, on the contrary," said Charles Grand, and continued, "It matters a great deal to me. I need to know what my customers like and dislike. If I don't please my customers I cannot stay in business. When you do shop here, what do you buy?"

Liberty placed her fork on her plate and allowed the waiter to remove her dessert dish and refill her coffee. "Let me see…well…I buy clothing…shoes and all that. But what I absolutely swoon over is your knickknack department."

"Knickknacks? How so?" Mr. Grand asked.

"I'm a figurine collector. Porcelain mainly."

Talon joined in and asked. "Do you have a curio cabinet for them?"

Liberty shook her head. "No, I have display shelves that my father made. They are done really well. My father is a carpenter in a furniture factory."

Alice spoke up. "Then when we are finished here, you shall go and pick out some figurines to add to your collection. Think of it as a gift from me to you for saving me from a terrible fall."

"Really, lunch is enough, and I didn't do that much."

Mrs. Grand clapped her hands together making her bracelets and rings flash. "We insist. My son-in-law can take you to the department when we're finished here. And Charles and I insist that you have all you want." The black feather on her red hat bobbed with each emphasizing nod. Her hat matched the bright red of the two-piece suit she wore.

Even dressed in the finest that Jonathan bought for her, Liberty still didn't feel close to being equal to anyone sitting here at this table. Well, maybe Jenny Bishop who kept glancing at her all during lunch. Yes, Liberty was well aware of Miss Bishop who was no doubt a fraud and not really a nurse at all. Wasn't everyone sitting here at this table a fraud in one way or another? Liberty wondered why Talon Montgomery didn't bring up the fact that he'd met her before today. That he'd flirted and insisted on walking her around the store, carrying her purchases? She also knew that she was the cause of him almost dumping his wife down the stairs. The moment they made eye contact his attention strayed from his missus. A strange reaction, Liberty thought. Learning that Talon Montgomery was at the theater the night Zelda DeLane was killed was the most interesting of all. She had to know more.

"Miss Fitzgerald?" Alice smiled across the table at her. "Do those at the theater still talk of Jonathan Drake being the killer?"

"I'm not sure who you're talking about? Oh...you mean the man found in Miss. DeLane's dressing room when she was murdered? Do you know him?"

"Oui," Mrs. Grand answered for her daughter. "Our families have been acquainted for years. My Charles here is a friend of Lincoln Drake...er...Jonathan Drake's father. I'm sure you're not aware of this fact, but Lincoln Drake owns The Drake hotel. It's very upper class, right in line with The Astor."

"So this Jonathan Drake is the son of Lincoln Drake? Interesting," Liberty smiled around the table at them all. "I have to say that there isn't a lot of talk right now about the murder. We're busy rehearsing."

"What revue are you in?" Talon asked.

"I'm in Leg's Galore. I'm also just a chorus girl. Someone who kicks high," she said and then laughed.

"Must be your long legs," Alice said in an envious tone.

"If you don't mind my asking, why are you in a wheelchair, Mrs. Montgomery?" Liberty asked, hoping she wasn't overstepping good manners.

Alice's eyes clouded as if remembering, and then she said, "I fell off a horse several years ago."

Yvette's brow wrinkled as she looked at her daughter. "My Alice was robust and healthy, but now she is quite fragile. The doctors hope that someday she'll walk again. So do we, Miss Fitzgerald, so do we."

They all became silent and Liberty thought now was the time to leave. She wiped the corners of her mouth and put the fancy monogramed cloth napkin on the table in front of her. "I'm afraid the time has gotten away from me. I really have to go. Please remain seated."

But being gentlemen, both Charles and Talon stood.

Talon went behind Liberty's chair and pulled it out for her. "Let me be of service and show you around."

Liberty allowed Talon Montgomery to escort her down to the first floor where his department was located. Imported ceramics from all over the world were clustered in colorful displays. Talon's hand seemed to linger on the small of her back, his fingers some-times going lower than necessary just like a possessive lover. Liber-ty allowed the slime to do so, wanting to secure more information from him before dismissing him.

"So, when is your debut?" he asked and paused before a dis-play of delicate figurines from France.

She moved closer to him leaving barely an inch of air between them and met his eyes with a flirty smile. "This weekend is my first night. You know, the costumes we wear leave little for the imagi-nation. I'd like to be in your head when you see them, just to know what you are thinking."

His eyes sparkled and he threw back his head in a jovial laugh. "Correction, please. I'd like to see you, Miss Fitzgerald, in a flimsy costume. The others I don't care about." He took her hand and ran his finger up her arm. "May I please say that you've been on my mind ever since I first waited on you in this very department? And here I thought you were married and buying clothing for your husband."

"You do flatter me, Mr. Montgomery. No, you're the one married. I was only picking out a few things for my agent."

"Talon, please call me Talon." He lifted her hand and while kissing it, ran his tongue over it.

"Talon," she said. "I like that name. It sounds dangerous—like a bird of prey. Are you dangerous, Mr. Montgomery...Talon? Did a bird scratch your face?" She flirted and leaned against him.

"Yes, I'm dangerous. No bird, just a display shelf that I walked into." His eyes undressed her and getting the message she was sending him, he said, "I want to see you."

"You will, at the Joyeux," she said and laughing moved away from him. As customers swarmed around them going about their shopping, she picked up a figurine of a Chinese woman carrying a water pole across her shoulders loaded with two pails, one on each side. The figurine was done in detail, exquisite, something that Liberty didn't have and something she wanted. "I'd like this."

Talon pointed at another figurine close by, the mate to the woman. "You cannot take the one without the other. Every woman needs a man in her life."

"Even if he's married," she said and pouted.

"Yes. But better if the man forgets he's married, or chained to a shrew. Will you rescue me, Miss Fitzgerald? Take me away from a fate worse than death?"

His meaning lodged in Liberty's mind. He was married, but didn't consider himself so. For Jonathan's sake, she should get as much from this man as possible. He was at the theater the night Zelda was killed. From the backside, he could pass for Jonathan, same height, same build, same coloring. Ideas were taking root. What was it Alice said? That Talon knows talented beauties? Meaning what? That Talon spent time with the Follies star? Or stars? Liberty couldn't wait to share her news with Jonathan.

"How about clothes, Miss Fitzgerald? You must pick out something to wear."

"Yes, I can do that." And she moved to stand right next to him. So close that she deliberately brushed her hand across the front of his pants. "I can do many things, Mr. Montgomery. As a nurse my talents concerning the human body run deep." She acted her part to an award winning performance.

Talon let out a moan and grabbing her hand pressed it tight against his erection.

Shocked, but not letting on, she laughed and said, "Naughty...naughty man."

"Mr. Montgomery," Jenny Bishop called out from an aisle over and came on. Her face was tight, as if she knew what they were doing.

Liberty stole one of the figurines out of Talon's hand, and

raised it high to show it off to Miss Bishop. "Do you like this one, Miss Bishop?"

"Nice, I'm sure," the woman said. "Mr. Montgomery, your wife is tired and she wants to leave now."

Talon signaled for a sales clerk. When one instantly appeared, he handed her the statues and told her to escort Miss Fitzgerald to women's clothing.

"Don't charge her for anything. Her purchases are gifts from Charles Grand."

Jonathan stood behind the window curtain, peering out, and waiting for Liberty to come home from shopping. She was supposed to talk to his father to find out where they would be hiding him next. He wanted to see Liberty's debut at the Follies before he went underground. And underground it would be.

He'd come to love Liberty with a strong passion. Loved hearing her talk, loved the crackle of her hair when she brushed out its long curly length that reminded him of fire, a hot fire, like she was. He was lucky to have someone like her who believed in him. He thought back over his life which in turn was little to think about. He'd accomplished nothing much. He'd been given gifts that some would have crawled on their knees across the continent to have. He'd squandered all that his parents gave him. And that included their love. He'd misused it as though it was nothing. When he thought of all his favorite foods his mother prepared for him only to have him say he didn't have time to eat them. Instead, he'd dashed out the door to play with his latest conquest. Liberty's family could have used all those meals that went to waste. Liberty would have loved to have the food to give to her patients.

Jonathan was sick of himself. If, and when, he got out of this mess, he was going to change, give what he could to charities.

And, he'd have to be the one making the money. Even though his father denied it, this murder charge had to impact his father's business in more ways than one. Jonathan hated that, hated himself for letting it come about. He wondered what would happen if he turned himself in. Could he have an attorney who would defend him and clear his name? No, he needed more information. He needed Liberty to get it for him.

From the window, he stared out at the sidewalk and was stunned to see the two detectives and behind them was another man who Jonathan recognized as Liberty's father. He watched as they disappeared inside.

"Damn it," he swore out loud and then rushed to turn the key in the lock making sure it was secure.

He stood in the bedroom doorway while they knocked and called out for Miss Fitzgerald. Jonathan hurried to shimmy under the bed.

"Oh…God," he muttered, and listened as the door was being unlocked and then male voices filled the living room.

"What do ye want with me daughter?" Keegan Fitzgerald's voice boomed.

"Listen, ah…Mr. Fitzgerald…is it?"

"Aye, I'm Keegan Fitzgerald, Liberty's father. Who in the hell are you?"

"I'm detective Jones and this here is Scala. We're investigating the murders that happened at the Joyeux Theater. Do you even know what we're talkin' about?"

"Can't say I do. Wait, I read about them in the papers awhile back." Keegan's shoulders stiffened and he became alert. Something was wrong here, for sure nothing made sense. And with that in mind he cautioned himself not to say or do anything that might jeopardize Liberty.

Scala glanced around and stopped in front of the shelf loaded with knickknacks. "Your daughter's quite the collector."

"Aye, I made the shelves for her as I did most of the furniture here. I work in a furniture factory."

"Well...that's strange. How does a dead man work and stand here before me?" Scala said while reading through his notes. "Dead, indeed."

Keegan swallowed hard, his mind racing, and being sharp as the nails he used in his job, he blurted out. "I am dead to her. In her mind that is. We've had a terrible row. She ordered me outta here, said I was dead in her eyes. Ah...me wee lass...the light in me heart wounded me deeply and I'm here to make amends." He put his hand over his heart, his eyes filled with tears.

"I don't suppose you know where her agent Emery Edison is? I take it he's not here?"

The detective's words made Keegan feel like he was drowning or standing in a total stranger's living room. He mustered a grin for the detective and wagged his finger at him. "Me daughter's life is her own. I'm not one to meddle. No, I don't know where Emery Edison is." And he could truthfully say he didn't. Hell, he didn't know the man at all. An agent? Why on God's green earth would Liberty have an agent? He felt like he was sinking in muck that closed over his eyebrows.

Jones shook his head at his partner. "I guess we'll have to come back another time...er...Mister...ah...Fitzgerald."

"Aye, that ye will. I don't know what ye believe me daughter's done, but she is kind hearted and wouldn't hurt a flea, not with her being a nurse and all."

The stares between the two policemen were enough for Keegan to realize he'd said too much. He couldn't help but wonder what in the hell Liberty had gotten herself into.

The one called Scala pocketed his notebook. "We'll call back. Ah…you might tell your daughter to expect us. That is if you're still not dead in her eyes."

Keegan held the door open allowing them to leave. He locked it behind them and went to sit on the sofa. He laced and unlaced his fingers. He tapped his foot and whistled while looking around. He'd come here to surprise Liberty, but now wasn't sure what to do. Glancing at the desk he'd made, he noticed a playbill for the Joyeux Theater. Going over to inspect it, he opened it and looked at a long row of dancers, counting sixteen women in all. A cluster of several scenes also held dancers and a close-up showed his tall beautiful daughter, Liberty, scantily clad, standing there with a headdress that stretched for the ceiling.

"What the feck!" he bellowed. Poleaxed! He was poleaxed, cut off at the knees. Going into the kitchen, he turned on the tap, and leaned underneath it to catch the water in his mouth. Straightening up and using the back of his hand to wipe his mouth off, his eyes bulged at the sight of a man's shaving strop hanging on the wall. Beneath it on the counter was a shaving mug with shaving soap and a brush in it. All nice and tidy. He felt inside the mug which was still damp.

Curiosity got the better of him and never one to snoop in his children's homes, he now did. He forced himself to go back out in the living room and to the bedroom's closed door that he opened. Inside the bedroom, he unlatched the wardrobe. Clothing for a man hung next to his daughter's and in the bottom of the closet was a dummy head wearing a blonde wig and beard. His skin prickled. Again that strange feeling that some kind of trickery was going on here.

Closing the closet door, he turned around to take a good look. The pink chenille bedspread was tucked against the floor along its entire length. It looked to him as if someone or something pushed it in while crawling underneath.

Keegan took a deep breath and growled, "If ye are or aren't Emery Edison, now would be a good time to show yourself. Or do I need to go call those detectives back?" His eyes widened in disbelief as a man shimmied out from under the bed. First his feet, then the rest of his body appeared. The dark haired stranger stood and met Keegan's gaze.

He held out his hand, "I'm Emery…"

Keegan's fist complied in a way of introduction that clipped the stranger's chin knocking him back on the bed.

"I'm Keegan Fitzgerald, and I want to kill ye for spoilin' me daughter. Ye feckin' bastard!" He struck the poise of a pugilist, hands fisted and held high.

The stranger rebounded off of the bed, and Keegan let fly with a left-handed jab. The man ducked. Keegan missed.

"Stop it! I don't want to fight with Liberty's father," he yelled, and held up his hands to ward off any more blows.

"I don't care what ye want or don't want!" His arm loaded with a curled fist darted out again. He missed.

"I'm not sleeping with your daughter! You should know her better than that. She's an honest woman who cares for others to the point of putting herself in danger."

Keegan straightened from his boxing stance and glared. "What danger? What's me lass gotten herself into?"

"Why don't you let me put a pot of coffee on? I'll tell you everything."

Keegan agreed. His arms fell to his sides, and he uncurled his fists. He still didn't trust this Emery Edison as far as he could throw a punch, which apparently wasn't far at all.

Liberty arrived home with two shopping bags filled with

packages. Unlocking the door and practically falling inside, she laughed and started to tell Jonathan what happened with Alice and Talon Montgomery when she saw her father sitting on the sofa and Jonathan sitting on the chair. Both were in a titanic stare down.

"Dad!" she exclaimed, amazed at the scene before her. "Oh…my…what are you doing—"

"Here?" he finished her sentence for her. "Well, me girl, this man…er…Jonathan Drake has been fillin' me in on yer life of late. Some things would make yer sweet mam turn over in her grave. But, this murder business I do want to hear all about." He appraised her with deep interest. "And iffen ye can't tell me what is goin' on in yer life, how can I be truthful with those detectives that come snoopin' around?"

She had the presence of mind to put her bags on the floor next to the sofa. She then removed her hat and coat and hung them on the coat rack. Taking her time, she fussed her hair back into place, and then fluffed at the skirt of her dress. Sitting next to her father, she swallowed, and stared at his thunderous face, not knowing where to begin, yet relieved that some of it was finally out in the open.

She noticed that Jonathan's jaw was red and swollen. No need to ask where that came from. "How much does dad know?"

"That I'm the accused murderer of Zelda DeLane. How you found me. And that I'm innocent. You're helping me find the real culprit before I'm taken to Sing Sing."

She proceeded to tell her father how she felt compelled to help Jonathan, that deep in her heart she knew he was innocent. Step by step, she recited her day at Grand's and all that she'd received out of good charity for saving Alice Montgomery from a gruesome tumble down the stairs. She was detailed about Talon Montgomery, his advances to her. But for her father's sake, she left off the part about her fondling Talon's privates.

"I know if I encouraged him, I could get information concerning the murder. Somehow, I just know it," she said.

Jonathan blew a lock of hair off his forehead and glanced at Keegan. "Yeah, Talon has an itch that needs constant scratching. He's a womanizer. I used to feel sorry for Alice, now I don't. I've decided she is getting what she deserves. Maybe she likes his attention diverted from her to someone else. Do you think he allowed the wheelchair to almost fall on purpose?"

Liberty stared at both of them and shook her head. "No, I don't. When he saw me on the stairs, he completely lost his train of concentration. He didn't do it on purpose. By the way, he has a scratch on his face. I don't believe his story on how he got it. His hands were also scratched, but nothing was said about them. How about we go sit at the dining room table so we all can enjoy a cup of coffee?"

Liberty poured three cups of coffee from the pot in the kitchenette. Putting them on the tray, she carried the tray into the dining room. She placed the cups in front of where they sat and slipped into her chair before Jonathan could get to his feet. Silence ensued while she put three cubes of sugar and cream into hers. Stirring her coffee, she found it easier to stare at her cup then at either her father or Jonathan.

Jonathan laced his fingers and cracked his knuckles. "Liberty, the detectives were here again tod—"

"In here—my apartment?" she exclaimed.

"Aye, daughter, here in yer apartment. I let them in. With me not knowing I was dead to ye, we had an interesting conversation." He took a sip of coffee.

"Oh...God...no, did that come out? They don't forget a thing they're told do they? I said you were dead so they wouldn't seek you out and talk with you. Thought if you were six-feet under they'd forget about you. Nor could I tell you about Jonathan here. It's all such a big mess. I'm sorry, Dad, so sorry."

Keegan nodded. "I told them I was dead to ye in yer mind. That we'd had a row. After they'd gone, that's when I figured out someone was in here."

Jonathan locked eyes with Liberty. "I've assured your father that nothing has happened between us. That you are still as pure as the day you were born, and I'm not a scoundrel who preys on single women."

Liberty choked on her coffee, spewing brown droplets across the front of her blouse. She grabbed a napkin and quickly dabbed at the fast spreading stain. "And if I wasn't still intact as you so nicely put it, that's my business and not Dad's."

"Weel, that's not exactly true. I'm still yer father and still look after ye. I want only good things fer ye, and being spoiled by an accused murderer isn't one of them. Now tell me about this here Follies thing yer into. And yer nursing that you've given up." He leaned forward.

"Jonathan and I thought that if I became a Follies dancer I'd be able to get backstage and maybe find out information that could help prove his innocence."

Keegan scoffed with disgust. "Daughter, the poor are better served with ye nursing them, educatin' them on clean livin'. Yer not going to get what ye want at the theater. How can ye scratch out such information when those two detectives can't seem to find the culprit? And sure as I'm sittin' here they think Jonathan Drake is guilty." He pointed a finger at Jonathan. "It's just a matter of time before they figure out that Jonathan and Emery Edison are one in the same."

Liberty grit her teeth before smiling at her dad. "It might surprise you to know I'm already finding out certain things. People have loose tongues, it makes them feel important to gossip and share."

"Your daughter's a good dancer too. She's beautiful on stage. All eyes immediately go to her."

Keegan took a swig of coffee. "Have ye seen her? Is that blonde wig and beard how ye go about?"

"Yes, to both questions. I've been out front during one rehearsal. We wanted to make it look like I'm her acting agent and have a right to be there. The spotlights are good to Liberty."

Liberty held her father's hand. Aging, gnarled around the edges, he was as endearing to her as her own life. She stared into his gray eyes that held nothing but love for her. "Dad, please don't tell anyone about Jonathan. Certainly not Blaine." She leaned forward. "I believe in Jonathan enough to know he's innocent."

"Speakin' of your brother, I asked him and his family to meet me here." Keegan squeezed her hand and asked, "What can I do to help ye and Mr. Drake here?"

"Wait a minute! Why is Blaine coming here? Oh for God's sake, Dad, your surprises are going to be the death of me. As far as Jonathan's concerned, for now please keep silent about him to anyone. I'm thinking now that you're in the know it'll be easier to fool the detectives."

Without a knock, the front door flew open and Liberty's two young nephews, Shawn and Kenny bounded in followed by her brother Blaine along with his wife Marybeth.

Liberty quickly stood and hurried into the living room. "Blaine—Marybeth!" she exclaimed, "How nice to see you."

Jonathan, without any time to react or hide, stood beside the table and shoved his hands in his pockets.

Keegan got to his feet and joining Liberty, said, "I asked them to meet me here so we could all go eat in a restaurant. In all the excitement of meeting Mr. Edison here, I forgot to tell ye."

Jonathan came into the living room to stand beside Liberty.

Kenny clamored over to Liberty's side and hugged her around the hips. "Grandpa says he's takin' us to…em…eat out." His enthusiasm for something that wasn't done much in his life showed in his wide grin.

Liberty removed his cap and tamed a few springy curls. "Oh…so that's why you are here, to take me with you?"

Shawn walked over to his brother's side. "Aye, Grandpa Keegan said we were goin' to surprise ya." Looking suspicious, he pointed a stubby finger at Jonathan. "Who's he?"

Liberty smiled at her nephews. "I'll introduce him as soon as we get your mother off her feet." She went to Marybeth's side and guided her to the sofa and helped her sit. Marybeth let out a groan as her pregnant body settled on the cushion.

"Better?" Liberty asked.

Her sister-in-law smiled back. "Yes, much better. I can't wait to have this child which is givin' me fits. Nothin' about this pregnancy is like my other two. Maybe it's a sign the child is goin' to be a girl. I'd like that so much."

Liberty noticed her brother's curious gaze was locked on Jonathan giving him the twice over.

Jonathan, not waiting for Liberty to introduce him, held out his hand to Blaine. "Hello. I'm Emery Edison. I'm a close friend of your sister's."

Blaine took his hand and pumped it. Releasing it, he pointed toward his wife. "That's my wife, Marybeth. My two lads, Shawn my oldest, and Kenny our youngest. Yer a close friend of my sister's?" His eyes took in Jonathan's bruised jaw.

Keegan joined in before Jonathan could reply. "Yer sister has been seein' Mr. Edison. That's why I asked ye over here, to meet the man that's taken with yer sister."

"So, you knew about Mr. Edison before today?" Blaine asked his father.

"Oh aye, that I did. And 'tis happy I am. Time for yer sister to settle down, stop her traispin' into sick people's homes. Thought I'd surprise ya all by goin' out and havin' a little toast on the town, ya might say."

Liberty had to hand it to her father. He'd jumped in with both feet and acted the part so well he could be on stage with her. The bit about the Follies she hoped would wait for another day. One bombshell, that she was seeing a man, was enough. And what's this about her dad taking them all out. That in itself was a big surprise. What did he have planned that he wanted to surprise her with? Well, she'd turned the tables on the big surprise, that's for sure. She could only hope he'd soon forgive her for getting him involved in Jonathan's mess. And she didn't want Blaine's family involved in the slightest. But, her brother had met Jonathan in his normal state, no wig, nothing.

She watched as Jonathan bent over Marybeth's hand and brought it to his lips. "Nice to meet you, Mrs. Fitzgerald." He then turned to the rest, her father in particular. "I'm afraid I can't join you tonight. Perhaps another time?"

"Aye, didn't know ye had other plans when I made mine." Keegan said and nodded. "Another time it is."

Liberty picked up the package from Grand's and took out the Chinese figurines. Holding them high for all to see, she announced. "Ah...Mr. Edison surprised me with these today." She directed a smile at him. "He knows my fondness for collecting porcelain." She handed the figurines to Jonathan who placed them on the shelf.

Marybeth smiled at Jonathan. "Mr. Edison, I can't tell you how happy I am that Liberty has met someone she likes. And if Keegan approves of you, then I find it easy enough to like you as well."

"Thank you, Mrs. Fitzgerald." Jonathan nodded and pulled

out his pocket watch. "I find I'm running a little late." He took Liberty's coat from the rack and held it for her to slip into. "Miss Fitzgerald, I'll see you tomorrow." He was the first to leave.

Blaine approached Marybeth on the sofa and putting his arm around her, helped her to her feet. He then nodded at Liberty. "Yer just full of surprises, little sis, yep, full of surprises."

Keegan held the door for them and they filed out one by one.

Chapter Fifteen

Jonathan found himself backstage in the Follies dressing room. After two weeks of being a background dancer for the Legs Galore revue, people were asking about Liberty. Who was she? And with so much attention on her, Sid Brawley put her in a new revue giving her a small part, one song.

Liberty just gave her premier performance and it looked like she was a hit. With the lights, glitzy costumes, and surrounded by leggy showgirls, Liberty became an illusion of talent. She sang her own song in her simple voice, but her onstage radiance had the audience forgiving or overlooking even that. There were no boos, only long applause and for that Jonathan was grateful.

When Foyle, the owner of the Joyeux, arrived backstage with his wife, Anna Pellum on his arm, he asked that his star Capucine and Liberty join them at the Broadway Restaurant. Jonathan as Liberty's agent was invited to come along.

Sidney Brawley, with his constant cigar in hand waved a piece of paper at Jonathan. "Miss La Roux…Liberty." He gestured both of them over. "I suppose after tonight, Mr. Edison, you will want more money for her? Well, I'm ahead of the game and have a new contract that Mr. Foyle insisted I draw up. Want to step over here and sign it?"

Jonathan cleared his throat and slipped his arm around Liberty. He spoke with authority. "I was already thinking on that matter. And after tonight's reception of her on stage, it's more than apropos that you pay her more."

Sidney clamped his cigar between his teeth and puffed while talking. "I see good things for our Miss La Roux here. My dear, you'll be making $700.00 a month. Hope your agent here doesn't plan on holding out for more."

Liberty curtailed her astonishment at the amount Sidney said. It was more than she earned in two years of nursing. Unheard of.

Jonathan took the contract. "I'm also concerned about her safety as I am sure you can understand, given current events at your theater. Can you reassure me that you will provide Miss La Roux with some security? I'd like to add that to her contract."

Sidney penciled in the security agreement, and at Jonathan's insistence, Liberty signed on the dotted line. Sid took the contract and after folding it, opened his suit coat and stuffed it inside the inner pocket. "I'll see ya at the Broadway."

Jonathan leaned close to Liberty's ear. "Look who's here," he said, and pointed to where Talon Montgomery stood amongst the crowd.

"Hmmm," Liberty muttered. "He keeps turning up, doesn't he? Let me get this stage makeup off so we can go."

Talon fought his way backstage after Liberty's premier performance. He pushed his way through tall leggy dancers, people scurrying around, only to be rebuffed when he tried to enter the dancer's dressing room. Deafening female chatter came out of the room where the words *Mr. Foyle* was bantered around more than once.

He stood aside and watched as a group of performers, Liberty being one of them hung on the arm of her blond agent, as they exited. They got into a waiting taxi and drove off. Talon hailed a cab of his own and followed.

They stopped at *The Broadway* restaurant where Foyle and his party were escorted to a large round table in the back. Others from the theater came in and joined them.

Talon, managed to bribe a waiter into seating him as close to the group as possible. He ordered food and listened with his whole body as champagne popped at Foyle's table. Sidney Brawley, the Follies manager, was promising Liberty a starring role. He told how everyone in the theater had eyes on Liberty.

Talon agreed with Brawley, Liberty looked like a goddess on stage, tall, regal, and with the lights on her sheer costume, every man in the theater took on fantasies about her and became hard with those fantasies. Talon's cock had swollen, and was doing it again by just thinking about her. He was glad the white tablecloth brushed his lap and hid his pleasure. His hand went to his crotch where he squeezed, the excitement of having an orgasm in a public place added to his titillation. His nostrils flared, he continued to stare and listen, all the while caressing himself.

"I can't really sing, Mr. Brawley," Liberty said, her eyes going to Jonathan almost pleading for help.

"That's no problem," Brawley answered and puffed on his cigar, sending blue smoke toward the ceiling. "Haven't you heard of lip-syncing?"

"No, I haven't."

"Well, it's where someone else sings while you move your lips to the words. From afar it looks and sounds like you're the one singing. I'll arrange it and you can practice this week."

Jonathan leaned back in his chair. "My little canary can do whatever you ask of her. With practice, she'll be perfect by your next big show, almost as perfect as Zelda DeLane was. You must miss her amazing voice and style?"

Brawley's forehead knitted into lines as he shot a glance at his boss. "An unfortunate event. I hope they find the man that killed her, hang him high, just like Josette was found."

"Did they ever figure out if Josette Jackson killed herself, or if she was murdered?" Liberty asked.

Sid Brawley shrugged and held up two fingers squeezed together. "I have about as much confidence in the cops that I have space between these two fingers. They are all a bunch of idiots as far as I'm concerned. Those two gals were murdered and probably by the same person."

Jonathan leaned forward and met Brawley's gaze. "Have you heard any more about Zelda DeLane's murder?"

"Nothing. But with Jonathan Drake being guilty as hell, what's there to hear?" Brawley took Liberty's hand and kissed the back of it. He then picked up his champagne glass and held it high. "Here's to Miss La Roux who just tonight signed a new contract for seven-hundred a week. Gauging from tonight's acceptance of her, I expect her to be the most exciting person on the theater circuit." Champagne flutes chinked together as they made a toast to her success.

Dark-haired and diminutive, Anna Pellum Foyle, who so far hadn't said a word, spoke up, "Isn't that a lot of money for someone who can't even sing?" She caressed her husband's arm. "I mean, how long has Miss Fitzgerald been with us? Two weeks? She admits her talents as a performer are limited. She barely dances and can't sing. What are you doing, darling?" Her gaze at her husband was bold and defiant.

Foyle, gray-haired, with a sharp stare, raised his eyebrow at his wife. "Sidney is doing what he's asked to do. I listened and watched the audience tonight. They enjoyed Liberty. When she was in the chorus, she stood a headdress above the others." Foyle kissed Anna's hand. "Besides, when do I have to answer or explain my business operations to you, darling wife?"

Chastised, Anna removed her hand from her husband, and sipped her drink. Her dark eyes glared at Liberty over the rim of her glass.

Capucine, also at the table, wisely said nothing and instead lifted her glass and drained it.

Liberty already knew she'd made enemies at the theater, and now she could add Anna as one of them. Anna, who as Foyle's wife, could wield great power on stage and off. And, who it appeared was extremely jealous of other stars. She wondered just how jealous Anna had been of Zelda DeLane. Was it enough to get her out of the theater permanently?

But as Brawley's thigh brushed against Liberty's under the table, she forgot to dwell on Anna's displeasure. So, that's the going price for becoming a star. She glanced at Brawley who took his cigar out of his mouth and smiled at her. His face glistened with sweat, and he stank of cigar smoke. Could she do it, go to bed with this barrel-chested man? She prayed she would never have to show her gratitude for making so much money. Yet, repulsed by what she was doing, and like every other star before her, she played the part and placed her hand on his trouser-covered thigh and squeezed, offering herself as a prize goose. She wanted to be done with the whole sordid mess of show business, wanted to take her doctor's bag in hand, be a nurse again, but she didn't think that would ever happen.

His eyes glistened in the candlelight as his hand pulled hers tight against his scrotum. He leaned close to whisper, "You're well informed of what is expected of you. I like that. Later this week, I'll be expecting you in my office."

Breathing a sigh of relief, she glanced over at a nearby table and spotted Talon Montgomery sitting alone, eating his dinner. First the theater, and now here, anymore he always seemed to turn up wherever she was. But right now she saw him as a means to get her hand away from Sid Brawley's privates. Liberty signaled to the waiter.

"Would you send a glass of champagne to that table over there? He's an acquaintance of mine."

"Nothin' doin'." Brawley shook his head and snapped his fingers at the waiter. "Ask the man at that table to join us."

Jonathan, who was talking to Capucine, watched as the waiter moved Talon and his dinner to their table.

As introductions played out, Talon Montgomery smiled and acknowledged everyone at the table. Standing next to Liberty, he brought her hand to his lips where he kissed it and took the time to press his moist tongue against her skin. He straightened and smiled as if he knew a secret.

"A rising star to be sure," he said, and walked around the table to sit next to Anna.

When Talon's gaze lingered on Jonathan longer than necessary, Jonathan started coughing. He removed his white handkerchief from his breast pocket and coughed into it. When finished he turned his head to whisper in Liberty's ear. "I've got to leave and you know why." Again he coughed and sneezed.

Liberty's smile went around the table. "Mr. Edison's not feeling well. With all the flu that's about, he's decided to go home and rest." She looked at Jonathan who kept his handkerchief pressed against this mouth. He did a brief bow and mumbled his regrets before taking his leave.

Talon tipped his head, and said, "A wise decision, I'm sure." This time he studied Liberty. "Your agent looks familiar. I feel as if I've met him before."

"I believe he would have said something to that fact if you had. Mr. Edison never misses a chance to say hello to people he knows. But then again, he was sick. This flu frightens me. It's like no other illness, and it's rapidly spreading."

Foyle offered his opinion. "Indeed it is. If it gets any worse, I'll be forced to close the theater until it passes. Even with my two lovely stars drawing the crowds in, I've noticed attendance is down."

"And here I thought it was my performance driving them away," Liberty said, and they all laughed.

Talon said, "I doubt that. I'm a connoisseur of the theater, and when I say you did a wonderful job tonight, believe my every word."

Anna smirked. "Are you sure you're not confusing her with me on stage?" She fluffed her hair and tilting her chin met Talon's gaze.

"You're both beautiful women who dazzle all of us in the audience. Not one star outshines the other. You're magnificent." Talon nodded at Anna.

Liberty thought him a wise man who knew not to put his foot in his mouth.

Jonathan moved through couples that were linked arm and arm and who stopped to kiss. He walked down the sidewalk filled with families out on the town. As he went, he occasionally glanced into store windows, admiring the displays, yet still startled to see his blond reflection staring back.

Several blocks away from the theater he passed an overweight, gray-haired woman who paused to stare at him. When he tipped the brim of his hat at her, she looked at her theater program and walked right past him.

Continuing on he stared across the street at Grand's department store where he paused to look at the large clock centered above the opening. He pulled out his pocket watch to compare the time. Both were right on. He waited on the corner and signaled at an approaching taxi to stop. He got in the back and swung the door closed.

"The Drake Hotel, please."

Turning to look out the back window, he noticed the elderly woman he'd just passed also got into a cab. He chided himself, what could a hapless woman have to do with him, tonight? He was excited, actually tingling inside that he was meeting his father. A long time in coming and he couldn't wait. Confident that his disguise would allow him to walk by the front desk and to the room his father had for them. Again he turned to look out the rear window and noticed that the cab with the woman was nowhere to be seen. He relaxed against the seat. The cab pulled up in front of *The Drake* where people scurried on the sidewalk. All in a hurry to get to their destination. The heavy door to the hotel was in constant motion. Fred Hastings, the doorman, a prominent fixture at the hotel, stood at attention, speaking to those going in or out.

Jonathan paid the driver and exited the cab. His throat squeezed tight and he tried to swallow, but couldn't. An upward glance at the *The Drake's* looming presence gave him pride in his father's accomplishment, of his ancestor's, and here he was on a path to make it crumble around them. He felt small and insignificant, a turd floating down the East River.

After looking both left and right, he squared his shoulders and nodded at the middle-aged doorman whose stomach was straining the buttons on his red uniform.

"Good evening, sir." Fred Hastings nodded at Jonathan, and pushed open the glass door, causing a gust of warm air to carry the comforting smell of rich cigars, perfume, and the voices of the guests out onto the sidewalk.

The men behind the desk were busy handing out keys and helping patrons. No one looked his way or paid him any attention. Unwilling to chat with the elevator operator, he headed for the stairs and started to climb.

He rapped four times on the door of 411. Within seconds it opened and he was pulled into the room by his father who embraced him. His father's strong grip made him feel like a little boy again. Jonathan welcomed the feeling. The smell of bay rum cologne filtered around him, his father's scent, the same as always.

His dad finally put him at arm's length and looked him over. "My, God, you're as handsome with blonde hair as you are with black. I wouldn't have known you." His eyes glistened with tears.

"Dad, I don't know what to say, only thanks for everything. Liberty and I are trying hard to find the real killer, but it isn't easy. I'm afraid we won't find him before I'm caught."

"Jonathan, son…taking in consideration all that you have tried and what you're saying just now, perhaps it'd be best if I hired a private detective to help out. Would you mind?"

Jonathan shrugged. "That might help, but with me being labeled the murderer, I don't know that a private detective could discover any more than Liberty and I have."

"I'll give you a few more weeks, if nothing breaks, then I'm going to the Pinkerton Agency and hire someone. But let's not talk about that, right now." Lincoln went to the bathroom door and opened it. "Son, I have a surprise for you."

Jonathan's mother stepped out. Stylishly dressed in a blue

two-piece suit that brushed her ankles, she opened her arms and crossed the room in seconds.

He scooped her up, embraced her as tight as he dared, and started to sob. They stood that way for a long time. Mother and son, holding each other as if to let go would separate them forever. Her gardenia perfume brought memories of the beautiful mother who held him and read stories to him. Of goodnight kisses and sheets tucked tight. She reminded him of good moments and not so good, especially his heart breaking behavior toward her before Zelda's death. Disappointment. Would he be given the chance to make things right with her? His father? He prayed so.

She pulled back to look at him and smiled at his disguise. "I'm so glad you are not a blonde in real life. And now, let's take those silly glasses off." She removed the glasses and stuck them in his breast pocket.

"Dad, why in God's name did you involve Mother in this?" Jonathan led his mother to one of the leather bound chairs, and held her hand while she sat.

"Ha! You have the nerve to ask that? You who have lived with your mother long enough to know she's as good as having a law degree. That she can flush out anything she wants by wearing the person down. Well, she wore me out with her nagging questions about you. Accusing me. Telling me that I knew where you were. So, here she is, and by God, I'm glad I brought her."

"Me too," Jonathan said and laughed. He knew too well what his father was going through. His mother could have led an inquisition in the old days. Flogged the truth out of the person. "Mom, how's Lona?"

"She's not feeling well. Listless. Losing Darrell has broken her heart."

He longed to comfort Lona, tell her that her heart would heal, that her world would right itself in time. Would his world ever right itself? He took a deep breath. "I wish she was here."

Earlene reached out to touch his arm. "I know you do. But she can't be told about you. As your father says, the less she knows the better it is for her."

"Does mother know about Liberty Fitzgerald?" Jonathan asked.

"Yes. I've told her everything."

Earlene smiled and shook her head. "I can't wait to meet this Miss Fitzgerald. All of us owe so much to her, especially with her being brave enough to give up her nursing job and go into a somewhat dubious theatrical career."

"Miss Fitzgerald is someone special, very special." Jonathan said.

When silence settled between the three of them, Lincoln spoke up. "We plan on going to the Joyeux to see her perform. I trust you are giving a wide berth to that place?"

Jonathan rocked on his heels. "I can't. I'm her manager, remember? And I have to be there to try and find the killer. But, I must confess, we are not finding out much. Nothing that would help me in a court of law."

"Son, please sit," Lincoln pointed at the other chair next to Earlene's. "Would you care for a drink? How about you, Earlene?"

"Yes, I could use a whiskey right now," Jonathan said.

"Me too, darling."

Lincoln poured them all a drink. He handed Jonathan and Earlene theirs, and then taking his up, he joined them and sat on the bed. "We don't have long. I've ordered this room to be left empty for an hour only. I hope by doing so I haven't caused suspicion, as I've never requested a room left empty for an hour."

"Certainly not enough time for me to enjoy being with you both. But, I'll take what I can get." Jonathan clanked his glass against theirs. "To my innocence," he toasted, and tilting his glass, knocked the whiskey back in one gulp, enjoying the burn. He crossed his legs and dangled the glass in his hand.

Lincoln reached into the breast pocket of his suit and pulled out his money holder. He counted out six one-hundred dollar bills and gave them to Jonathan. "Do you have any idea who killed Miss DeLane?"

"No. My mind's a blank when it comes to that. There is…was…no reason for anyone to kill her." Jonathan accepted the offered cigar from his dad and the flaring match that followed.

"A jealous lover perhaps?" Lincoln puffed on his own cigar then leaned forward. "Son, I doubt you were the only one in her life she took to her bed. Were you aware that she kept more than one man on a string at the same time?"

"Dad—" Jonathan interrupted but Lincoln shushed him.

"You of all people know that actresses are a fickle bunch and spread their wares around. It's called financial gain, or solidifying one's income."

"Lincoln, darling, how would you know all of that?" Earlene darted a hurtful glare at her husband.

Lincoln grinned and held his hands up in mock surrender. "For God's sake, Earlene. I'm a professional man who knows about life. I…er…I have never taken an actress to bed. But I know that anyone in business, any type of business, wants to move ahead, make money, and be secure."

Jonathan tried to enjoy his cigar, the richness of its tastes, but it soured in his mouth and he stubbed it out in the ashtray. "Mom, you know Dad. That he loves you. That's not the issue here, right now. It's what Liberty is trying to find out, if anyone else was seen backstage that night. So far, anyone of interest is slow to material-ize." He sucked in a deep breath and rolled his empty glass be-tween his hands. "Those two detectives, Jones and Scala want me or I should say Emery Edison to come down to the precinct. I don't dare. By now they probably know that Emery Edison doesn't really exist."

Lincoln snuffed his cigar out and stood. "I agree, and imagine they have figured that out. Probably can't find a damn thing out about you before the killing. Be careful, Son, be extremely careful." He patted Jonathan on the shoulder.

Jonathan noticed that new lines had formed around his father's eyes and mouth. More gray invaded his dark hair and beard. "Dad," was all Jonathan could say before his throat closed tight and he willingly allowed his father to pull him into another embrace.

His mother stood and held out her arms to encompass both Jonathan and Lincoln. The three of them held one another tightly.

"Mom, I love you," he said, his voice breaking. Damn it, he didn't want to go. He longed to stay here with them. He wished to go where he pleased without wearing a scratchy disguise. Have Liberty next to him and walk out together in the daylight. Be free.

Earlene stood back and dabbed her tears that squeezed out.

"The next time we're together, I'll be a free man. I promise."

"I'm going to hold you to that promise, darling boy," she said, and drew in a deep shuddering breath.

"I'll lead you out of here," Lincoln said.

The phone jingled, and with a puzzled look on his father's face, Lincoln answered it. "Yes?" That was all he said before slamming the phones receiver back in place. "That was the desk. The detectives are here. Hurry—get to the roof, Jonathan! I'll try and head them off. Earlene, quick—can you go down the fire escape?"

"No, I can't. Give me a key to the room across the hall, I'll hide there."

"Don't let the cops see you," he said and handed her a skeleton key. "I'll come and get you when it's safe."

The woman, who had followed Jonathan Drake here, sat in a plush chair close to the front door and facing the elevators. After an hour of securitizing each and every guest coming and going, she was beginning to wonder how she'd missed the man she'd followed. She was the one who had made a phone call to the police precinct, to the detectives on the case, telling them that Jonathan Drake was in the hotel.

She no sooner stood when two men entered the hotel in a flourish and flashed their badges at the desk clerks. The woman smiled most salacious, and watched as one rushed toward the elevator and the other headed off in the direction of the stairs. She was most efficient in doing her job. But then she always did as ordered. Opening her clutch purse, she took out her mirror and stared at herself. Man or woman, it didn't matter, her disguise was better than Jonathan Drake's ever could be.

Jonathan hurried toward the stairs leading to the roof. He could hear footfalls not far below. Trying to stay out of sight, he slipped off his shoes, tied the laces together and slung them over his shoulder. He hurried up the darkened stairwell with only a simple electric light on the wall to guide him. But he'd taken these steps many times from when he was a little boy and then as a grownup, especially when an irate husband found out about his wife's little adventure with playboy Drake. His long legs propelled him upwards, taking the stairs three at a time. Behind him came the faint clump of the detective's shoes as he noisily climbed.

When he reached the rooftop door, Jonathan opened it and closed it silently behind him. He put his shoes back on and ran in a crouched position, heading toward the adjoining roof. He listened as the door opened and slammed shut. Light-footed and swift, he sprinted to the next roof and the next. When he came to a roof separated by several feet or more, he backed up and ran, leaping into the air, landing with a crash and feeling the pain of airless lungs. He crawled to hide behind the cooling shaft to catch his breath. His pounding heart sounded like a kettle drum. He waited and not detecting anyone coming after him, he used the stairs and escape ladder to drop down to the sidewalk.

He brushed the dirt from his suit and straightened his cuffs. Once again, he hurried toward his sanctuary and Liberty who he knew would be waiting.

Lincoln pulled an unsuspecting maid inside his room forcing the towels she carried to fly out of her hands. Seeing a wide-eyed Earlene peeking out the slit in the open door across the hall, he signaled for her to shut the door.

Ordering the slim maid to ask no questions, Lincoln helped her strip to her corset cover and jump into the bed. He quickly lit his cigar and pocketed the one Jonathan had been smoking. He splashed whisky into Jonathan's and Earlene's empty glasses and handed one to the open-mouthed maid. He snatched her maid's cap from her head making her reddish-blond hair escape its pins and tumble around her face. Next he flung off his suit coat and tie, toed off his shoes, dropped his trousers and shirt, and dived onto the bed where he took the startled maid by the chin and kissed her soundly.

"Act like you're enjoying me," he urged, and listened to the key turning in the lock. The door was flung open revealing Detective Scala standing there.

As if on cue, the maid screamed and pulled the covers up to her throat. Lincoln jumped from the bed and stood in his underwear. "What in the hell is the meaning of this?" he sputtered, wearing his affront to no end.

Detective Scala, with disappointment shrouding his face, ignored Lincoln and pushed passed him. Going first into the bathroom where he did a quick look around, he returned to the bedroom, and groaning, he got down on his knees to peer under the bed.

"Where's Jonathan Drake?" he asked, as his face flushed from exertion. He wiped his face with a handkerchief.

Lincoln grabbed his pants and shirt, and got dressed. "I don't know what you're talking about. I haven't seen Jonathan since the night of the murder. Your insistent spying on me is getting tiresome."

"Who are you?" Scala asked the maid.

She stuttered, "Lizzie Fields…I'm…a Lizzie Fields."

"Are you Mister Drake's lover?"

"For the moment, yes. I mean…er…that I'm Mister Drake's latest." Her brow furrowed over brown eyes that now rested on her employer.

He was quick to come to her rescue. "I was bored at home, so came here to have a little romp with Lizzie. My wife you see…ah…doesn't give me what I want. Lizzie or any maid working here does and can." Lincoln lied through his teeth, willing to give up his spotless reputation to save his son. "I trust you will use discretion and not inform my wife of this?" He looked at the door left wide open by the cops. He stared across the hall where Earlene hid and where her door silently closed. She'd heard all that was said.

Detective Scala's glance at Lincoln was sly, as if he'd heard it a dozen times before. He pocketed his notebook. "I want to talk with you in private." He nodded towards the door.

Lincoln gritted his teeth and ground out. "There is nothing to

say. But I'd like to know why you are here in my hotel and harass-
ing me." He shut the door behind him and stood in his stocking
feet, glaring at the detective.

"Mr. Drake, we got wind that your son, Jonathan Drake was
here," Scala said.

Surprised, Lincoln squared his shoulders, his jaw. "I think
someone was playing games with you. Jonathan never comes
around here. I suggest you start trying to find who killed Miss
DeLane because my son is innocent. He isn't capable. You're wasting time—mine and yours." Inwardly, Lincoln prayed that Jonathan got clean away, for if he didn't, his own world would crumble
along with his son's.

It wasn't long before the other detective, Jones came up to
Scala and shook his head. He took his handkerchief from his
breast pocket, flapped it open, and wiped sweat that trickled down
the sides of his face and forehead. "If Drake was here he got away
and I sure as hell didn't hear anyone on the stairs. I could have
been following a ghost." He folded his hanky and shoved it into
his pocket.

"We'll be leaving you. Sorry to have interrupted
your…ah…indiscretion," Scala said.

When Jones's brows knitted in question, Scala said, "I'll fill
you in later. Let's go."

Lincoln watched the detectives head for the stairs before going back inside the room. Lizzie Fields had dressed and stood next
to the bed.

Lincoln pulled out his wallet and took out several large bills.
"I'm buying your silence here, Miss Fields. Praying that in your
heart you will stick to our story."

She accepted the money and did a quick curtsy. "I have sealed
lips, Mr. Drake. I need my job."

"That's good to hear. And now, I'll leave you to clean this

mess." He put on his shoes, his suit coat, and running his hands through his hair, he did a quick glance around the room before going to rescue Earlene.

Scala and Jones walked away from *The Drake*, and away from getting their man. The crowds around the hotel started to thin with the occasional guests still arriving.

Shoving his hands in his pockets and wanting to beat the hell out of anyone named Drake, Jones practically roared, "After that major screw up, I need a cup of coffee."

Scala matched Jones' scowl with one of his own. "I'd call it a major fuck up. I need more than a cup of coffee."

The two headed toward a restaurant midway down the block.

Jones opened the door of the bistro. Inside, it was noisy with chatter, smoke-filled, and a lot of scurrying to and fro by waiters. A friendly mustached waiter seated them off to the side at a square table with a white tablecloth. A flickering candle stuck in a wine bottle lit the area. After taking their drink order, the waiter left them to peruse the menu.

"I busted in on Lincoln Drake in bed with a maid." Scala laughed and looked at his partner. "So what we hear about the mighty sin-free Lincoln Drake turns out to be false."

Jones couldn't help but smile back and raise his brow. "Could be. But maybe not. True, you did walk in on Drake without knock-ing, and giving him a chance to stage the place, but..."

"What do you mean, but?"

"While you searched the room, did you notice anything out of the ordinary?"

Scala glanced at the ceiling in thought. He snapped his fingers. "Hell yes! Now that you mentioned it, I noticed several folded towels were on the floor right inside and outside the door, like the maid dropped them. Maybe from being pulled unexpectedly inside the room. Spur of the moment type of thing."

Jones nodded. "My conclusion exactly."

The waiter brought their coffee and after taking their orders, quickly left. Both men sipped their black coffee.

"Pulling a maid into the room at the last second would go along with Drake's reputation of never cheating on his wife." Scala frowned and took another sip. He grimaced and said, "This coffee tastes like shit, makes me sorry I gave up my whiskey flask."

Jones chuckled. "You probably don't know what coffee taste like without lacing it with spirits. When did you give up your flask?"

Scala flipped his suit coat open and tapped the flask he still carried in the inside pocket. "Right now, trying to be a good cop. And out of respect for my partner who makes my life miserable when I do take a drink."

The waiter arrived with steaming plates and put them on the table.

Scala's meal was a mouth-watering thick steak, potatoes, gravy and asparagus.

Jones was having breakfast. Three eggs, sausage, toast, and pancakes with maple syrup.

"So," said Scala, "did you see any sign of Jonathan Drake on the roof?"

Jones blew out a deep breath. "No. Didn't hear him on the stairs either. But then he'd know his way around the hotel in the dark. The man is like an eel that slips around, eluding us."

"Just like this Emery Edison person."

Jones stared at Scala. "Yeah, the man who doesn't exist, or should I say the agent who up until Miss DeLane and Josette Jackson were murdered didn't exist. Makes one wonder doesn't it."

Scala cut his steak, making pink blood ooze out. He put a half done piece in his mouth, chewed and then took a sip of coffee to wash it down. "I have my thoughts on that. Hope I'm right." He used his fork to point at Jones. "Regardless, whoever tipped us had something of interest. Knew what they were talking about."

Jones dipped his toast into the yolk and put the dripping piece in his mouth. He chewed and swallowed. He took another loud slurp of his coffee and rattled the cup against the saucer. "Sergeant did say it was a female who called, right?"

"Sure was. Nice soft feminine voice." Scala buttered a roll and bit into it, taking half of it into his mouth. Butter trickled across his pudgy fingers that he licked before wiping the rest on his napkin. "Someone certainly knows more about this case then we do."

Jones noticed and smiled at the elderly woman seated in the table next to them. Elderly and alone, how sad.

Liberty, having arrived home by a cab that Mr. Foyle insisted on paying for, wondered what had detained Jonathan. The hour was late, after midnight. Longing to undress and go to bed, she hesitated to do so in case she had to go search for him, but where?

She put the kettle on and glanced around. With the money she now made, she could afford a bigger place. But who was she to put on airs. After proving Jonathan's innocence she planned on returning to her nursing job and her low wages. When she cashed her first paycheck from the theater, she would give some to her dad, her brothers, and then most of it to the Wald foundation. To Liberty, the money was made in deceit, but could be put to good use.

The tea kettle started whistling just as the key rattled in the door. Snatching the kettle off the burner, she hurried into the living room. Jonathan stepped inside. Sweaty, dirty, his mustache was askew and his beard was missing.

Liberty locked the door behind him. "My—God—Jonathan,

what happened? What went wrong?"

"Plenty." He shrugged out of his filthy suit coat and hung it on the hat rack.

She took him by the hand and led him into the kitchen where she filled a wash basin with water and put a washcloth and bar of soap in it.

"I hate this damn wig." He took it off and threw it onto the floor.

"We're going to have to buy new, this is all damaged. Where are your glasses?"

"In my suit coat pocket, I guess."

She pulled loose what remained of his mustache and fake eyebrows, revealing the man she loved best with his jet black hair. After dipping the washcloth into the water and soaping it up good, she started washing his face. His eyes, those glorious shades of sky blue, peered at her. When she had his face clean, he took her hands within his and turning her palms upright, tenderly kissed each one.

"I'm tired of running. Tonight I placed my father in serious jeopardy. My mother was there. I don't know how it turned out for him, but I was almost caught by those detectives, Jones and Scala." He took off his tie, shirt, and threw them to the floor.

"Don't despair, we are close to finding the killer," she said and tried to smile, but couldn't. She knew within her heart that they weren't experienced enough to find a dead mouse, let alone the cat that killed it. "But, until we do find the killer, it's time you stay with Dad in my brother Teague's flat. It isn't under any kind of surveillance like mine. And, maybe you should consider staying away from the theater, especially with Scala and Jones always snooping around."

"I thought I was safe with the disguise." He flicked an ironic smile.

"Not if someone has seen through it and knows it's you. And that person who has seen through your disguise also knows everything about you. I've come to the conclusion we've been going about this all wrong. Jonathan, please think strongly of who constantly visits the theater and who would know your routine concerning Zelda."

"Are you referring to Talon Montgomery?"

"Yes, I am. From the back you and he look a lot alike."

Turning the faucet on, he put his head under the running water and let it sluice over his hair. When he straightened, Liberty dried his hair and torso, all the while meeting his wary gaze.

"Know what I like about you?" he asked, and when she shook her head, he said, "Your faith in me, that I'm innocent. Sometimes I feel that with you in my corner we can prove all the wrongs in the world. But reality encroaches and I know within my heart that we can't. Hell, we can't even find Zelda's killer."

"If we could just convince those detectives of your innocence their time would be better spent finding the real murderer." An errant droplet of water dripped from a lock of his hair onto his chest. She dabbed at it with the towel, stopping to kiss his chest. Compelled to do so, she rubbed her lips across his thick chest hair, loving how it tickled. Tonguing his nipple, she forced it to peak into a hard nub, hoping to take his mind off the brick wall they were up against.

His face was covered with concern as he stopped her. Taking the towel from her he put it on the counter. "Liberty, you know that I can't offer you anything beyond the here and now." He palmed her face, his thumbs caressing her cheeks. "God knows I don't want to hurt you."

"There is nothing between us, so how can you hurt me?" she answered, her lie piercing her heart a little more. How she longed to tell him that she'd fallen in love with him. It had happened along the way and she hadn't seen it coming. Her eyes became moist.

His gaze traveled over her face, searching, and then he said, "I wonder when my tastes went from blondes to a fiery redhead with a heart of gold.

She couldn't help but smile at his comment and watched him untie his shoes and take them off. While kneeling, he removed her shoes, treating her as though she were made of glass. Sexual anticipation flared between them and she helped him to stand. He lowered his head, and she met his lips with tenderness and heat. His fingers wove into her hair, feeling around, finding the combs holding her hairdo in place. He pulled them loose allowing her hair to tumble around her shoulders in a bright copper halo. She nipped up his throat until she reached his chin where she kissed his stubble and moved on to his lips. Soft and warm he tasted as her tongue sought his. He allowed her to search, tantalizing him, teasing him. She sought his pants where she loosened his belt and pulled his suspenders off his wide shoulders. She opened his fly and pushed his pants over his hips. He began his arduous task of getting her out of clothes. Lacy corset cover, lacy corset, frilly drawers, white hose, all landed in a heap.

"I warn you," he said in a husky voice. "There's no stopping me this time."

"Then don't stop."

Excitement rippled through her when he gently lifted her into his arms and carried into her bedroom. Her body craved his, wanted him inside her, wanted fulfilled, as if it would be the last thing they would do together.

Without turning the light on, he placed her on the bed. The light from the living room filtered in, placing them in shadows as he lay beside her and ran his hand over the curve of her hip, her ribcage and up over her breast that he cupped. He tongued her nipple, the feeling so wanton that she moaned and allowed him to have his way, teach her the art of making love. His fingers sought her cleft and its hidden delights.

"Touch me," he commanded and encouraged her to explore him, and she obeyed. Gently, she cupped his sacs, causing him to groan and guide her hand to wrap around his penis.

"Come here, nurse," he said and pulled her up to sit on top of him. "You're so beautiful. I can't get my fill, will never get my fill of you." He snaked his hands up over her breasts, delighting her with his deft lovemaking. He reached to the back of her neck where he pulled her down into his kiss. He rolled her over and landed on top of her. "Do you want me inside you?"

She ran her hands over his chest, skimming her fingers through dark chest hair. His body was well-shaped and she craved every inch. "Yes, oh yes. I've waited for this, for what seems forever."

She sucked his bottom lip into her mouth, she played.

His hand parted her legs and his fingers quested, feeling her, inside and out, sending delicious heat with every touch. And when he had her moist and almost crazy with desire, he asked, "Do you want me now?"

She nodded, her eyes locked onto his, her mouth swollen from kisses. "Yes, make it now."

"Tell me if I hurt you." Knowing this was the first time for her, he slowly guided himself into her. She moaned and a brief shiver rippled throughout her whole being.

"Are you all right?" he asked.

"Fine…I'm enjoying every part of you."

He was gentle. He pushed, until her body allowed him inside hers. Jonathan began a slow rhythm, the bed springs creating a lulling tempo all their own. His was a lesson in lovemaking and she the willing pupil. She wrapped her long legs around him pulling him into her as much as possible. He became wild with urgency like this was the last time they'd ever be together, intimately.

Afterward, they lay together, his arm around her and her one leg thrown across his thighs.

Liberty could overlook that no words of love were uttered by him. And even if he did say the words she longed to hear, how could he commit to loving her when his future might include a slow walk to an electric chair.

Chapter Sixteen

Alice, wearing a negligée of sheer blue crêpe with lace trim, waited in her bedroom, listening for either Talon or Jenny to appear. She sat propped up in bed with several fluffy pillows behind her trying to read a book. Concentration eluded her. Her nerves were frayed, on edge. Across the room, her lovebirds softly trilled to each other underneath their covered cage.

A soft feminine knock on her door foretold that Jenny had arrived.

"Come in," she eagerly called out, and watched as Jenny came in and took her time closing the door behind her, locking it. Alice held out her arms, beckoning.

Jenny, wearing a smug grin of success, crossed the room and in swift movements, she turned off the electric lamp next to the bed, peeled off her clothes, and went to throw open the thick velvet curtains of lavender. She postured, standing like a warrior princess with her strong body, her full breasts and dark thatch lit by the moon outside.

"Do you want the pipe?" Jenny asked and was already going

to the wardrobe for their pleasure.

"Not tonight, I'm too anxious. I need to know what happened. Please tell me." Alice opened her sheets allowing Jenny to slip between them. Her body was cold against Alice's. "My dear, Jenny, you're so cold. Here let me warm you."

They snuggled, bodies pressed together, hands seeking feminine places, their mouths closing over the other's, tongue's searching.

At last, when Alice could no longer contain her curiosity, she spoke. "Did anything interesting happen tonight?"

Jenny chuckled, making her breasts jiggle underneath Alice's hand. "Plenty and it's just as you suspected. How astute you are."

"Once you have a man in your arms, you're not likely to forget his face, the contours of his head, nor the shape of his lips. I'm happy to know my suspicions are true." It was Alice's turn to chuckle and pinch Jenny's nipple into a firm point.

Jenny slid her arm behind Alice's head and pulled her close. "You forgot to mention the shape of his cock. Is he large, is he small, is he fast or is he slow."

"Shame on you, Jenny," Alice couldn't help but laugh at the thought. "But alas, I never knew what was inside of Jonathan's pants. Oh, we courted, he felt me and I felt him, somewhat. But you must remember, I was a chaste young thing and behaved myself."

"How boring a life you led."

"But no longer, thanks to you, Jenny, thanks to you. Please tell me that your call to the police was successful, that they got their man?"

"No. He got away. Tell me, sweet Alice, what are you going to do about Jonathan Drake and Liberty Fitzgerald?"

Alice put her finger across her lips and hemmed and hawed. "I'm not sure. If our plans had come to fruition tonight, we would have gotten rid of one, and had one left. For now, we've done enough by alerting the detectives that Jonathan was at the Drake. I'm just disappointed that they bungled their job and lost him. But still, we certainly know where he's hiding, don't we?"

"Do you want me to make another call? This time telling where they will find Jonathan...ah...Emery Edison?"

"Not yet. I like playing this game, pulling strings. Poor Jonathan, here lately he's always at the wrong place at the wrong time. You know, years ago, I actually wanted him to ask me to marry him. But he didn't. He was too much of the playboy, and only gave me what he wanted me to have, bits and pieces of his life. Certainly, I wasn't good enough for him to marry."

"Your father's dream but not yours?"

"Something like that, at first. But I did come to love Jonathan. I wasn't the cripple I am now. I was a woman who could dance, flirt, and ride horses."

Jenny took Alice's face and turned it toward her own. "You're that woman, don't forget, you're still that woman very much." She placed Alice's hand between her legs. She shifted allowing Alice's fingers to probe even deeper.

And so I am...thought Alice. Remembering, always remembering how it was to be held in Jonathan's arms while they danced, the magic his life brought to hers. But no matter how she tried, it was beyond her ability to make him love her. He was always looking around the next corner for another conquest. But that was another life, and it was sad that he was blamed for Zelda's murder. But now that he was, it had become very convenient for her to have the police think so. And, here she was tied to Talon, a man with no ambition other than to pocket her father's money. Oh...how...she would show her husband that she wasn't the sick, cloyingly, meek parasite that he called her. Somehow, she was going to make him pay.

When Jenny began kissing her abdomen, everything that Jenny told her about tonight simply flittered out of her mind. She moaned as Jenny kissed her pubic curls and then tongued her deeply.

Talon pressed his ear against his wife's bedroom door. Hearing the moans coming from within, his mouth creased into an all-knowing smile. And he whispered a prayer of thanks to Jenny for taking over his duties as a husband. He'd come to abhor even touching Alice.

Putting his hands in his pants pockets, he walked down the hall to his bedroom where he unlocked the door and entered. Crossing the room he stopped next to the tall dresser which held his personal items and opened his gold cigarette case. He removed a ready-made cigarette that he lit. Puffing on it, he opened the window, and stood there blowing smoke out into the cold night air, wondering how this was all going to end. After smoking the cigarette to a nub, he left the window and went to stub it out in the crystal ashtray on his nightstand.

He figured he had about an hour before Jenny felt it safe enough to slip inside his room. She'd come wearing Alice's pussy smell on her mouth like lip rouge, and wanting to ride a real man's cock. Well, he'd be waiting and most happy to oblige.

Talon removed his black suit coat, arranged it carefully on the wooden valet, and brushed off a few pieces of lint. After stripping down nude, he took his clothes and hung them in the large closet where his shoes, pants, and shirts were neatly arranged. No one could ever accuse him of being slovenly; tidiness was what he was all about. Neat and tidy.

Remembering how he lived as a young boy, he couldn't stand dirt, slovenly people or poverty. Brought up in San Francisco without a father, he ran errands for his widowed mother who owned a dress making shop. He'd lived in places Alice and her parents never knew existed, or if they did, they would never be able to put their minds on how it was to live hand to mouth, and have bill collectors knocking on the door.

When Talon grew into a virile man in his early twenties, he came to appreciate the red light district and whores who crooked a finger at him, called him pretty man, and gave him what he wanted for practically free. He became an artist at fucking and his brush was his phallus.

He'd still be in the city by the bay if the earthquake hadn't happened. His mother's business along with her in it was flattened. The whorehouses with the rouged-cheeked women and overflowing corseted breasts were gone in a pile of rubble and fire. With flames nipping at his heels, Talon made it to his mother's shop where he tried to find the cigar box where she hid her money. Still in bed, and pinned by a ceiling beam, she held out her hand to him, pleading.

"Where's the money!" he yelled

"Help me," was all she could say as blood trickled out of her mouth.

He jerked her head up by the hair, and with disbelief covering her face, she pointed to where the box was.

"Son, help me!" she screamed.

As the air became hot with the fast encroaching fire and the tinny sound of the horse-drawn fire wagons with the firemen urging them on, Talon found the blessed money. Without so much as another look his mother's way, he left.

The box, still smelling of cigars, held a wad of neatly stacked bills. Twenties, and ten's, all together, it came to three-hundred dollars. He tossed the box into the crackling flames, and put the money in his money clip. Schooners were sailing constantly out of

San Francisco headed toward the east coast. He bought a ticket for New York and sailed away from the old and into the new.

Life's little knock-outs as he called them seem to cycle in and out of his life in increments. Never having a father around was the first. His mother's death was the second. And although he would never think to call what he did to her as murder, he'd certainly left her to burn to death in the rubble. Did he have qualms over it, no he didn't. His third big leap was causing Alice's accident on the horse. But in his mind that wasn't his fault either. Hell, horses were an unpredictable lot, and so was the man he'd hired to frighten her. But nothing compared to his grand finale, Josette. The woman would still be alive if she hadn't gotten herself with child. He did have to admit that her death was the hardest. Her last performance he called it.

He'd waited for her at her apartment. Only this time he was the one in the bed, between not so clean sheets that gave him the shivers. Excited to see him, she'd stripped off her clothes and joined him. He roughed her up, pretending it was what she wanted, but she protested, saying he might hurt the baby.

The mere mention of what he wanted to forget further enraged him. He suggested they go get something to eat and she agreed. She said she was sick most mornings and talked him into letting her quit the revue. They went to the theater so she could gather her personal stuff from her dressing room. The theater was dark and empty. He said he wanted to see what the stage looked like in total quiet and guided her there.

He picked up a rope from the floor. "Come here, Josette."

"What are you doing?" Upon realization, her pretty face blanched, and seeing the rope in his hands, she tried to run.

He grabbed her by the necklace and jerked her back against him. "I told you I'd take care of you, didn't I?"

"No!" she screamed.

She fought like a wild woman, slapping at him, scratching at his face, drawing blood. Enraged, he slammed her against the floor. Her eyes were wide and accusing, she shrieked, kicked. He tightened the rope around her neck and pulled. Her eyes bulged; she grasped at the rope and struggled.

His face turned red with exertion, hers turned purple.

He continued to squeeze. Finally she went limp, and when he was certain she was dead, he hauled her body up to the balcony. He took care to remove her clothes, fold them all nice and tidy. All the while she stared at him with lifeless eyes.

He hung her from the balcony. Her body swayed back and forth. To him, she looked like an angel without wings…

…With a groan of pleasure, he slipped into his bed, liking the sound of the crisp sheets that he insisted upon having changed every day. His hand wrapped around his erect penis that the mere thoughts of Josette's murder brought on. He stroked himself. *Ahh…Jenny, you better hurry*, he chuckled. He cared not for the woman, only that she was fiery in bed and she kept him abreast of what was going on in Alice's small world.

Chapter Seventeen

Jonathan sat on the lone chair in Keegan's Fitzgerald's flat, brooding. The space was small with a sofa, the chair and a bureau with a lamp and a few framed pictures on top. It had a kitchenette with a cook stove, a bedroom that fit a bed, a dresser, and nothing else. One wall close to the front door held an oval shaped picture of Teague Fitzgerald posing in his army uniform. What Jonathan could make of the man, he looked like all the Fitzgerald's. Just this week Keegan had received a letter from Teague and shared it with Jonathan. The letter said that Teague was stationed in Spain, that he was fine now but had been ill with the Spanish Influenza. Hundreds of soldiers died with the illness. And like everyone else, Teague thought the war would soon be over.

Keegan came from the kitchenette area holding two glasses of Irish whiskey. He handed one to Jonathan and then sitting in his chair, he held it high in a toast.

"Sláinte," he said.

"Sláinte," Jonathan echoed.

They both downed their whiskey in one gulp.

Keegan fit a white cigarette paper into the roller, and tapping tobacco out from a drawstring bag onto the paper, he rolled a cigarette for Jonathan. After handing the cigarette to Jonathan, Keegan took his pipe from the end table and proceeded to tamp tobacco in the bowl using his finger. Taking out a wooden match, he scratched it against the side of the matchbox. It flared and he leaned forward to light Jonathan's cigarette, and then his own pipe. He puffed, releasing the flavorful smoke inside room.

After taking several more puffs, Keegan relaxed against the back of the sofa eyeballing Jonathan as if he was the devil himself. And Jonathan knew that's what Liberty's father thought of him. The devil.

Jonathan stood and asked, "Want another whiskey?"

"Don't mind if I do," he said and handed over his glass.

Jonathan returned with the drinks and gave Keegan's his. Sitting down again, Jonathan said, "I'm going to see Liberty tonight."

"Lad, that's not a good idea. Liberty told ye to stay away from the theater. Ye should listen."

"I know. It's just that I want to be with her. Especially before I leave for Quebec." He sipped the whiskey, feeling the burn it put in the back of his throat and all the way to his stomach. He still bore bruises from his escaping run from the Drake hotel and ensuing rooftops. With both he and his dad almost getting caught at the hotel, Lincoln thought it best for Jonathan to leave the country, and had purchased a ticket for him to sail in a few days. As much as he wanted too, Jonathan couldn't take Liberty with him. But with Jonathan safely out of the country the time had come for his dad to hire a private detective.

"Ye know," Keegan said and smiled, "My girl reminds me of her mother. Full of spit and fire, even in the old country, my Mona was. She could wallop anyone who gave her displeasure, and a lot of people did."

"You don't think much of my kind, do you?" Jonathan asked.

"What d'ye mean by yer kind?"

"Well, rich."

"It's the other way around isn't it? Ye don't think much of my kind. The poor."

"You're right, not until I met Liberty did I have any thoughts for the working class, the lower class, and the destitute."

"Ye still don't know what it's like to be destitute. Now if Liberty hadn't found ye that day on the roof, and ye had to fend totally for yourself, then ye might know the meanin'. Destitute is what I was back in Ireland. Back before I brought me family here to America. I was a furniture maker in the old country. Tying to earn a livin' by ownin' a small shop. I'd make a coin or two. Buy food, a scrap here, a scrap there. My lads were little. Teague was five and Blaine a mere three. My mum and Da were both alive then. My Mona was a midwife. She'd help women bring their wee ones into the world.

"One day she was helpin' a young mother deliver her second child when the baby was turned and not wantin' to come out. I went for the doctor, but when we got there, it was too late. The young mother was dead, the child dead, and the husband in a rage. He attacked my Mona, cut her arm something terrible. I fought the man off, but things were never the same. He made it his life's goal to torture us. He burnt down my store and saw to it that no one would hire my Mona to deliver their babies. I'm certain this is where Liberty got her wanting to be a nurse from. Her mam.

"It took me two years workin' odd jobs to scrape enough to purchase passage for us. By then, Liberty was growin' in me wife's belly. I vowed I'd never let another child of mine grow up listening to the kind of hatred the young husband kept spewin' about us. It wasn't fair. So I brought us here to a country that I thought bigotry wasn't a word even known. But it was and is."

"Are you meaning the classes? The rich the poor?"

Keegan nodded. "I guess I am."

"Mr. Fitzgerald, not all rich men are snobs. A lot of wealthy tycoons who built railroads, banks, and hotels, started out as poor as you claimed to be. Someone has to start somewhere." He tapped his head. "And someone has to have the idea, put money, sweat, and the shirt off their backs to make it happen. And when they are lucky enough that it does happen, who can blame them for hiring workers, make a go of it?"

"I don't begrudge anyone becomin' successful and I don't begrudge the gap. What I do dislike is the actions of some who are rich and feel they are above all others. I hate the distain they have for us. And like ye said, someone has to do the work to make a business a success. I'd like to believe that my furniture making has been a big factor in the success of the company I work for. My designs that is." He patted the sturdy chair arm and smiled. "This is my design. Came out of my noggin. I like it."

Jonathan leaned forward, his cigarette ash falling on the floor. "You know, when I get out of this mess, my name cleared and all, I'd like to show your designs to my father. I bet he could use them in his hotel suites."

"Have ye learned anything, lad? Have ye learned enough about us on this side of the City to see we're not as ye envisioned us to be?"

Jonathan stubbed his cigarette out in the ash tray. "I've learned a lot from Liberty. And I've changed from that self-centered playboy I was, to someone more fruitful, someone who cares about the other person on this side of the City."

"Well, lad, we're going to see how convincing ye are because yer going to come clean with Blaine who is on his way here. Blaine's a bitter man. Accordin' to him, the world is against him. He thinks there's no hope for the rich. In his book yer all a bunch of assholes." Taking several more puffs on his pipe, he laid it on the ashtray.

A loud knock sounded on the door and Blaine Fitzgerald opened it and stuck his head in. "Da, it's me. I'm here without my family, just like ya asked."

"Come in, son, come in." Keegan beckoned Blaine inside. "I have someone I want ye to meet. But, ye have to be careful and not fly off the handle as yer known to do." He motioned for Jonathan to join them.

Jonathan once again faced Liberty's brother. He watched as Blaine squinted, studied him, and finally said, "We've already met, aye? Thought there was something phony about ya. You're not Emery Edison, are you?"

When Jonathan nodded and started to speak, Keegan cleared his throat. "Well me lad, yer right on all accounts. This man is Jonathan Drake."

Blaine tipped his head in thought, again Jonathan could see the wheels turning trying to place the name. "Ah...yeah...now I remember. Jonathan Drake, your name was in all the newspapers. You're the man who murdered that star at the theater."

"I didn't kill her," Jonathan blurted.

Keegan spoke up, "Yer sister's been helping Jonathan here prove his innocence."

"In whose eyes!" Blaine's hands formed tight fists. "Innocent—hell! How do you know he's innocent? How does Liberty know for sure?"

"Calm down, lad, just calm down," Keegan ordered.

Jonathan stepped back an arm's length out of Blaine's reach, just in case he let fly with his fabled Fitzgerald temper. "I care deeply for your sister. She cares enough to help me."

Blaine smirked. "I should turn your sorry ass in. Let the police haul ya out of here."

"Hold on there me boy. Your sister believes he's not guilty. He's been staying with her for weeks now. Iffen he meant to harm her, he'd done so by now." Keegan put his arm around his son's shoulder. "Blaine, for once in yer life, can't ye see the good in someone? Want to help them? Turn the other cheek? If I can accept Mr. Drake here as being truthful so should you. I say he's an honorable man who someone has framed. Teague's place here is the last bastion for him to hide out."

"Why are ya tellin' me?" Blaine stuffed his fists in his pockets and rocked on his heels, his temper squelched to a simmer. "What can I do?"

Jonathan seeing this, said, "I'd like to shake your hand as the real me with no deceit, Drake to Fitzgerald. I just need you on my side, to help me and your sister if needed. Let me tell you my side of things, my story, and see what you think when I'm done. And, if you're still of a mind to punch me, I'll let you do it."

Blaine stared at Jonathan's outstretched hand. Finally and appearing reluctant to do so, he shook hands. "No matter what, I'm a Fitzgerald. My word is like granite. I'll help ya, nor will I betray ya. But, if you harm a hair on my sister's head, I will kill you."

"I'll drink to that," Keegan said and went to get the whiskey and another glass.

Chapter Eighteen

Liberty sat at her dressing room table powdering her face, neck and shoulders with a large, fluffy powder puff. She'd begged Jonathan to lay low and stay away from the theater. They both felt the noose tightening around him. Someone knew who he was as Emery Edison, and that same someone also knew he was at the hotel and alerted the detectives.

With Jonathan hiding out at her father's flat she couldn't go see him for fear of being followed. And both admitted they were running out of options. The theater turned into a dead end with no clues and no slip of the tongue to point out who the murderer might be. Jonathan was so discouraged that he talked of giving himself up. She'd argued with him, asking for more time, and no way was he to even consider going to the police. Yet, they both felt that someone with a whole lot of knowledge was looking over their shoulders. And now, with the current happenings at *The Drake* hotel, it was out of their hands. Despite her arguing against it, Lincoln Drake was sending Jonathan out of the country. Neither Lincoln nor Jonathan would tell her where or how, only that he was leaving soon. It was better she didn't know.

Liberty's shared dressing room was normally filled with laughter and jokes. Tonight there was no laughter, only muted discussions between Liberty, Simone, Fantine, and Magnolia, who all sat at the well-lit dressing table putting finishing touches to their makeup.

Simone, along with Fantine, and Magnolia, were a step-up from the regular chorus dancers and two steps below the big stars. The three went on stage before Liberty and did a ballerina act. When they were done, the lights were dimmed and they blended in with the rest of the chorus girls doing a slow runway walk, showing off the ornate costumes that were the envy of all the theaters.

Apollo, the weight-lifter, and Simone's lover, had his own act and had already gone on for the night. Still wearing his costume, fitted tights over bulging muscles, he stood teasing Simone about something that happened earlier in the day while taking a stroll in Central Park.

Fantine, sitting next to Liberty, appeared listless and was coughing even more. Her eyes were red, making Liberty wonder if she was coming down with the flu, and if so, how the girl was going to get through her routine.

Mick, doing his duty, poked his head in. "Ladies, you're on in five. Get out there."

"Mick," said Fantine as she approached him, "I'm too sick to work."

"You're a little late in tellin' me this. Ya hafta go on." He scoffed. "There's no one else. Liberty, you have twenty minutes to get your ass out there. Don't lag."

The three women with their toe shoes clicking against the wooden floor, and looking like fairy tale princess's in their frilly white tutu's, just stepped out of the dressing room when Fantine threw up. The stench of partly digested food was strong as it splattered against the wall, the floor, and Fantine.

"Oh…my God, Fantine," Simone said and pinching her nose and mouth, stepped clear of her fellow performer.

Magnolia and Apollo stopped to stare.

Mick waved his hands in disgust. "Damn it, Fantine! You've ruined your costume. Fitch!" he bellowed, "Fitch—get the mop bucket and clean this up."

Liberty ran to the door and knelt beside the stricken dancer still on the floor and crying. All the symptoms were there for the Spanish Influenza. Liberty put her hand on her forehead. Fantine was burning up. "She has the flu, she can't possibly perform."

Mick scowled and said, "How do you know that?"

"Because I'm a certified nurse. I joined the theater for something new and exciting. Mick, listen to me. Fantine is extremely ill. Please send for a doctor."

Mick got to his feet. "Simone—Magnolia—you'll have to do your bit without her. You," he said and pointed at Liberty. "Get away from her—damn it. Don't need ya getting sick too. Be ready to hit the boards when I say so. Apollo, stay back. Don't need ya getting sick as well."

Liberty watched two other stage workers hurry over, and after talking with Mick, they took Fantine by the arms and feet, and left by the back stage door. Fitch clamored over with a bucket and mop and set about cleaning up the stinking mess.

Liberty darted back to her dressing table and leaned forward to smear on her lip rouge. Worried about what the flu was capable of, she figured it would rampage throughout all the theaters.

The door opened and Fifi the seamstress came in holding folds of gossamer material, the skirt to Liberty's costume was done in brilliant peacock blues and aqua. Liberty steeled herself for the fondling she knew would take place.

Finished with her makeup, Liberty moved behind the screen

and took off all her clothes. Fifi draped the heavy skirt over the top of the screen and moved close to Liberty where she whispered in her ear.

"I've remembered one tiny detail the night of Zelda's murder." She placed a soft kiss against Liberty's cheek, and before Liberty could react, Fifi dropped to her knees and buried her face against Liberty's pubic curls, her breathing labored.

Liberty unwrapped Fifi's arms from where they were clasped around her hips. She then took hold of the woman's hands and held them tight.

"What do you remember, Fifi? You better tell me. Otherwise you're to help me with my costume and nothing more."

Still on her knees and looking upwards, Fifi said, "I remember a seamstress here that night. She was a stranger. We hadn't hired anyone new."

"What makes you think she was a seamstress?"

"Because, she wore a tape measure draped around her neck, and carried this funny little wicker basket with a pin cushion inside it. She was coming from the dressing room area and headed toward the stage door. She didn't see me, nor did she belong back here."

"How long before Jonathan Drake was found with Zelda did you see this seamstress? What did she look like?"

"I find it strange that you are so interested in Miss DeLane's death. What could it possibly have to do with you, oui?" Fifi stared up at Liberty.

When she tried to finger Liberty's pubic area. Liberty had enough. She grabbed Fifi's hands and pulled her to her feet. "You will tell me what I want to know right now!" She pushed Fifi against the wall and gripped her face between her hands. "Now!"

"Non, threats will not scare me." But her face betrayed her, her eyes held fear for only a moment, perhaps wondering just what

Liberty was capable of.

"Then I will go to Sidney Brawley and tell him you can't keep your flirty paws off me. Foyle likes me. So does Sidney."

"Ah…more threats. You're intimidations don't faze me. I'm the best costume designer in New York. Do you think that you can get me fired? No. I'm ordering you to come to my sewing room after you're finished."

"Why can't you tell me now?"

"Because, mon chère, I'm to be pleased as well. No pleasure, no information. You have…ah…how do you say…dodged me long enough."

Feeling used and dirty but with no other choice, Liberty nodded and accepted each piece of clothing that Fifi handed to her, from sheer glittery stockings, to a skimpy sequined aqua colored brassiere, and a long skirt with a side slit from ankle to waist. Next up was the headdress, a turban of blue feathers which fit tight against her head and was topped with tall billowy peacock feathers. She slipped into her high heels topping her height out at six feet and towering over Fifi who Liberty wanted to squash like a bug.

Stepping out from behind the dressing screen, Liberty waited for Fifi to bring the billowing skirt she'd brought in with her. Attaching it around Liberty's waist, the colorful skirt was sheer with long skinny rods sewn every two feet in the skirt. Liberty grasped the two handles sewn into the fabric and lifted the skirt, forcing it to fan upwards and around her like a flared peacock's tail. She held the tail aloft while Fifi walked around it, searching for imperfections that might make the costume come apart during the performance. There were none.

Fifi clapped her hands and grinned. "You wear my design well, and you will give every man out there decadent desires."

"Please, Fifi," begged Liberty. "Just answer my question, what did the woman look like?"

The door flew open and Mick stuck his head in. "Two minutes, Miss La Roux—two minutes."

Fifi, who usually never bothered to help the dancers, now did so. She got behind Liberty and held the skirt up by the tail while Liberty took her place off stage.

Liberty flowed on stage in a breathtaking gasp of the audience, the music going to a loud crescendo. She strolled, and fitting her hands into the cloth handles, flared open the skirt's peacock tail to form a huge circle up, around, and behind her, extending five feet or more beyond her height, the look magnificent. She continued to parade around the sparkling stage, slightly nodding toward Foyle in his private balcony, acknowledging the crowd, and making eye contact with the gentlemen near the stage. She cruised off the stage where Fifi removed the skirt, and shoved a large feathery fan into her hand, allowing her to return to the stage where the dancers showcased her before she started her song.

The men in the audience stared at her as though they wanted to devour her, the women simply looked envious. Just as she was about to end her song, she put her hands together and cocked her head upwards. Startled, she stared directly at Jonathan. In disguise, the man she loves was in his father's box and peering out from behind a velvet curtain, trying to be inconspicuous.

My God, why was he here?

Could the man never follow orders or good advice?

Her song faltered to a warbling end as the detectives stepped inside the balcony and closed in on Jonathan. When she would shout out a warning, her heart dropped as Jonathan bailed over the side of the balcony, leaped to grab the stage curtain and scrambled down its velvet luster like a monkey on a vine.

The trumpets last note lingered and fizzled to silence.

The dancers on stage crashed together in the middle of their routine.

At first, the audience was shocked into silence, and then jumped to their feet. The men pumped their fists at Jonathan. Their shouts mingled amongst the women's high-pitched screams.

Liberty feared for his life. No way was he getting out of here.

Bedlam broke loose as Jonathan limped up the side aisle trying to get away. Liberty watched as Detective Jones did an amazing leap to grab the curtain and follow Jonathan to the floor. With his head lowered like a bull to a matador, he sprinted after Jonathan.

"Stop that man!" he shouted above the din.

Most stepped aside to allow Jonathan a hasty retreat, others grabbed at him ending up with a piece of his suit-sleeve that they threw in the air. They slowed him enough to allow Jones to catch up, and take him down with a gut-busting tackle.

Liberty, along with the other dancers, stood on the edge of the stage. Her hand covered her mouth. With the audience on its feet, she barely made out Jonathan's blonde head above the din. Seeing detective Jones's gray head right next to Jonathan's blonde one, she could tell he was boxed in, surrounded. When the stocky Scala, with his gun pulled shouted at everyone to stand back, the crowd parted like the Red Sea, giving Liberty a perfect view of what was going on.

Jonathan was spun around and handcuffed. His gaze met Liberty's, and with a shake of his head warned her away. Stunned, Liberty stared as Jonathan was led through the chattering theater goers. Catcalls of *hang him* echoed above the pandemonium.

Liberty started off stage, but the emcee grabbed her by the arm.

"Stay here!" he hissed, and shouted orders for the dancers to get back in line. He yelled for the drummer in the pit to do a drum roll.

The drummer hit the skins hard followed by the crash of the cymbals.

"Ladies and gentlemen, don't say we don't put on a realistic show! And now let us continue with our lovely song-bird here, Miss Liberty La Roux."

How she was able to finish the song she didn't know. But she did and when she ran off stage to thunderous applause someone attached the skirt again.

"Liberty—Liberty—they demand a bow from you. Go take it."

She was pushed back on stage where she bowed, and blew kisses at the still excited audience. She lifted the skirt back up, and once again became a strutting peacock, ending her charade in the theater. She didn't care if she'd be accused of harboring a fugitive; she had to find where they took Jonathan. Lincoln Drake, she must call Jonathan's father. Why did Jonathan come here tonight? She knew he was tired of hiding out, wearing a disguise. Why didn't he stay put? Oh…God…why…why…

When she ran backstage, those that weren't on stage were chattering in excitement. "My, did you see that? Liberty—you're agent, Emery was arrested—here—tonight of all places!"

With the awkward skirt flaring out around her, the inserts banging against her legs, she pushed aside excited performers, and went for the wall phone. She took off the tall headdress and let it fall on the floor. She grabbed the receiver and clicked the metal hook hard until an operator answered. Talking into the mouth piece, her voice shook as she directed the operator to get her Lincoln Drake.

"Please be home—please be home…" she prayed.

"Hello," he answered in his familiar voice, so like Jonathan's that it rattled her heart.

"Mr. Drake—it's me—Liberty. Jonathan's been arrested." The sharp intake of his breath was loud in her ear.

"Just now?"

"Yes. They just took him away. I'm at the theater." She paused for a moment. "I think they took him to the precinct where Scala and Jones work out of."

"Miss Fitzgerald, I'm sending a car for you—"

"No! I'll grab a taxi, it'll be faster."

"Then I'll call my lawyer. Meet me at my hotel—please." He hung up.

Lifting the skirt of the costume, she hurried as fast as allowed. Inside her dressing room, she looked around for Fifi, but the seamstress wasn't there. Several of the dancers were. "Magnolia—please help me get out of this darn thing!"

The young dancer approached and started opening clasps in the back. "Liberty, I'm so sorry for what's happened with your agent." She started coughing and couldn't stop, her eyes watered.

Free from the throes of peacock feathers, material, clasps, wires, and everything else inhabiting Liberty's body, the skirt fell to the floor in a stiff puddle.

"Magnolia, you have the flu. Please see a doctor right away."

"It's just a cough. Half the audience out there was busting a cough during the first song."

"No, it isn't just a cough. That's how the flu starts." Liberty changed as fast as she could, jammed her hat on her head, skewered it with a hat pin and fled.

She meshed into the crowds on the sidewalk, and lifting her long skirt, she stepped into the street right in front of a taxi, and waved her arms to bring it to a screeching halt.

The short drive took far too long. Liberty was relieved when they stopped in front of *The Drake*. She paid him just as the Drake's doorman opened the cab's door.

She darted inside the hotel lobby where her hurried stride took her to the concierge's desk, and Mr. Edgar Hill who sat behind his name plate.

"I'm Liberty Fitzgerald. Mr. Drake told me to meet him here." Her chest heaved in and out, straining her corset. She tried to steady her breathing.

Alarmed, the concierge with the haughty face came around his desk. He took her by the arm. "Do you need anything? A glass of water, perhaps?"

"No—yes—I don't know."

"Miss…ah…Miss Fitzgerald, Mr. Drake telephoned me to say that if you arrived before he did that I was to take you to his office." He face became gentle.

Thankful she didn't have to explain any further, she looked at him through tears and nodded. "Yes, please." She followed him down the hall, to Mr. Drake's office, and to the same place she'd come such a short time ago telling him his son was innocent and that he needed help.

She collapsed into the nearest chair. The concierge, Mr. Hill, left her alone only to return a minute or two later with a glass of water. After handing her the glass, he asked if she needed anything else, when she said she was fine, he left her alone. Trying to take the drink, her hand shook so hard the glass rattled against her teeth. Finally she was able to take a sip.

Lincoln Drake came through the door as he did in life, with a cyclone like intensity. On his heels was an attractive older woman dressed in a blue coat. Following behind her was a dark-haired young lady who greatly resembled Jonathan. The young lady was attired in a warm red coat. Both wore black hats with thick high crowns and wide brims.

Liberty stood to face the three, surprised to see that two women were accompanying Mr. Drake. Mr. Drake put his arm around the older woman and was quick with introductions.

"Liberty Fitzgerald—this is my wife Earlene and my daughter Lona." He didn't wait for them to acknowledge one another before he picked up the phone and asked for the nearest police precinct. He kept dialing and calling, talking at length, trying to find his son.

Earlene Drake smiled and stood next to Liberty. "Miss Fitzgerald, Lincoln told me that you've helped our son tremendously and at a loss of your own nursing career. We can never express our gratitude enough."

Lona Drake echoed her mother's sentiments and took it a step further by kissing Liberty's cheek. "You will never know how much I admire you," she said.

Lincoln slammed down the phone. "C'mon, I've found Jonathan."

He ushered them out the door where they got into his chauffeured Studebaker. He told his driver to take them to the precinct in lower Manhattan. They sat there, all on edge, listening to Liberty tell about Jonathan's arrest.

Earlene Drake reached out a gloved hand and covered Liberty's with it. "Jonathan must love you very much to put aside the danger of getting caught, just to be near you."

Liberty swallowed the knot in her throat and nodded. Earlene's words were an eye opener. And leave it to a woman to sort out the obvious.

Upon arrival at the precinct's booking room, Liberty, flanked by the Drakes, pushed through a jostling crowd to approach the tall desk with a stern-faced cop standing there trying to restore order. Reporters from the newspapers, cameramen, people in handcuffs, a young man throwing up, it was bedlam. Cops came pouring out of the back, blowing whistles, and yelling for the crowd to shut up. The disgusting smell of vomit filled the room.

Lincoln managed to garner a policeman's attention and tell him why they were there.

The policeman blew his whistle so loud it almost broke everyone's eardrums. The room fell silent. "Which one of you ladies is Miss Fitzgerald?" he asked.

"I'm Liberty Fitzgerald," she said and stepped forward. "Where is Jonathan Drake, can I see him please? Are detectives Scala and Jones here? I need to talk to them. Jonathan is innocent, he didn't do anything."

"Miss Fitzgerald, you are under arrest for aiding and abating a fugitive." He grabbed Liberty by the arm.

Flashbulbs went off, cameras clicked, and reporters grinned.

"Wait! You can't do this," she exclaimed and glanced at Lincoln Drake. "Mr. Drake, help me."

"I'm calling my lawyer immediately. He'll get you out of here." He pointed at the cop who held Liberty. "I demand to see my son."

Ignoring Mr. Drake, the officer escorted Liberty down the hall and into a dark room. He pulled a chain coming off the ceiling light to flood the area in a bright glare.

Liberty looked around at the bare room with its lone wooden table and several chairs. "Why are you doing this? When can I see Jonathan?"

"Miss, just sit here and be quiet." He shoved her onto the chair's seat, and left the room.

Alarmed, Liberty hurried to the door to find it locked. She pounded on the hard wood, yelling to be let out.

From the moment Jonathan entered the Joyeux Theater, he worried that he'd made a huge mistake in trying to get a glimpse of Liberty. He'd been hiding out in her father's apartment a little over a week now. And finally he was able to relax for the first time in weeks, and not fear a knock on the door with the detective's busting in. But he didn't have the one thing he craved more than life.

Liberty. He simply missed her. And that need drove him to seek her out tonight. Just a fleeting glimpse from his balcony, that's all. With luck, she wouldn't even know he was there. Just one glimpse of the woman he'd come to love with unrelenting passion. A woman he wanted to spend his life with, make babies with her, and throw his money behind something good for a change, like a clinic, a clinic for the poor to get health care.

No longer the playboy snob he once was, he wondered when the change came over him, when Liberty had changed him. He couldn't remember. He knew she'd disliked the man he was, and he didn't much care for the man he used to be either, selfish, and only thinking of himself.

And now, sitting in this cold jail cell, he could kick himself for not changing sooner. But he'd have to get behind a long line of wronged people to be able to kick himself.

He had come to admire Keegan Fitzgerald, yet tonight, he'd ignored Keegan's pleas not to leave the apartment. Keegan tried telling him that Liberty would stop by over the weekend to see him before he left the states. He'd told Jonathan that he should be on Liberty's timeframe, not anyone else's. Certainly Liberty knew when it was safe or not to visit. But he'd told Keegan, he'd be careful and always looked over his shoulder. Well, tonight, he'd failed horribly.

As always, and like so many times before, he'd gone into the theater through the backstage door. Smiled at Fitch, the young messenger, smiled at the seamstress Fifi, and hurried to his father's balcony box. He didn't see any sign of the police. But once Liberty made her entrance onto the stage, he, like all the men in the theater was enthralled. My God, she was an enchantress, tall, magnificent, and her costume breathtaking. Her skin glowed like a fiery sun, and he wanted to shout out that she was his woman, the love of his life, that he was innocent and to please let them alone to live their lives. When she spotted him, he smiled and would have blown her a kiss but the detectives and cops had him surrounded. They grabbed at him. Missed. The chase was on.

He'd gone over the balcony causing every head in the theater to look his way. He prayed the curtain would hold, and it did, thick and velvety in his hands. He'd landed wrong when he jumped off the stage, turning his ankle. Had he gone backstage, he might have escaped out the back door, but he panicked. He was caught, like a fly in the detective's web. When they pressed the hard steel of a gun barrel against his ribs and told him to surrender, for the first time in his life, he obeyed.

Both detectives joined him in the interrogation room with its stark walls and lone light bulb hanging right over his head. His arms ached from being handcuffed behind his back. The detectives didn't bother to remove them.

"Well, now, it's nice to finally make your acquaintance, Jonathan Drake. I'm detective Jones."

Jones approached Jonathan and pinching the end of his fake mustache began pulling it off. Jonathan felt the angry tug on his skin, but sat there, not flinching, allowing the detective to unmask him. The beard wasn't so easy, while it was slowly peeled away, he felt as if his face was being scraped with a dull razor. Next, his blond wig was snatched off and put into a paper bag along with the rest of his facial hair.

"Well, there you are, gone from Mr. Emery Edison to Jonathan Drake in an instant. What part did Miss Fitzgerald play in all this? How long has she been helping you? From the beginning?" asked Scala who was sweating like he was the one in the hot seat. He took a handkerchief from his suit coat and dabbed the perspiration from his face.

"She knows nothing." Jonathan said, his mouth going into a tightened slit.

Scala laughed. "Don't insult us. You lived with her." He got closer. "We have Miss Fitzgerald in custody. Just like on stage, she sang like a bird. Told us, her new audience, all about you. What do you think about that?"

"You're lying!" he shouted, and jumped up from his chair.

Scala shoved him back down by the shoulder. "Ah…then she does know all about you. That you're Jonathan Drake the man who murdered Zelda DeLane."

"Leave her out of this." Oh…God…what did he just do? Now his Liberty was arrested. "Listen, I didn't kill Zelda. Why would I? I fancied her, more than that."

"Really?" sneered Jones. "Why don't you tell us about that night? We've never heard your side of the story."

"Could I have a cigarette first? Some water?"

"Sure," said Jones. He removed the handcuffs, and taking a cigarette case from his suit coat pocket, lit one and handed it to Jonathan. He opened the door and hollered for water to be brought in.

"Start talking," Scala ordered, and again he wiped the sweat from his forehead and used his handkerchief to cover his cough.

"I met Zelda backstage after her show. The night was Friday. I usually attended the Saturday night performance, and then I would perform with Zelda afterwards."

Jones crossed his arms, his body rigid. "Why only Saturday nights?"

Jonathan glared at the cop. "Because, Zelda liked to spread her…ah…charms around. She'd never have just one beau. She liked many who bestowed her with expensive jewels."

Scala cleared his throat and got closer to Jonathan. "I'd say jealousy is a good enough motive to kill the star. Perhaps you got tired of sharing."

"No, it gave me a reprieve. Zelda had a rigorous sexual appetite." He lied. He'd heard the rumors that were flying around backstage that he was about to be replaced in her bed by someone else. Never one to share, he hated the thoughts of doing so.

Jones squinted at Jonathan. "You're saying you weren't man enough for her? Another good reason to kill her. Your manhood was in question. She let ya know about it by taking other lovers."

Jonathan blew out his breath. "No, not at all. I believe she loved me best. Or should I say the best that Zelda could give. Listen, here's what happened. I was sitting on the chair next to Zelda's makeup table. Fully clothed. She was naked and I was playing with her leg well...feeling her up. Next I know, I'm hit on the head and when I come to I'm stripped and on top of her dead body."

"Yeah—yeah—and I'm the Prince of Egypt," quipped Scala, spewing spittle while leaning close to Jonathan's face. "What about the knife in your hand? The stagehand, Mick said you were holding a knife and that you tried to use it on him." Relentless, Scala was like a giant drill that kept taking chunks out of him.

Jonathan wiped the detective's spit off his face. "That's just it. The knife was in my right hand. I'm left handed."

"Left handed, huh?" Jones wrote in his notebook. "What did you do with the knife?"

"I switched it to my left and when Mick came after me I used it to defend myself. The man was going to kill me. I don't know what happened to the knife after that. I lost it during the fight."

Again, Scala came at him. "So someone comes out of the blue, knocks you out, overpowers Miss DeLane, kills her, strips you bare and stages the whole thing to look like you did it?"

"Exactly," Jonathan said.

"Hmmm," Scala muttered.

"What happened to my clothes? They were gone and I assure you I was fully dressed when I went to the theater. And I sure as hell was wearing them when I was sitting at Zelda's dressing table. Hell, she was the one who started taking my bowtie off. It was a game between us." He wanted to shake the truth into them, make them believe him.

"We found your duds, shoes included, behind Zelda's dressing screen. All in a neat folded pile. Explain that." Jones said.

This was news to Jonathan, the first he'd heard his clothes were found. God, he could feel the hot seat getting closer. "I'm tellin' you I had my clothes on before I was hit on the back of the head. What about my wallet? I had a wad of bills in a money clip."

"Wallet only, in the right hip pocket."

"I don't carry my wallet in my right pocket. I always have it in my left side." He demonstrated by using his left hand. "Ask my dad. Ask my mother—sister, anyone who has ever been with me. The killer must have taken my money clip."

"Right side, left handed, who gives a damn." Scala's face paled. He licked his lips. "Why did you run?"

"Because the stage hand, Mick, was going to kill me. All of them would have torn me apart. The only thing I could think of was to get away."

"Mick Brown said he saw you slashing Miss DeLane's throat." Jones drew a finger across his own throat.

"He's lying."

"Ah, you wouldn't by any chance know Zelda's Friday night beau?" Scala pushed his handkerchief back inside his pocket.

"I'd been told Talon Montgomery."

The detectives shot each other a questioning stare.

Jonathan said, "You know, Talon Montgomery of the Grand's department store fame. He's married to Charles Grand's daughter, Alice."

"And you know these people how?"

"Years ago, I took Alice out on dates, that's all, a few dates. It was expected. High society debutante stuff. We all ran in the same circles…ah…isn't that how we're described? High society snobs?"

"Do you know what other men, Miss DeLane was dating?"

Jonathan shrugged. "You'll have to ask those at the theater. I'm sure she also gave out favors to the men who work there as well as those who own the show."

"You mean Foyle himself?" asked Jones.

"The list is long," Jonathan said.

"You know, by not running away, you could have told us all this sooner."

"Not with you believing I'm guilty. Roasting in the electric chair at Sing Sing didn't appeal to me either. Still doesn't."

The door opened and a blue-coated policeman stepped inside to whisper in Jones's ear. He let out a deep breath, and shook his head before motioning for Scala to step outside.

"Well, we have some interesting happenings. Two people have stepped up saying they are Zelda DeLane's killers," Jones said, and waited for his friend's fiery Italian temper to explode. It didn't take long.

"What?" Scala's words burst forth. He used the back of his hand to wipe sweat from his upper lip.

"Two men just came into the station saying they killed Miss DeLane."

Scala thrust his hands in his pockets and rocked on his heels. "Oh, and who in the fuck are they?"

"None other than Keegan and Blaine Fitzgerald. They both are claiming to have done Zelda in."

Scala put his hand against the wall to steady himself. He was sick. Too much pasta, too much of anything good. And now this, a kink in their murder case. A tiny kink, but a kink no less. "We both know who Keegan Fitzgerald is. Who in the hell is Blaine Fitzgerald?" Leaking sweat, he felt like a red-hot furnace, and he took out his handkerchief to dab at his face, again.

"He's Liberty Fitzgerald's brother. They think that by admitting to killing Zelda DeLane that Liberty couldn't have harbored a fugitive, so we have to free her."

"Did they say that?" Dizzy, he needed to sit down.

"No. I'm just surmising that's what they're thinking." Jones's eyes narrowed while staring at Scala. "Are you all right? You look flushed, feverish."

"I'm fine—fine. Shake the truth out of the Fitzgerald's, then send them home. Christ, just when I was startin' to believe there was something to Drake's story. His being left—" Scala, jerked his tight collar loose. Vomit surged to the back of his throat forcing him to spew his supper on the floor behind him. Hearing Jones shouting for help was the last thing Scala heard before the floor came up to meet him.

When shouts of confusion sounded outside the walls of the small interrogation room Jonathan was in, he went to the door and tried the handle.

It opened.

He peered out to see Scala on the floor with Jones bending over him.

Without thought, Jonathan yelled. "If Miss Fitzgerald's here—get her. She's a trained nurse who knows what to do."

Jones pointed at Jonathan. "Get your ass back in there." He quickly turned to a nearby policeman and ordered. "Bring Miss Fitzgerald here, quick!"

Chapter Nineteen

Liberty knelt beside the downed detective and placed her hand on his forehead. It felt hot and moist. His eyes fluttered open, red-rimmed and bloodshot, they stared at her in confusion, finally realizing it was she.

"Don't worry, and don't move. It's ironic, but now it's my turn to ask you some questions. Do you feel tired, does your body ache?"

He perceivably nodded to each answer.

"Does your head hurt?"

"Yeah."

She pointed to the vomit spattered on the wall and floor. "I already know the answer to that one. Detective Scala, you're very ill. I've called for an ambulance."

His hand clasped her lower arm and squeezed. "What's wrong with me?" His words trailed off into a cough.

Liberty removed his hand from her arm and proceeded to unbutton his white shirt revealing a barrel chest furred with dark and gray hair. She tilted her head to press her ear tight against his chest and was satisfied to hear a good strong heartbeat. That made her diagnosis easier. She raised her head, alarmed to see that Scala's nose started to bleed.

Taking her floral handkerchief from her pocket, she wiped the blood away. "I can't say for sure, but I'm afraid you might have the Spanish Influenza. If so, then you're highly contagious."

He started to rise and said, "I don't need an ambulance. I have work to do."

Liberty gently helped him to lie back against the floor. He was no longer able to fight.

Jones, appearing unafraid of catching the flu, bent to talk to his partner. "Scala, don't worry. I'll handle things here." He closed Scala's suit coat and told him to be patient.

"Detective, we need blankets to cover him with," Liberty said.

Detective Jones beckoned two policemen standing nearby. "Grab some blankets from the cots, hurry!"

The two cops disappeared down the hall.

"Miss Fitzgerald, both your father and brother are in the jail and are claiming that they killed Miss DeLane."

"Oh my word. The silly fools."

"Yes. They are fools," Jones said.

The policemen returned with several wool blankets and a pillow. Liberty accepted the blankets and knelt to cover Scala. When she raised his head to put the pillow under it, he didn't stir. Worried, she got to her feet.

"Detective Jones, everyone who has come in contact with Detective Scala in the past twenty-four hours will need to be looked at. This flu is virulent and spreads from person to person at a rapid pace." She rather liked being a person of authority again, yet was uneasy about her dad, brother, Jonathan and his family being here.

"What about you?" Jones asked.

"I had the flu this past spring. I pray I'm immune. What happened to Mr. Lincoln Drake and his family? They came in here with me."

"Thought it best they weren't here. I sent them away. Lincoln Drake said to tell you he was getting lawyers for both you and Jonathan." Jones crossed his arms and leaned against the wall.

Again she repeated her question about who Detective Scala had been in contact with.

Detective Jones shrugged. "It would be easier to tell you who Scala hasn't been around. We've been in several restaurants, the Joyeux theater, we were all over backstage today, came in contact with everyone working there, seamstresses, doormen, ticket takers. And, that's not mentioning everyone here, the cops who have gone out on beat." He looked at Liberty, his face paled. "My wife. Scala was at my house for dinner night before last."

"I'm not sure of the incubation time for this flu. It used to be approximately four days or so. It's hard to diagnose from the common cold, and I'd love to tell you that your family is safe, but I can't. They need to be watched over."

Two attendants wearing face masks hurried in carrying a stretcher between them. They lowered it to the ground and carefully placed Scala's body on it. Liberty asked what hospital they would be taking him to.

"No hospital, Miss. They're starting to overflow. We'll be taking him to the armory where doctors have set up a triage type of hospital."

"Overflowing?" Liberty grabbed the attendant's arm. "Armory?"

"Yes, ma'am. Lots of people are sick." He tipped his cap at her and picked up his end of the stretcher. They hurried away.

Like an unwanted pest, this illness crept around the city, infecting, killing, and Liberty hadn't been aware when it turned so deadly. But now that she knew, she had to get back in touch as soon as possible. She turned to Detective Jones. "Unless you're going to keep me in a cell, I must help nurse the sick. And in order to do that, I have to call Emma Taylor at the clinic, immediately."

"Against my better judgment I'm releasing you to work in the armory so you can help nurse my partner back to health and I can keep an eye on you. You still have charges against you that will not be dropped."

Liberty thought long and hard about what he said. "I understand. Do you want me to swear on a bible that I will not take off for parts unknown?"

Jones' scoffed.

"May I use your telephone please?" she asked.

"Yes. But it's late, will anyone be there?" Jones escorted her to the sergeant's desk and phone.

"The flu doesn't function on time nor does it discriminate. I've got to request that health workers come to this precinct—now." She took the cone shaped earpiece and put it to her ear, using her other hand, she clicked the receiver and asked the operator to connect her with the health organization.

The flu hopscotched throughout the precinct, sparing some but sickening most. Liberty's father Keegan, and her brother Blaine became ill, so did Jonathan. With his feet manacled and shackled to the bed in the armory along with the other ill cops, Jonathan fought for his life.

When he wasn't choking on his vomit he'd become delirious. At times he dreamed he was home in his bed and his mother taking care of him. Her lovely face loomed close to his, telling him how much she loved him. She sponged cool water on his face, and dribbled some inside his mouth, helping to slack his thirst. As he sank deeper into his delirium his mother disappeared and he was being led to the electric chair to fry for Zelda's murder. And fry he did. Laughing, Scala threw the switch. Jonathan's body danced, shook, and sizzled, and as smoke started coming off his body, the stench of burning flesh became strong. Mick the stagehand materialized and replaced the electric chair. Mick with his hands around Jonathan's neck began squeezing, shouting, *"you killed Zelda."* Jonathan tried to cry out, but couldn't. Everything went dark. He could hear a woman's voice in the distance urging him to fight, to hang on, that he would be well. He didn't want to fight. He wanted to die, to be put out of this hell he was in.

When his fever broke, Jonathan opened his eyes, barely seeing, yet somehow knowing Liberty was nearby. And she was, dressed in a blue nurse's uniform with a long white apron. His beautiful Liberty was right beside his bed. He groped to feel her, to put his hand on her hip, to make sure she wasn't an angel.

"Are you real?" he asked, his throat hurt to talk.

"Welcome back to the living, Mr. Drake," she said from behind her mask. "Open your mouth so I can take your temperature." She slipped the thermometer under his tongue and ticked off the needed five minutes before removing it.

"Am I going to live?"

She cupped his face within her palms as her eyes lovingly searched his face. "Yes, I believe you are. Your temperature reads 100 degrees. Down from 104. Darling, I'm so happy. I was so frightened that you were going to die."

"My...Dad?" he asked.

"I haven't heard anything from him. He left for home right after Scala collapsed at the precinct. When I have a moment, I'll try to call him."

The smell of vomit and diarrhea was something even Liberty

could never get used too, and the strong odor permeated the armory's spacious rooms. Large canvas curtains had been erected between each bed trying to give the patients some semblance of privacy. Loud moans of the sick prevailed, along with coughing, retching, and bedpans hurriedly put under a patient.

There was no cure, rendering the doctors and nurses helpless, realizing they had a pandemic on their hands. All they could do was take temperatures, pulses, sponge faces, bodies, and pray.

Along with doctors and nurses pressed into service, Liberty's friend Helen Cartwright was at the armory helping. It felt good to have a fellow worker from the public nursing agency here. Liberty owed a lot to Helen who stepped in and took her patients when Liberty was given time off. It all seemed so long ago, certainly much longer than the short two months since she'd first met Jonathan.

Seeing that Jonathan was out of danger, Liberty, tired to the bone, her nurses uniform long ago soiled from vomit, left his side and was immediately beckoned by Doctor Curtis to follow him. Walking behind the elderly doctor with his long gown of white, she admired the doctor who retired years ago, but pressed back into service by the shortage of doctors needed to battle the flu.

They moved from bed to bed, taking temperatures, both dreading to see the patient who'd developed a blue tinge to their skin, knowing death would soon follow. They gently covered the dead with their bed sheet. Doctor Curtis kept his mask on, signing death certificates and placing them on the covered body. Liberty mentally added the dead over the ones who got well and realized that the grim-reaper was winning. The ones who were still alive, Liberty sponged them off, trying to comfort each and every one. She removed their grasping hands from her apron, and would tell them that they had fought the battle and tried to reassure them that they would survive. Some did, most didn't.

When it came to her family, she tried not to give differential treatment, but she couldn't help it. She'd spent her meager off duty hours next to her father's bedside, wetting a sponge, showering him with all the love she could give. She held his arthritic hands, kissed them, and was reluctant to leave his side. But she did, only to move to her brother and from there to Jonathan. In short, she never left the armory, choosing to grab a nap on a cot in a small room for the doctors and nurses.

"Liberty, there's someone at the door to see you. She says her husband is here—that you're her sister-in-law." Helen, wearing a mask, and holding a wash basin filled with fresh water smiled with her eyes. Diminutive, Helen, was also a member of the suffragette movement, and Liberty knew to never let the nurse's short statue fool her. Helen was fierce when it came to her beliefs.

Liberty put her hand on Helen's arm and stared at large brown eyes peering over her gauze mask. "It must be Blaine's wife."

"I'll take over with Doctor Curtis," she said, and joined the doctor who was moving between the sheet draped beds.

Just in case someone was foolish enough to let Marybeth inside, Liberty hurried to the front window. Keeping her mask in place, she peered through the glass and spotted Marybeth standing on the sidewalk next to the street. Liberty opened the door and stepped outside, not daring to go any closer to where her pregnant sister-in-law waited. Marybeth's face was pinched and white, the baby due in several months.

People, all wearing masks scurried by. When they spotted Liberty's nursing uniform they couldn't get past the building fast enough.

"Oh...Liberty," Marybeth cried, and started toward Liberty.

"Please, don't come any closer." Liberty held up her hand to stop her. "Marybeth, as much as I want to hug you, I can't. We don't know for sure how this disease travels."

Marybeth's shoulders fell as she dropped her outstretched hand. Tears coursed down her cheeks. "Can't I even see Blaine?" she sobbed.

Liberty shook her head. "It's too dangerous. If you got the flu who would take care of your boys? What about your unborn child? No, it's best you don't go anywhere near Blaine. He's doing better than dad and some of the others. Do you have a mask?"

Nodding, Marybeth pulled one out of her coat pocket.

"Please wear it at all times, on the trolley, every time you step foot out your door. Keep the boys home from school. If you do get sick, please call me and I'll send help."

Marybeth's brows pulled into a frown. "Are you sure Blaine isn't dead—that you're just saying he's doing better to make me feel better?"

"For God's sake, Marybeth, I don't lie, and I'd certainly never keep anything so dire from you. No, Blaine's alive, he's very sick, but he is still alive."

She stifled the urge to take Marybeth in her arms. "Please go home where you're safe. Don't let any stranger in unless it's a nurse. Be sensible, please. I'll send Blaine home as soon as he's well—I promise."

"Then promise me you'll be truthful with me about all things." Marybeth put her gauze mask over her nose and tied it against the back of her head.

"Oh…Marybeth…of course I will."

No amount of doctoring could save Detective Scala. His skin took on the fatal blue tinge associated with near death. Liberty, now at his side, thought he might show compassion for Jonathan, but when he fumbled for her hand and in a moment of defiance he muttered, *"Drake is...guilty,"* she felt nothing for the man who made hers and Jonathan's lives miserable. He quickly lost conscious, and blood stained sputum foamed from his mouth. Had he chose to say that Jonathan was innocent, might have made her feel differently, but he didn't. Even in death he accused. She was almost glad he was dead. One less detective to dog Jonathan.

After she filled out the death notice with time of death and no next of kin, she took the sheet he laid on, and used it to tightly wrap his body. When he was trussed up like a mummy, she went to put his name on the list for the soldiers from the armory pressed into death detail. They made their rounds twice a day taking the dead to mortuaries marked for the claimed and marked for the unclaimed.

Liberty now stood beside Jonathan's bed. While he slept, his legs twitched causing the manacles to rattle against the bed frame he was anchored to. Lifting the sheet she could see that his ankles were abraded and bleeding from the metal anklets. She wanted them off and thought to telephone the precinct to send someone over with a key. She spotted Scala's suit coat hanging on the pole at the end of his bed next to his shrouded body. Wondering if he had a key that would fit, she crossed the small space between beds. She searched his suit coat pockets for a key. Elated, she found what she sought in the breast pocket. Returning back to Jonathan, she held her breath and prayed while putting the key in the lock. She turned the key opening the shackles.

"Jonathan?" she said and squeezed his hand within hers.

"Scala?" He turned a ravaged face toward her.

Liberty shook her head. "He died a few minutes ago. This flu can't be contained. They have closed the theaters, schools, all public gatherings for now."

"Must find Fifi and make her...tell you about the strange seamstress...the one who..." he broke off coughing.

"I know—I know, find the seamstress who shouldn't have been there the day Zelda died. I'll go see Fifi when you and my family are out of danger. I can't before then." She kept sponging his face, until it appeared he'd fallen asleep. Satisfied that he was, she went to stand next to her father's bed.

Something was wrong. His pallor was slate colored and waxy in appearance. Nor could she detect a rise and fall of his chest insuring he still breathed.

"Dad?" She took her stethoscope and bent close to his chest. But she already knew what she'd hear. Nothing. No heartbeat thumped in her stethoscope. Only silence. Her stethoscope dangled. When had the dreaded bloody foam appeared? How had she missed his final moments? Alone. He'd been alone. Damn it, no one should be alone. He died while she was with Scala, Jonathan, the manacles.

"Oh—God—no," she wailed. *Not daddy. Not daddy. Noooooo.* She clutched the sheet on the bed and fell to her knees, sobbing. The light of her life, her daddy was gone. No more hugs, no more teasing from the man who meant more to her than anyone ever could.

The influenza was like a slithering, hissing, deadly, coiling mass of unseen airborne death that didn't care who it felled. Would her father have become ill if he wasn't helping Jonathan and been infected by Scala? Possibly yes, more likely no. "Daddy," she murmured, "I swear to you that I'll see Jonathan free, prove his innocence, that you haven't died in vain." Her father had accepted Jonathan's innocence on her word that he was. All she had to say to him was that she believed in Jonathan. Her belief was good enough for her father, and he never doubted her, accepting her word as his, siding with Jonathan and giving him shelter. It was the only thing solid she could hold onto.

Like a puppet, she stood and took the sponge from the water

basin and squeezed it out. She lovingly closed her father's eyes and washed his face, the bloody spittle from his mouth.

"Liberty?" Blaine's voice floated across the aisle. "Is it Dad?"

She couldn't answer. How could she tell her sick brother that their father, the anchor for them both was dead? *No—no—no! Too much death, too much heartache.*

"Miss Fitzgerald?"

She wasn't aware of the doctor taking the sponge from her hand. Finally, he took her by the shoulders and turned her to look at him. She stared into the sad eyes of Doctor Curtis.

That's all she saw anymore, eyes peering over white gauze masks. She wouldn't know what the doctor looked like without one. This is what the world had become, nothing but eyes. Eyes showing pity. Eyes showing sadness. Eyes showing…what? Certainly not hope. And then there was the mask. Masking off the smile, the grin, laughter, kisses. And if the mask truly worked, her father would still be alive. She tore off her mask.

"I'm sorry, so sorry Miss Fitzgerald."

Again Blaine called out, "Liberty—damn it—what's happened?"

Liberty couldn't move. She stared at the doctor, trying to contain her hysteria. "Doctor, he died alone. I was with another patient—my God—alone—alone in a room full of sick people, he died alone. I wasn't here," she wailed.

Doctor Curtis shook her. "Stop it! Stop blaming yourself. Your father's been out of his mind for several days. He wasn't aware of anything."

"Your words don't make me feel any better," she said and drew in a breath, a hiccup, a shudder.

"Go to your brother, I'll take care of your father." He replaced her mask and retied it.

She approached Blaine's bed. He looked wane, exhausted, yet, somehow the worst was behind him, that he'd recover and go home to Marybeth. But would she ever recover from losing her dad? Would Blaine? No. Their father was the pillar of the family, his strength was their strength. His hands, so talented in making something of beauty from a piece of wood, stilled. She met Blaine's fever ridden stare and prayed for guidance.

"Dad's dead, isn't he," Blaine said, saving her the words.

Nodding, she took off her mask and blew her nose on her handkerchief. She wiped her eyes and replaced her mask, thinking the darn thing wasn't working so well.

She took Blaine's hand within hers, but he pulled her down against his chest. His arm went around her and his racking sobs were loud against her ear. When finally they had no more tears to shed, she straightened and stared at her brother, seeing a softer side of him.

His voice was weak as he said, "I'm trying to remember when I last told Dad that I loved him."

Liberty wiped his face, his tears. "He knew you loved him. He knew we all loved him. Oh…God…how can I tell Teague when he is over there fighting in a war?"

"Don't tell him, not yet anyway. I don't want him grieving while trying to fight. Liberty, Dad wanted to be buried next to Mom. His plot's paid for." He wiped tears that just kept coming.

She'd forgotten all about the paid arrangements, and was grateful that Blaine reminded her. Squeezing his hand, she said, "I'll see that he's put next to Mom." Her voice sounded hollow to her. Strange words, and even stranger to be spoken here and now. But it was the first thing to come to mind, and she would dig the grave herself if it meant keeping him out of a mass gravesite which seemed to be the norm, right now.

She felt Blaine's forehead. It was sweaty, and somewhat clammy, but no fever. He was over the worst of it. He would live to go home to his family.

"Marybeth was by earlier. I refused to let her enter the armory. She said to tell you she loves you." Again tears crept down her brother's cheeks and disappeared into the pillow. She knew he was feeling helpless not being able to be with his wife and boys. And help bury their father.

"Can you call her and tell her I'm better, and about Dad?" he asked.

"Yes, I will. I already told her you were getting better."

Blaine studied her, and to Liberty, he never looked more like their father than he did right now.

"Sis, I'm proud of you. You saved my life."

"I don't know about that, I'm only doing what I'm trained to do. If I could find out why the flu happens and a vaccine to cure it, then I'd say I'd saved your life. Right now, I think it's your ornery temperament that's saved you." She tried to smile, but couldn't. She could hear several nurses wrapping her father's body in his sheet. To her, their administrations made it final, more believable that her daddy's gone, forever.

Taking a sponge from the water basin, she squeezed it out, and wiped Blaine's face. How strange this flu was. Why did some get better, some die, and some like her who had it once became immune? She glanced over the top of the privacy curtain and stared. The ward was fast filling up with dead, shrouded bodies. She left Blaine and went to look at Scala's body and then at the manacles on the floor next to Jonathan.

Muted voices and noise from outside forced her to hurry over to the window to look out. Two army trucks gathering bodies had arrived. One for the claimed and one for the unclaimed. She glanced at her watch pinned to her bodice. Today they were early. Stopped alongside the trucks was a cab bearing more sick patients. A doctor, last name Smith, and Liberty's fellow nurse Helen Cartwright, hurried outside to assist. The cab driver ran over and started gesturing at the doctor. Soldiers wearing masks got out of the trucks and stopped to talk with the doctor.

Liberty turned back and hastened over to Jonathan's bed.

Putting her hands on the sides of his head to meet his gaze, she leaned down and spoke against his ear, "Jonathan, can you act dead? I'm getting you out of here, but you must be silent."

He continued to stare at her, puzzled, his brow knitted.

She shook his head none too gently. "Please listen to me. I'm going to declare you dead. Fill out a death certificate and get you out of here while I can. I can't let you recover here, if you do, Jones will take you back to jail. Don't worry, I'll telephone your father and tell him to get your body at the morgue for the unclaimed. He'll have to take you back to dad's place to hide."

When he started to nod off again, she swore under her breath and slapped him hard against the cheek.

"Jonathan, listen to me. You must not move, stay calm and don't move! Can you do this?"

"Liberty..." his voice wavered, his eyes met hers, he nodded.

She grabbed the sheet and wrapped him as tight as a mummy. She then put the manacles on top of his body. Praying that none of the doctors or nurses would accompany the soldiers in here, she watched them enter and Doctor Smith point her way. Then along with Helen who was supporting a sick woman, the doctor put his arm around a male patient and escorted them down another aisle.

Acting quickly, Liberty entered Jonathan's name and no next of kin on the paper and pinned it to his shroud.

"Ah...nurse, we're here to pick up the dead." The taller of the four soldiers tipped his cap at her, even with the mask on, his eyes looked fearful, showing he'd rather be on any other detail.

She glanced across the aisle to see Blaine watching her. She couldn't worry about what he thought, not now.

"The three bodies are here," she said and started for Scala's body. "Two for the unclaimed mortuary, and one for the claimed."

The shorter of the soldiers peered at his list. "I have two listed. What's the name of the latest?"

"A mister Drake. He recently died. His body is still warm," she answered in a calm voice.

As the masked soldiers approached, she pointed to Scala's body where one of the soldiers bent to read the certificate.

"This is in order," he said.

"Yes, that's Mr. Scala. And that one over there is Mr. Drake. Both have no kin. Hmmm, are you still taking them to Chillers and Slate's Mortuary, or is it full?"

"Close to being full, but not yet. They have taken to burying the bodies with no kin in mass graves in Potter's Cemetery." The soldiers got on each end of Scala's body and lifted him.

When they returned for Jonathan, she held her breath silently praying that Jonathan wouldn't call out or squirm or do anything to let them know they were carrying a live person. She escorted them to the front door that she held open allowing them to go through and where she watched to make sure all went well. They got into their truck and drove off.

The remaining two soldiers from the other truck stood next to her father's body. She hurried over to them. "This is my father," she said fighting back tears. "He's to be buried next to my mother. The orders are pinned to the shroud."

"I'm sorry for your loss," the soldier said. "We'll be gentle with him. You can claim his body tomorrow and see to his burial." He peered over his mask at the writing and was satisfied to see that Liberty would be by to pick up her father's body.

She went to stand next to Blaine's bed and both watched their father being carried away. Holding Blaine's hand, Liberty took her hanky and dabbed at her eyes.

"If you want your plan to work, you better go call Lincoln Drake and let him know what's happened. That his son has died," Blaine said in a quiet voice.

"You saw what I did?" she asked him.

"Yes. If you hadn't done what you did, I would have suggested it. Good for you, Liberty."

"Coming from you that means a lot to me. I've never known what you thought about me helping Jonathan, his being wealthy and all."

"I was dubious at first. But then after hearing his story and it all falling together, I was on his side. One thing for certain, when we die, other than how you're put into the ground, it doesn't matter if you're rich or poor. We all rot the same."

Liberty shook out the thermometer and ordered him to open wide. After timing it, she pulled it out and was pleased to see his temperature was almost normal.

"Sis," he said, "When you get the time would ya go check on Marybeth and the kids?"

"Yes, I will."

"I need to speak with Lincoln Drake please," Liberty said to the housemaid who answered the telephone.

"I'm sorry, but he's recovering from the influenza. The whole household has come down with the illness. Their daughter Lona passed away with it yesterday."

Liberty sucked in her breath and slowly let it out. "How sick is he? Can he talk at all?"

"Who is this?" she asked.

"Tell him Liberty Fitzgerald is calling about his son."

The maid paused a second before saying, "Please, wait a minute." Liberty could hear the woman's footsteps running from the room. She didn't have long to wait before Lincoln Drake came on the line.

"Miss Fitzgerald?" his voice sounded weak. "What's wrong?"

"Mr. Drake, I'm sorry to tell you that Jonathan passed away today."

"Oh…God…No!"

She could hear him pounding on something hard, his desk perhaps. "Mr. Drake, please listen to me. Jonathan's body was taken to Chillers and Slate's mortuary a little while ago. You need to get there as soon as you can."

"You don't sound upset, I thought you loved Jonathan."

"I do *love* Jonathan, very much."

"Love?"

"Yes, I *love* Jonathan."

There was a long pause and Liberty could only pray that he understood what she was trying to say. And in case the operator was listening as they always did, she hoped she didn't have to say more.

"My father died today and I'm devastated. I understand you lost your daughter yesterday. I'm so sorry to hear about her. I know how you feel, like your hearts ripped out, shattered." She became silent for a moment, trying to hold back her tears that were threatening to fall for everyone she knew. "Can you get your son's body? If not, I'll try and get there myself."

"No, Miss Fitzgerald. I'll go now. How can I get in touch with you?"

"I'll be here at the Armory on Bowery Street."

"Ah…have you made arrangements for your father?"

"Yes, he's supposed to be buried next to my mother in the Restful Haven Roman Catholic cemetery. He has a plot there. Mr. Drake, how is your wife doing?"

"Earlene has turned the corner but is still weak, and now with

Lona's passing, she just lays there inconsolable."

"I'm so sorry about your daughter, so sorry. Is there something I can do for you?"

"I expect my grief is the same as yours. And, I've come to the conclusion that the doctors really don't know how to cure this illness but act like they do. The numbers are going to go even higher, I'm sure." He sounded bitter, like a man who just lost everything. His children, his world.

"I believe you are right. No one knows how to stop this epidemic."

"Chiller and Slate's?"

"Yes. Please hurry." She replaced the receiver.

Chapter Twenty

Alice peered out the large dining room window. The month of November just started. Everything was gray outside with a darkening sky and deep shadows.

The house was silent and Alice never felt more alone. The flu had rampaged through the Grand's household with a vengeance. The illness showed no mercy and took her mother Yvette shortly after she became ill. Alice's jaw tightened at the thought of losing her beloved mother. Tears stung her eyes and her life now felt as barren as the tree branches looked. Her father, still fighting the virile strain, seemed to be slowly improving, but losing his wife played into his slow recovery. Several maids died and those left practically refused to leave their rooms, and did so only when ordered.

She held onto the heavy velvet curtains as if to let go would propel her into a dark hellish abyss that she would never climb out. Her activities over the past few months were more likely to get her there faster. She dabbed at her tears and blew her nose on a monogramed hanky.

Alice wondered why she didn't get sick. Talon didn't get sick either. She figured the evil surrounding them both kept them safe from the grim reaper. Or maybe that old saying, 'Only the good die young,' had something to do with her and Talon avoiding the flu. But if that were true, then how could she account for her precious Jenny coming down with the illness and almost dying. Jenny fought back and survived. Maybe that was the Devil stepping in and watching over his spawn.

They'd kept *Grand's* open. Some of the help seemed to be immune to the disease. Alice thought the store should close, but her father, claiming he'd be ruined if they did, put Talon in charge. And, since there was a quarantine notice on their front door along with a black wreath denoting Mother's death, Talon moved into his office at the store.

The door opened and their maid, a new hire, Beatrice Lane, came inside carrying an empty tray. She placed it on the sideboard. Wearing a white mask with fearful eyes staring out, she curtsied at Alice and said, "I've fed Miss Bishop. You're father refused to acknowledge my knocking on his bedroom door."

"Thank you, Beatrice. That'll be all for tonight."

"Shouldn't I clear the food away? Take it to the kitchen?"

"I guess so," Alice said aimlessly. It was her mother's job to tell the help what to do, and it being her mother's duty for so long, Alice was at a loss. She squared her shoulders and said, "Yes, please do."

Pushing the large wheels on her chair she rolled inside the den and to her father's desk where she removed the telephone's black receiver and rapidly clicked the handle several times. The operator came on and transferred her call to Talon's office at the store.

"Grand's department store," he said.

"Talon, it's me."

"Ah…Alice…dear, it's good to hear from you. How is everything at home?"

"Not too well. Dad refuses to come out of his room. He's taking mother's death extremely hard. And other than a few servants here, I'm alone."

"How about Miss Bishop? Has she recovered?"

"Yes, she's doing much better. Hopefully, she'll be up and around in a few days. Ah…have you heard any news about Jonathan Drake?"

"What's the interest in Jonathan Drake? Why do you care?"

"Just that we were at the theater the night he was caught, that's all."

"Alice, I'm sure he's still in custody, not that I give a damn. I'd like to talk longer, but I need to go and make sure the store's empty so that we can lock up. I'm not having much fun being here around the clock."

"I know. You should be able to come back home in a few days. At least attend Mama's funeral. Maybe you can get through to Father since no one else can. I'm worried about him."

"I know. Why don't I come by tomorrow night and see what I can do?"

"All right. It looks like everyone here is over the worst of the flu. Please come home."

He clicked the phone off and Alice replaced the black receiver onto the cradle. Talon may be a horrible man, but he was the lesser of dying or being alone.

Alice went into Jenny's room located in the servant's quarters, on the first floor and down the hallway. She wheeled her chair close to Jenny's bed.

"How are you feeling? You look better, much better." Alice brought her lover's hand to her lips and kissed it. She noticed that Jenny was wearing a pretty nightdress, all lace and blue crèpe de chine.

"I'm still shaky. I've never had anything like this flu before. I'm drained, and my limbs feel like they are made of lead."

"That's how my father said it affected him. I just got off the telephone with Talon. He will be coming by tomorrow after the store closes."

"Is he now? So are you feeling the need to have your husband near?"

"Not really. But with Mama dying I need family around. I'm heartbroken over Mama."

Jenny's eyes locked onto hers. "Yes, Alice, I know how much you loved your mother. I'm sorry, so sorry." Jenny frowned. "Is your father doing all right?"

Alice pulled in a deep breath. "I'm not sure. With Mama's death, he's become like a recluse, and really doesn't care if he completely heals. He's still upstairs. No matter how often I knock on his door he refuses any and all company. The doctor hasn't been around since yesterday and come to think of it, I don't believe I've talked to Daddy since he's left. I know Doctor Evans said that Daddy would in time overcome his depression from losing Mother. That we needed to be here for Daddy but to allow him time to heal. I've never really given much thought about Father and his desires, his love of Mama. I guess I've been too self-centered to consider anything other than myself and Talon's peccadilloes." She looked around the drab room to see a few knick-knacks, a tall dresser, rocking chair, but not much else.

Jenny plucked at the quilt covering her and asked, "Have you any news about Jonathan Drake?"

Alice leaned back against her chair. "Funny, I asked Talon the same thing tonight. Thought with his carousing he might hear something, but he said no, he hadn't heard."

"I'm tired, Alice. If you don't mind I'd like to sleep."

A rainstorm started, light at first, but then it came down in torrents of misery. Lincoln Drake, not knowing what he was going to encounter, left his automobile parked a street away. The street lights helped him to see his way. He was getting soaked as he ran toward the mortuary.

Dashing inside, he stood dripping wet and fumbled his handkerchief from his breast pocket that he used to wipe his face and hair. The stench was horrific, making him gag. He slipped his gauze mask over his nose, but it didn't help. Staring about the dim room in which a single light bulb in the center of the ceiling created more shadows than anything else, he didn't see another living person. Another room just off of the main area from where he stood shed a light through the open door that was filled with coffins. No one, an attendant or otherwise, appeared to be about.

Glancing around, he was taken aback by the amount of bodies stacked on the floor like chopped wood, wondering if people knew what was happening, that their loved ones had been discarded like yesterday's garbage. It amazed him how a living breathing soul one day could become a decaying wrapped mummy the next. But what stuck with him most was the fact that these people had no one to claim them, to mourn over them, bring flowers to their graves.

Still weak from the flu, he looked around, dismayed and wondered how he would be able to find Jonathan. He moved with caution amongst more than fifty sheet-shrouded bodies, pausing only when he turned the tag over to read the name. Most were adults. Several were whole families who had perished. He ached enough, but was comforted to know his precious daughter's body hadn't been treated like this. Just this day, her body was taken with dignity by private hearse to the funeral home where generations of deceased Drake's were seen to with care.

Lona.

Daddy's girl. Why didn't God take him and not his child who was just starting to taste all that life had to offer? The moment he took his dead daughter's hand within his was the moment he started doubting God. A God that he'd been brought up to love and worship. Well, no more, and the bodies in this morgue gave him even more reason to doubt. If God wanted to strip the earth bare of all criminals, the people who harmed others, then do so, be selective, instead He let loose a scourge on all humans, the innocent.

Lincoln wiped at his eyes and continued searching. In a far corner, he found Ernesto Scala, the detective who was determined that Jonathan was guilty. Jonathan was next to him. Lincoln knelt and slowly opened the sheet. As his son's waxy features came into view, for a second there, he thought Jonathan was dead.

"Damn it," he swore and put his ear against Jonathan's chest. Feeling the soft swelling of his chest and hearing a strong heartbeat, Lincoln expelled the long breath he'd been holding. He felt Jonathan's forehead which was hot and clammy. Still sick.

Detective Jones made himself go into the armory. He needed to check on Scala and hoped he was recovering. The moment he opened the inner door to step into the ward the stench of vomit and loose bowels assaulted him. He fumbled for his mask and put it on. Moaning and coughing behind the makeshift canvas barriers could be heard all over. When he entered the area where Scala's bed was, a dark-haired woman lay in place of Scala. Apparently she was in the bad stages of the flu and he quickly backed out. Scala must be improving and moved to the ward for the recovering. He rushed over to where Jonathan Drake was being held. Only Drake wasn't there either. A small boy was leaning over the side of the bed and vomiting on the floor.

Jones backed out and glanced around, hoping to find Miss Fitzgerald. A harried looking nurse came toward him carrying a bedpan.

"Sir, you shouldn't be in here. Don't want you getting sick, now do we?" Looking at him over her mask, she shifted the empty bedpan in her hands. "Do you need help?"

He showed her his badge. "I'm looking for my partner Detective Scala who was in that bed over there. I'm also trying to find Jonathan Drake who was under arrest and in that bed across from my friend, Scala. Where are they? Have they been moved to the recovery room?"

The nurse crooked her finger at him. "Let me check the list for you." Placing the bedpan on the floor, she picked up the list of patients, living and deceased. She flipped through several pages and finally glanced at him.

"Is your friend…Ernesto Scala?"

Jones's skin prickled and he said, "Yes." Able to read faces for more years than he could count, he could see what was written on the nurse's. Her eyes were a dearth of sadness. "He's dead, isn't he?"

"I'm so sorry…so sorry."

Jones swallowed hard. "And Jonathan Drake? Where is he?"

She looked at her list and cleared her throat. "His body is at Chillers and Slate's mortuary, along with Mr. Scala's. Chillers and Slate's are taking on the dead with no next of kin."

"Is Liberty Fitzgerald on duty now?"

The nurse shook her head. "No, she's off for now. Due back tomorrow evening. Her father died today so she is in bereavement and handling his funeral."

Pulling his pocket watch out, he glanced at the time. 6:30 P.M. "Is there a telephone nearby?" he asked.

"Yes, right over there on the entry desk."

Jones quickly dialed his precinct. "Who can get to Chillers and Slate's mortuary fast?" he asked the policeman who answered.

"Good—get several guys and meet me there. Hurry!" He hung up and ran toward the front door. Christ, he prayed that what he suspected happening, wasn't. And if it was he was going to arrest one Miss Liberty Fitzgerald so fast she would never see the light of day again.

Just as Lincoln started to lift Jonathan from the floor, his son opened bloodshot eyes.

"Dad, is that you?" He fumbled for and gripped Lincoln's suit lapel.

"Yes, it's me. Hurry, let's get you out of here." He struggled to get Jonathan upright.

Jonathan's bare feet no sooner made contact with the floor, when his legs buckled and his weight almost pulled Lincoln down. Lincoln put his arm around Jonathan and started dragging and walking him toward the door.

"Oh...God...I'm sick," was all Jonathan could say before leaning over and heaving.

When he was finished, Lincoln hefted him up fireman style. Staggering under his son's weight, he left through the small empty office and out the back door. Outside, he didn't know if he could make it to his automobile, and wanted to kick himself for parking so far away. But, he had to try. He decided to cut through the cemetery and stepped inside the iron gates where rows upon rows of headstones blocked his view.

Jones left the armory and ran out into the rain where he pulled his coat collar tight. He hailed a cab that slowly chugged to a stop. The driver got out and proceeded to push past Jones.

"Wait!" yelled Jones and flashed his badge. "I need you to take me to Chillers and Slate's mortuary."

"Mister, ya might not want to use my cab. It's now an ambulance for the sick, by order of the mayor." He opened the back passenger door and leaning in, helped a very sick man to get out.

The nurse that Jones talked to earlier scurried out to take the failing man around the waist and help him inside.

Jones jumped in the backseat and ordered the cabbie to drive. "I'm past caring about this damn influenza. It can't hurt me more than it already has. Now get the lead out and take me to the morgue."

Jones glanced out the window that was streaked with rain blurring the street lamps. The driver wore a mask, hoping the damn thing would protect him. Jones scoffed. Both he and his wife wore masks too no avail.

The driver spoke, "You lose anyone to the grippe?"

Jones stared at the back of his head. What business was it of this man, and instead of telling him to mind his own fucking business, he said, "Yes, and you?"

The driver nodded. "It took my little girl. My wife and son are back there in the armory hospital, fightin' for their lives. Thank God for the doctors and nurses. Can't say they do much, though. Just make the sick comfortable. I guess." He paused for a brief moment and then continued. "My little girl—my Madeleine." He started crying and used his mask to wipe his eyes. "You?" He was finally able to say.

Yes, Jones had lost a loved one. His wife Clara, sweet, patient Clara who spent so much time alone while he was out chasing criminals succumbed almost a week ago. He'd telephoned both his sons. Frederick and his family were all right. Garth had the flu but was recovering. Having already buried his wife, Jones's house was empty, his life even more so. He dreaded becoming like Scala, with no one to give a shit about him. Scala who was scheduled to be dumped into a mass grave. *Had to bury the dead fast so they couldn't continue to contaminate, according to city hall.*

He lit a cigarette and thought he could get out and push the cab faster than it was going. The morgue was only five miles or less from the Armory, but for someone just getting over the flu it felt like a hundred miles. Over half of the police force were out sick, and those standing were reluctant to go searching for anyone. Couldn't blame them.

The cab pulled over. "Sir, we're here." The driver glancing out the window at the mortuary crossed himself.

Jones paid him and got out. He was moving too slow for his liking, his limbs felt lead-filled.

Two uniformed policemen hurried up to Jones.

"Have you been inside yet?" Jones asked.

"Nope, waiting for you to show. You didn't say on the phone what we were looking for, ya just said to get here."

Jones realized his mistake as soon as the cops spoke. He could blame it on the flu that still had him in its grasp, or he could blame it on being rattled from Scala's death and not knowing if Drake was dead or alive. He felt sure it was the later.

In the distance a belching stream shovel was digging a massive grave. Several men stood around it holding up lanterns. Lincoln, bent over from carrying Jonathan over his shoulder, and seeing the digging, tried to hurry, but couldn't. He followed a path between the headstones, some tall, some short, which protected him from being seen. Still he couldn't see where he stepped. His shoes squished in the mud, almost sucking them off his feet. Lincoln managed several more steps before the ground opened beneath him. He tumbled into an open grave, landing hard against a coffin, smacking his chin, his elbows and anything else that broke his fall. Stunned, he lay there gulping in air. The weight of Jonathan's body pushed Lincoln's face further against the pine box that a putrid odor emanated. He shoved Jonathan off his head.

Lincoln used his coat sleeve to wipe the blood trickling from his busted chin. If Jonathan was injured, it would have to wait because he couldn't see anything in the dark pit.

"Are you all right?" Lincoln asked.

Jonathan grunted a yes. The storm whipped up heavy torrents of rain to wash the mud down their faces.

Hearing voices coming on, Lincoln got close to Jonathan and put his hand over his mouth, cautioning him to be quiet.

"They have to be here, couldn't have gotten far." Lincoln recognized detective Jones's voice. Damn, the man was a constant.

The loud steam shovel burped as it was shut down. In the distance voices carried, followed by silence. Lincoln, a little over five-ten, stood on the coffin and peered out. About a dozen men were standing around the steam shovel and appeared to be having a lively conversation. The detective and cops gestured, sweeping the cemetery with their arms. The steam shovel driver was shouting at them, his arm rapidly pumping and pointing towards the mortuary. The engine started back up with a loud rattle and the bucket was lowered into the large hole. Death and burial won this round.

Lincoln bent low and grabbed Jonathan's hand. "We have to get out of here—now. Can you make it?"

"I'll try," was all Jonathan could say.

Lincoln helped Jonathan to his feet. They wobbled on the slick coffin. "Here, son, put your foot in my hand."

"What…"

"Quick," Lincoln interlaced his fingers together forming a stirrup, urging Jonathan to step on it.

Jonathan placed his foot against his dad's palms, put his hand on Lincoln's shoulder and with a grunt was boosted up and out of the grave. He landed flat on the ground and that's where he stayed, until he put his head back over the open grave and heaved.

Lincoln jumped upwards, and grabbing the edge of the grave, he pulled himself out. Standing next to his son's side, he hoisted Jonathan's long body over his shoulder.

He dodged through tall headstones and left by a side gate where he came out onto the street and continued to walk. Spotting his automobile a half block away, and now winded, he put Jonathan down where he leaned him against a brick wall.

"Jonathan, we're almost to my auto, can you make it?" Lincoln, breathing hard, pointed at his car.

"I don't think so," he said and spewed his guts out again.

"Come on. We're almost there." Lincoln practically dragged Jonathan to the car and opened the door for him. He helped him lie down in the backseat, he cranked the car, and then ran around to slip behind the large steering wheel. He drove to Liberty Fitzgerald's father's apartment located several miles north of where Liberty lived.

Lincoln was thankful that Keegan Fitzgerald's apartment was on the ground floor. He leaned Jonathan next to the door and fumbled for the key over the door right where Miss Fitzgerald said it would be. He half lifted, half carried, Jonathan into the apartment and into the bedroom where he stripped his muddy shoes and clothes off, and put him to bed. He pulled the quilt up next to his chin.

Leaving him alone, he went into the kitchenette where he found a tin basin under the sink. He filled the basin with hot water, grabbed the bar of soap, and took it back to his son.

He wrung out the washcloth and cleaned Jonathan's face and upper body. Before Lincoln knew what was happening, he collapsed to his knees and was sobbing and praying to that very God he'd forsaken. Begging The Man to heal Jonathan, to leave him with one child and not take both. When his sobs finally subsided, he raised his head to stare over at Jonathan who was watching him, his face full of questions.

"Where...are...we?"

"Back at Keegan Fitzgerald's."

"Where's Keegan?"

"Son, Miss Fitzgerald's father died today. My gratitude for the Fitzgerald family expands every day. This can't be easy for Miss Liberty. I wouldn't blame her if she never wanted to lay eyes on any of us again."

"Where is she?"

"I'm not sure. She called me and told me that you'd died, and to get your body at the mortuary. When she said she *loves* you, instead of *loved* you, I knew what she meant to say but couldn't. That you were alive and I was to get you from the mortuary. That's all I know."

"This damn grippe...killed too many—" He started coughing and Lincoln was quick to hand him his handkerchief.

"Yes it has." And the horrible news that Jonathan's sister Lona was dead from it would have to wait. His son had gone through enough horrors for one day.

Standing inside Fifi's apartment building foyer, Liberty buzzed the number next to Fifi's name. When there was no answer, she took the lift to the fifth floor and got out.

After knocking on the seamstress's door and again receiving only silence, Liberty tried the doorknob. The door slowly opened and the smell coming to meet Liberty was recognized instantly. Putting her mask on, she found the bedroom. Fifi was in bed, covered to her chin. Her mouth covered in bloody foam hung open in a grimace, her eyes unseeing. Liberty put her fingers next to her neck and felt for a pulse. There was none.

Liberty glanced around, searching for what she didn't know. She went through all the drawers. She looked in the wardrobe, feeling all the clothes, putting her hands in the pockets. The table next to the bed held a glass of water and a lamp with its light still burning. Peeking out from under the bed was a book. Liberty picked it up and started leafing through the pages. It was a journal of sorts, but mostly listed Fifi's list of conquests. Their accomplishments in bed. She read about herself. How Fifi hated her freckled skin, but was determined to overlook that. How she planned to have a good time with Liberty if the stupid girl let her. Liberty fanned through the book back to the date that Zelda died.

Fifi had written in English with a spattering of French here and there. She wrote about her love for Zelda, about Zelda's sexual desires, of Zelda's ability to bring Fifi to a climax more than once a night. She told of seeing another female seamstress, someone who didn't work for Foyle, someone who she'd seen coming from Zelda's dressing room about an hour before Jonathan Drake was discovered on top of Zelda. The seamstress was tall for a woman, dressed in a floral blouse, straight black skirt, and carrying a small basket with a pin cushion sticking out of it. Fifi noted that her clothing was tacky, not at all of the quality of the Follies sewer's, and even herself. And what seamstress didn't wear a pin cushion on her wrist? We all do. Fifi wrote about her love for Zelda and how Fifi hoped Jonathan would fry for what he'd done.

Liberty put the book into her doctor's bag. Taking the bed sheet, she commenced to shroud Fifi's body, all the while thinking that the woman would never again prey on a young dancer with stars in her eyes. She filled out the death certificate, guessing at the date of death, but did list the Joyeux Theater and Foyle himself as next of kin. Before leaving Fifi's apartment, she put in a call to the authorities to come and get Fifi's dead body.

Tired to her very core and as Liberty trudged up the steps to her own apartment, she hoped to get a few hours of sleep before going back to the armory. Confident that Lincoln Drake found Jonathan at the mortuary, she rounded the last flight of stairs to her apartment only to find several policemen waiting at her door.

"Miss Fitzgerald?"

"Yes?"

"You're under arrest."

Her mouth fell open in surprise. "What for? I've done nothing wrong. I'm needed at the clinic to help with the flu."

The cops took her by the arms. "Detective Jones said you would say that. He sends his regards for a job well done. He also said you would know what he's talking about."

Lincoln Drake took care of Jonathan throughout the night and well into the next day. When he deemed Jonathan was able to be left alone for a while, he returned to his own home to check on Earlene. He no sooner stepped out of his automobile, still wearing mud-caked clothes, when Detective Jones walked up to him and shoved him against his front door.

"What do you think you're doing?" Lincoln said.

"I'm arresting you for helping your son escape. Where is he, Mr. Drake? Where are you hiding him this time?"

"I don't know what you're talking about."

Earlene opened the door to find Lincoln in handcuffs. "What on earth is going on? Lincoln? Why are you being arrested?" Still wan looking from her bout with the flu, she slowly started for her husband's side.

Detective Jones put his hand out to stop her from coming any closer. "He helped Jonathan escape from the armory hospital, that's why."

"You have no proof that I've done any of that," Lincoln said.

Jones shrugged and picked at the dried mud on Lincoln's suit coat. "From the looks of you, I'd say you were mucking around a cemetery, getting all dirty. What do you say? Where have you been until now?"

"That's no proof. Yes, I was at a cemetery seeing to the burial place for my daughter. I'm putting her next to my parents. I slipped and fell into an open grave that was right next to where I was standing. I was also at the funeral home across town picking out a coffin."

"You are going to have to prove every word, Mr. Drake. It doesn't take a day and a half to arrange a funeral. In the meantime, I'm still arresting you." He ordered the two cops that were with him to put Lincoln in the waiting paddy wagon.

"Where are you taking him?" Earlene cried out.

Lincoln yelled at her from the back of the paddy wagon, "Contact Hollis Webster, our attorney. Have him meet me at the precinct."

When Earlene appeared confused, Jones approached and told her where he was taking her husband.

Earlene thought for sure the whole world had gone mad. Trying to absorb Lona's death and now this with Lincoln, and she still didn't know if Jonathan was alive or dead. Her family was being ripped apart. She closed the door and went to make her call.

Talon spent another busy day helping out customers, mostly servant's sent by their rich employers, and desperate people seeking anything that gave them hope they wouldn't get the flu. And those brave enough to shop in *Grand's*, he met with a wide smile.

But how could they not, when he had lined the store's shelves with a hot selling *Sanitas Fumigator* for treating influenza, lung and throat afflictions. He even put a half dozen of them in the front display window. They sold faster than the Paris knockoffs and ready-made clothes that women typically fought over. When they asked about the flu remedies he was selling, he assured each and every one that they worked.

Next to a stack of gauze masks, he sold camphor bags for people to wear around their necks. Anything for a profit, he'd become a fleecier of people and did it quite well. He reminded himself of the salesmen who used to sell fake medicines and were called snake-oil salesmen for lack of a better word. As the stuff flew off the shelves and he couldn't keep enough in the store, he didn't care. He'd put a sign in his window reminding people of the City's government law that to spit on the streets was illegal and if caught would cost them five-hundred-dollars. He even extended the City's law to include the inside of his store. If they spit in there, they paid Talon the fee, too hell with the government.

Only after it turned dark outside did he put the *Closed* sign in the window next to the front doors. Upon leaving, he along with a few die-hard employees, ten altogether, and most who had the flu in the spring and felt immune, prepared to go home. As they gathered their coats about them, opened umbrellas against the rain, and said goodnight, he nodded at each one. Alone, he turned to lock the doors.

The masked cab driver let him off in front of the Grand's mansion. He stopped to stare at the imposing brick and stone building with only a few windows showing lights within. The tall imposing door bore a large black wreath. He wasn't all too sure that he wanted to step inside a house teeming with influenza.

He picked up his small valise, one that held his toiletries while living at his office. His changes of suits and shirts he simply took off the rack. He longed for a hot tub to soak in, fill Charles in on the latest figures from the store, which, thanks to those damn worthless flu remedies were keeping the store above water. First off, he planned on seeing how Alice and Jenny fared. He came into a house that was quiet, too quiet for his liking. No maid was there to greet him, so he shrugged off his wet coat and hat and draped them on the stair rail's post.

He glanced in the parlor, silent as a tomb and where the fireplace was draped in black bunting. On the mantle, lit and elegant candelabra's flanked the large oil painting of Yvette Grand. Even with the fire burning, the place was as cold as death. Unable to stand at the shrine any longer, he sought out Jenny whose bedroom was down the hall in the servant's quarters.

After knocking, he eased the door open to find Jenny propped up in bed, reading a book of all things. He'd never thought about her being able to read or write for that matter. She glanced from the page to stare at him, to close the book, to smile at him, to open her arms wide, to invite him in.

Wearing his mask and not wanting to take any chances, he sat on the bed but refused to take her in his arms. "You don't look like you've been sick. I expected a walking skeleton."

She frowned at him. "Well, I have been sick, very sick. This flu is nasty and I'm just happy to be alive."

"How happy?"

"You know how happy."

"Show me," he said. Feeling it safe to do so, he removed his mask and grinned, and was awarded with a wide smile that reached her brown eyes.

"I can't do that. You should go see Alice. She's been waiting for you since dinner. She thought you'd be here to join her."

"Couldn't get away." He stowed his disappointment of Jenny not wanting him in her bed. He could wait, but he could also take a few nibbles with him. "Let's pretend I'm Doctor Montgomery, here to listen to your heart," he said with a chuckle. He untied pink ribbons and parted her lacy night robe to reveal her large breasts that he immediately cupped with both hands. The fullness of them overflowed his palms. "Doctor Montgomery has missed this…er…these." Using his teeth, he locked onto her large dusky nipple and commenced to suck as hard as he could.

She moaned and taking his hand pushed it under the covers. "What does Doctor Montgomery have to say about this?"

He pushed the covers aside and slipped his fingers into her slit and began working them. "Ah…yes, Doctor Montgomery finds that you have a fever between your legs."

Alice, wheeling her chair down the hallway, heard Talon's voice coming from Jenny's room. Anxious that he was home, she peered with caution through the partially opened door into Jenny's room. Momentarily abashed, her mouth tightened as she watched her husband making love to her maid. Blood pounded in her temples. Humiliated, she wanted to rush into the room and attack them both, tear at Talon, pummel Jenny until her face was a bloody pulp, but she didn't. Instead, she became a voyeur and watched as Talon made love with his hands, his mouth, his lips. Jenny undid his pants, pushed them off over his buttocks. She took his rigid penis between her hands, stroked him, and finally guided him into her.

Incredulous, Alice thought she was going to be sick as she watched her husband's hips thrusting, his bare buttocks going in and out. Jenny moaned with pleasure and met his surging climax. Talon fell against her in a trembling heap.

"I'm glad you're so much better," he said. Jenny's legs wrapped around his torso and she pulled him tight.

"Do me again," she said.

Alice fisted her hand against her mouth to keep from yelling accusations. Foreboding spread throughout her. And as the bed-springs squeaked and her husband and Jenny's cries of passion echoed out to her, Alice backed her chair up. She wheeled away from the bedroom, down the hall, across the foyer, and into the parlor where she tried to compose herself.

How dare Jenny do this, not with Alice knowing all that she did about her maid? And, Talon, dear twisted Talon who visited prostitutes and theater actress's to fulfill his sexual needs. What she'd just witnessed between Jenny and Talon was not a spur of the moment happening. They acted as though they'd been making love with each other for years.

Alice sobbed. She'd given Jenny her heart, her soul, and Talon stole it. He dirtied her love for Jenny. How could Jenny allow him to touch her? She couldn't, not if she loved Alice as she claimed. Alice looked at her mother's portrait, her eyes, her smile, and felt she'd betrayed her. Daddy would make it better, Daddy would help her get a divorce from Talon, send Talon and Jenny packing. Daddy would glue her life back together. Daddy...who was up-stairs in his bed and...

The grandfather clock on the wall loudly ticked and gonged seven loud times. Finally, when she composed herself enough to face her husband, Alice wheeled back into the foyer and called out, "Talon, are you home? Talon?" She waited, and he soon appeared from the hallway, neatly dressed, every hair in place.

"Yes, I just got in and was looking around for anyone. The house is too quiet," he said.

Smiling, he came toward Alice and dutifully bent to kiss her cheek. A chaste kiss on the cheek with lips that just a while ago was licking Jenny's pussy. How could he be so callous?

"Are you all right? Alice, you're not getting sick are you?

You're flushed." Alarmed, he felt her face.

"Warm, hot, or maybe stone cold. How do I feel, Talon?" God, she wanted to slap his lying mouth off.

"You feel warm, but maybe it's the excitement of seeing me?" He chuckled and taking her hand, put it against his lips. "I'm so glad to find you well. But, I'm worried about your father. Has he allowed anyone to talk to him?"

Oh? And just how worried was he that he made love to Jenny before seeing her father? "No." She put her hands on the large wheels of her chair and started toward the parlor, but he insisted on doing it for her. And while he walked behind her, pushing, she talked. "Daddy will not take food, or anything. Maybe you can get him to eat something." She hoped he could.

"I'll try. Why don't I go up now? Have the maid fix a tray and I'll take it to him. Ah…do we still have servants?"

"I've hired someone new. Beatrice Wilson. I'll go have her prepare another tray. How about you, are you hungry?" she asked.

"Yes, I am, but I can wait."

"You and I can talk later, then." She eyed him, wondering just when he stopped loving her, if he ever did. Certainly, he married her for money, prestige and to climb the social ladder. And she'd married him for what she thought was love. She was naive, delusional, and she hated him.

Talon put the tray filled with hot dishes on the hall table. He situated his mask and then knocked on Charles's door. After waiting for a polite minute or two and with no response, he used Jenny's set of servant's key to unlock the door.

"Charles?" he called out. Still no answer, and with dread, he pushed the door wide open and was met by a dark decaying presence. The room stank of vomit, feces, and of death. He swallowed the bile that pushed to the back of his throat, forcing him to hurry to the window and throw open the heavy drapes and the large window. Pulling his mask off, he leaned out the window and threw up. Taking out his handkerchief, he wiped at his forehead, and gulped in the clean night air, breathing, trying to rid himself of the overpowering stench. He hoped all of the flu germs had left the room, and prayed that he wouldn't become ill with this devastating disease.

Dreading to do so, he turned toward the bed. "Charles?" he said and approached the man's bedside where he turned on the electric lamp. Talon peered at a face with wide-open eyes, and at a mouth drawn into a death grimace and one where bloody foam dribbled down his chin and onto the sheets. From the looks of him, Alice's father had been dead for a least a day or more. My God, why didn't Alice realize something was wrong when Charles refused to open the door, refused all food? Talon wondered if after losing his wife if Charles wanted to join her in death. He'd heard of that happening before.

With no other choice, he closed his father-in-law's eyes, and folded his hands across his chest. Unable to look at Charles's face any longer, he covered it with the sheet. Talon paused to take in the large room, decorated for a man, and lived in by a man. The dark mahogany dresser held a fancy tortoiseshell tray with cufflinks, a pocket watch, a gold pinkie ring, and Charles's billfold. Pausing to finger the items on the tray, Talon slipped the ring on his finger and held it out to admire the diamond set within the gold. It was a perfect fit, and he decided to wear the ring. He finally left the room.

He sought out Alice who was waiting for him in her bedroom suite. She took one look at his face and broke into sobs.

"Daddy's dead, isn't he?"

"I'm afraid he's been gone for a day or more. Perhaps after

losing your mother he didn't want to live anymore. Alice, I'm so sorry." He bent over and picking Alice up out of her chair, he carried her to her bed where he laid her down. He removed her shoes, and pulled the blanket over her. "I'll go make arrangements to have your father's body removed." He paused next to the bird cage. "Did you know your birds are dead? I'll have the new maid, what's her name…ah…Beatrice remove the cage."

Alice turned against her pillow and gave way to more tears. He left her alone, unwilling to even try to understand her grief. He couldn't. He was a taker, and it was the way he went through life and always would. He knew that Charles had accepted him only because of Alice, that the man would do anything for his daughter.

He would need to have Charles' will read as soon as possible. Hell, he only hoped the lawyer in charge of Grand's affairs was alive and well. And he really hoped that Alice and he as her spouse were set to inherit it all.

Chapter Twenty-One

Liberty had Lincoln Drake to thank for sending a lawyer to represent her. Spending two days in jail was enough for her.

Chester Miller, middle-aged with brown thinning hair and blue eyes, cleared his throat and removed papers from his brief case. "Miss Fitzgerald, Lincoln Drake has posted bail for both you and himself. I will be taking you out of here today. But, you are forbidden to leave Manhattan, work, or do anything to jeopardize your case."

Liberty could only stare at him through the bars of her cell. "My nursing skills are needed to help the sick with this Spanish Influenza. How am I to live without working? I must pay my rent, buy food."

"I understand, but these are orders from the police. They don't want you anywhere near the armory or a hospital. Mr. Drake has made arrangements for me to give you money. He said for you to accept it and that you will see him soon."

"Do you know anything about Jonathan Drake? Is he still ill? Where he's been taken?" She wanted to take the slow moving man and shake information out of him.

"I'm afraid I'm not privy to that information. And, Miss Fitz-gerald, please don't speak about those circumstances while we are here in this police station. The walls have ears. As far as anyone knows, Mr. Drake left the mortuary on his own. We're calling it a mistaken death."

"Privy!" the words exploded from her. "You should know all about his whereabouts."

"Once again, I must caution you to hold your tongue. I'm told I'm to deal with you and you only."

She scoffed and grabbed the bars with both hands.

"Miss Fitzgerald, you must know that Detective Jones is livid concerning the way his fellow detective was treated."

"I took the best care of Detective Scala that I could. He died. I couldn't help it. My father died," she said and continued, "I'm glad I made it look like Jonathan died. I'd do it again if I had the chance. Yes, I'd do it again!" She left her attorney standing there and went to sit on her cell's small filthy mattress. "I've had no time to even mourn for my father, to see to his burial," she railed at Mr. Miller and started sobbing again.

It wasn't long before the jailer came to open the cell and allow her out.

Outside, a wagon filled with several coffins rattled by. Every-one wore masks. Her lawyer put his on, and handed one to Liber-ty. They waited until a chauffeur-driven car bearing Lincoln Drake and another man pulled up. The chauffeur got out and opened the door for them. They got in and Liberty removed her mask to stare at Lincoln Drake who greatly resembled the man she loved. Albeit much older and with hair turning grayer each day, the resemblance was reassuring to her.

"Miss Fitzgerald, I'd like you to meet my attorney, Hollis Webster."

The white haired man with yesterday's mutton chop sideburns took her offered hand and shook it. "I'm pleased to make your acquaintance I'm sure. And please be assured that anything said in my presence is privileged information and will not be repeated." He was stiff, formal, and to the point.

"Mr. Drake, thank you for posting my bail. I'd still be in there if it wasn't for you."

"No thanks needed. I was in the same jail, only down a few cells. My lawyer here, Mr. Webster, cannot represent us both, but Mr. Miller will do a good job for you."

"Mr. Drake, I have something here for you." She reached into her doctor's bag that had been returned to her and pulled out Fifi's journal. "Please read the page I've dog eared."

Both Miller and Webster stared at the journal.

Inquisitive, Webster, the senior lawyer asked, "What's that? Something to do with the case?"

"Yes, I believe it may be a clue to the real murderer." She watched Lincoln read the entry about the seamstress, someone Fifi had never seen before. He handed the book to his lawyer who quickly read the marked page before passing it to his colleague Mr. Miller.

"I would imagine there are a lot of seamstress's working at the theater." Miller, her attorney closed the journal and handed it back to Liberty.

"That's where you're wrong. True, there are several head seamstresses like Fifi. And they have a handful of sewers working under them. But, everyone knew everyone. If there was someone new, she would have been introduced to Fifi, and interviewed by her. Please, listen to me, people didn't just walk in off the street and go to work there without Sidney Brawley hiring them or taking them around and introducing them to all the help, it didn't happen. Foyle's productions were in competition with all the other theaters and shows. We employees signed a written agreement to keep everything that happened inside the theater a secret. And that included everyone from a stagehand, seamstress, songwriters, and performers. Fifi wrote it in this journal that the woman was seen by her leaving the theater less than an hour before Jonathan was found with Zelda. I'm sure it's an important clue." Liberty's gaze went between the two men.

"And, this…hmmm…Fifi, this seamstress is willing to testify?" Webster asked.

"I'm afraid she succumbed to the flu. I found her dead," Liberty answered.

"Is this clue admissible as evidence then?" Lincoln said.

"I'll have to get all the particulars before I can determine that. Mr. Drake, it just might be for the best of all if Jonathan turned himself in. Clear his name with a trial." Webster cleared his throat.

Liberty was stunned to hear the lawyer even say such a thing. "You're wrong, Mr. Webster. Jonathan will have to clear his name before giving himself up. I see how the justice system works in this city. There is none." Liberty leaned back against the seat.

Lincoln took a deep breath. "Miss. Fitzgerald, don't give up hope. I'm hiring a private detective, should have done it weeks ago. You and I will continue searching for this mystery woman."

Miller sputtered, "Miss Fitzgerald is supposed to remain in her home. She's not to work in a hospital, she's not to go near the Joyeux Theater…she's—"

"We understand," Lincoln said while putting his hand over Liberty's. "However, neither Miss Fitzgerald nor I intend to stop trying to prove Jonathan's innocent. Because he is…you know. I'll not see my son imprisoned for something he didn't do."

Liberty let it known that she planned to go to the theater.

"You can't," lectured her lawyer.

"I have too," she argued. "Please hear me out. I was on stage singing when all heck broke loose and Jonathan was arrested. Then everyone got sick and I started nursing them. I'm going to the theater as a nurse and not a performer. I need to know what is going on there."

"Maybe she's right," said Mr. Webster.

"What if I escort Miss Fitzgerald to the theater," Lincoln volunteered.

"Yes, that will be fine," Webster spoke and nodded.

"Trying to get Jonathan away from the morgue is all they have me on, yes?" said Lincoln Drake. "And they have no proof I did it."

Webster looked at his client. "Yes, that's why you are out of jail right now. They have to prove the charges, and they can't. No one saw you."

"If Jonathan wasn't in a real jail then how can I technically be charged with stealing someone out of there?" Lincoln asked.

Mr. Miller cleared his throat. "Because, he was still under arrest. Manacled to the bed, I'm told." Miller cut his eyes over at Liberty. "For Miss Fitzgerald here, the charges are more severe. Planning and abetting Jonathan's escape. Mishandling of detective Scala's corpse. Also helping to hide Jonathan since the murder. Yes, indeed, quite long."

"I gave the utmost of care to Detective Scala. He died, and I tagged him just like all the others. I didn't abuse his corpse in anyway."

"That's not what Detective Jones is saying. He said you had his partner's body bound for a pauper's grave...er...to be buried in a pit with those who have no loved ones to claim them. He's angry as hell."

Liberty looked out the window, noticing they were stopping in front of a stately brick mansion built close to the sidewalk and enclosed with a black wrought iron fence.

"Is this your home?" Liberty asked Mr. Drake.

"Yes. We'll only be here for a while," he answered. "I want you to say hello to my wife, Earlene. You briefly met her and my daughter Lona at the police station. She can use another woman's company right now. Earlene's devastated by Lona's death. Lona was our only daughter, my pride and joy," his voice broke and he quickly looked out the window.

Liberty remembered how proud Jonathan was of his family, his only sister. "Mr. Drake, Jonathan was very fond of his little sister. How's your wife holding up?"

"Holding up is about it. The accusations against Jonathan almost had her breaking, and now this. Jonathan doesn't know about Lona."

"Mr. Drake, I must find out about my brother, Blaine. Last I saw him he was in the armory hospital. I don't even know if his wife and little boys are all right."

Lincoln's grin for her was reassuring. "Once inside, I'll find out for you." Lincoln ordered the chauffeur to take the lawyers back to their office.

The limousine no sooner pulled away when Liberty turned to Mr. Drake. "Is Jonathan safe? Is he at my father's?"

"Yes, he is. He's relapsed. No doubt from being in that morgue and lying on the cold floor. It also didn't help to have him dumped into an open grave while we were running from the mortuary."

Liberty's mouth fell open, but she didn't have a chance to ask any more questions for the front door opened and Earlene Drake stood there. She held a delicate hanky in one hand, her eyes red from crying. She reached out for Lincoln and he took her in his arms.

"I was so frightened," she said, and clasped her husband's broad shoulders. "What has happened, you must tell me," she insisted. Spotting Liberty standing there she put out her hand and grasped Liberty's within hers.

"Earlene," Lincoln said and continued, "You remember meeting Miss Liberty Fitzgerald the night Jonathan was arrested."

Earlene squeezed Liberty's hand a little tighter. "Yes, yes, of course I do. How can I ever repay you for what you have done for our son? Please—please come in."

After they settled her into a floral cushioned chair in the sitting room, Liberty accepted a hot cup of coffee from the Drake's servant. Looking around, Liberty compared the home Jonathan was raised in, to the home she was raised in. The furniture in here was richly made. It was foreign without an inkling of the familiar. She wanted to be at her apartment and the memories she had with Jonathan there. Her bed where they'd shared conversations, sweated together, and shared their bodies in the most intimate moments of her life. The teacup he'd drank out of. Yes, she wanted to wrap herself with Jonathan's memory, here she couldn't.

She hadn't been given a moment to grieve for her father, to attend his burial. With the whirlwind of dead bodies, going to Fifi's apartment, and being arrested, she wasn't allowed to go to the cemetery to make sure it was done and done right. As tears came to her eyes, Liberty thought about her dad, his talents, but most of all his love for his family, and her love for him. Unlike a lot of fathers who simply existed and left their children to find their own way in life, her father didn't. He spread his love between all of them. Liberty learned well from her father's teaching. She set about trying to make each person that she came in contact with live a better life. She didn't' want to see the sacrifices her father made for her education go to waste.

Wiping her eyes, she shuddered and looked around. The difference between her life and Jonathan's was apparent. But what was also apparent was the love the Drake's have for their son. Lincoln fought hard for Jonathan, put his reputation, his life, on the line to clear him. Both of the Drake's were devastated by Lona's death.

When Earlene plied her with questions about the first time Liberty met Jonathan, Liberty told almost all. Their personal moments were not to be shared.

Lincoln placed the telephone receiver on the desk and came over to her. His face was solemn and at first she thought something bad happened to Jonathan.

"Miss Fitzgerald," he said and put his hand on her shoulder. "I've made those inquiries about your brother and have him on the telephone. He wants to talk with you."

Liberty stared at the waiting phone. Nothing but bad news waited on the other end, of this she was sure. With Lincoln's help, she slowly stood and made her way to the telephone. She put the cone-shaped receiver to her ear.

"Blaine?" she said.

His muffled reply confirmed her fears. "Sis, I called my apartment manager. He tells me that my family is sick. No one's seen them for days. He says the sickness went through my apartment building like loose bowels after bad food."

"Are you still in the hospital?"

"Yes, I had a relapse—help me. Sis, please see to my family."

"I'll go right away. Blaine, don't worry, I'm sure everything is all right."

She hung up and looked at Lincoln and Earlene Drake. "I've got to go check on my brother's family."

"My dear," said Earlene, "Let Lincoln drive you. You'll get there faster. And, if I can do anything, please let me know."

Lincoln took Liberty's tan-colored coat from the coat rack and helped her into it. She buttoned it.

"As Earlene says, you shouldn't do this alone," Lincoln said.

"Miss Fitzgerald?" Earlene asked in a soft voice. "May I come with you, be of help?" Her eyes pleaded, and Liberty knew the woman wanted to get out of the house, away from the memories assailing her of her daughter.

"Yes," she said and took the woman's hands. "I'd like that."

Lincoln helped his wife into her coat and then opened the door for them.

Jonathan sat on Keegan Fitzgerald's sofa. Even with a heavy quilt tight against his neck, he couldn't get warm. He'd cranked the radiator up as far as he dared and still he'd pulled every blanket off the bed and wrapped it around himself. The cold reminded him f his time on the rooftop wearing Zelda's cape.

For the second time in a matter of weeks he'd beaten the devil influenza. Especially with the reports saying that if a person re-lapsed they died. He had much to thank his father and Liberty for. He knew she'd pretended like he had died to get him out of the armory, and that his father saved him from the morgue, fallen into a grave, and somehow got him here to Keegan's apartment.

The apartment was lonely without Keegan. He couldn't even turn on a light for fear the cops were watching and he'd be found out. A two-day-old newspaper on the floor dated November 11th, had announced the end of the war.

Jonathan, so far had only ventured down the hallway late at night to use the toilet. He hadn't bothered to bathe yet, but changed from his vomit covered clothing to one of Keegan's suits, his Sunday best. The pants were too short, the waist tight, he didn't care. He also had the start of a beard and mustache, black, with no more blonde disguises.

He stared at the photographs on the bureau, knew them by heart. Several pictures were of Keegan's family back in Ireland and of them here in America. There was one with Liberty and her brothers, all three smiling and poised in their best clothing. With the armistice having been signed, Teague, the one fighting in Europe was due home soon. Teague would live here as he did before going into the army. Jonathan wondered if Teague Fitzgerald knew his father was dead. He didn't think so.

Wrapping the blanket around him like an Indian Chief, he padded his way over to the kitchenette and poured a cup of coffee. He missed Liberty. *Missed*—hell—he longed for her. Her family made ultimate sacrifices for him and he could never repay her for all they did. He hoped that Keegan and Blaine didn't get the flu from going to the police station. But Liberty's brother Blaine said that the grippe was going through the furniture factory before they went to jail, that it was closed right now. If the flu didn't take a person out physically, it took away their means of earning a living.

His forced isolation was getting on his nerves, he wanted to call Liberty, see how she fared.

He'd fallen in love with a freckled-face, red-headed spitfire. Liberty. Her name meant just the opposite to him. He felt no liberty right now, only shackled to an apartment, shackled to a life on the run, to hide out constantly. He wanted the freedom her name meant. He wanted the liberty to walk around a free man, he wanted to be free of the accusations that settled on his shoulders and trailed him everywhere. He wanted to be free to walk the streets with the woman he loved. Liberty. He wanted Liberty. To hold her close, smell the lilac fragrance nestled in her hair, touch her soft skin, kiss her eyelids, kiss her lips, tell her he loved her, wanted to marry her, start a family with her. Oh…yes…he wanted all those things and more.

He picked up a picture of Liberty in her nurses cap, an oval shaped photograph of a father's pride and joy. Keegan told him how proud he'd been of Liberty when she graduated from nursing school. Jonathan could see a need for the health care that Liberty brought to most. He could also see a need for a clinic to treat people in the tenements, the poverty stricken areas where diseases prevailed. A need to teach people about prevention. He could help the Lillian Wald foundation branch out, build a clinic and name it after the Fitzgerald's. The idea took root and started to grow. No matter what happened with him, prison or the electric chair, he wanted a clinic built and staffed.

He opened the bureau drawer and searched for paper, pencil, and a ruler. Finding what he sought, he went into the kitchenette and sat at the table. In the room without windows, he turned on the overhead light and started to draw. He drew a building, a clinic. He drew it from the inside out. He drew rooms to treat patients, rooms to do small operations. He drew an outside façade, not too fancy, but sturdy looking and one that would beckon people in. Across the top of the page he penciled, Keegan Fitzgerald's Clinic.

If he survived this mess, his calling would be not to design skyscrapers, but hospitals, clinics, anyplace that took care of the sick. He'd been humbled in many ways and this was the most humbling of all.

He listened to the wall clock chime three times.

Liberty got out of Lincoln's automobile and asked them to remain there until she found out what was going on. She glanced at the gray overcast sky. The clouds matched the world as it was right now, she pulled on her mask. This was a world she didn't recognize. One of scurrying people with heads down, eyes averted, wearing masks, and wagons going by picking up the dead. It was medieval, and felt like the plague had descended upon the earth, again, and this time it was just as deadly.

Close by, raggedy dressed youngsters, three girls and a boy, jumped rope. Two girls twirled the long rope while another girl jumped. The boy watched. With each slap of the rope against the sidewalk they chanted, *"I had a little bird—its name was Enza—I opened the window and In-flu-enza."* They giggled and started the chant again when Liberty grabbed the rope and stopped its decent.

"Why are you out here playing? Shouldn't you be inside with your family?"

A thin dirty-faced girl, glared back. "My mom's dead. My dad's workin'. I ain't got no family inside. None of us do." She stuck her tongue out in defiance. Her companions gathered close to her, all stared with grim faces, distrustful.

Liberty could only nod. She swallowed, who was she to tell anyone what to do? Her heart went out to the children who long ago lost their innocence, lost all hope.

"Miss Fitzgerald," Lincoln called her name.

She walked slowly back to the automobile where Lincoln had his hand out the window offering her some money. "Give this to the youngsters. They might be hungry."

She accepted the bills and going back to where the kids were jumping rope, she held the money out. "Here, get something to eat, and you can thank Mr. Drake over there." The rope dropped and the kids ran over to her with grasping hands taking the money.

Climbing the steps to Blaine's apartment building, Liberty hurried inside and up one flight to the second floor where she took the key from over the door and used it.

The smell hit her first and she could be blind and would know exactly what it was.

Decay.

She kept her doctor's bag clutched in her hand.

"Marybeth?" she called out.

When no one answered, she tried again. "Marybeth? It's me, Liberty. Blaine's sent me to check on you." She hurried into the bedroom and suddenly stopped. Her hand went to her mask and she looked on in horror.

Marybeth and Shawn lay together in death. Their skin stretched a slate blue color. Liberty backed out of the room and ran into the boy's shared bedroom. The bed was rumpled and unmade. No sign of Kenny.

"Kenny!" she screamed.

A sob came from under the bed and she got on her knees to peer underneath it. Her nephew was scrunched against the wall. Tears slicked his cheeks. She reached for him.

"Come here, Kenny."

He did as told. He squirmed out from beneath the bed and collapsed into her arms. She held his small body, allowing his hot tears to soak into her coat. When at last he stopped his loud sobs she leaned back to make eye contact. Taking out her hanky she wiped at his tears that pooled underneath his eyes and spiked his lashes. He felt clammy, but not with the flu but from being upset and crying so much.

"Auntie Lib, Momma and Shawn don't move. They're sick." Again, he started to cry.

"My sweet, sweet, Kenny, do you know how many days it's been since they stopped talking?" she asked, knowing he was old enough to know, yet too frightened to remember such.

His small shoulders shrugged and again he snuggled against her, balling the material of her coat inside his hand. She cupped the back of his head and pulled him close.

"Did you get sick, Kenny? Did you vomit?"

He shook his head. "Nope."

"Kenny, I have to take care of things here and then I'm going to take you to my place. I'd like you to stay inside your room here until I say it's all right to come out."

"Why can't I stay with Momma and my brudder?"

Liberty drew in a deep breath and said, "Kenny, it's because they have died. You know what death is?"

"Maybe."

"Do you remember church where the priest spoke about heaven and hell?" She waited for him to nod. "Well, that's where your momma and brother have gone. They're in heaven."

"Without me?" he said, his voice quivering. "Why are their bodies still in the bed?"

"That's because their souls are with God in heaven. Those bodies that you see in the bed are no longer alive, they can't see or move." She tilted Kenny's chin. "I'm going to put clean clothes on you and take you outside. There are some people out there who are going to help us."

"Where's my daddy? Is he dead?" His face scrunched up and he looked like he was going to cry again.

"No, Kenny. He's better and getting well, and he should be home soon."

When Kenny nodded, Liberty got to her feet. "Can you show me where your clothes are kept?"

He opened a drawer in the dresser. "These are my things. Shawn has two drawers, I have two."

"Let's see," Liberty said and pulled out a clean pair of brown wool knee pants, a shirt, suspenders, and black hose. When she started to help him out of his undergarments, he pulled away.

"I can do that, I'm eight."

"Yes, you are but before you do, I want you to wash all over. Then put on your clean clothes."

Liberty waited for him and finally he appeared. His blonde curls were tamed with water. His blue eyes searched her face.

"I'm going to pack clothes for you and then I'm taking you outside to the people waiting in an automobile. Kenny, you have to be a big boy for your auntie, because I have to notify the authorities to come and take away your momma and brother's bodies."

"No!" he screamed, his eyes gone wide.

"I'll be here. I'm not leaving you alone again, never alone, Kenny do you understand?"

When he just stood there in agony, his mouth clamped into a firm line, Liberty nudged him. "Do you understand? I'll not leave you alone—I'm here."

And when he finally nodded, she took his satchel and his hand and guided him outside to where the Drake's waited.

Lincoln got out.

Liberty shook her head at him. "Both Marybeth and Shawn are dead. This is Kenny. I have to go back inside, would you mind watching him?"

Earlene leaned out the open window. "My goodness, what a pretty little boy. Come here child."

Lincoln opened the door. But Kenny squeezed Liberty's hand and shook his head. "No," he said. "I want to be with Aunt Lib."

Liberty forced him to look at her. "I have things to do in there. I won't be long. This is Mr. and Mrs. Drake. They aren't going anywhere without me."

Lincoln smiled at Kenny. "My wife needs protection. While I help your aunt, would you mind guarding my wife out here?"

"Mr. Drake, You shouldn't risk the flu."

"I've had it once. I don't believe I can get it again."

"You might relapse. Just wait here until I have their bodies taken away."

He finally agreed and helped Kenny into the backseat with Earlene. He got back behind the wheel.

When a hearse drove by, Liberty hailed them and asked them to wait.

Liberty went back inside her brother's home. There she filled a basin with water, got a sponge and taking a deep breath, walked into the bedroom. She commenced to wash Marybeth's face and arms. Seeing her burgeoning stomach, Liberty removed her stethoscope from her doctor's bag, and putting it into her ears she put the other end against Marybeth's mounding abdomen. She listened in hope, but there was nothing but silence. The baby soon of this world wasn't to be. Cleaning her nephew's body and mourning over his angelic face so still, she wrapped both bodies in sheets and pinned their death certificates on each with orders to be buried in the Fitzgerald plot.

Marybeth's read: Marybeth Fitzgerald and baby.

Shawn's read: Shawn Keegan Fitzgerald.

Liberty felt hollow, like someone took a knife and scooped out her insides, starting with her brain, organ by organ, emptying her out until there was nothing left to keep her body functioning, nothing but an empty shell.

She signaled for the men to come inside and remove the bodies. She gave them written instructions of what funeral home they were to be taken to. Following the men and stretchers outside, Liberty watched as they loaded the bodies inside the hearse. She joined Kenny whose big eyes stared out the automobile's window at the hearse.

She climbed into the car and putting her arm around Kenny, she sat there wondering how she was going to tell Blaine about Marybeth and Shawn.

Alice sat in her wheelchair that was pulled against the dining room table. She stared down the long length of it to where her husband sat in all his duplicity, stupidity, cutting his steak with precision. She wondered what he would do if she told him that his lover Jenny was a cold blooded killer. But, how could she say anything when she was equally guilty? Her plans went into the commode when Jonathan was the man with Zelda that fateful night and not Talon. Oh, how easy it was to have been if everything had gone according to plans, a deceitful plan, a deceitful bait setting her husband up as the murderer. He was to be in Sing Sing prison by now, or already fried. Oh...yes, Talon of the cheating heart and who sickened her just to look at.

And now she discovers that not only is he cheating on her with women in the theater, but that Jenny who she thought of as hers, her lover, someone to call her own was in bed with him as well. She'd believed Jenny was forever, someone to grow old with, travel, see the world, and help her to run *Grand's*. But now, seeing Talon and Jenny together brought the thought slamming into her mind that she was the one being set up. She wondered if she was next. They could easily murder her and make it look like she died from the flu.

Poison.

She stared at the food on her plate, the scalloped potatoes, and the peas. Were they tampered with?

..."I say," Talon's words filtered down the table. "Alice, are you well? You're not getting the flu, are you?"

When she didn't respond, he clanked his knife against his water glass. "Alice?"

"Yes, I hear you, Talon. I'm fine. But the loss of Daddy is getting to me" She wiped her eyes with her napkin and tried to suppress her sobs.

"Don't forget you and I have a meeting with your father's attorney later this week to go over his will," Talon said with no feeling whatsoever.

Alice stared at him. The ass, the unmitigated ass, no tears, no emotion to show he was in mourning. Well, he wasn't, and why should he be? He was getting what he married her for, or was he?

"His will? Ah…yes, Daddy's will."

Talon sipped his coffee from a decorated cup rimmed with gold. He replaced his cup back in the saucer. "If this sickness doesn't subside soon, there will be nothing left of your father's fortune to discuss."

"Is it that bad?"

"Yes," he answered and wiped his mouth using his napkin. "Only because this flu is keeping people away from the stores in droves. No one dares to shop and risk getting ill. Those that do shop come into the store to buy flu remedies. I've stocked plenty of them. But, I'm sure your father's lawyers are gathering information as to where the stores finances are today compared to where they were when your father made out his will."

Alice, having been told by her mother that her father changed his will recently, knew exactly how it read. Her father never cared for Talon, and it appeared that the will would be very enlightening, indeed, very enlightening.

She was now sandwiched between the evil of Jenny and the evil of Talon. Had they made vile plans where Alice was concerned? Jenny knew too much. Alice studied Talon who returned her gaze with one of his own and with a deadly smile to match.

"You should eat your dinner. You'll need your strength for the funeral and meeting the lawyers."

A loud knock sounded on the front door and with no servant around, Talon stood and went to look out of the dining room window.

"It's the hearse. They are here to take your father's body to the funeral home, and it's about time." He hurried from the room to leave her sitting there, alone.

Glad that he was taking care of the arrangements, horrified to be here in this house with him and Jenny, she didn't know what to do. She could only wonder if Jenny told Talon that it was Alice's idea to betray him, that he was supposed to be the one framed for Zelda's murder. Jenny said that from the back both Talon and Jonathan looked alike. That she had to use the knife. It wasn't Jenny's fault that Zelda DeLane juggled both men like a circus performer. That particular night, both Alice and Jenny thought it would be Talon. But now Alice knew the truth of it all, that Jenny knew damn well Talon wouldn't be there, and that Jonathan would. How nice. Jenny altered Alice's plans to get rid of Talon so that she would end up having him all to herself. But all good plans go awry and the big thing they didn't count on was Jonathan's escape, and Liberty Fitzgerald's hiding him. Oh...yes, she and Jenny knew Jonathan's every move after that night at the Joyeux. But they didn't count on the flu. And the one big colossal sized obstacle that Alice didn't count on was Jenny being Talon's lover.

It was all becoming too much. Her mother and father's death was a crushing blow, and now this enlightenment about Jenny and Talon being laid out for her. Alice's eyes welled with tears. She used her napkin to dab at them.

The side door opened and Jenny strolled into the room with a bold confidence. She nodded a good evening and walked over to the sideboard to dish up some dinner. How blatant of the woman. She should be eating in the servant's quarters.

But Jenny came over right next to Alice and after putting her plate on the table, she kissed Alice on the lips. A long drawn out kiss with Jenny's tongue searching inside Alice's mouth, and with Alice wanting to bite Jenny's tongue off.

Jenny finally took her seat. "I'm famished. It feels like forever since I last ate." She smiled at Alice and patted her hand. "How about you? Are you eating?"

Alice nodded. "Shouldn't you be eating in the servant's quarters?"

Jenny forked her potatoes and paused. "Other than the cook

and Beatrice, there's no one left. Besides you and I are close enough that we can share a meal or two, don't you agree?"

Alice swallowed, almost choking on her spit. "Yes, you're right. You are my companion after all."

Jenny ate with gusto, buttering her buns, eating peas and steak, followed by two glasses of red wine. A change had come over Jenny, more self-assured of her position within the household, more in control of everything. It was like a reversal of fortune.

"Here," Jenny said. "You haven't eaten a thing. Let me get you food that's hot. The steak is cooked just like you like it." Before Alice could stop her, Jenny got to her feet and went to get Alice a fresh plate.

Returning, she put the plate down in front of Alice. Alice's stomach churned. Was the food safe? Did Jenny slip something into it?

"Truly, I'm not hungry." She started to roll her chair away from the table but Jenny put her hands on the large wheel and stopped its motion.

"You need to eat. Really, Alice, it's what your mother would want. For you to stay strong in such trying times." She grinned and teased. "Don't make me force feed you like a naughty child."

Alice cut the steak and putting it into her mouth, chewed. Flavorful and mouthwatering, she didn't know if she could taste poison or not, and thinking it would be hard to poison a piece of steak, she continued to chew. After all, Jenny didn't know Alice had saw her husband licking Jenny out, reminding her of a dog gnawing at a bone. Now Alice must act as if nothing changed between this evening and last. Nothing at all.

So she cleaned her plate and waited to keel over.

She didn't.

"Where's Mr. Montgomery? I thought he'd be here with you,"

Jenny said.

"The men from the funeral home came to take Daddy's...ah...to take him away." Tears sprung anew and she couldn't help but sob. More for the predicament she now found herself in than for losing Daddy. Oh...God...why did she ever start this?

"Rather late, isn't it? I'd have thought they would have come earlier, this morning perhaps."

Alice shrugged. "It's because they have so many bodies to collect. How morbid sounding." She started to roll her chair back, when again Jenny put her hand against the wheel and stopped her.

"Let me," Jenny said and came around behind her chair to pull Alice away from the table. She started rolling it toward the elevator. "Here, here, Alice darling. Let me put you to bed and make you feel all better. Would you like that? Would you like me to make you feel better all over?"

Alice could only nod.

Chapter Twenty-Two

The window curtains were opened just enough to allow Jonathan to peer out. He watched as a woman, dressed in black and with a wide brimmed hat and veil covering her face, climbed the steps to the apartment's door. She carried a floral shopping bag.

Across the street, two blue-coated policemen stared at her briefly, and then lolled against the building, talking, blowing on their hands, trying to stay warm. The police, with Detective Jones leading the way, searched Keegan Fitzgerald's place, and while they did so, Jonathan hid in the bathroom until they left. With the two police watching the place, Jonathan figured they thought he'd show up here sooner or later. Certainly anyone or anyplace that had anything to do with Liberty or her family was under suspicion.

When a soft knock sounded on his door, he was surprised. No way would Liberty come here and put him in jeopardy.

Jonathan leaned against the door, his hand on the knob, debating if he should open it or not.

"Who is it?" he said.

"Darling, it's me, mother."

He cracked open the door, a mere inch at first. "Are you alone?"

"Yes, very much so." Her voice so familiar and one he hadn't heard since he'd been at The Drake with her and Dad.

He opened the door and grabbing her by the hand, whisked her inside, closed the door behind her, locked it and took her into his arms. He held her tight, the familiar curve of her back through her coat, her Jasmine perfume, the large brimmed hat that tilted and threatened to fall. Mother. He clasped her at arm's length and simply stared. His eyes filled with moisture, he couldn't help himself. Once again a little boy in short pants needing his mother's love.

Earlene smiled and put the shopping bag down allowing the canned goods to shift. "Jonathan," was all she could say before bursting into tears.

Jonathan stared at her. She was bone thin, her beautiful face looked tired and faded since he'd last seen her. Was he the cause of this? He hoped not, but knew deep inside he was to blame. That she was dressed in black didn't get by him either. Even her wide brimmed hat was black with no colorful adornments.

"Mom?" Her face told him something dire had happened. He wondered if his father had been arrested—again. She fidgeted with her purse, clasping and unclasping it until he asked her to stop.

She wet her lips and spoke. "Jonathan, the flu...well...oh God...I don't know how to tell you this...but—" Her eyes searched his.

"Tell me what?" Jonathan's skin prickled and he grabbed her hands. "Dad?"

"No, son. It's your sister. Lona has died...the flu..."

"Oh...my...God." Tears glazed his eyes. He led her to the sofa and helped her to sit. That Lona died hit Jonathan in the gut. He slumped next to his mother. He should be home with his family during a time like this. He'd been close to his sister, his only sibling and he couldn't even attend her burial. God damn it, he hated his life and what it'd become.

"Have you had her funeral?"

"Yes, it was a rushed affair. All funerals are rushed nowadays. Something about getting the dead into the ground fast might stop the flu from spreading."

"And Dad, is he all right?"

She nodded. "We were all ill. It was touch and go for all of us there for a while. Your father was sick when he helped get you away from the morgue." She stared at Jonathan, and he wanted to comfort her, to take her in his arms, and he did just that.

"Mom, I'm so sorry about all of this. I never meant—"

"Darling, I know. Your father doesn't dare come here to see you. He asked me to tell you that he is still working with Miss Fitzgerald, and that he has hired a Pinkerton detective. He said not to give up hope." Her eyes glistened with tears and she opened her purse to take out a hanky.

"I doubt very much that a private detective will be able to find out any more than Liberty and I did."

"It's your father's way of trying everything possible. He wished he'd followed his instincts and hired the man sooner."

"Mom, let me make us some tea. Let's talk." He suggested and she smiled.

"I'd like that very much. So you know how to make tea?" She smiled and hitched in a breath.

"Yes, I can make tea and cook. I have to if I want to eat." He went into the kitchenette and put on the kettle. He took two cups out of the sink and washed them. After filling the cups with tea-bags, he poured the boiling water over them and motioned for his mother to sit at the table with him.

She used her spoon to put two sugar cubes into her tea and dunked the teabag inside her cup. "I guess you can bless the person who invented teabags?"

"Yes. But I can make tea with a tea strainer. I've learned a lot these past few months. Mostly what a big shit I was, excuse my language, but it's true. I was becoming a terrible person."

"Are you saying you've changed?" She sipped her tea.

"And how. After I'm proved innocent, I'm going to build a clinic for Miss Fitzgerald."

"You are?"

"Yes, I'm going to design it and build the clinic in a neighborhood that doesn't have anything like it."

"I see." She put her hand on Jonathan's. "Are you in love with Miss Fitzgerald?"

He stared at his mother's sad face, noticing the lines next to her eyes, and bracketing her mouth. "Yes. But Miss Fitzgerald is too good for me. She's too good in the way of someone like me not being good enough to lick her boots. She's too good in the way she has lived her life compared to mine. I simply wouldn't put her in a position to have to turn me down."

"Does she love you?" She reached over to flatten her hand against his cheek and turn his face to meet hers.

"I don't know."

"Then we must find out. Son, if you let someone like Miss Fitzgerald slip away, then you haven't changed at all."

"Mother?"

"You heard me. Don't be a fool."

He grinned and for a brief moment he could forget where he was and why he was here. Hiding.

"Darling boy, I must go."

"I wish you could stay longer," he said and rose to help her from her chair.

"I'll come back soon and bring more groceries."

"Tell Dad I love him and thanks."

He took her arm and started walking toward the door with her.

"Mom—I'm innocent."

"I know." She smiled and tiptoed up to kiss his cheek.

Jonathan closed the door behind her and went to the window to stare out. He watched as his mother breezed down the front steps, paused to put her mask on, and then crossed the street right in front of the policemen who tipped their hats at her. She bravely nodded back, and continued on her way.

Jonathan sat down on the sofa and allowed tears to slick his cheeks. Sick at heart, he mourned his sister. Why had she died and he lived? Lona was such a good person, not like him at all. He wanted to hold her, see her lifeless body, and without doing so, her death was hard to accept. Oh...God...Lona, his little sister, so full of life. They played together as youngsters in the nursery. And he, the older brother tried to teach her how to share. But she didn't want to share anything, especially toys. She'd stamp her foot in her girlish way, and say mine, making her head full of black curls bounce. She'd turned into a lovely young woman with so much to live for.

Wiping his cheeks, he lay back on the sofa, staring at the ceiling, hating how cut off he was from everyone.

Alone, he was so damned alone.

Chapter Twenty-Three

Alice became ill. Her insides roiled and erupted with vomit spewing all over the Persian carpet. Jenny, who cared for her at first, now sent Beatrice in to wash her brow and make her comfortable. Wasn't that all they could do with the flu was make the patient comfortable and either wait for the end, or praise be to God they got well? Did Alice have the flu or was it something else? She didn't know and became suspicious, refusing all food for fear of being poisoned.

Whom could she trust? Doctor Snead, her parent's old friend and family doctor must have fallen ill as he didn't answer a summons from her. Alice wondered if Jenny delivered the request or simply tossed it away. Yes, dear sweet, Jenny, a master at deception, at murder, was pure evil. And her evil made a novice out of Alice who had been horribly duped.

All of Alice's scheming plans had combusted, gone up in smoke, and now the tables were turned. She'd become the target. Alice knew too much about Jenny. And, Jenny knew too much about her. They were a threat to each other. But to the schemers,

Talon and Jenny, who must think with Alice out of the way, dead from the flu, they would be the only ones left to enjoy the fruits of her father's labors. *Grand's*, and all the trappings that came with it.

But little did they know the only thing that might save Alice was her father's will. While Talon didn't know what was in it, she sure did, line for line. Months ago her father had divulged to Alice and her mother the contents of his will. Upon his death, her mother and Alice inherited the stores, the entire fortune to be equally shared, but even that inheritance had a clause requesting that the stores were to be managed by Yvette Grand's remaining family in Paris, the Therriault's. When her mother passed on, Alice would inherit all. Upon Alice's death, Grand's and the entire fortune would go to the Therriault's. Talon Montgomery was to receive five-hundred dollars for all he did at Grand's, but he would no longer be associated with any of the stores. Yes, Talon would be better off not harming a hair on Alice's head. But did he know that?

Alice was sure Jenny told him he was the target at the theater and not Jonathan. That Alice wanted him out of her life, and short of murder she was willing to set him up. Put him in prison and then divorce him. But Alice was the one being conned, not Talon. Both he and Jenny had made even better plans. Who could have known the influenza would become a catalyst in moving everything along at a rapid pace?

Again, who could Alice trust? Who could identify her illness? Most of all, she needed to clear Jonathan Drake. She'd read the paper telling how Liberty Fitzgerald helped get Jonathan from the armory hospital. They were still looking for him. And Miss Fitzgerald had been banned from nursing. That in itself was a shock as all doctors and nurses were needed to fight the flu.

Remembering that Liberty Fitzgerald once worked for the Lillian Wald foundation, Alice had phoned there. A woman by the name of Emma Taylor answered and gave her Miss Fitzgerald's address. She also said a message might reach her faster.

Alice, with no one to trust, had to rely on Beatrice Wilson the new maid. She'd summoned the timid looking, mousy-haired Beatrice to her bedroom. Trying not to vomit, Alice pulled her close to the bed. Beatrice's small blue eyes stared at her over her mask. When Beatrice started to wring out a washcloth and wipe her face, Alice raised her hand to stop her.

"Don't. Not now. Beatrice," she paused and continued, "Did you know Jenny Bishop before she hired you to work here?"

"No, Mrs. Montgomery, I didn't. I never thought I'd be able to work for such fine people as you are."

"Are you sure? Did you know Mr. Montgomery before?"

Beatrice's forehead wrinkled in puzzlement. "No, Mrs. Montgomery, I didn't, I swear on the bible. Are you feeling better? You don't look it." And she proceeded to wipe Alice's brow.

Alice grabbed Beatrice's wrist and held tight. "Please, I need you to deliver a message to the person at this address. The note's in my nightstand here, top drawer. Beatrice, you mustn't tell anyone about this, especially Jenny Bishop. And my husband is not to be told. Don't return unless you have Miss Fitzgerald with you. Understand?"

"Mrs. Montgomery, I don't know how to tell you this, you being sick and all, but I've seen your husband and that Jenny Bishop doing things…well…they are doing you know what all over the place. It's not right, him being married to you. I think marriage is sacred and all." She opened the drawer and removed the note.

"Beatrice, I believe my life is in danger. You must get this note to Miss Fitzgerald."

Beatrice accepted the folded message and appeared excited to be doing something other than attending to Alice. "I understand, and yes I can do this." She tucked the piece of paper inside the cuff of her blouse. "Maybe I should buy something from the grocery store to show Miss Bishop when I return?"

That Beatrice, a simple maid, realized the seriousness of the situation made Alice pause. "I could use some peppermint candy. I have this horrible metallic taste. Please find something to settle my stomach, ask the druggist for help."

Alice pointed to her purse on her dressing table. "There's money for cab fare and the peppermint. Beatrice, please hurry."

Beatrice no sooner left when Alice was bending over a bedpan, puking. Her symptoms mirrored the flu, leastways, like her mother and father had. Her heart started beating rapidly and she prayed she'd still be alive when Miss Fitzgerald arrived. She lay back on the pillow, her eyes filled with tears of remorse.

Liberty recognized the plainclothes policemen that took turns across the street watching her apartment. Just waiting for her to lead them to Jonathan. Well, they should give her some credit for being smarter than they were.

After the fiasco at the armory and morgue, the health department of New York City deemed they could get along without one Miss Liberty Fitzgerald's help. And that was saying something, especially with the shortage of nurses and doctors to help fight the contagion.

She wondered how long it would be before Detective Jones realized that Jonathan was at her father's place. Blaine and Kenny were living with Liberty for the time being. Blaine couldn't bring himself to step foot inside his home that was filled with memories of his loss. He mourned Marybeth, Shawn, and their dad.

Liberty spent hours reading to Kenny, trying to dispel the boy's memories of witnessing his mother and brother dying. Kenny constantly woke up screaming, and sobbing. Liberty gave her bedroom to her brother and nephew and she took the sofa.

Blaine, still weak from the flu's grip, was useless. Liberty bought food and brought it home to prepare. Her only income right now was the money she'd earned from the theater. A large amount to be sure, but with no income coming in to add to the pot, she had to be careful. Even the furniture company Blaine worked for kept it doors shuttered for the time being. Not that he was able to work, he couldn't. He'd cocooned himself in her apartment just existing.

Liberty heard the soft knock on her door, and going to the window she checked to make sure the police were still there. They were, both leaned against the building wearing masks and lifting them to steal a puff off their cigarettes.

When Blaine started to get up from the sofa, she signaled for him to stay put. Drying her hands from doing dishes, she cracked open the door. A woman, a stranger, stood there holding a dripping umbrella. Dressed in a heavy over coat, her hat glistening with rain, she dripped water on the floor.

"Are you Liberty Fitzgerald?" she asked from behind her mask.

Cautious, and thinking this to be a police trap, she asked, "Who are you?"

The woman's brow pulled together as if Liberty's question wasn't expected. "I'm Beatrice Wilson. I have a message for you," she stuttered.

"A message?" Certainly Jonathan wouldn't be foolish enough to try and contact her through a message. "From who?"

The lady leaned close and said "Alice Montgomery."

Oh…yes…*Alice* of the Grand department store fame. *Alice*, as in Talon Montgomery's wife. *Alice* as in the very woman Liberty had saved from a terrible fall in her wheelchair. Intrigued as to why Alice Montgomery would be sending her a note out of the blue, she asked the woman inside.

"Please, come in out of the cold and have some hot tea." She held the door open allowing Miss Wilson to pass by. After taking her coat and hat and putting them on the coat rack, she led her into the dining room.

"Take a seat," she said and indicated with her hand where the woman was to sit. "Blaine, do you and Kenny want some tea?"

When they both shook their heads, she concentrated on making tea for just her and her guest. She filled a tea strainer with tea and dropped it in the tea kettle that was always filled and kept hot on the stove. After placing two cups and saucers on the dining room table, she joined Miss Wilson.

"Thank you," the young woman said and gingerly put two sugar cubes into her cup.

Liberty did the same, and only after taking a sip did she say, "Miss Wilson, you said you have a message from Alice Montgomery."

Miss Wilson opened the clasp on her black purse, and taking out the message, handed it to Liberty. "Yes. I er…I work for the Montgomery's."

Finding this information interesting and puzzling, Liberty held the letter in her hand. Finally she opened it.

"Dear Miss Fitzgerald. I need your help. My life is in danger. I know who really killed Zelda DeLane. Please come to me as soon as you can. Alice Montgomery."

Liberty's skin prickled from her toes clear to her scalp. She sucked in her breath and let it out slowly. My God, at long last, after all the searching, she held Jonathan's freedom in her hands. Instead of being elated, as here was his proof of innocence, she was cautious, thinking it might be a setup.

"How are the Montgomery's?" She forced herself to act nonchalant while sipping her tea.

"Well, Mrs. Montgomery's parents have succumbed to the grippe. Mrs. Montgomery is ill. Her companion, Jenny Bishop was sick but she's recovered."

"And what of Talon Montgomery?" With his vile slippery ways, Liberty thought he just might be the killer.

"He appears to be quite healthy. Never brought to bed with the contagion."

"How about you, Miss Wilson, have you been ill?"

She nodded and took another sip. "Yes, I had it last spring. Terrible stuff, this influenza."

Ah, once again someone like herself who had the flu last spring is immune to it this time. Liberty wondered about that. How could it be? But now was not the time to ponder.

"How do you find the household there?"

"Well, there's just me and the cook now. Miss Bishop has taken over running the place. She and Mr. Montgomery appear to be quite cozy, if ya know what I mean."

Liberty most certainly knew what Miss Wilson was referring to. The man had roaming hands and roaming eyes. How convenient for him to have a sick wife and someone as robust as Jenny Bishop under his roof. Hmmm.

"Miss Wilson, can you tell me anything else?"

"No, ma'am, I haven't been there that long. Oh…wait, when Mrs. Montgomery gave me the note for you she told me not to let Jenny Bishop or Mr. Montgomery know that I was bringing the message to you. She was quite adamant about it."

"Did you have any trouble getting away?"

'Well…er…like I said, with Miss Bishop and Mr. Montgomery being so friendly with each other, I waited until they were…well indisposed with the other—"

"Were they in bed together? Is that what you are trying to say?" Excited, Liberty could hardly stop herself from running out of here.

"Yes, they can't seem to stay away from each other. Doing it right underneath, Mrs. Montgomery's nose, they are."

"Now, listen, what I want you to do is to return to the Montgomery's house—"

"They live on Fifth Avenue, in the Grand's mansion."

Liberty turned her letter over and asked Beatrice to write down the address. "As I was saying, you need to go back to the Grand's home. Ah…were you instructed to stop and buy something to bring back?"

Beatrice nodded and smiled. "Yes, Mrs. Montgomery gave me money to buy her some peppermint candy. She hopes it will take away the metallic tastes in her mouth."

"I see. Well…you must also pretend that the cook sent you and you must buy something else, like bread. Under no circumstances are you to tell anyone that Mrs. Montgomery sent you here. Tell her that I'll be along shortly to see to her welfare. Can you remember that?"

"Ah…Mrs. Montgomery told me not to return without you."

"I understand that. But, if I come with you, they just might be angry enough to let you go. Let me stop by as if you and Mrs. Montgomery don't know I'm coming. Please, tell her that."

Miss Wilson smiled and agreed to Liberty's orders. She finished her tea and stood.

"Miss Wilson, do you have enough money to buy bread and meat along with the peppermint and still have cab fare?"

When the maid shook her head, Liberty gave her a dollar. She then saw the woman out.

Liberty pulled on her warm long woolen coat, her hat, and got her medical bag. "Blaine, I'm going out for a while." She showed the note to him.

His eyes widened and he whistled in amazement. "You

shouldn't go there alone. Want me to come with you?"

"I'm going to get Detective Jones. I want him to read this," she said while taking the note back from Blaine.

"See that you do—I mean it, sis, you don't know what you're getting into. What about the cops outside?"

She smiled. "I'm going out the back door."

Detective Jones sat on his sofa, alone in a house too quiet, alone in a world he hated. He couldn't understand why he got sick with the flu, recovered, and why others died. He held a photograph of his family. All four of them, his wife Clara, his sons, Fred and Garth, and he, all were smiling.

After losing Jonathan Drake again, he'd almost turned in his badge, but for Scala's sake, he didn't. He owed it to his partner to carry this through, to see justice done. But most of all, he owed it to the star, Zelda DeLane. He'd never attended a play, the revue, or any of the other stuff put on. He was always too busy to take his wife to the theater, even when she asked. Now it was too late. He'd never enjoy an outing with her, hear her soft voice, or see the sparkle in her eyes. He was a big fool. And where did it get him? What? Nothing, and now he was a lonely man sitting in a lonely house, feeling sorry for himself. All Jones knew is that he hated life at the moment. The thought of walking off the Brooklyn Bridge into the East River appealed greatly to him right now.

Would life get better? He hoped so.

Jones sighed, and after using the bathroom, left for work.

Beatrice moved like a slug on her way home. Along with the peppermint candy, she stopped to buy the suggested bread and few things that cook would use.

When she got home and entered through the backdoor, a highly agitated Jenny Bishop was waiting for her.

"Where have you been?" Miss Bishop demanded, hands on hips, her chin thrust out.

"Out shopping for Mrs. Montgomery," Beatrice said and held her ground.

"What could Mrs. Montgomery need that we don't have here?"

Beatrice knew her answer was critical. Not only for Mrs. Montgomery, but the fate of her own job. "Peppermint sticks. She had a craving for peppermint candy. Thought it might make her feel better."

Jenny Bishop grabbed Beatrice's floral shopping bag from her grasp and opened it. She pulled out the loaf of bread and shoved it in Beatrice's arms. She held onto the meat that was packaged in butcher paper. When she couldn't find the candy, she glared with triumph at Beatrice.

"I say you are lying. What did Alice send you out of the house for?" Her mouth sat in a firm line, her eyes glittered with distrust.

Beatrice put the bread back in the shopping bag. She then unclasped her purse and took out a small wrapped package. "I would have liked for Mrs. Montgomery, the head of this household, to open this. But if you insist—"

"Is that the candy?"

"Yes. I didn't want the sticks to break so I put them in my purse." Oh...my...she thought, when the nurse, Miss Fitzgerald arrives, her little scheme will backfire on them, and that's when she will lose her job.

"Very well." Jenny relented. "Take the candy upstairs to Mrs. Montgomery."

Alice fought the bitter taste in her mouth. Her limbs felt like heavy cannon balls, like she couldn't raise them. She didn't think this was the flu. Something else for sure.

When the door opened to her bedroom, Alice's foreboding turned to relief when Beatrice slipped inside. But Alice's relief was short-lived when she saw that the maid was by herself.

Beatrice stood in the open doorway and looked out into the hall as if searching for someone. She spoke up in a loud voice, "Mrs. Montgomery, I did as told. I got your peppermint sticks. I hope they settle your stomach." She shut the door and approached the bed.

Alice accepted the wrapped candy but could only fumble at the wrapper. "You'll have to open it for me. Where's the nurse...ah...Miss. Fitzgerald?" she whispered.

Beatrice leaned down and began peeling the paper away. The sharp smell of peppermint invaded the area. "She's coming. But she said if she was to accompany me that I might be fired."

"Smart woman, indeed." Alice took a deep breath, and bit into the red and white stripped candy. It crunched as she chewed. Her stomach rose and fell as bile surged to the back of her throat.

"Oh...God," she groaned, and Beatrice was quick with the pan to catch her vomit. When she stopped, Beatrice handed her a hanky to wipe her mouth. Alice lay back on her pillows.

"Beatrice, go downstairs and wait for Miss. Fitzgerald, please." Too weak to do anything else, she could only say. "Thank you—thank you so much."

Liberty got to the precinct and was met by a desk sergeant wearing a mask. When she asked for Detective Jones, she was told he hadn't come into work yet. The sergeant said he didn't know when Jones would be in.

Liberty asked the sergeant for a piece of paper and wrote a note to Detective Jones telling him what Mrs. Montgomery said. She asked that he meet her there at the Grand's home. "Will you give this to Detective Jones, and tell him I've gone to the Montgomery's...well to Charles Grand's house on Fifth Avenue?"

When he took the note and set it on his desk, to be forgotten no doubt, she said, "Please, don't forget. It's important that you give this to him. It might mean life or death."

Seeing she was serious, the sergeant said, "Wait a minute. I'll call Jones at his home." He dialed and when there was no answer, he shrugged. "Might be on his way here. Sure you don't want to wait?"

"I'm positive. But do you mind if I use your phone?"

Again another lift of his shoulders.

She called Lincoln Drake. "Mister Drake, I have proof of Jonathan's innocence. I have a note from Alice Montgomery saying she knows who killed Miss DeLane. Can you get to Jonathan and tell him this news?"

"Who is the killer?" he practically yelled in the phone.

"Mrs. Montgomery didn't say. But I believe her. I'm sure it's Talon Montgomery."

"Let me pick you up and go with you. We could meet Jonathan and all go together."

"No, we can't do that. What if it turns out to be a hoax? I mean...I'm sure she is being truthful, but what if she's not? What if she's working with the police to smoke Jonathan out?"

"Then let me go with you. You might be in danger."

He thought the same as her. Could Alice be trusted? "Mr. Drake, I'm willing to take that risk. I'm at the police precinct right now and have left a message for Detective Jones to meet me at the Grand's house."

"I see. Please reconsider, let me accompany you."

"Just tell Jonathan what's going on." She replaced the receiver and noticed that the desk sergeant had stepped away from his desk and her note had fluttered to the floor. She retrieved it and this time she used a bottle of ink to hold it in place.

Hurrying out the door and not seeing a taxi, she ran to catch a trolley that had just stopped to let riders off. She jumped on and quickly took a seat near the exit. Only a few brave people were using the trolley and those that were wore masks, reminding her to put hers back on. Most of the people kept their eyes averted. They passed a street cleaner with his cart of brooms and trash cans. He too wore a mask. Everything was topsy-turvy. The normal waves of people scurrying around dried up to a trickle.

She stayed on the trolley as far as she could and after getting off, waved down a taxi. She exited the cab in front of Charles Grand's front door, and stood staring at the stately brick home that was wedged right next to another mansion. It appeared the rich in Manhattan built up and not out. The black wreath with its black ribbons fluttered in the breeze, foretelling that death had visited here. She briefly remembered meeting Mr. and Mrs. Grand at the store. Liberty lifted the large brass knocker and banged it against the brass plate more than once.

The door was opened by Beatrice who swung the door wide. "Yes? May I help you?"

"The health department sent me here to see how this household fares. We are aware that several people here have died from the flu. Has anyone else come down with it?"

Beatrice asked Liberty in. "Yes, the lady of the house, Mrs. Montgomery is ill. Could you see to her?"

"Whose there?" Jenny Bishop hurried to where Liberty and Beatrice stood inside the front door.

Liberty showed her medical bag. "I've been asked by the health department and the family doctor to check on everyone in here. He says that two have died so far."

Jenny Bishop's eyes narrowed in speculation and she asked, "Who's the doctor that sent you?"

Liberty was quick to say, "Why Doctor Snead of course. He is the family doctor is he not?"

"I know you—we had lunch together at Grand's." Jenny moved closer as if to intimidate Liberty.

It didn't work. "Oh...yes...you and I met at the restaurant in Grand's store. I'd just saved Mrs. Montgomery's life—her wheel-chair almost fell down the stairs." Liberty pointed at Jenny. "Then you know that I'm also a nurse and was one before I joined the theater. My one big folly in life I must say...joining the Follies, not nursing."

Jenny nodded. "I'll take you to Mrs. Montgomery. She isn't feeling well. I suspect she has the flu."

Liberty followed Jenny up the winding stairs and down the hallway to what she figured was Alice's room. Jenny opened the door where the smell of vomit was strong. She led Liberty over to Alice's bed. Alice stared at the two as if trying to figure out who they were.

Liberty placed her doctor's bag on the nightstand and took out her stethoscope. She leaned over to put it on Alice's chest and while she did so, she sniffed the woman's breath that smelled slightly of fish and garlic. She listened to the heart and didn't like what she heard. Alice's heart was beating too fast. She then held her wrist to time her pulse. It all fit together so neatly, but she had to do one more thing to make sure.

"Mrs. Montgomery, are you able to use the bedpan for me?"

When her patient nodded, Liberty went into the adjoining bathroom and spotted the white enamel bedpan on the tiled floor next to the commode. Making sure it was empty she brought it back into the room.

She turned to Jenny who was standing guard. "Would you mind leaving me with my patient?"

"Yes, I would mind." She crossed her arms.

At that moment, Talon Montgomery in all his handsomeness entered. "Ah, the lovely star, or is it nurse, er...Fitzgerald." He snapped his fingers and smiled. "That's it! Today you're a nurse, right?"

"I am, and what of it? Your wife is extremely ill...with the flu or something else. I'm here to treat her." Liberty felt cornered like a helpless bird, caught by two cats with their claws out going for the kill.

"Treatment? Flu?" Talon clasped his hands behind his back and ventured forth, his gaze never leaving Liberty. "I didn't know there was any treatment. Just make the person comfortable, isn't that what the doctor's say? Comfortable?"

"I've only begun to examine her," Liberty retorted, keeping both Talon Montgomery and Miss Bishop in her vision. "She may have typhoid fever. Why don't you leave me to my job, let me determine what she has."

"Maybe I should stay here and assist," Jenny Bishop volunteered.

"Good," said Liberty, "you can help me get her on the bedpan."

"I can get on...bedpan without Jenny's help..." Alice offered, sagging even further into her mattress. She took a deep breath, her eyes frightened.

"Mr. Montgomery, why don't you step outside while we do this?" Liberty suggested, and was relieved when he shrugged and turned to leave. Again, and from the back he looked so much like Jonathan that Liberty was jarred. My...word. She glanced to see Jenny Bishop staring at her with speculation, like a dangerous animal, or someone with intent to harm.

Still rattled by Talon's likeness to Jonathan and visions of a dressing room, Jonathan sitting there, of being hit on the back of the head, of being set up, Liberty grabbed the bedpan. With Jenny taking Alice's legs, and Liberty her torso, they lifted Alice to a sitting position and Liberty slid the bedpan under her bottom.

"Hold onto me, Mrs. Montgomery," Liberty ordered and felt Alice's arm go around her shoulders. When Alice's urine stopped tinkling against the enamel pot, Liberty slipped it from underneath Alice. After they tidied her bottom, Beatrice arranged the covers back over Alice.

Liberty carried the bedpan into the bathroom where she saw the urine was a dark brown color.

Nothing could help Alice Montgomery. The arsenic she was being fed was doing the job intended. It was killing her. Liberty didn't think Alice would survive more than a day or so, and figured she'd been given the poison for several weeks or more. How convenient. Do away with the wife, her parents, keep your mistress, and inherit it all.

Who killed Zelda? Liberty needed the information from Alice.

She walked back into the room and spoke to Miss Bishop who hovered next to Alice's bedside. "I'm fairly certain she has typhoid. Unless you've had typhoid fever, you might want to leave the room. Typhoid is a killer, worse than the flu."

She watched as Jenny Bishop's features changed from mock concern to one of self-preservation. She nodded and left, leaving the door ajar.

Liberty squeezed a sponge out over the wash basin and gently wiped at Alice's forehead. "Can you tell me the name of the person who killed Zelda DeLane?" she whispered.

Alice grabbed Liberty's hand to still her efforts. "What's wrong with me?" she managed to ask.

Noticing that Jenny Bishop lingered outside the door, liberty put her mouth right next to Alice's ear. "You're being poisoned. Arsenic—"

"What?" Alice exclaimed, drawing upon strength she didn't have.

Jenny poked her head inside. "What's going on? Is Alice all right?"

"Yes, I just told her she has typhoid and not the flu. Why don't you go get some broth to feed her?"

Hearing Jenny's footsteps on the stairs, Liberty forgot about Talon's whereabouts. "Tell, me, who killed Zelda?"

Alice looked at her. "Am I dying?"

"Yes. You've ingested too much of the poison to reverse it. I'm sorry, but there's nothing any doctor can do. Please clear Jonathan—please. You can write it on a piece of paper and sign it— yes?"

Alice crooked her finger, beckoning. Liberty leaned forward to listen.

"I killed Zelda—"

"What? You? How could you—you can't even walk?" Finding it hard to believe, Liberty recoiled at such devious news.

Alice took a deep breath and said, "I planned it. Jenny did the killing. We thought Talon time to be there. Wanted him gone from...my...life. Hate him."

Liberty hurried to the nearby writing desk and opened the drawers searching for a piece of paper and pen. Finding what she sought, she went back to Alice and asked her to write what she just said. She helped Alice to sit up and put the fountain pen in her hand.

When Alice finished scribbling, saying that she and Jenny Bishop were the killers, that Jonathan Drake was an innocent pawn, Liberty shoved the note into her doctor's bag.

"It's not easy to hear...Talon...killing me, with Jenny's help."

Alice started crying, softly. "Be careful...both deadly...deceitful."

"Listen to me, Mrs. Montgomery. I've got to go for help. But I'll be back as soon as I can."

Alice nodded.

Liberty grabbed her bag and rushed out of the room only to collide against Talon Montgomery's hard chest. He caught her by the arms and squeezed, holding her like a trapped animal.

"Where are you going in such a hurry?" He glowered at her.

"To get medicine for the typhoid fever your wife has. Have you had the fever Mr. Montgomery? If you haven't, you will most likely get it. Would you mind letting me go?" Liberty now wished she had Lincoln or even a cop next to her.

He released her, his eyes the color of storm clouds. She hurried down the stairs and took her coat from the coat rack. She opened the door and started to step outside when something hit her on the back of the head, knocking her out.

Chapter Twenty-Four

Jonathan opened the door to let his mother into Fitzgerald's apartment. Earlene Drake was in a dither, practically jumping up and down, and for the queen of sophistication this was surprising.

"Mom, what's happened?"

She tried to catch her breath, finally getting herself under control she blurted. "Jonathan! Miss Fitzgerald called to tell us she has proof of your innocence. Alice Montgomery sent Liberty a note saying she knows who the murderer is."

Jonathan trembled with excitement. "Where is Liberty now?"

"She told your father that she was on her way to see Alice Montgomery."

"Oh God! No! Liberty might be in danger. Where's Dad?" He thundered.

"In our car on the next street over. Hurry," she said and thrust a bag at him. Inside was a red wig and beard.

"I don't have time to put this beard on," he exclaimed while shoving the wig on his head.

She took the beard and hooked it over his ears. "That will

have to do." She grabbed his hat and jammed it on his head.

They both donned white gauze masks and left the apartment. When they got to the door leading outside, his mother grabbed Jonathan's arm and interlaced it within hers.

"Stay on the inside," she ordered.

"I can't, no manners in that," he said. "Let me walk on the outside, it'll draw less attention."

They held their breath and boldly walked down the street opposite of the police. His mother threw back her head and laughed, practically sashaying along, acting the part. They were ignored by the police.

Detective Jones made his way to the precinct. Not much was happening. No prostitutes clogged the area. No push cart vendors with flailing arms and shouting in a foreign language at each other, accusing the other of stealing his territory. No murderers, no automobile collisions. The grippe had closed some police stations and was coming close to closing down the City itself.

Jones went to his desk, cluttered with food wrappers, manacles and Scala's badge. Why his desk? The badge should have been turned into the police chief. He picked up the gold-colored shield and held it.

He'd been with Scala for over ten years, long enough to bond like brothers, long enough to know what the other thought without speaking. He missed Scala. Scala had left a will with instructions that in case of his death Jones was to have Scala buried next to his dead wife, in the Scala's family plot. Scala being the last of his family's line had designated Jones as his beneficiary and left all his possessions to Jones.

Jones ran his hand over his face, feeling the grooves living had etched. His mustache was a bristle patch of gray under his nose, his chin and cheeks felt like sandpaper, and he wasn't sure when he'd last shaved. Blowing his cheeks out, he expelled a long breath of air, picked up wanted posters and flipped through them. Seeing Jonathan Drake's photograph staring back at him, he paused. The damn picture was posted all over the city. How in the hell how Drake eluded them so far?

He was tired of wearing this damn mask, looking like a bandit, a criminal that he would put in jail. Anymore, it was hard to tell the good guys from the bad ones. Several robberies were committed with the thief wearing a gauze mask, looking like he was trying to stay healthy, instead his intentions were criminal. Removing his mask, he flipped it into the garbage can next to his desk.

A slender, brown haired man, wearing a gray suit and gauze mask underneath a gray fedora, approached Scala's empty desk. He took off his suit coat, and placed it on the back of the chair, before he sat down.

Jones couldn't believe they'd already replaced Scala. He wanted to run the newcomer off but couldn't. Policemen were a premium, especially right now with the flu rendering so many good men useless. Yet, there was something very familiar about the guy, his build, especially his blue eyes that stared over the mask.

Spotting Jones, he stood and came over to him. Holding out his hand, he said, "Detective Jones?" The voice sounded just like Jones's own son, Garth, a cop in another precinct.

"Garth?"

Garth Jones took off his hat, removed his mask, and grinned at his father. "I believe I'm your new partner. For a while anyway."

Jones fighting back tears pulled his son into a bear hug. When did he get so tall and handsome? Looking at Garth was like looking at Clara. He'd inherited his mother's brown hair, straight nose, but his blue eyes were just like his old man.

"My God—should you be here? Is it safe?" Jones asked.

Garth nodded. "Dad, I told you I already had the flu. You need family around you. I applied for a transfer and got it. I also made detective. Junior grade, but I'm here and want to learn from the best detective there is. You."

Jones couldn't believe he heard right, that his son who he thought never gave him much thought just said that he was the best cop in law enforcement. The large knot in his throat prevented him from speaking, so he nodded and handed Garth a wanted poster with Drake's information.

Garth looked it over and smirked. "Yeah, we've all been on the lookout for this guy." He removed a note pad and pen out of his jacket pocket and started to put them in the desk drawer. "Whoa, what's this, evidence? Or did Detective Scala have a lady friend who got mad at him?" He handed Jones a gold, heart-shaped locket."

"Shit," Jones exclaimed. "We forgot to put that in evidence." He accepted the necklace from Garth and turning it over in his hand, he spotted the fine slit where the locket came together. He put his fingernails in the slit and opened the locket to reveal a picture of a man. Talon Montgomery. Jones was rattled, how in the hell did they miss this? Better yet, how did they forget about it? Vital clues just staring them in the face and they'd slipped up big time. "Is there a scrapbook in there?"

Garth opened the drawer further but no scrapbook. He opened a side drawer and found the scrapbook tipped on its side.

Jones came around his desk and opened Josette's scrapbook. He hurriedly turned the pages until he came to a picture with the man's head cut out. Heart shaped, and with Josette leaning against his shoulder. Jones could tell it was the same nightclub as in the other picture. Another photograph snapped by a roaming camera girl.

"Jesus Christ," Jones exclaimed and looked at his son. "The

killer's identity has been under my nose for weeks. Shit!"

The desk sergeant interrupted the two by coming over to Jones's desk. "Didn't see ya come in. A lady left this for ya." He gave Jones the note and started to leave when Jones swore and stopped him.

"Wait. What time was Miss Fitzgerald here?"

He pulled out his watch and squinted at it. "Oh, about two hours ago."

"Damn," Jones swore again and handed the note to his son. "Well, detective, there's nothing like getting your feet wet. Let's go."

Alice knew she was dying. She also knew that something must have happened to Liberty Fitzgerald to keep her from returning. Drawing on strength she figured long gone, she pushed the covers off of her body. Wearing a sweat soaked pink nightgown, she stank like death, like rotten flesh. Seeing that her wheelchair was too far away to reach, she held onto the sheet and tried to lower herself out of the bed, but she fell onto the floor in a thud. She started pulling her withered body toward the chair, her legs useless. She used her elbows, her hips, she crawled on her stomach like a snake. Finally, she was able to grasp the seat of her chair and the door handle where she slowly pulled herself into her wheel chair. Her head pounded, her vision blurred and she took deep breaths, trying to fill her damaged lungs.

Weak from getting to her chair, she trembled as she reached for the door. Opening it, she peered out into the hallway, shadowy, and with the sun setting everything looked sinister. She wheeled to the end of the hallway where the elevator was located and made especially for her chair. The black bars going across the front of the elevator were locked. It was never locked, and always left open for her to use. Her skin prickled, she was cut off.

She wheeled away from the elevator and toward the stairs. To her, they looked as steep as a two-story building. She took hold of the banister's slick mahogany, and using all of her strength, she heaved herself out of the chair and onto her bottom. Using the banister rails, and holding tight, she lifted her behind and bumped down another stair. She used her arms and buttocks to inch along, slowly going stair-by-stair. Halfway down, she became nauseated and couldn't help but retch, the odor strong of garlic.

"Going somewhere, my dear?" Talon's voice floated up the stairs.

Alice, breathless and with her lungs burning, looked at her husband, the man whom she'd come to despise, hate. "The elevator's locked. Did you...do...that?" she managed to say.

He started toward her. "Yes, I did. For your safety. Why are you here on the stairs?"

"I—I—I'm not sure. I..." Tears of frustration formed.

He reached her side. "Maybe you felt guilty over the admission note you wrote to Miss Fitzgerald." Talon removed the letter from his pocket, flashed it at her and put it back in his suit pocket.

Her scalp prickled. "I don't know what you're talking about," she said and shut her eyes, blocking out his cunning ones. She flinched when his hands circled her arms in a tight grip.

"Yes, my dear, you do. Too bad your plans went so awry. But you were always the target, never me, and you and Jenny Bishop were never to be."

"Jenny?"

"Oh," he said and leaned close to her ear. "I overheard what you told Miss Fitzgerald." He clicked his tongue. "Poor Alice. How does it feel to be dying inside? How does arsenic feel? Your lovely Jenny is good at murder, quite accomplished I must say."

So Nurse Fitzgerald was right about the arsenic. It was all so clear to Alice now. She laughed and cried, it no longer mattered to her, she'd be glad to die, get it over with. Dying was better than going to prison. Her only regret was that she wouldn't see Jonathan Drake walk free. It appeared that her husband and Jenny Bishop would come out victorious after all. "What have you...done...with Liberty Fitzgerald?" She gasped for air.

"Don't worry your pretty head about her."

He lifted Alice, like a groom holding a bride, and she was loath to put her arms around him, but she did. Solid feeling, strong, yet diabolical hostility seethed from him. He started up the stairs, his storm-gray eyes mere inches from hers. When he reached the top of the stairs and walked a few feet, she thought he was going to take her to her bedroom. Let her die there. But he paused next to the balcony railing and kissed her cheek.

"Goodbye my sweet, Alice. Goodbye."

Sensing what he was about to do, she screamed, "Talon...no! Please...no..."

Again, he nuzzled her cheek, licking it with his tongue. "Don't fight it, let it happen. I understand, once your dead your soul has free reign." His voice sounded eerie.

Unable to help it, she vomited on his suit front, a vile and stomach turning smell.

"You stupid pig!" He roared in disgust and moved to toss her.

Alice grabbed at the railing, held tight, her useless legs dangled. She was too weak to hold much longer. "What about the will? You get nothing," she yelled in desperation. Desperate to what? Die in bed and not be broken like a doll on the floor below?

He blanched white, looked unsure of what she said. "You're lying."

"My cousins in Paris get everything. You get nothing."

He no longer cared, her stench overpowered him, he wanted free of her. He became brutal, almost breaking her fingers, trying to pry them loose.

"Die—you damn albatross—die." He tossed her over.

Alice screamed. She grasped at nothing but air. The marble floor met her with a skull busting splat. Her limbs twitched as her blood seeped red on the floor around her head. She stared up at Talon with accusing, lifeless eyes.

Across the foyer and in the locked den, Liberty heard the commotion. She figured she was next. Taking a hypodermic needle from her doctor's bag, she filled it with morphine and put it in her pocket. Easing to stand behind the door when it opened, she waited.

The door swung slowly open.

"Miss Fitzgerald?" Jenny Bishop called out. "I'm sorry to keep you waiting, but we had to take care of Mrs. Montgomery first. You know, the rich always come first."

Liberty didn't make a sound.

Jenny chuckled. "I know you're behind the door. In this small room here, where else would you hide? Just accept your fate. It'll be easier that way."

Liberty pushed the door closed and sized up Jenny Bishop who held a knife in her right hand. They were the same height, only Jenny was a little stockier. But Miss Bishop was used to killing. Liberty was used to healing.

"I stopped by the police station before I came here. I left Detective Jones a copy of Mrs. Montgomery's note implicating you and her. That you actually did the killing. He'll be here anytime."

"But you don't know for sure that he got the message? It sounds like he wasn't there." She raised the knife and advanced. "Unless he's here in the next few seconds he won't be able to save you." Jenny slashed at her.

Using her doctor's bag as a shield, Liberty stopped the first thrust. The knife embedded in the leather bag, puncturing it.

Liberty pushed her bag into Jenny and fled out the open door. Jenny was right behind her.

They ran across the foyer where Alice's bloody and crumpled body lay.

Liberty paused and turned to catch Jenny's onslaught head on. She tried to plunge the needle into Jenny's neck but Jenny grabbed the needle and twisted Liberty's hand. She bent her hand backwards. Pain shot up Liberty's arm. Using her free hand, Liberty slugged Jenny in the face, almost breaking her knuckles. Jenny, the stronger of the two, pulled Liberty to the floor with her.

Straddling Liberty, Jenny raised the knife.

Chapter Twenty-Five

Lincoln Drake no sooner stopped in front of Charles Grand's mansion, when Jonathan tore off his disguise and bounded from the car.

"Jonathan, wait!" Lincoln opened his car door. "Earlene, you stay here," he ordered. "Son, I'll go around back and try to get in that way."

Jonathan flung open the black metal gate in front of the imposing house and took the front stairs two at a time. He tried the door. To his surprise, it was unlocked.

He pushed open the door to find Liberty and another woman tussling on the floor, fighting like two alley cats. The woman held a knife that she was getting ready to plunge into Liberty's chest.

"Liberty!" Jonathan shouted and started forward.

Liberty held the woman by the wrists, keeping the deadly blade from striking her. She bucked her attacker off. In a flurry they rolled apart.

Jonathan reached down and grabbed Liberty up.

Liberty pointed. "Jonathan, thank God! That's Jenny Bishop,

Alice's maid. She's the one who killed Zelda."

The maid looked deranged, her eyes like an animals, her teeth bared like she wanted to rip him to shreds. He put Liberty behind him and just as he started to lunge at Miss Bishop, a shot rang out.

Jenny Bishop grasped her chest. Blood flowed out between her fingers as her eyes turned toward the stairs, seeking someone. Her legs buckled. She slumped against the floor.

Both Jonathan and Liberty knelt beside her.

Liberty tore the woman's bodice open and saw blood pumping out with each heartbeat.

"Please," Liberty said, "Clear Jonathan's name—now."

Talon Montgomery, carrying a gun, rushed out the front door.

Jenny stared after him. She didn't speak.

Lincoln Drake, along with Detective Jones, and another man burst into the foyer from the hallway. They glanced around at the carnage. Beatrice and the cook cowered behind them.

Jones paused next to Jenny Bishop. "Is she dead?"

"Yes." Jonathan jumped up and pointed a finger at Jones. "And I didn't shoot her. Nor did I kill Zelda. I'm going after the son-of-a bitch who has framed me."

Liberty nodded toward Jenny Bishop. "And this woman right here was the one who cut Zelda's throat."

As the younger man who was with Jones knelt beside Jenny, Jones ordered him to stay here and take care of things.

"Not a chance," he said and told the two policemen with them to remain behind and get more cops here.

Jonathan and Liberty along with Lincoln ran out the door, followed by Jones and the young detective. They dashed outside where the sun was starting to set and watched in shock as Talon drove off in Lincoln's car with Jonathan's mother still in it. Earlene turned to look out the back window, her eyes wide, waving, signaling for them to follow.

Jones yelled, "Get in the paddy wagon. We have to get him before it gets dark." He led the four of them across the street and got behind the steering wheel. While Liberty, Lincoln, and the young detective hurried to get inside the back of the wagon, Jonathan ran to the front, grabbed the crank, and gave it several good spins to start the car. When the engine rattled to a start, he jumped in.

Jones drove off. "Is that your mother in the car?" he asked.

"Yes it is!" Jonathan replied. "Hurry, I'm afraid he'll harm her."

Liberty, sitting on the wagon's bench seat, and right behind Jones spoke to him through the bars. "Do you believe us now? That Jonathan is innocent?"

"New things have come to light here recently. I still need to hear it from the murderer's mouth." He tossed over his shoulder.

"Well, you can't." Liberty yelled, "Both of them are dead. Talon Montgomery has the evidence in his pocket. A signed confession by Alice Montgomery herself. He took it from me."

"My father's dogmatic, and needs proof in black and white. I'm Garth Jones."

"It isn't going to get any more black and white than this!" Jonathan glared at Jones.

They followed Talon, taking a corner too fast and almost overturning. The unwieldy, slow moving paddy wagon a hindrance lost sight of Lincoln's Studebaker.

"It's way up there!" Jonathan pointed.

He watched in amazement as the car came to a stop in the middle of the street. Earlene Drake bolted from the backseat and started running. Talon Montgomery rushed from the car and chased her down. Manhandling her, he put his arm around her chest, tore her hat off and flung it away. He held his pistol to her head, dragging her backwards into an alley.

"Christ," said Jones. He pulled the police wagon over next to Drake's automobile. They all got out.

Several masked bystanders gawked at the police wagon.

The four of them started toward the alley. No sign of Talon and Earlene.

Jonathan feared for his mother. He reached the end of the alley to come out onto another street.

Liberty, having caught up with him, pointed. "There they are!"

The two took out after Talon.

They chased him, their feet pounding against the pavement. They rounded another corner to find Earlene standing there, abandoned.

Overjoyed, Jonathan scooped her into his arms. "Mother, my God, I thought he was going to kill you. Are you all right?"

She caught her breath. "Yes, I am. Please don't let him get away." And she reached out for Lincoln who cocooned her within his embrace.

Jones caught up with them. Again, the pursuit was on.

They crossed the street and entered another alley.

Talon was climbing a fire escape and had almost reached the top of the building. He paused to shoot at them. The bullet ricocheted off the cobblestones, sending sparks flying.

"I'll go this way." Pulling his own pistol, Garth started running along the street, staring upward, keeping Talon in his sights.

Jonathan leaped upward to grasp the bottom of the fire escape ladder. He pulled himself onto the rungs and turned to grab Liberty, who was being lifted by Jones. Jonathan, with the two behind him, climbed hand-over-hand, hurrying to catch Talon.

He bolted over the top of the building. Talon had already reached the next rooftop. Jonathan ran and leaped, crossing the five-foot-space. He landed and rolled, bruising his shoulder.

He heard Liberty and Jones behind him. A quick glance showed Liberty had hiked up her skirt and tucked it in her waistband. Her long legs propelled her to land next to Jonathan who reached out to prevent her from falling.

Next, Jones clattered down, his breathing loud and labored.

Jonathan continued on, leaving Liberty and Jones behind. He chased Talon as if the Devil was nipping at his heels.

He drew close to Talon and grabbed him by the collar of his suit coat. Talon threw his arms out, breaking Jonathan's hold. When he started for the next building, Jonathan tackled him around the legs. The pistol flew out of Talon's hand.

Jonathan's knuckles scraped against the building's roof, but he held fast. Talon kicked free, landing a booted foot square in Jonathan's face.

Stunned, and feeling like his face had collapsed into a mass of splintered bones, Jonathan let go and the man scrambled to his feet. Dazed, and with his nose bleeding, Jonathan followed. Again they jumped across to another building. Talon ran, and when he started to cross over to the next building, he miscalculated and barely made it over.

Jonathan backed up and ran hard, leaping, going midair, landing beside Talon. He grabbed Talon by the coat lapels.

Talon put his hands up to protect his face. "Don't hit me," he yelled.

Ignoring the coward, Jonathan, threw a punch that connected hard against his mouth. Jonathan's anger reached a boiling point, each hit was for the last months of hiding, of being labeled a coward, a murderer, a hit for Lona who he'd been kept apart from. With piston like intensity, his fists pummeled the man, smashing into Talon's face, crushing his nose. When he heard Jones yelling behind him not to kill the man, only then did he stop and turn to see Liberty and Jones coming on.

Talon moved to the edge of the roof where he stood grinning at Jonathan through a blood covered face. As they came closer, Talon saluted Liberty. "I'm only sorry that I didn't get to taste your wonderful delights, Miss Fitzgerald."

"Don't!" she yelled, sensing he was going to jump.

From his pocket, he took out the condemning note, and flung it away. "Go find the truth," he said and stepped off the roof.

They watched Talon's body bounce against the side of the building before he hit the sidewalk in a loud splat. He stilled.

Liberty went after the note. She dropped off the fire escape and chased the fluttering piece of paper.

When it landed next to Garth Jones, the detective opened the note and read it. Upon her approach he handed the grubby piece of paper to her. "Well, this is black and white enough for even my dad to believe. I always did think he was chasing the wrong man."

"Really?" Thrilled, Liberty turned to where Jonathan and Jones were coming into the alley. She joined them, and with beaming satisfaction, she handed Alice's note to Jones. She then approached Talon's broken body. His legs were twisted at odd angles, and a splintered bone stuck through his torn pants leg. Knowing it was useless, she knelt next to him, and felt for a pulse.

Looking up at everyone, she shook her head. "How fitting that he dies from the fall. I heard Talon and Alice fighting and could tell he threw her over the balcony." Liberty took Jonathan's hand within hers. "Talon was poisoning Alice with arsenic. He must have gotten impatient for it to work."

Garth Jones stood next to his dad. "Mrs. Montgomery and Jenny Bishop weren't the only ones Talon killed. He was the one who murdered Josette Jackson and hung her in the theater."

Jones read the note. "This is good enough for me."

Jonathan asked to see it. He read the words clearing him of any wrong doing and handed it back to Jones.

"No hard feelings here, Drake. I was just doing my job."

Jonathan pulled Liberty tight against him. "The only good thing to come of this is that I met Miss Fitzgerald. Had I not been accused and ran, I would never have met her."

Liberty put her hand on Jonathan's cheek, her eyes soft with love for him. "Your nose looks broke. Let me put iodine on your cuts." She smiled most wickedly.

"Oh, no, you don't," Jonathan replied. "Never iodine. That stuff kills!"

Jones laughed and turned to watch as the paddy wagon driven by Lincoln Drake and with Earlene in the passenger seat pulled up.

Earlene, not waiting for Lincoln to help her out, opened the door and exited the wagon by herself. She came to stand next to Jonathan.

"Are you free?" Earlene asked. And she too put her hand on his cheek checking him out.

Liberty smiled and answered for the battered and bruised man she loved. "As free as the Statue of Liberty itself."

Jonathan kissed her, long and desirous. Liberty clasped his suit lapels, holding him against her, never wanting the kiss to stop.

Finally Jones cleared his throat and said, "All right now don't want to arrest ya for indecent and lewd behavior in public."

Jonathan broke the kiss to push an errant strand of red hair off of her forehead. "Arrest me if you want, detective. Acting lewd is a far cry better than being arrested for murder."

Epilogue

Summer 1919

Jonathan and Liberty stood watching the steam shovel bite deep into the ground, digging out the foundation hole for the clinic Jonathan had designed. The clinic to be named, *The Keegan Fitzgerald Clinic*, was being built on a lot in the Hell's Kitchen area where it was needed the most. Blaine and his brother Teague were to build the furniture that would be used in it. Lincoln Drake had set them up in a furniture factory of their own.

Earlier in the day the site was swamped with important people. From Mayor John F. Hylan along with Lillian Wald who cut the ribbon to commence the building, to Lincoln and Earlene Drake. Liberty's brothers, Blaine and Teague, and her nephew Kenny proudly represented the Fitzgerald family. Other dignitaries posed for the cameras, and now all had left.

The flu had abated leaving thousands upon thousands dead in New York City alone. Millions in the City survived the grippe and were now trying to get on with their lives.

The bright lights on Broadway were back on. The theaters, especially the Joyeux, were raking in the patrons now. Liberty had gone back to see who survived. Most did, even Magnolia Moore who had a quick smile for Liberty. Foyle found another star, *Desiree Devine*. But no amount of coaxing from Sid Brawley and Foyle himself could get Liberty back into a costume again. She wished them well.

The Drake hotel survived the scandal and Jonathan was also busy updating its look. His big plans for the expansion of motels across the country were still in his mind. Between his designs, his father's money to build, and the Fitzgerald's talents for furniture building, both families would not want for anything ever again.

Charles Grand, it was determined after his body was exhumed, had been poisoned with arsenic. And although they couldn't prove it, the detectives surmised that Mr. Grand was helped to meet his maker by Jenny Bishop and Talon Montgomery. All of Grand's holdings, his stores, his home, were taken over by his wife's relatives from Paris.

The murder plot had originated with Alice wanting to frame Talon. But little did Alice know that Talon and Jenny were working against her, plotting to get her and her family out of the way so they could take over Grand's. They could have gotten away with it if it hadn't been for Liberty Fitzgerald and her willingness to help Jonathan.

Jonathan took Liberty's hands within his and turning them palm up, placed a kiss on each one. "I have something special in mind for you."

She cocked her head at him, taking in his handsome, clean-shaven face, his strong jaw, and determined eyes. "Might I ask what you have in mind, Mr. Drake?" She smiled unable to take her eyes off his tall, strong body wearing a gray linen suit, his hat a summer straw with a black band around its crown.

"How about a ride on a ferry?"

"I can't imagine why, but if you insist, who am I to say no."

He whistled for a taxi.

When they arrived at the ferry terminal, Jonathan bought two tickets, a nickel each, and guided Liberty onto the passenger ferry. The ferryboat, with a single funnel and a lone American flag flapping in the breeze, slipped from the dock and started toward Staten Island. Its horn blasted loud sending seagulls flapping skyward.

Arm and arm, along with a crowd of people, Jonathan and Liberty watched Manhattan's skyscraper's recede and the water turn into a rippling silver sparkle.

"Do you want to sit inside, or stay out here?" Jonathan asked, his eyes searching her face, his arm around her shoulder.

She looked at the women and men chatting amongst themselves. "Let's remain out here." Liberty moved toward the rounded nose of the ferry with its security gate barricading the opening.

Both of them tipped their faces up allowing the warm July breeze to whip around them. Liberty, dressed in a summer blouse of white and an ankle-length skirt of light blue, held onto her wide brimmed hat with its lone feather briskly waving.

When the ferry stopped at the Statue of Liberty's dock, Jonathan grabbed her hand and took her ashore along with a dozen or so other people. Jonathan deliberately lagged behind the crowd, allowing some privacy for him and Liberty. They made their way to the base of the statue that reached for the sky.

Jonathan stopped and surprised Liberty by getting down on bended knee. He stared into the face of the woman he loved.

"Jonathan," she exclaimed, "what are you doing?" Her russet eyebrows rose in amusement as she stared at him.

He fumbled inside his suit coat pocket, searching, and just when it appeared he'd lost what he sought, he took out a small velvet blue box.

"Miss Liberty Fitzgerald, I'd be honored if you would marry me."

Liberty's heart sang with delight as she smiled radiantly at the man she'd come to love so much. "I would be happy to marry you, Mr. Drake. More than happy, delirious, delighted—I love you, Jonathan."

Still on his knee, he removed her glove and slipped the shiny engagement ring on her finger. She admired it, and with a turn of her hand, made the diamond sparkle. Jonathan stood and looked her over seductively before claiming her lips with his. Right here in public, he kissed her long and hard, his tongue seeking until she met his ardor with her own. When their kiss finished, he surprised her by removing the hat pins from her wide brimmed hat and took it off.

And as the sun burnished her hair, he kissed the freckles on her face. "You will never know how much I love you, Miss Liberty Fitzgerald. But I'm willing to take a lifetime to try and show you just how much."

This time no family or a detective was around to stop them. They held each other tight. Standing in the shadow of the statue, they knew the future would be bright for them, and that together, inch by inch, mile by mile, they could change the world.

"How about August? I think that's a lovely month for a wedding," she said.

He nodded.

They both turned to tilt their heads upward at the statue, her meaning never more profound than now.

Freedom.

The End

Author's Notes ℃

I set this story in one of the most influential, inventiveness, and medically devastating times in our existence because I love the richness and the wealth this era brings to a tale. While I like to think I am so well informed about history, in the scheme of things I probably know very little. But in my ignorance I believe I have crafted a work of fiction in, A Deceitful Bait, that will not only entertain the reader, but will take them back in time, to a time, that I am so thankful those that came before me had the presence of mind to invent, build, create, and simply believe.

My next book to be released, The Caged Countess, a medieval set in 1306 Scotland, will take the reader even further into our past, one where a king's word was the rule of the day, a knight fought and gave up his life, and where men and fealty ruled the women of the era. Again, I'd like to thank the builders, the fabulous craftsmen whose work still stands today.

Since writing is such a solitary enterprise, and with only me at the computer typing away with my mind a whirl of words that I try my best to put down on paper, I have my close family that I must thank for such wonderful support, especially my husband Ty. Thanks to my daughter Whitney for all the hard work editing, and to my dear author friend Anna Brentwood for the same. I must mention Jodi and Debbie from Jan's Paperbacks in Aloha, Ore, who are true believers in my stories. I can't say enough about fellow author and friend, Maggie Lynch, who formed Windtree Press and asked me to join.

And, dear reader, I'm thanking you most of all.

Mercer Addison

"It is never too late to be what you might have been."
Quote by writer: George Eliott (1819-1880)

Mercer Addison, a late bloomer in the publishing world, took on this quote as her motto, not only for inspiration, but that age doesn't matter when you really desire something. Mercer (pen name only) has lived in the Pacific Northwest, and the state of Oregon all her life. She resides in the Portland area with her wonderful husband Ty, and their little dog, Gracie.
www.merceraddison.com
Other books by Mercer:
Even Nectar is Poison
Five o'clock Whistle

www.ingramcontent.com/pod-product-compliance
Lightning Source LLC
Chambersburg PA
CBHW051322250626
47155CB00007B/2421